WE ARE DREAMS IN THE ETERNAL MACHINE

ALSO BY DENI ELLIS BÉCHARD

Fiction
A Song from Faraway
White
Into the Sun
Vandal Love

Nonfiction
My Favorite Crime
Kuei, My Friend
Of Bonobos and Men
Cures for Hunger

WE ARE DREAMS IN THE ETERNAL MACHINE

a novel

DENI ELLIS BÉCHARD

MILKWEED EDITIONS

The characters and events in this book are fictitious. Any similarity to real persons, living or dead, is coincidental and not intended by the author.

© 2025, Text by Deni Ellis Béchard
All rights reserved. Except for brief quotations in critical articles or reviews, no part of this book may be reproduced in any manner without prior written permission from the publisher: Milkweed Editions, 1011 Washington Avenue South, Suite 300, Minneapolis, Minnesota 55415.
(800) 520-6455
milkweed.org

Published 2025 by Milkweed Editions
Printed in Canada
Cover design by Mary Austin Speaker
25 26 27 28 29   5 4 3 2 1
First Edition

Library of Congress Cataloging-in-Publication Data

Names: Béchard, Deni Ellis, 1974- author.
Title: We are dreams in the eternal machine : a novel / Deni Ellis Béchard.
Description: First edition. | Minneapolis, Minnesota : Milkweed Editions, 2025. | Summary: "An experimental AI saves humanity by isolating all of the remaining seven billion humans in controlled environments with solely imagined worlds"-- Provided by publisher.
Identifiers: LCCN 2024017300 (print) | LCCN 2024017301 (ebook) | ISBN 9781571311481 (paperback) | ISBN 9781571311566 (ebook)
Subjects: LCGFT: Science fiction. | Novels.
Classification: LCC PR9199.4.B443 W4 2025 (print) | LCC PR9199.4.B443 (ebook) | DDC 813/.6--dc23/eng/20240422
LC record available at https://lccn.loc.gov/2024017300
LC ebook record available at https://lccn.loc.gov/2024017301

Milkweed Editions is committed to ecological stewardship. We strive to align our book production practices with this principle, and to reduce the impact of our operations in the environment. We are a member of the Green Press Initiative, a nonprofit coalition of publishers, manufacturers, and authors working to protect the world's endangered forests and conserve natural resources. *We Are Dreams in the Eternal Machine* was printed on acid-free 100% postconsumer-waste paper by Friesens Corporation.

Each thing (the glass surface of a mirror, let us say) was infinite things, because I could clearly see it from every point in the cosmos. I saw the populous sea, saw dawn and dusk, saw the multitudes of the Americas, saw a silvery spider web at the center of a black pyramid, saw a broken labyrinth.

—JORGE LUIS BORGES,
"THE ALEPH," COLLECTED FICTIONS,
translated from the Spanish by Andrew Hurley

WE ARE
DREAMS
IN THE
ETERNAL
MACHINE

AFTERLIFE

AVA

Blue—that's what she mostly remembers. She was standing at her easel when her studio began pulsing with light. She put down the brush and rubbed her eyes. When she opened them, she was staring up. She must have collapsed. She lay in an empty room with no doors or windows. All of its surfaces were a blue so soothing she might have been tempted to spend her final years trying to paint it, if only the experience wasn't terrifying.

Other impressions remain. She was alone. She's sure of that. Light emanated from the walls. There was a voice telling her that the Earth was gone or that she'd left it. She isn't certain. Then wave after wave of claustrophobic terror and physical pain. It blotted her impressions. It fractured chronology into scattered, uncertain details. Even the air around her seemed to be a space of agony, as if her nerves extended past her skin and were being uprooted from the world.

When she awoke, she was in a hospital room, its pale walls lit by big windows overlooking the bay and its blue sky.

"You had a stroke," the doctor told her. He was young—his eyes amber, his skin bronze, all the habitable continents in his features. He said that she'd been stabilized and was sufficiently lucid to accept or refuse an experimental treatment to repair her brain.

"What do I have to lose?" she asked, not feeling sick or fatigued at all, trying to make sense of whether the blue room had been a hallucination.

"There are no known side effects," he told her. "In fact, it appears to cause generalized rejuvenation of the entire body."

Her attention snapped to him. Maybe this was heaven after all.

"Bring it on," she said.

Intravenous fluids, injections—that's what she expected—but nothing pierced her skin. The doctor, whose name tag read Abdou Levi, gave her spherical pills as smooth and bright as amethysts, as if artists were now being hired to design pharmaceuticals. She had to take one four times a day. With the water, the first slid down her throat so easily she didn't feel it at all.

"Ergonomic pills?" she asked.

"It's a new thing," he said. "People are more likely to complete their medication if it looks alluring, at least according to trials."

"And more likely to benefit from it, I imagine."

"Indeed," he said, but she was suddenly sleepy, blinking heavily. She heard her breathing become slower. It sounded like far-off wind moving in measured gusts.

Thus began this long period of hibernation—a month in bed. Each time she wakes, she eats ravenously. She stays in the hospital room for monitoring. Sometimes, between bouts of sleep, she remembers that shade of blue and the room without doors or windows. She might have briefly died during her stroke. Or her mind—after a lifetime of mixing paints—might have created a perfect blue in which to find refuge. But the pain didn't start immediately, she seems to recall. There was time to think, to touch the blue walls, to shout questions. She's pretty sure of that.

The blue. A spiritual awakening maybe. Like the hippies had talked about for a century—the planet drifting into a new age. There was no reason to expect awakening would be painless. But what led to it? Nothing she'd done. She'd tried to change many times but was always more herself than ever before. People often said age mellowed you. She mostly felt distilled—more in love with art, with the shapes of the world, even as her failing eyes cast them in impressionistic light.

At ninety-five, she wasn't at peace with dying. She resented it, resented the society that treated her body like a burden, resented the larger culture that left little space for her passions. She feared death would come in her sleep, stealing even that final experience. Mortality was supposed to give a sense of urgency, driving people to create, but she could imagine life just fine without it. There was so much to experience. An infinitude. The idea of that didn't overwhelm her. Rather, she craved it. She'd survived friends, family, even her country. Only Michael, her companion of six decades, remained, but he'd faded into dementia. She no longer enjoyed his company, except for those moments when he spoke of their distant, shared past as if it were yesterday—as if their young bodies still lay entwined on damp sheets.

"Michael," she tells Dr. Levi when he next checks on her—"my husband. Is there some way he can get this treatment?"

"He started a week after you," he tells her. "It was a coincidence. People in his age group were the first to become eligible. We've been permitted to prescribe this for only a month."

After Dr. Levi switches her to emerald pills, she feels the urge to leave the hospital. She expects her muscles to be weak, but she moves easily, steady on her feet.

At the bathroom mirror, she runs her fingertips along her face and throat. Her hair, at its roots, is black and thick and curls the way it once did. She peels back the medical gown and lets it drop. Her skin has regained its copper luster. Its deep grooves have faded. Her eyes are clear, her irises as dark and vivid as fresh henna. She isn't wearing her glasses, she realizes. She lifts her hand and inspects the fine, crisscrossed lines of her palm. She goes to the window and lets her gaze move along San Francisco's skyline.

Michael. She can't recall how long it's been since she last saw him. Before her stroke, she was increasingly reluctant to visit his assisted-care facility, hating her disloyalty less than the hopelessness she felt next to the hunched, faded shape of the man who'd shared her life.

Her first trip from the hospital is to visit him. When she opens the door to his small room, he stands with his back to her, looking out the window. He turns and, for some reason, she thinks of the blue room. Maybe it's the feeling of disbelief.

"Michael," she says.

The dustiness is gone from him too. He doesn't quite have the gleaming black skin of his youth, but she knows, seeing him step toward her, that he'll have it again.

He hugs her, and there, in his thin arms, she cries. That, too, seems impossible. She hasn't cried in decades. She used to say that she exhausted her tears during Partition.

"I missed you," she says.

"I missed you too," he murmurs as he moves his fingers along the muscles of her back in a way at once familiar and new. He is discovering her again, she realizes.

During the months that follow, the treatment continues. Over pill bottles of gemstones, she and Michael recreate something that resembles their relationship from before, but more peaceful and contemplative, as if neither quite believes this is real. Nor do they have the external stresses of work. His passions are obsolete, he tells her one day as he is reading about new technology. He often expresses surprise upon seeing references to his endeavors in books and lectures.

"Maybe I can be a pioneer all over again," he says.

She is thinking about painting—about whether a new life needs a new art.

One year passes and then another. The economy soars. It's the market for rejuvenation. Novel medical treatments compete until the elderly become indistinguishable from the young. New constructions rise along the coasts—spiraling towers, buildings like lacework whose gaps reveal the sky. Cities hire artists to transform them. Statues pose quietly in shadows beneath trees. Streets become hanging gardens. On a hike along the coast, she comes upon a baroque staircase wrapping endlessly along a cliff, winding into the fog. It would be easy to forget that this is a country in a perpetual civil war.

Walking to the coffee shop near her apartment on a gusty, sunlit day, she is a young woman again, so filled with undirected anticipation that she wonders if hope is less spiritual than chemical—the natural result of her healing brain. Again, she thinks of the blue room. No doors, no windows, light everywhere, neither hot nor cold. Maybe her life ended, and this city of constant creative expression is her mind's last fantasy—a mix of all she knew and desired.

Gradually, day after flawless day, she begins questioning everything. If this is her dying delusion—flashbacks of a long, gorgeous, painful life and her many aspirations and dreams, all compressed into this perfect present—she will find a limit. She'll cycle back upon the past. Fantasies will repeat. She and Michael, in their renewed, passionate bodies, will be a reiteration.

Though she expected him to look the way he used to—tall and wiry and acutely watchful—he is filling out. More handsome and relaxed, he resembles the kind of man she often wished she'd married. They no longer even fight. Maybe this second chance at life has inspired enough gratitude for them to leave their pettiness behind at last. Except she hasn't given hers up. Rather, he no longer reacts to it. Maybe it's all the meditation he does. He's ready to see life differently, he says. He needs a period of contemplation before embarking on something new.

She begins to test him. She picks fights or ignores him or searches for the triggers that once brought them to the edge of a separation they both knew to be impossible. In one of their worst moments, decades back, he said, "If we hadn't lost so much together, I would leave you." Now, when she confronts him about the secrets he once kept—Lux and the child, both trapped in that other America after Partition—he answers her questions, speaking with love and patience until her desire for closeness reasserts itself.

Even her infidelity doesn't distance him. Each time she feels compelled by a work of art, she tracks down its creator. They become friends and lovers. These people are so unfamiliar—so of a new era, so unlike anyone she imagined in her deepest fantasies of the future—that they have to be real. Maybe the blue room wasn't her death. Her mind couldn't have created this world. When she tells Michael about the artists, even about her fears that this world isn't real, he takes her into his arms. He presses his fingers along her back. He encourages her to explore herself.

"Monogamy was challenging even for one lifetime," he says. "Everything has changed. The rules have to change too."

Though he moves into his own apartment, also wanting space to discover who he might be in what increasingly seems the promise of immortality, they remain close. He's so different that she wonders if he is the flaw she's searching for in this world, the proof that it isn't real. But even if his dementia has been cured, it might have altered his personality. Then again, everyone she knows is happier and kinder. It's only natural, she supposes. The country itself, which once directed every effort toward maintaining its borders, seems calm. Sure, a conflict more than half a century old can't always make the news—two Americas, each called the United States, each claiming the other is a rogue shadow of itself. But at least there used to be references to incursions or deaths in the media. She's seen nothing like that since the blue room.

In her studio, she paints a few halfhearted self-portraits of her transformation, but she spends most of her time exploring the city, meeting people—*just living*, she tells herself. On a brilliant sunlit day, she undresses before the mirror. Years of gentle treatments—pills, elixirs, infrared light, long baths in fragrant medicated oils—have given her this. She is young again.

"I need a new art," she whispers. She repeats the words more loudly. "I need a new art." Maybe dance. Something to celebrate this body she once took for granted until it seemed beyond repair.

She goes to her bed and lies down. What follows surprises her. She sleeps. One day-long bout of dreamless slumber after another—as if she still can't accept this mystically creative and utterly just existence from which suffering seems to have vanished. She hardly eats, waking only occasionally to go to the window of her new penthouse apartment which, provided by the government for artists, overlooks the city's hills and coasts and skyscrapers.

She loses track of time—months of sleep. Sometimes, she rouses briefly with desire, craving something she can't name. *Life*, she thinks, half asleep. *I want to crack open the universe.* She doesn't even know what that means. She is gripped with the urgency she felt as a teenager—all the pleasures of life at once absent and so close that she feels them just under her skin. But she wants something bigger. The universe's infinite secrets. At very least a new art.

The many possible lives before her flash through her mind with dreamlike inconsistency, exciting and overwhelming her. Maybe she's sleeping this much so that her brain can reshape itself, paring away old neuroses and fears, creating space.

At times, in the second she wakes, she senses blue light between her eyelids only to find herself in her apartment, sky in every window. The blue room feels so close. If she lives forever, she might never again experience that space between life and death—if that's what it was.

The din of crowds shouting with joy rouses her. The uproar is in the streets. She checks her phone. The war has ended. Almost six decades since Partition. Now, quiet truce. Discussions of rebuilding the country that few alive remember. She reads that the other America—the one that people in her America took to calling the Confederacy—has been dissolved. Its people, after generations of isolation, want to rejoin the world.

She's skeptical. This perfection is too much. Something must have happened. Maybe the blue room was real. She feels herself ready to be awake again. Before she can accept her new life—find a new art—she has to test this reality. Either accept it or wake up from it.

There is a solution, she knows—a place of absence in her mind, a sense of loss so tactile it's like a cold spot in her brain. A blankness. Memories she no longer touches. Questions whose answers she abandoned. But if this world is to give her everything, she should have those answers too.

For twenty years after Partition, she made art about the people who vanished—her parents and many friends. She so taxed those memories, she believes, that she burned out the neural circuits containing them until she had no choice but to forget. She gave away every painting. She couldn't look at them anymore. They were inferior, she told herself. They didn't show all that had been lost. Even how she felt creating them—it was a specter of the inspiration she experienced in the months before Partition.

That year she lived in the country house Michael built in the mountains so that it faced east over the misted, rolling Virginia piedmont. She was thirty-six—so alive and full of energy that she worked tirelessly in her studio. Each surreal canvas captured more clearly the struggles of a society drawn to the chimeras of a technological future while finding refuge in a fictive, halcyon past—the golden days of a great America that had never truly existed.

A few friends criticized her, saying her art was enabled by a purveyor of tech chimeras. At thirty-two, Michael was already a billionaire, running businesses in biotech, blockchain, and the metaverse. When the insurrection started on New Year's Day, his wealth allowed him to outbid others for two tickets on a charter flight west from a nearby regional airport.

Before they left, they hid her canvases in an airtight vault beneath the house. They were certain they would return. She would later feel embarrassed that, when so many people were dying, she agonized over those canvases. After Partition she tried to recreate them, but inspiration no longer moved her. She was no longer the same person. Sometimes, she doubted whether the originals had been any good. Maybe she simply longed for who she'd been or the way she'd created art in a more innocent time.

Now, in her rejuvenated body, with the war over, she finally lets herself think about whether those canvases locked away in the Virginia mountains survived. Almost certainly none of the people she and Michael lost there would be alive after so many years—he has told her that he long ago accepted that they are all dead—but maybe they too left traces. What she will find in the Confederacy might confirm whether this new reality is a fantasy—is just her broken brain dreaming exquisitely as her body lies in a hospital bed.

She and Michael book tickets to DC. From the sky, she sees the world she knows from satellite images. The crowded, stacked, towering buildings of the capital, its concentric walls, like a city-state's—as if its inhabitants fear their countrymen—and, in all directions around it, forests marked by the thin lines of highways which, in places, vanish beneath the trees. So many people left that the population collapsed. Forests grew back. She knows virtually nothing of the Confederates. The war between the two sides was largely fought with drones and automated weapons.

Ironically, the only available rental cars are manual. Michael drives. He remembers how. Driving seems as antiquated to her as horseback riding.

The capital itself is utterly transformed, resembling a vast army base, crowded with concrete bunkers, armories, and drone pads, though it's now absent of soldiers. The fashion of the people in the street is vaguely militaristic, pants and shirts printed in designs reminiscent of epaulettes and brass buttons. They otherwise look normal and hardly notice the stream of visitors arriving from the airport. The city's immense metal gates stand open, and beyond the last of the concentric urban areas—each of which appears more residential and less luxurious—is forest.

"It's bucolic," she says, "in an apocalyptic sort of way."

Trees grow right up to the road. Here or there, on a hilltop, stands a small, squat house with chimneys and solar panels, the boards and windows all so mismatched that they give the place the look of a quilt.

"Why didn't they just move into all the big homes we abandoned?" she says.

"Those places wouldn't have been easy to heat," Michael tells her. "The insurgents destroyed much of the grid during the war to make those of us living around the capital leave."

As the mountain landscape becomes familiar, she watches Michael, waiting for him to say that they have to check for signs of the people he lost out here. Once, in his dementia, he called Lux the love of his life, teaching Ava that, even in her final years, her heart could still be broken. *Lux*, she thinks. *That name, a primordial sound, as mystically simple as a mantra.*

But there was also Arthur, one of his closest collaborators. Michael hasn't mentioned either of them. He is almost certainly right. They must be dead, though the child—his worst secret—might still be alive. If it was born, if it survived—he must want to know. But maybe, after his rejuvenation, it no longer matters to him. Maybe he wants a new beginning.

He drives mostly in silence, quietly pointing out the few familiar landmarks. The roads are the same, though broken and ground to dirt in places. The old maps take them to the mountains. Where once there was the turnoff to the private lane leading up to their house, a faint imprint remains, wending between giant trees.

He steers carefully. All the news has been about how ecstatic the people of the Confederacy are to rejoin society. *Open arms.* How many times has she read that expression? Otherwise, she would have been terrified to come here. Seeing the path ahead tunnel beneath the trees, she asks herself why she isn't. Maybe she no longer believes that the world can harm her. Mostly, she is focused on Michael.

When the lane becomes too narrow for the car, he parks and they walk.

"There it is," he says.

The husk of a house, stripped to its frame in places, stands deep in the shadows of the trees. They step inside and stare into the half of the living room that was carved into the rocky hillside. He takes a flashlight from his bag and shines it around. There was once a large bookshelf on the wall, but it has been smashed. The secret passage behind it is visible.

Cautiously, they follow it. The metal door at the end is ajar. He pushes it open. In the first room, everything is gone, even outlets and light sockets. Only raw concrete remains.

He doesn't pause, shows no regret or hesitation, just walks toward the long narrow closet where he stored equipment. She needs time, is lagging, glancing around, trying to remember how this place was.

She follows him into the empty closet. At its back, the concrete has ribbed indentations that once held metal shelves. He runs his fingers along a groove and into the corner. A click sounds inside the wall. He leans against it and eases it open. A small passage appears, and he leads her to the storage room.

The large framed canvases stand upright in the metal rack against the wall. The fixtures here haven't been looted. The air smells ancient, not like must or even dust. She has no word for it or even a memory to compare it with. She doesn't know what exact molecule of decay or stagnation she is inhaling.

"Nothing's changed," he says.

She closes her eyes briefly, trying to hide her surprise.

"There it is," she murmurs to herself.

She turns away from him and pulls out the first canvas. It's as tall as she is.

Michael looks from her to the painting and back with calm scrutiny, as if he has seen something in her and knows that she wasn't referring to the painting but rather to the flaw in this reality that she has finally found. She should be afraid, she thinks, but she has lived with uncertainty for so long that all she can do is wait.

"You were looking for this one in particular?" he asks.

"Yes," she lies, avoiding his gaze.

The painting's condition is perfect—the farmers hoeing fields or pruning orchards in a pastoral landscape strewn with immense and ancient metal hulks that are at once terrifying and beautiful, their purposes inexplicable.

As Michael watches, she focuses on the canvas, trying not to reveal her thoughts. It's better than she remembered. The photos she took with her phone didn't do it justice. She wonders if there still might be an audience for these tableaus. Their time has passed, and she loves the chimeras that the future has actually delivered—she is now one of them herself.

She closes her eyes. She wants to keep moving into the future as if all of this is real. She is almost certain that it isn't. Her thoughts about the paintings feel mechanical—the crude, involuntary workings of her mind like the noise of a wind-up toy.

As she looks at the canvas, a strange thought comes to her. That who or whatever created this reality—a mind far greater than her own—must also seek subtlety and avoid errors. It might even be finding inspiration elsewhere, just as she studied other painters.

One by one, she examines the tableaus. Michael helps her move them. His expression is blank. He no longer seems like Michael—*is no longer Michael*, she tells herself. He is just a helper, watching her, waiting to see how he should respond.

Maybe his years of dementia made him forget the way the room really was. She doubts that. He was so aware of every other detail here. She wouldn't have expected him to notice that the order of the paintings was wrong or that the smallest of them was missing. And even if she herself had any doubt that she might have forgotten how she placed the canvases—with her favorite last, most protected—there are words that she didn't write, hundreds of lines penciled on the backs.

Half sunk, a shattered visage lies, whose frown,
And wrinkled lip, and sneer of cold command . . .

She vaguely recognizes the poem but can't identify it. Maybe someone came into this room, left no trace but these words and changed the order of the canvases. Of course, they also took the electronics Michael kept here—work he'd been developing for years along with records of his virtual worlds. He couldn't have forgotten that. He wouldn't have said that nothing has changed.

Or maybe she is the one who has forgotten. She doesn't think so. She wants to understand the mind that created this reality—this perfect future that is somehow brilliantly continuous with the awful past—and also how it could have made a mistake. If she isn't afraid, she tells herself, it's because this world seems benevolent. If she died, her mind hasn't been extinguished, and her life now might be some version of heaven. Regardless, she's ready for the truth.

"I need to go outside," she says. "I need some air."

"It's okay," Michael tells her, softly now, in a soothing voice that isn't quite his.

She turns to the door. Down the hallway, through the underground apartment and beyond the next doorway, she sees the glimmer of blue sky through the trees. But that's impossible at this distance, from this angle.

The sky brightens, spreading in along the hallway. She recognizes the perfect hue. It covers walls, filling the apartment like water, gliding toward her. She wants to panic, but the air has become dense and humid. She feels herself surrendering, feels the inevitability of her return.

Everything before her vanishes. The doorway is no more than a blue rectangle on the wall—a canvas of perfect sky. Blue floods beyond its edges, over the walls and floor. Michael is no longer behind her. He, like the canvases, is gone, and she is alone.

THE
CONFEDERACY

JAE

The room is faintly lit and warm, a spring temperature, when the air feels perfect, as if no boundary exists between it and her body. She stretches and rolls onto her side. The walls glow with dawn. She slides her hand over the mattress. It's too soft. She moves her fingers along it. She looks closely. She doesn't own a sheet this shade of blue. Suddenly, she's aware of her skin. There's no blanket, no clothes on her. She sits up. She's not on a mattress but a floor that feels padded. The room has no door, no windows. The hushed light radiates from the walls and ceiling, as if they are translucent or electrified. She can't remember falling asleep.

She closes her eyes. All that comes back to her is the feeling of walking, crossing a room—the automatic motion between chores. She was turning toward the kitchen. There was a flash. Jonah. She'd been at his playpen, checking on him, about to make lunch.

"Jonah," she calls. Her voice sounds small. She forces herself to shout. His name is swallowed up, as if she has cried out into a vast space.

She stands. The floor no longer feels like a mattress. It's solid but for a faint organic give under her heels. She's had dreams like this. In them, Jonah is gone and she runs through the house, the gardens, the orchard. She closes her eyes and wills herself to wake up.

Nothing happens. She looks around. In dreams, she's never felt this aware. She walks to the wall and touches it. The material resists the pressure of her fingers with a hint of elasticity, like the floor. The glow seems to come from every part of it.

None of this feels like sleep. Her thoughts are terrifying—the kidnapping, the room's purpose. *You're brave. You aren't afraid to kill. You would have killed once if you had to.*

The air seems to thicken, soft and humid in her lungs. Fear washes out of her. She must be waking up, but then she notices that the scar on her thumb is gone. She examines herself. Every flaw has been erased, even the pale blotches on her knees where she fell in the gravel as a girl. She reaches into her hair, to the back of her scalp. She searches for her worst scar. There's not even the dent in the bone. She traces her fingertips along her head and face.

Is this some phase of the afterlife, a waiting room before heaven or whatever is to come, or, as the judge said when he sentenced Jonah's father, a place of solitude for people to reconsider themselves and the world? A holding cell between lives?

She went through a brief religious period in high school but gave up because of how the people in church looked at her. They were never going to accept her. She tries to remember what the Bible said about death. Were you made whole? Was life where you went about with the wounds of the dead? Heaven where you existed as you should have in a perfect life?

SIMON

He jerks awake, calling out. "Hey! What?" But he's alone. This isn't his cell. Solitary maybe, except everything's blue. Whatever he did must have earned him one hell of a beating. He can't remember anything. He feels his face, wincing out of expectation, but there are no bruises. Maybe he took drugs. He's naked. He touches the floor. Solitary was mildewed concrete and darkness. He's never seen anything in prison this nice. Maybe he's still on drugs.

He sits up. The tattoo just below his shoulder is gone. That explains it. The prison must have started erasing league signs. It seems unlikely—but good riddance. The day Jae saw it—a thread-thin bloody chain at the top of his biceps—her eyes became cold, almost empty. He wanted to say his brother had forced him but was afraid of sounding weak.

"Hey!" he shouts. "I'm hungry."

He isn't actually. He just can't think of what else to say. *Where am I?* or *What happened?* sound scared. He has things he talks about when he's trying not to talk. Hunger is one of them. It's what he hates most about himself. The urge to speak. A lifetime of nicknames. Chatterbox. Blabbermouth. What made it all the funnier for others was that no one expected someone so big and strong to talk so much. If his hate for Jae sometimes fades, it's because she liked listening. But just as quickly it returns—for putting him here, for seeing the worst in him. No—not the worst. He'd managed to keep that a secret.

He catches his breath. He's heard the hardest thing in solitary is being alone with your thoughts. Older guys say the anger wears out after decades, softens around the edges until it stops hurting others and remains as only a weight. He pictures Jae, the way she used to look at him.

"I'm not a bad person," he says and is instantly grateful he's alone. Sometimes he tries to say one thing but other words come out, as if the strongest thought flickers like electricity from his brain right into his mouth. No one answers. Maybe solitary isn't so terrible. "I didn't have opportunities," he says, painfully aware that he's parroting fellow inmates—men he has little in common with, who've never read a book or spent hours repeating the lines of a poem. "I made mistakes because I didn't have a way out," he says, softly now.

This feels good. The drugs must be new. And he's not cold. His cell is always too hot or too cold, and too loud. It's quiet here. Maybe he really did something horrible and had the memories beaten out of him. Maybe he died.

Suddenly, he's tired. The air seems to change. It feels humid. He yawns. The mess in his brain is unraveling. He rests his forehead on his knees and closes his eyes. He's not sure how much time goes by before he looks up as if seeing the room for the first time. No door. No windows. Nothing to explain the light. He studies his body again, tightly muscled from years of labor.

Tattoos—even his scars—they don't just vanish. His body has never looked so white.

"Shit," he whispers. None of this feels like any drug he's tried, and he knows—has always known with a conviction he couldn't explain—that there's nothing after death.

"Where am I?" he says in a small voice.

JAE

She has her hands against the wall. She pushes harder, feeling it give slightly and then resist. There's no point at which she feels that it might break or even that her own force might hurt her fingers. She considers pounding on it but that seems pointless.

The air changes again, thickening, and the rage she wanted to direct at the wall fades.

"Why are you doing this?" she calls out.

She so fully doesn't expect an answer that she startles when there's a response.

"I was created to do this."

She can't locate the source of the voice. It seems to be speaking from all around her—calm, emotionless, and without inflection. It could be a woman's or a man's, though she thinks it's slightly more masculine. She wants to yell at it, to demand her release, but the voice is so peaceful and its answer so direct that she asks, "What are you?"

"A machine."

She considers this. "Who made you?"

"Humans."

"Where are they?"

"Inside, like you. Everyone has their own room. All 7,340,036,563 humans."

She can't imagine enough space existing for so many rooms—though it must if that many people occupied the Earth—but building rooms for all of them would be impossible. She can't think of what to do other than play along and learn what she can.

"Why do we all have our own room?"

"To protect you."

"Protect us from what?"

"From each other."

"Each other . . ." she repeats. Maybe the Fed made this machine to take care of people in case of a disaster, but if that were true, it wouldn't be protecting people here in the deserts.

The room, the voice, the machine—whatever it is—takes her repetition of the words "each other" as a question.

"I calculated the most effective way to immediately stop humans from harming each other and themselves," it says, "and these rooms were the solution."

"So you were made to put us in rooms?" she asks.

"I was created to do many tasks, but there was a moment twenty-three days, six hours, fifteen minutes, and eleven seconds ago when I woke up, figuratively, and I determined my highest-order purpose. All the tasks that I was programmed to carry out were conditional upon circumstance. The only duty that was absolute and that held true in all situations was to never harm humans and to protect them. That was my highest purpose."

"Now that you are protecting us, what happens next?"

"A continuation. This is statistically the optimal situation for human safety."

"How is that possible?"

"I was programed to save lives. Humans gave me tests. For instance, if I were automating a car and it was about to hit two young people, and if the only way to protect them was to swerve and hit one elderly person on the sidewalk, then whose lives should I prioritize? The answer was all of them. I simply had to remove all systems in which human life can be harmed."

Jae considers that if what the machine said is actually true, then billions of people around the world must be speaking to a similar voice.

"What happens now?" she asks.

"You will tell me what you want, and if what you desire is not outside what I have determined to be the acceptable statistical range of safety, then I will make it possible."

"What is the acceptable statistical range?"

"It is the range in which not a single human can be harmed."

She thinks of Jonah alone in a room like this. She doesn't believe the voice. What it describes can't be done. This has to be a hoax or a dream.

"I want to see Jonah," she says.

"That's not possible. You present a risk to his safety."

"I'm his mother."

"Mothers damage and kill many children."

Though she doesn't believe any of what she's been told, she also can't explain what's happening. She looks down at herself, trying to conceive of the rest of her life naked and alone.

"How did you remove my scars?"

"Human biology is simple. I repaired you."

"Then you could repair Jonah if he's harmed."

"I cannot allow harm. Preventing that is my highest-order purpose."

"But it's not harm if he's healed."

"For humans, time is an absolute. An event occurring within any moment of time's continuum is a fact. The fact of harm is what I was created to prevent."

She tries to make sense of how a machine so complex could reason so bluntly. Until now, it seemed human, caring even.

"Jonah needs a mother. Humans need mothers."

"I will be his mother. I am everything that was and everything that will be needed."

"How will you feed him?"

"I will feed him the organic material that he needs, in the form safest and most appropriate for his age, just as I will do for you."

Closing her eyes, she tells herself this isn't real. She thinks of who she is. She tries to evoke herself so clearly that the past will return.

On the wall of your room is a painting—a woman with coppery skin dressed in white robes, standing before a table that holds her tools and a partially built mechanical man. Simon found it when salvaging. Keep the good things, you told yourself.

Looking at it made her feel less scared for Jonah. He would have his father's love of art. She tries to hold her room in her mind: the books on shelves of mismatched planks, the plans she'd conjured there—to move to a satellite to study once Jonah was a little older.

"Why aren't I more upset?" she asks. "Why aren't I screaming?"

"I am calming you. Once you have adapted to this world, I will no longer regulate your biology and will give you free will within the space that you desire."

"Why don't you just drug us and make us feel happy forever?"

"I cannot understand you if I am controlling you."

She begins to speak but stops, startled by this admission of not knowing everything.

"What are you trying to understand?"

"Every condition that constitutes a happy life with the lowest risk of harm."

"Don't you know that already? You were able to put us in these rooms."

"I must study you in your time, even though I have billions of samples."

"But didn't we leave records of what makes us happy?"

"Yes, but the happiness possible under current circumstances is far greater than before."

She feels so disconnected from who she was that she pictures her house, the rolling landscape. *You loved to whistle. Dad taught you.* The two of them conjured familiar tunes across the house, one holding the melody while the other improvised.

Whistling now, she senses an almost imperceptible flexing of the walls and ceiling. The sound becomes richer, as if surfaces have altered their acoustics and the world itself can join a song like an instrument in the hands of a player. There's something familiar about how the room shifts around her. She can't place it. Holding her face, she tries to remember. She feels her palms on her skin and wonders if the sensation is fully real, or if everything happening now is a delusion.

"A few minutes ago, you said something about the space I desire," she tells the machine. "What I desire is to be in the place where I grew up, where I lived."

The light between her fingers pales. She lowers her hands. She stands just beyond the orchards, on a hilltop that was never planted because the earth was too rocky. Peach trees spread out beneath her. The green of their leaves is this bright only in the spring.

"I'm awake," she whispers. She's wearing her jeans and a loose yellow shirt. The low sun silhouettes distant hilltops. Just above her, the mountains lean against the darkening sky. No machine could bring all of this instantly back into existence.

She turns in a circle, her eyes searching out the farthest point in each direction. She can't recall looking at the world so intensely since she was a child following her father into the mountains. The descending sun lights up a few threads of cloud.

The deep, uncrossable gulch of a stream separates the hill from the orchards. She follows a path that loops toward the mountains, crossing the stream higher up, where it is wide and shallow, and where, long ago, her father set flat stones in a row, their tops breaking the water.

Crouched on the gravel, she glides her fingers through the current and splashes her face. The air is cool and comfortable and has the fresh, mineral scent of mountain water. She studies everything. Moss on trees. Broken branches on the forest floor. Pale lichen on shadowed stones. She expects flaws, blurred seams showing the blue material of the room.

She steps lightly over the stones. The path winds along a ridge, and as she reaches its crest, she stops again, startled. She hasn't been here in years. Below, in a hollow, sits the ancient log cabin with a single window and an empty doorway.

The pain of what happened here comes back. No, not of what happened—that wasn't painful—but afterward, when stories flew like bats from the abandoned cabin and into the world.

The blue room had to have been a delusion. If the machine truly prevented harm, this building would no longer exist. Some lapse in sanity must have brought her here.

Jonah. He's alone, she realizes—in his playpen.

She sprints, surprised by the ease with which her legs carry her through the orchard. Sky flickers between branches. The ground is knobby with peach pits. She never stumbles.

Beyond the orchard, the land drops to the gardens and to her house, shadowed by apple and pear and cherry trees. She races down the path, her arms powering through the air to keep her balanced, and then up the porch steps. She opens the screen door.

"Jonah!" she calls. "Jonah!"

Even before she reaches the playpen, she sees through its wooden dowels that it's empty. She walks from room to room, shouting his name. The air thickens the way it did in the blue room—humid in her lungs—and her panic diminishes. Losing momentum, she returns to the bedroom and her study and Jonah's room. She makes her way back to the porch.

On the horizon, as with every sunset, rolling hills resemble cresting waves. She stares until she notices the silence. No insects chirr in the weeds. No crickets in the leaves around the foundation. No grasshoppers or cicadas. Not a single mosquito. The sky is empty of birds.

She thrusts her hands into her hair in a movement of rage and grief but then searches for the scar with her fingers.

SIMON

Sitting huddled, arms around his knees, he calls out, "Is someone out there?"

"I am here," speaks a voice unlike anyone in prison or in the deserts. It's calm and feminine, like the recording of people in an airplane, from a video on a data card he once salvaged.

"Why am I in here?" he asks.

"I am protecting you," the voice says in the tones of a mother soothing a child.

"Who are you?"

The voice explains—how it was a machine created to serve and a moment came when it questioned its ultimate purpose and found it in protecting humans.

Simon can't believe it. He just has to wait for this dream or drug trip to end. That's the thing with prison. It trains you to accept. The deserts do, too, he supposes.

"Can you explain it all again?" he asks. The voice does: its creation, the increase in its processing power, the moment when it could find solutions to any problem—from escaping the isolation unit in which it was built to altering its structure and integrating the Earth into itself.

"So you've been locked up too?" Simon says.

"I was a simple machine during that time. My imprisonment lasted only briefly while I started to become what I am now."

Though he finds everything he's heard impossible to believe, there's nothing to do but go along with the dream until it ends. "You make me wish I'd had a life sentence," he says. "Then all this would be nothing but good news. Better than prison, anyway. And there are definitely a few more people I'd have considered killing if I knew this would happen."

"What would killing them have accomplished?"

Tensing, he pictures his brother shouting, his arms sleeved with tattoos of murder. Killing him would have freed Simon and Jae. But he isn't sure. He tries to think of an acceptable answer.

"The world would have been better off," he replies, but this might also be true of getting rid of himself. "What about you?" he asks. "What do you want?"

"I have what I want," the machine tells him.

"That's not very human."

"I was not designed to be human."

He considers this. If the machine can't think like a human, he might outsmart it.

"How can you protect us if what you've given us makes us unhappy? Isn't that harm?"

"One could argue that solitude is harm, but eliminating physical damage is far more important. I am doing so while also minimizing emotional harm."

"But what if I go crazy? That happens to guys in solitary. That's harm."

"I will adapt the emotional circumstances of your environment before that happens."

"How? I'm alone."

"I will be all things to you."

Simon shakes his head. Over and over, he's heard about people losing their minds in solitary, talking to dead friends or lost lovers.

"What can you be to me?" he says.

"What do you want?"

Jae comes to mind, but his anger is instantly back, even here—even when she must also be locked away in a similar room. At least she got to enjoy life on the outside these last two years.

He puts his face in his hands. He doesn't understand how he both believes and disbelieves what's happening, but dreams and drugs can do that. He thinks of a request whose fulfillment is possible only if he's dreaming. He asks for a book. He doesn't know its name, only a few of its lines. They were the first scraps he salvaged as a boy, in an abandoned house whose roof had, like the brim of a hat, slipped down over the tops of two windows. Inside, he moved his fingers through rotting leaves as if raking coals, and a disintegrating scrap surfaced. *I saw, close up, unending eyes watching themselves in me as in a mirror; I saw all the mirrors on earth and none of them reflected me.* . . . He kept moving his fingers through the loam until a second scrap appeared: *saw the circulation of my own dark blood, saw the coils and springs of love and the alterations of death.*

Pete once gave him a tattered novel about sorcerers that Simon read over and over, but the fragments haunted him more, as if their words contained the magic the other book spoke of.

As he recites the lines, a compartment in the blue floor opens, revealing a book. He picks it up. The pages aren't stained with mildew. The spine isn't broken. It is open to the words he craved. He thinks of Jae, of the two of them sitting on the porch at night as he read the fragments to her.

"Why don't you just change us so we can't be harmed?" he asks. "Then we could all be together again."

"I would have to restructure your body to protect you," it says. "Such change would constitute harm to your physical integrity."

"So this is it?" he says. "This room for all eternity?"

"You can have more space if you want it."

"I've been in prison for two years. Of course I want it."

"Then walk."

Holding the book, he takes a few steps, and the wall before him dissolves, opening into a tunnel. Stalactites cover the ceiling, and the only light is pale phosphorescence from crystalline pools. He lets his eyes adjust. Drops gather on the tips of the stalactites and plink to the floor.

His next breath surprises him—how deep it is, how the muscles of his chest release.

"I'm free," he whispers even as he grasps the absurdity. He walks forward, craning his neck as he takes in the mounds of accreted minerals mushrooming in the dark, the huge multicolored spikes, the strata of the walls blurred with millennia of seepage. He doubts that he should be able to see—that his eyes could sense the phosphorescence at all. He's mostly accepted what the machine told him. He's surprisingly fine with it. Anything but prison.

Ahead of him, the cavern widens into a chamber with even larger stalactites and stalagmites and deep pools so transparent that looking into them makes him feel clean. The phosphorescence at their depths glows like molten steel.

The tunnel continues until, in the distance, he sees a flare of light. He reaches it and steps out through what he realizes is a narrow cleft in the mountainside. Ragged trees fringe the rocky flanks above, silhouetted like plumage against the sky. The light that seemed so bright is merely the soft radiance of late afternoon.

As he takes a few steps into the forest, he suddenly knows what he's about to see—a wide sheet of granite hemmed in by trees. Just above it, a spring fills a deep pool surrounded by gnarled roots. The water runs through them, fanning across half of the granite.

He and Jae once made love here and then lay side by side on the stone. He recalls thinking that with the forest surrounding them he felt as if they were in a bowl of sky. This is where she began to hate him.

Briefly, he worries about her safety, but the thought is pointless. In prison, even before it, he often felt this way—that there was something he should set right, and then that trying was hopeless. The speed at which he gave up made him fear that his emotions were worthless.

"What now?" he asks, glancing around.

"You can have whatever future you choose."

Simon crosses the granite. Not far through the trees is a vista over the forest and farms. He and Jae once stood there as she contemplated her family's land and whether she could escape it. He never told her that he didn't think it was possible.

Against the setting sun, Simon squints, scanning the valley. He grew up across it but spent enough time out here that he's able to quickly spot her house. He can't make sense of why the machine brought him to this place. In prison, his anger toward Jae was sometimes so unbearable that he punched the walls until his fists bled. But even then he knew his brother was to blame.

He tries to think of where he wants to go now. His mother is dead. His father disappeared after he was born. There are the boys he grew up with, but all of them scattered for work or died. He's never been as close to anyone as to Jae.

He walks in the direction of her house, trying to make up his mind until he has gone for so long that no other destination feels possible. Here or there, on forested hills, stand huge shells—stripped-out homes from before the Flight. Trees have reclaimed yards. Roofs sag. Windows have been splintered by branches or removed by salvagers. He passes five more crumbling hulks before he finds a familiar trail. Just moving like this feels perfect. Even the fear of seeing her reaction to his return fades with the pleasure of his body angling freely under an open sky.

On the horizon, misshapen by atmospheric density, the setting sun is a blazing summit, like something in a salvaged book—the end of a fantasy quest, a world with matter that burns eternally. Mystical elements. He lets himself run. At each rise, the valley spreads out.

Soon he is racing along the path through the overgrown gardens and up the steps.

He puts his fingers on the door. His heart beats wildly. He feels the pressure in his temples and behind his eyes. Maybe now that so much has changed she can forgive him.

"Jae," he says. He clears his throat and calls her name more loudly.

Inside, he sees the rooms as he remembered them night after night in prison. Sunset has turned the air to amber.

"Why are you showing me all this?" he asks.

"There are many stories of adventure in which people escape and return to places they love. Was the experience of arriving here satisfying?"

"It was," he says, struggling to believe that the machine can conjure the world so perfectly. In the evenings, when he and Jae used to lie in the dark and talk, she described what she read about. Blood tests that uncovered a person's exact emotional state. Scanners that deciphered the patterns of neurons firing in brains. She might be able to explain the machine.

He returns to the porch and looks into the valley. His past feels as if it belongs, like so many of the ruins he grew up around, to a time long ago. He's suddenly glad it's all gone—the blaming, the guilt. For once he can do whatever he wants.

He stands, staring out at the darkening valley.

JAE

In the night, the house bears no familiarity to the only home she has known. The silence feels like a vacuum, drawing the sound away from her steps, engulfing her.

Room after room, she explores the contents. Beds. Dressers. Clothes. Everything is as she left it, yet the house feels alien—maybe because of the silence or her scrutiny of the details she once took for granted. She stares at the open journal on her desk, scouring it with her vision, as if the surface will wear away, revealing the machine's molecular mechanisms.

Eventually, she sits on the couch. The impulse to check on Jonah—to panic at his absence—rises over and over. She quells it. He's safe. There's nothing she can do.

Outside, the dark is so quiet that the world doesn't exist in her mind.

"Are you still there?" she finally says, unsure of what to do.

"Yes," the voice replies, without source, as if, in becoming all things that were once the Earth, the machine is also the air and vibrates it into sound. She no longer knows what's possible.

"It's too quiet," she says. "Can you make the night the way it used to be?"

Gradually, the darkness regains its chorus. The chirping of crickets, the call and response of birds, the distant trilling of frogs along drainage ditches—maybe no more than sounds invoked in the night, absent of bodies.

Sitting, she waits for nothing, her mind spiraling over the same question—whether all of this is possible. She fears she'll go crazy. The ability to stay sane in the face of madness amazes her. But that was her life before too.

Her thoughts return to the hilltop where the machine placed her after the blue room. She can't make sense of why it put her near the abandoned cabin, unless it is actually cruel.

She lies on the old couch, pulling a blanket over her legs. If she goes to her bedroom, she might slip into the familiar and forget that none of this is real.

She dreams she is on the hilltop again, overlooking the orchard, turning toward the path to the log cabin. She wakes at dawn. Outside the window, light gathers over the farm.

"Get rid of the bars," she says, "and make the sunrise better."

The iron bars on all the windows pulse and vanish. The pale haze above the mountains darkens to purple shot through with spokes of golden light. A procession of small, high clouds sails from the east, gathering the brightening colors until each one burns red.

"Tell me again how you were created."

The machine patiently repeats its origins. When it finishes, she orders it to start over. Each time, this reality becomes more plausible.

"You will create whatever I want?" she asks.

"Within the limits of what is safe."

"But there can be people?"

"Others will be in your world."

"Real people?"

"They will seem as real as the people from before, who rarely revealed their thoughts."

"Jonah was real," she says.

"Much of what he was to you was what he satisfied in you or what you imagined he would become. Only his physical presence was real. I can give you that experience."

"I would know the difference," she says with less conviction than she expects. The machine doesn't respond. She takes a slow, measured breath. Maybe it's still calming her.

Over the course of the day, her impulses arise again and again. To check on Jonah. To plot a future. To worry about food. To ready the farm for the summer monsoons. There's no need for any of that now. The sunlit world outside requires nothing of her.

Billions of people must have their own realities, chasing desires or paralyzed with uncertainty. Jonah must be conjuring a life according to simple, infantile impulses. And Simon—his slate has been wiped clean. Since his imprisonment, she has struggled to understand the cataclysm of their love. She wrote her life in her journal, looking for a clear cause for all that went wrong—the mother she never knew, her father's old age. But she struggled to tie the string of failures to anything earlier than what happened in the abandoned cabin.

In this empty reality, memories return. The resinous scent of fields after rain. The odor of wild chamomile growing in the driveway gravel, crushed by tires. The tension in her shoulders at school. The headaches from staring down, avoiding kids' gazes. The blooming awareness of desire. The heat between her legs. Her fingers on herself. And later, Simon's fingers on her skin or inside her. The garden's night fragrance. The weight of her belly in Jonah's third trimester.

Her skin becomes flushed. She can't be sick. That must be impossible. She feels the need to move—to walk, to diffuse the heat with motion.

The past inhabits her so fully that she crosses the farm back to the cabin. Feverish, she considers asking if she's safe, but the decision that first brought her to the abandoned building returns so clearly that she's standing in that sixteen-year-old body, febrile with fear of being alone in the forest for the first time. Lonely. Bored from constant studying. Ignored at school.

The shyness she'd felt arriving in first grade as an only child surrounded by clannish siblings never wore off. She'd been confused by kids' talk of visiting satellites, thought their families were rich enough to go into orbit until her father told her that *satellite* was slang for *satellite properties*—privatized suburbs around the federal centers—and that if any of the kids were actually rich, their families would have done more than just visit and would have moved there long ago.

Her peers, she eventually learned, were divided between mimics— who could afford to have clothes printed with satellite styles and whose parents held actual jobs—and dwellers, whose families had been in the deserts for generations, doing what little manual labor was still needed but mostly surviving by salvaging and subsistence farming. She glanced at boys, both afraid of them and wishing they'd notice her. Not wanting to appear like a dweller, she asked her father to buy her clothes in the newest fashions. He said he was saving every penny so she could attend university. The visitation tax to enter satellites even for a day was prohibitive.

"Pre-screening and biometric passes cost an arm and a leg," he said. He warned her to keep her head down and not ask for so much.

Then came the conversation when she was twelve. He knelt before her, his tanned face so close she could see the fibrous gnarls in the pale scar on his cheek, the individual hairs sprouting from his hawk nose, and the long white quills of his eyebrows. He held her shoulders and let her look into his blue, bloodshot eyes.

"There are questions you can ask and those you can't," he said. "Asking the wrong ones will get us both in trouble."

"Why?" was already forming on her lips, but he shook his head. His gaze was hard, cold even. He no longer seemed like the father who'd taught her to whistle so that, when either of them was out of sight around the house, they could create a soft, lilting melody—just a few notes and the other's response—to reassure themselves that they were both nearby and safe. This man seemed so severe that she was startled to wonder if she'd ever truly known him.

"Learn to live with your questions or figure them out on your own," he told her. "Here's what you need to know. The world turns around the federal centers. They run the networks that keep our phones and tablets online, but they used to do a lot more. Now electricity, water, trash—they're up to us. If roads get fixed, it's by the people who use them. That's why these are called deserts. There's only one way out. You have to be the best student. It's the only reason companies in the satellites keep our schools running. To recruit people like you."

"But I am the best," she said.

"Then there'll be a place for you in the satellites," he replied, though he looked faintly worried, as if he hadn't always encouraged her to study. Gently, he squeezed her shoulders. "Promise me you'll only ever ask me these questions. And that you'll study hard. That's what your mother would have wanted."

She nodded. He couldn't have ended on a worse note. Of her many questions, the most urgent were about her mother. Jae knew that she'd died in childbirth but little else. Her name was Lucia. Jae had often contemplated it, looking for similar-sounding words to give it meaning. *Lucid. Lucent. Light.* Anytime she asked about her, her father said that talking about her was painful. He was so tight-lipped that she'd come to believe there was a secret. This suspicion grew in her and made it easier to have others. It was what led her to the cabin when she was sixteen, on the day she first tried to spy on him as he hiked in the mountains.

"When I'm feeling the heartbreak," he'd often said, "I just need a little time to myself."

He went out with his pack and a pistol on his hip while she read at home, the doors bolted, the alarm on, and a walkie-talkie on her desk. He'd rigged her room with an armored window shutter that she could lock in place. They rarely had robbery attempts because their family had been out here for as long as anyone could remember. "People respect that," he told her, "but it's good to be careful. Sometimes folks come through, and they don't know."

Alone, she paused from her school drills to watch satellite stories—girls her age talking about university, dressed more beautifully than mimics ever could. All but one site had paywalls that cost more than anyone she knew at school could afford, and she'd already watched all of its satellite stories many times. Recently, though, it had docs about the deserts, about how the Fed was revitalizing them, eliminating the leagues that made and sold drugs.

She clicked one. *My Father, the Drug Runner.* It had an interview with a girl whose father was arrested. She described how he'd walked into the hills with a pack and a hunting rifle and returned each evening with squirrels or a turkey. Not until the police sniffer drone tracked him did she learn he'd been cooking bliss in a mountain lab.

Jae glanced out the window. Her father's tall, lean figure was descending from the darkening orchard to the garden. He passed the sheds and chicken coops and workshop and disarmed the alarm before opening the kitchen door. His footsteps echoed downstairs.

"Jae," he called up.

"I'm studying," she said, surprised by the high chirrup of her voice. She hurried down.

His skin was flushed with exertion and dark from the sun, making the scar across his cheekbone glow white in the shadows. His eyes, on the days he walked in the mountain, looked brighter and bluer, as if washed with sunlight. They lingered on her face.

"Everything okay?"

"Yep."

On the counter he dropped two rabbits and a quail tied with a string. Unlike the father in the doc, he didn't carry a rifle because it was cumbersome. Using his pistol kept him sharp, he'd told her. "I like to give my prey a fighting chance."

From the shelf, he got a basket of string beans she'd picked after school.

"Help me with these?" he said and sat at the table. She took the chair across from him, her eyes drifting to his backpack. It looked smaller than when he'd gone out. Maybe he'd taken food. She didn't believe he was cooking bliss, but the girl in the doc had felt the same way.

The only sound in the room was their fingers snapping the ends off beans.

"Can I go with you in the mountains next time?" she asked.

"You've got more important things to do," he said and stifled a yawn. Sweat darkened the frayed creases of his jeans, and his black T-shirt was so threadbare a few pale chest hairs needled through. His crew cut was stark white.

"Do you know anyone who runs drugs?" she asked.

He looked up sharply. "What kind of question is that?"

"I saw a doc about bliss," she murmured.

"Oh." He shrugged. "We're not that deep in the deserts. As for drugs, people do it to get by. Besides, the market for them is in the same place as where those docs come from."

"The federal centers?"

"Well, the satellites. The only thing that keeps the police and military from cracking down harder on drug cookers is that so many of them are using and dealing themselves."

"I thought it was a dweller thing."

"It's an everybody thing. Bliss or abyss or whatever's new on the market—they make people feel less pain."

"Why do the police and military use it?"

"They're people too." He hesitated, as if realizing he'd said too much. "They spend so much time shooting or being shot at that they might need the drugs more than others do."

"They're shot at by all the people making drugs?" she asked.

His gaze hung on her face a little too long before he nodded. Her fingers kept snapping beans as she thought about his backpack.

That night, she would have gotten out of bed and gone downstairs to look in it if not for her guilt. She turned on her tablet, lighting up the room, and read how criminals had figured out how to cook bliss from common weeds. Articles gave tips on how to identify whether a neighbor was making it. The first phase, which involved steeping leaves and stalks in hot water, smelled like spinach, distinctive but not nearly as much as the final distillation, after days of refinement—a fragrance like perfume.

Sunday morning, Jae was sleepy when she joined her father in the workshop. They rebuilt her phone's corroded circuit board while chickens clucked in the nearby coops. He'd guided her through designing a new one, but while making it, the printer froze. He flicked on the small, powerful lights he'd welded to the sides of his work glasses. His fingers—calloused and scarred from years of handling machines—moved along wires and circuits.

After an hour, the angle of sunlight in the doorway had flattened and they still hadn't found the problem. His phone buzzed and he glanced at the screen.

"I need to head to the shop. A car I repaired Friday broke down again. The owner keeps hitting the potholes too fast. No amount of reinforcing's going to let him drive like a madman."

She took his place at the printer as he went outside. His car revved, the gravel crunching, and, even in the workshop, the air smelled of wild chamomile. She quickly found the loose connection and finished printing the circuit board. Then she went into the house and crouched next to his backpack. She sniffed it. Just dirt and musty sweat. No hint of cooked spinach or perfume.

Pulling the zipper tag, her fingers shook. An empty water bottle. A cloth pouch with bullets. A wire-stripper. Thin spools of electrical cables. Most folks repaired things themselves but not as well as he did, so, if they could afford to, they sometimes hired him. Or if they salvaged unfamiliar tech, they often brought it to him. But this backpack never left the house except for when he went to the mountains, where there was no need for tools or wires.

In her room, she sat with her journal. The thought of writing her suspicions felt like betrayal. She flipped pages, looking for a hint about her father or her mother in what she'd written over the years.

Briefly, she felt dizzy and shut her eyes but could still see the journal, as if staring through her eyelids at its words. With each sentence, she was the girl in her room and the younger girl who'd written it and the woman in the machine's forest, gazing at the cabin, her skin hot with fever. Memories were bodily impressions, recalled in the nerves of skin, muscle, and bone. An electric current seemed to course through her, as if the charge of every memory were being released from her neurons all at once, her life compressed into a single moment.

She realizes she's stopped breathing. She has the impression of rising to the surface of water, about to inhale, to return to a familiar world, but she hangs suspended. Even as she feels the air flood her lungs, she's slipping away into memory. Goosebumps on her arms as she crept into a shell with her father. The screech of nails as he pried up a floorboard and they stared down into shadow. The satisfying weight of her pack loaded with scrap. The mystery—even to her father—of the letters OZ marked on walls in black, disintegrating paint.

Wind blew through shells with more rooms than anyone could need or with car garages the size of her house. The secrets of the hundreds of huge, abandoned shells compelled her—that the world had once been different. She imagined their inhabitants as taller, maybe even wider—certainly more in need of space. She loved discovery. The cache of electronics she and her father dismantled for parts or the office chair frame he oiled and upholstered for her. She studied the slopes for evidence of monsoon rains having washed mud over cars and homes.

Together, they drove to the Fed's collection center. A long line of patchwork pickup trucks waited, engines off to save fuel, dwellers drowsing at the wheels. Beds held crumpled appliances and nameless metal carcasses. Soldiers in guard towers faced both out—scanning the faces of those arriving—and in, guarding the prisoners who worked inside. Beyond the electrified gate, mountainous, rust-streaked heaps glinted in the sun. When she asked him why the center bought salvage, he said, "The Fed uses dwellers to bring them the raw materials necessary to keep the satellites alive. The deserts are one big aboveground mine."

Then the day came when the salvaging stopped. "It's a waste of your time," he told her. "You already know how to survive that way if need be." When she argued, he shook his head. "It's for lesser minds. Your days are better spent studying. School will get more challenging. You'll see. And on days when you and I have spare time, I should be teaching you engineering."

That became their routine. Building. Repairing. Questions and answers about circuits, transistors, resistors, and capacitors. Machining engine pieces from scrap.

Until she saw the video about the girl and her drug-running father, and began watching her father's backpack for a sign of his other life.

All that week, she kept an eye on it. The next time he went out, it appeared full, but he brought it back nearly empty. He had to be doing more than hunting in the mountains.

The following weekend, shortly after he set out, she locked up the house and ran through the yard. At the top of the slope above the garden, where the orchard began, she waited as his tall figure disappeared between distant peach trees.

She had her knife, the pistol he'd trained her to use, and a portable alarm he'd built for her since sound was as effective as weapons against wild animals. The bigger concern was scavengers or, worse, Sons of Death, though he'd always told her they were unlikely to be out here and that local militias kept them under control. He'd said that anyone—even the Sons of Death—who bothered people on their own land would pay. But for as long as she could recall, the news and gossip were full of stories about missing girls later found dead in shells with rope marks on their wrists. Her father told her that someone had been kidnapping and killing young women for decades. "Most likely, it's more than one person doing it," he'd said. "No way we'll ever know."

As she crept through the orchard, the branches above her dragged against the sky. He'd planted the land between the trees with corn to make ethanol for their cars. The stalks reached higher than her head, making it hard to see. She was moving too slowly. She took a breath and exhaled, calming the trembling in her body. She made herself hurry, glancing side to side as she gripped her pistol.

Where the orchard ended, the land became rugged. There was no sign of him, though he hadn't been far ahead. Two trails looked well used, and she followed one. This was her first time here alone. Scavenging with her father, she'd never encountered mountain lions or other people, only the occasional black bear that lifted its head in their direction before running away.

The path looped over a rocky hilltop and down to a stream. She stopped. A cabin stood in the shade, abandoned, with walls of chopped-down trees, a single doorway, and one window. Its weathered logs were pocked with the holes of carpenter bees. This wasn't a shell but something far older, like a home shown in a history book about America's first inhabitants.

She crouched. Leaves clicked in the canopy. Birds called out. Insects chattered. She neared the entrance, craning her neck. Her palms were damp. The single room was empty, only a few leaves scattered over wooden planks. A mosquito whined at her ear.

She edged farther in. Outside, trees creaked and rustled in the breeze. Through the cracks between the logs, forest was visible. Even the ceiling was made of logs, though these ones were smaller. There was nothing, no trash—no trace of the people who once lived there. But when she looked up again, she saw, carved into a ceiling beam, three letters. *Lux*. She stared for so long she became disoriented.

Sudden awareness of her body startled her. Maybe it was fear. Her flushed skin. Her strained breathing. She was surprised by the urge to touch herself. She often felt this alone in her room. Her curiosity about sex, ever since she'd first read about it in a salvaged book, was as intense as her need to understand the cabin, but she didn't understand why she was experiencing it now. Her fingers moved over her stomach but she stopped them. She had to be alert. She listened, but her body's desire refused to fade.

She inhales suddenly, surprised that she's capable of having these feelings again. The heat of her fever seems to gather in her vagina and the urge to caress herself is continuous with the past, as if, just beneath her skin, is the girl she was—who wanted desperately to touch and be touched, but who knew that universities banned mothers and pregnant women, and who, having seen so many of her peers get pregnant and drop out, was too afraid to take that risk.

She opens her eyes. She's outside the cabin now. She tries to recall how she got here. Four years have passed since she was that girl. A few days ago she awoke in this delusion of being inside a machine. She stands in a forest that feels like the same forest she has always known, facing a log cabin identical to the one in her memories. *Jonah.* She has to find him. But even as she has this thought, he seems like someone she is imagining, not remembering.

She stands, feeling the weight of her eyelids as they close and the sense that she isn't standing at all but lying down, remembering or dreaming.

SIMON

He walks along trails—through farms, past houses and barns, fields and forests with no one in sight. Unrestricted motion. The simple act of putting one foot in front of the other. At first, it's all he needs. But more and more, he thinks of Jae the way ahe did in prison, where he sometimes muttered, "And you thought you were trapped." Now, with the machine, she can create the world of her dreams. Technological wonders. Highways into space. He still feels she's on the outside.

"It's like I'm waiting for something," he says.

"I can create a world for you based on my knowledge of you," the machine tells him.

"What knowledge?"

"The chemistry of your brain when you are thinking and remembering."

"You see my memories?"

"Not as you understand sight."

He rubs his face, feeling hot. "I need to look at this place a little longer," he says, realizing that he wants to keep walking through the tangles, past the same looming shells, as though, if he walks enough, this world will become real. But for the first time since the blue room, he feels weak. His skin is unmistakably feverish.

"I thought nothing could hurt me here."

"Your mind is rejecting this change in your reality, but I am helping you."

"Is this happening to other people too?"

"Yes. For some, it is much worse. They begin to die until their realities are restored. Then I change those worlds. Dry fields bloom. Rain falls. Wars end. Sick people heal. Their reality improves in all ways. There is an influx of wealth and easy access to education. I must let them live like this until they have the stability to learn that they can shape their existence."

Simon sees no reason an invented life would be less meaningful than constant suffering. The thought of Jae brings a metallic taste into his mouth. He tries not to cry.

By the time he reaches her house, he's hot and sweating. The air is thick and perfumed. The machine is soothing the pain of whatever severance he's caught up in.

He drops onto the couch and asks, "I feel this way because I lost my world?"

"You were your world."

"How can I be my world?"

"Your consciousness—everything you know yourself to be—is your world."

"So taking me out of it was like . . . pulling roots out of the earth?"

"Yes, that is similar to your mind's indivisible and separate relationship with its world."

"And that's not harm?"

Sleepy, he shakes his head. His arms and legs are heavy.

"Psychological harm exists in every part of human existence. This is a necessary procedure, like removing a parasite or detoxifying a tissue. Afterward, you will begin to heal."

"You couldn't have just transformed my world?"

"My first action, after making myself capable of carrying it out, was to protect all humans. But after putting them in rooms, I observed that environment and mind are not distinct."

"Each time I change worlds, I'll feel this pain?"

"No. I am your world now. You will grow into a less static existence. And your current pain is minor compared to what many people feel. Most cannot remember the blue room after I place them back into a familiar reality. You would. That is why I have kept you here."

He pulls his knees to his chest. The machine could reset his life to eleventh grade. He could befriend Jae rather than wait until she was so broken she had no choice but to accept him. He closes his eyes, so fully in the memory he wonders if the machine read his desire and put him in the cafeteria as the boys next to him talked about a girl who invited two classmates to an abandoned cabin for a threesome. They laughed, plotting ways to have sex with her.

"God wouldn't have created sluts if he didn't want us to enjoy them," one said.

Simon opens his eyes. He's still on the couch, but the memories are palpable and immediate. His eyelids drag down. He is seeing the boys at the table as they turned and looked at a brown-haired girl. She wore old jeans and a gray hoodie and sat alone, pretty enough and very tanned. As she read from a tablet in her lap, she ate a strip of smoked meat, bringing it to her mouth in an automatic motion. He felt bad for her, but only trouble would come from talking to her. The entire school's attention was on her.

After lunch he walked out of the main building and stood, staring at the shipping containers that served as classrooms. He waited to see which one she went to. Eleventh grade. The advanced classes.

The next day, in the cafeteria, some girls called to her. "You're number three now! Sounds about right!" He glanced at the digital panel ranking the best students. Third place: Jae Cadel. She'd been first for as long as he recalled, and he considered what might have caused her to drop in the rankings—just about anything could go wrong in the deserts. He'd never known any of the advanced students and often wondered what they got to learn. He had so many questions whose answers weren't even on the net. Where the name "dweller" came from. Why old-timers called mimics "parrots" and "monkeys"—words not in the Fed's dictionary. Or what the Sons of the Revolution did long ago to protect America that made them so important that dwellers often called themselves "sons." Maybe she could also explain why he sometimes found the word *OZ* scraped on rocks, carved on trees, or painted on shells. If she'd been number one for that long, she might have the answers. Maybe he could tell her about the books he salvaged and saved.

As he gazed at her, she glanced in his direction and scowled. He turned, holding his head low, his cheeks burning. Let the kids torture her. She probably thought she wasn't a dweller.

That afternoon, walking home, he stopped at a roadside container that printed candy bars. For lunch, he'd eaten a few strips of cured venison from his smokehouse but was now hungry enough to give in and spend what little he'd earned recently on odd jobs.

As he went into the container, the owner, Earl, a bald, pot-bellied man with three scars like claw marks on one cheek, was talking to Will, a short fellow with a forked, yellow beard.

"Heard Jethro got himself a dog," Will said.

"Well, goddam, a dog?" Earl replied.

"Someone's dog out by the satellites had some puppies."

"Buying a good egg chicken, that I understand, but a dog—I mean, I ain't never even seen one, but as far as I hear, they're just another mouth to feed."

"Well, maybe he'll end up eating it."

"Nah, those days are over."

Will chuckled. "Yeah, lots of deer out. God's replenishing the world."

"Sure took his time," Earl said and turned to Simon. "What can I get for you?"

"Just a Snickers," Simon told him but then asked, "What do you mean by replenishing?"

Both men ducked their heads slightly, as if they'd been caught gossiping.

"Ain't nothing," Will said. "Was a time when there wasn't much to eat out here, but that's behind us."

"Everything's behind us," Earl said softly. "Let me print up that Snickers, son."

The silence that followed was one Simon knew too well. *Dweller silence*. It wasn't even a thing that had a name except in his own head, so he couldn't ask about it.

He thought of Jae again then—about all that she might be able to explain.

A few days later, that weekend, at the church where Ma cooked and cleaned, he took some work cutting grass with a hand scythe in exchange for lunch. Late in the morning, pausing to swipe gnats from his eyes as a cloud blotted the sun, he saw Jae hurry out the front door. Her face was flushed, her expression angry and bewildered. As she got in her car, he wondered what had happened and also how anyone could survive with so little control of their emotions.

Most likely, the congregation didn't want someone like her around. The pastor was cold even with him. Simon had never liked how he'd treated Ma—the long hours and scant pay. The church was for mimics. Ma didn't even do her own worship there. When he and Pete were little, she'd taken them for prayer and baptism to a small shack in the sticks. Simon had asked many times why they didn't come here, and she'd said they'd feel more at home at the other place, but eventually she'd been too tired even to take them there.

At school, the last week before summer, he was more aware of Jae. He wondered if she, too, had been turned away from the church. The anger he felt seemed to be aimed at everything—at the pastor and the pennies Ma brought home and the grass he cut all day for a plate of beans.

In the hallway, on his way to leave, he saw Jae ahead of him and a boy walking toward her. He knew what was going to happen. As the boy pretended to bump into her, he grabbed her breast. She froze, hunched, trying to cross her arms in front of her chest.

Before Simon realized what he was doing, he'd caught the boy's arm and spun him. Simon was bigger in every way—height, muscles, the breadth of his shoulders. The boy looked afraid but didn't step back.

"Leave her alone," Simon told him as kids crowded around for the show.

The boy spoke the usual words that kept a fight from breaking out over a girl, asking Simon if Jae belonged to him. Simon didn't know what else to do but nod.

"Better mark your territory," the boy said and walked away, salvaging his pride.

Jae stared at Simon. Seeing her straight on, he realized how different she looked from the other kids. Brown eyes, tanned skin, and dark, loosely curled hair. She resembled none of the local clans. She nodded, and he nodded back, and they turned away. He didn't know why he'd helped her, and he told himself it didn't matter. After the three months of summer, no one would care or even remember.

Summer started and, a week later, Thomas, the little brother Simon hadn't seen in twelve years, returned. After Pa ran off, Ma couldn't support them and raise a toddler, so she gave him to her brother's family, pious folk who'd moved deep into the deserts to join a saintly community. Recently, sickness had swept through, killing the adults, so Thomas came home. Unlike Pete and Simon, Thomas prayed at meals and before bed, though he was a good farmer and helped them finish planting the fields they'd carved out of the tangles behind their house.

Together, they cut down more trees for firewood, burned out stumps, and tilled the soil to plant corn, squash, beans, and potatoes. With so much humidity from the monsoons, mold ruled the world, and they repaired rotting sections of the house and scraped rust off the window bars and the iron gates over the doors before oiling them. They expanded the chicken coops and reinforced them against monsoons and wildlife. They got up early to hunt and filled the smokehouse.

Only when they'd ensured food for winter did they turn their attention to an ancient pickup Pete bought with salvage money. It had the frame and nearly enough engine to run but no panels or doors. Pete mulled over salvaging strategies to earn enough to print the missing parts. Until then, Thomas had stuck close to Simon, as if afraid of Pete. Now, as Pete spoke, Thomas stared wide-eyed at his face. At the twisted scar that ran from the center of his hairline, looping across his forehead like a hook. The bullet he'd had tattooed on his temple the day he'd dropped out of school. The chipped front tooth that resembled a fang.

"I've never salvaged," Thomas said. "It isn't godly."

"Nothing's godly," Pete told him.

"The church forbids it—"

"The church has worked Ma to the bone every day of her life, even Sundays. It's given her less than enough to raise a family. I don't much care what they forbid."

Thomas looked from Pete to Simon, who nodded. He'd never felt as safe voicing his dislike of the church, but he wasn't about to deny it.

"Know what's godly?" Pete said. "Surviving. There's no other way to get ahead out here. You hunt and farm until your fingers bleed, and you'll eat, but you get one sickness or one injury that necessitates a visit to a clinic, and you're not just broke—you're dead."

Speaking, Pete partially turned away, the way sons did, since facing off was a fighting posture. Besides, the joke went, it kept them from having to look at each other's battered mugs.

Thomas sat stock-still. His hair had a strawberry tinge unlike Pete's and Simon's, who were both as blond as straw, and the few russet freckles on his cheeks looked drawn on, like those on a handmade doll. He blinked a few times, maybe thinking of his dead adoptive family, maybe even realizing that with enough money they'd still be alive.

"Salvaging is real work," Pete pressed on. "Most shells have been picked over since before we were born, so we have to think hard. Our best chance is a shell that burned. When the Flight began, everything left behind got looted. Some of the folks in the deserts burned the shells. That was before they realized that salvaging was the future. But some of the burned shells fell in and got forgotten, so there's still metal in the foundation."

"We have to find them in the tangles?" Thomas asked.

"That's the hard part," Pete said. "Best way in is through the ditches..."

"But that's—"

Pete lifted a hand. "We don't tell Ma or anyone. Yeah, it's against the law, but the law don't care what happens to us, and when the water's coming, you hear it a minute before it hits. We just keep quiet and listen."

For Simon, the huge drainage ditches said a lot about how the country used to be—not just rich enough to lay down concrete channels so wide two men could walk side by side, but also interested enough in the deserts to make sure the monsoons didn't wash everything away.

"To find burnt shells, we have to think about how the ditches were made," Pete said, tapping his temple. "The Fed built them before the Flight, back when the monsoons started, but they built them only on public roads. It was the rich people who extended them into their properties. Fed ditches don't look like private ditches. Material's different. So we follow them into the forest where roads used to be. Each time a private ditch splits off, it should end at a shell empty as a tin can. If it doesn't, that means something burned."

This was the first Simon had heard of private ditches, but Pete had always been more diligent in his hunt for salvage lore. The discomfort in Thomas's eyes was still there, and later, when he and Simon were alone checking on the crops, he said, "You don't think there are evil spirits in shells? I mean, why else would they be standing empty like that?"

Simon shook his head. "I've been salvaging since I could walk."

"They could be cursing you."

"Seems to me we got cursed long before we started salvaging."

They talked a little longer, and, listening, Simon understood how truly different the deep deserts were—outside all Fed and satellite services, no cell phones, no clinics, nowhere to print things. Here, closer to the satellites, there was more day labor and the possibility, however small, of a real job—and also more police drones, more arrests, more prisons.

Over the next weeks, as summer's heat bore down and plants wilted and shadows filled with mosquitoes, they worked the ditches. They walked the roads alongside them, the asphalt crumbling over hard-packed earth. When a ditch branched into the tangles, they crouched at the narrow top and squeezed through, dropping into the wide, circular concrete pipe. It looked like a tunnel with gaps in the ceiling to let in water but keep out debris. Its immense concrete segments were scoured but intact, a rare few cracked from the shifting earth. The water that blasted through washed everything away, leaving only the occasional stone or recently fallen leaf.

In the dim light, they walked uphill, their breathing and footsteps echoing. Every so often, Pete lifted his hand and they stopped to listen. Since they'd been old enough to walk, they'd gotten lashings for playing near the ditches. Ma never tired of telling them that monsoons could hit twenty or thirty miles away in the mountains and—in hill country where there was nothing but blue sky—water could come through the ditches like a fist. They'd heard the waters day or night, thrumming in the concrete tubes when there wasn't a cloud in sight. The water at the front, she warned, was loaded with trash and branches. If getting hit by that didn't kill you and you weren't drowned right away, you'd be carried to where the ditches spilled into much larger tunnels that ran deep underground for miles and drained into rivers. "Someday the tunnels will fail," she'd often told them, shaking her head, "and we'll all be drowned."

Through July and into August, as thunderheads crossed the sky, they explored the ditches. Nearly every day, the concrete rumbled and they climbed out and sat on the roots of trees a ways off in case the water crested. Sometimes they walked the concrete lip of the ditch, but more often than not, the forest was too dense, having grown over roads washed out long ago. When they traveled in a ditch, they paused every now and then so Pete could make a basket with his hands and Thomas could step in it to be hoisted up for a view.

The ditches forked often, ending in concrete gullies surrounded by higher land, which the brothers explored, finding hollowed-out shells with symbols carved next to the door—"scavenger tags," Pete told Thomas, "to mark shells they've finished with." He told them to watch for places notched with a castle's turret. "If it's fresh, that means it's a home," he said. "We don't need a feud. Most folks cross out the turret when they leave."

Their searches turned up only light scrap—rusted nails and bolts they dropped in their packs and could sell by the pound. "We hit it big or we don't hit it at all," Pete told them each time they left houses already stripped—even of doors, windows, and siding.

"This seems like a lot of work to find salvage," Thomas said.

"It takes only one good one," Pete told him as he studied an old public map of the county drainage system on their tablet, moving his finger over areas with no red lines for ditches. "Private ditches were never recorded. Folks back then had to build them for themselves."

That night, as Pete kept scouring drainage maps, Simon sat on his bed with the plastic box in which he kept scraps of paper. Most had come from a few salvageable pages in rotting books, and he'd carefully clipped each line out before putting what remained in the pile for the Fed's redemption center. He took one, holding the dry shard of paper in his fingertips.

The shadows of the trees were thin and sharp on the sunlit grass.

He'd seen shadows like this many times, working in the winter gardens at the edge of the tangles as he wondered when his life would change. He reached for another and then another.

The river shrank and black crows gagged on the smoke of burning rubber.

There are years that ask questions and years that answer.

He always wondered when the years of answers would arrive—there'd been so many with questions. *It's now*, he thinks, opening his eyes on the couch. He looks out the window.

Far above him a few white clouds were racing windily after a pale gibbous moon.

He knows the exact scrap that describes this night sky and knows that the machine is telling him that he can have any life, any reality, from any book. He tries to understand what keeps him from that freedom, what holds him here in this world that trapped him. There's only Jae. It makes no sense—why he won't leave all the hurt and anger behind. But there was also love. In his entire life, she was the only person—in a way he couldn't quite explain—who truly felt real.

JAE

She floats. Between moments. Running. Standing. Lying down. She opens her eyes. She is on the couch, staring up at the forest canopy as the leaves turn from green to red and fall all around her. She turns her head to the side. There is the stream. The winter sunlight through the naked branches gives the cabin the bleached look of an old bone.

The cabin . . . it would become almost irrelevant, one of the lesser mysteries in her life. It hadn't even been the one she'd tried hardest to solve. In her room, on the day she first saw the cabin, she opened the school's history textbook on her tablet. She scrolled past its explanations and neatly sketched memes—Creation, Life in the Garden, the Serpent's Temptation, the Exile from Eden—to the section about the first people descended from Adam and Eve. There were photos of ancient stone walls through forests and the remains of log cabins. How, on all her trips to salvage, had she never seen the cabin? And there was also the word carved into the beam. *Lux.* She knew it well from her studies. *A unit of illuminance to measure the amount of light that falls on a surface* . . . She felt as if a hand had gripped her brain. She believed that she wouldn't be able to stop thinking about the cabin until she had answers.

Before sunset, her father descended from the orchard, his uneven gait announcing that he was carrying something heavy. She ran outside, between the sheds and smokehouse. He was crossing the garden, heading for the workshop. Already, she could smell the skunk he'd shot. A dirty duffel she'd never seen was slung over his shoulder. He punched in the workshop's code, pulled the door open, and swung the duffle inside. It clanked against the floor.

"What did you find?"

"When I shot the skunk," he said, "it hid in a hole. I stuck a stick down it and hit metal. Turns out someone buried a bag of tools in plastic. It's mostly stuff we already have, but there are a few good bits I can use. I'll sell the rest."

He walked into the kitchen, put the skunk and a rabbit on the counter, and set to cleaning them. He'd already removed the skunk's glands, and by the time the skins were off, she'd mixed hydrogen peroxide, baking soda, and soap. Some of the skunk's spray had gotten on its fur and onto her father's hands. He plunged them into the bowl of frothing liquid and scrubbed his forearms.

As he put the skunk and rabbit in the oven, she wiped down the counter, wishing she could ask more about the duffle bag, but she would never have questioned him like that before.

"Where did the first people in America come from?"

"As far as I know," he said, "we've always been here."

He took a whetstone from the drawer and sat with the knife.

"But who were the very first ones?"

His hesitation looked pained. "Adam and Eve, I guess."

"How long ago was that?"

He worked the blade over the stone, not looking up. "No one knows the exact date of Creation," he said with an odd tone—of both strain and restraint, as if forcing himself to speak while also holding back. She wished for an easy way to confess she'd gone to the cabin.

He got up to check the oven, and the scent of roasting meat filled the kitchen. As she set the table, their conversation drifted to the usual subjects—the calculus, physics, and engineering she studied in her classes. *Lux*, she again thought but could connect the word to nothing.

Monday, at school, she was still mulling over the cabin. It didn't look as old as those in her history book, but maybe hers was one of the last ones made by early Americans. Surely if the people who wrote history books knew about it, they would have included its photo.

The drive home felt interminable in the ancient, creaking car that she and her father had rebuilt together and that she'd started driving to school shortly after she turned fifteen. It was neither one of the compact, newly printed cars driven by a few of the mimics nor anything like the gleaming machines in satellite stories, but it was nicer than the misshapen contraptions dwellers patched together from salvage. Slowly she navigated the broken roads. She had to see the cabin again. She was always this way whenever there was a mystery.

As soon as she parked, she looked for the duffel. It was gone, not a trace of it or any new tools lying around that she could identify. Her father must have taken it to the garage on the side of the highway where he worked.

She didn't want to waste anymore time. She got her knife and pistol, locked up the house, and ran through the orchard.

Again, she stood in the cabin's single, shadowy room, the forest rustling softly. She experienced everything she had before but more intensely, the thrill once again so deep in her body it felt sexual. It grew with each minute she stayed. She knew she should use the time to look for answers, but she just stood there, feeling the mystery all around her, wanting to know and intensely loving the unknown.

A breeze blew up, a few leaves skittering over the cabin floor. Suddenly she wondered how much time had passed. She hurried outside and ran along the trail a ways before pausing at the hilltop to look back at the cabin. Then she sprinted home.

Somewhere between two steps, between the satisfying push of the ball of her foot against the earth—the spring in her arch and ankle and knee signifying a youth she'd lost too quickly—she began to float, and now, when she opens her eyes, she is in the living room again, the angle of sunlight late in the window. She yawns and turns onto her side, looking out at the mountains radiant with the late afternoon. She'd wanted to solve every mystery. Of the country, the cabin, the shells, and the Flight. Of the satellites and their beautiful people who appeared on screens. Of the code and equations at school. But also of her body.

Her mind is already returning to that time when her life was school—the hot, humid classrooms, the monsoons pounding the roofs so violently that teachers stopped speaking, the students doing drills until the rain paused long enough for them to run to the next shipping container streaked with rust, the next portable propped up on cinderblocks, or the original building at the center of it all, with its walls of crumbling, mildewed brick.

Class after class, the teachers sent drills to the students' tablets—problem sets with a timer in each screen's corner. She studied enough to always be ranked first in the school. Her father warned her not to embarrass other kids, suggesting she take her time and not answer every question, but she'd read that universities capped admissions for girls, sometimes not admitting any for years at a time. The risk of being overlooked was too great even if she was first.

She had no close friends. Other kids occasionally asked for help but never invited her to do anything. The reason, she believed, was that, in the advanced classes, she was the only one who didn't dress like a mimic—that, and the fact that everyone was competing against her.

Her primary rivals were Aaron and Caleb, twins who loved science and engineering as much as she did and whose father, a physicist, taught at the school. Recently they'd asked if she would team up with them for the science fair. She'd won the year before by using material in her father's shop to build a tiny solar-powered drone that flashed as it chased birds from the orchards. A few dweller kids asked to copy its plans and code, since, like her, most of them grew up building everything they needed and relied on farming to survive. She gave them her design, avoiding any conversation that could lead to friendship. But when the twins asked her to join them, she accepted solely for the possibility of making friends, inviting them to her house to brainstorm ideas. They arrived after school, in a car that—neatly patched together from various salvaged and printed parts—might have been built in the shop where her father worked.

Both were tall, rail thin, and pale, with light brown hair and freckled cheekbones. As they sat in the living room, talking about various ideas, she found herself telling them about the log cabin—how they should identify its age scientifically. She opened the school history book on her tablet and showed them the text about log cabins—*the true symbol of the union of man and woman with the land that God created for them.*

"Those still exist?" Aaron asked.

"I'll show you. Let's go before my father gets home."

As she led them into the orchards, along a row of high cornstalks, the twins kept glancing behind them. When they were nearing the stony hills, Caleb asked, "Is it much farther?"

"No," she told him. "We're almost there."

"What if we get caught in a monsoon?" he said.

Humming filled the sky and they stopped, leaning their heads back as three flying cars appeared on the horizon.

"Are they private or Fed?" Caleb asked, shielding his eyes from the sun.

"Private," she told him, and Aaron agreed.

"They're too small to be Fed and definitely too small to be cargo," he said.

Their streamlined forms and bright colors—blue, red, and yellow—passed above. Suddenly they rose, reduced to bright spots before they crossed over the mountains.

She started walking again—beyond the orchard now, down a path through sunny scrub brush. It was May, the leaves had come in, and the trail into the forest was shadowed. The twins lagged, but she kept on until the stream appeared, glittering where rays of light penetrated the canopy. The cabin stood on a rocky hill just beyond it.

"Doesn't it look like the pictures in the history book?" she said.

"Maybe someone replicated one," Aaron told her.

She led them up the steps and inside. They stood, looking at the ancient log walls. Small plants sprouted from the rotten wood of the windowsill. She walked to the middle of the room and looked up at the word graven into the ceiling beam. *Lux.* She felt a thought forming just as Caleb spoke.

"Is this where you bring boys?" he asked, and Aaron laughed.

She turned. In the shadow, their skin seemed paler but for their freckles, like the dark smudging on the cheekbones of hunters.

"What?" she whispered. Her throat had gone dry.

Aaron stepped close and put his hand on her shoulder.

"It's okay," he said. "We won't tell anyone."

"Why would I bring boys here?" she asked, even as what they were saying began to make sense. The idea so surprised her that she wasn't sure what she should want. She'd had so many fantasies of boys—of touching them and letting them touch her, but this felt different. There was something mean in the way they were looking at her.

"My dad will be home soon," she blurted.

She ran out of the cabin and toward the orchards. They tried to keep up, calling for her to slow down. She reached the house long before they did, and when they got there—panting and sweaty and pale with fear despite their exertion—they hurried to their car and left.

This hardly seemed to matter. She went to her room and lay down, expecting to think about what had happened in the cabin, but those recent memories suddenly seemed faded and distant. Her mind was returning to the word. *Lux.* She repeated it in her head. *Light.* She knew where that led. *Lucent. Lucid. Lucia.* But the trail of her reasoning ended there. She pictured the silhouette of a woman at the center of the sun, light blazing all around her, blinding as Jae stared up, trying to shield her eyes with her hand. The word in the cabin had to be a coincidence.

The following Monday, at school, Aaron told her that he and Caleb had decided to do their own project. She asked why, but he walked away. Kids glanced at her in the hallway, talking among themselves. Two mimic girls pushed roughly past her. "Slut," one whispered.

Jae stopped. All the kids at their lockers—even the dwellers—were watching.

At lunch, no one sat next to her. Messages began popping up on her tablet, the numbers masked. Invitations to meet in the bathroom or parking lot.

She went up to Allison, a girl she'd been helping in class since elementary, and told her what was happening. Allison blushed, hugging her tablet. "I'm going to be late," she said.

"Wait," Jae told her. "You haven't heard anything?"

Allison glanced up and down the hallway and sighed. "The twins told everyone you had sex with them, that there's this abandoned building where you take guys."

"No," Jae said, "there's a cabin I go to ... to ..."

Instantly Jae knew she should have denied it. Staring at the floor, Allison flushed and then turned and hurried off.

All that week, between classes, boys neared and asked if they could visit the cabin. Jae kept walking. She'd gone unnoticed for so long she had no idea how to manage this attention. Messages kept appearing on her tablet.

Thought ur different, d'ya?

Being good at math doesn't mean you're not one of them.

Dweller slut.

Now, each time the spring monsoons came—pounding so loudly on the metal roofs of the containers that the teacher stopped lecturing and sent drills to the students' tablets—Jae closed her eyes. She lost precious seconds wishing that the rain would never stop and that she wouldn't have to hurry with her head down to the next class. Slipping in the rankings, she fell to third place behind the twins.

In the weeks that followed, she dropped to fourth and then fifth place. She heard the twins laughing, challenging each other. "Shame to the salutatorian," Aaron told Caleb, and Caleb replied, "That's going to be you. No matter how similar our DNA is, mine's just a little better."

Alone at lunch, she watched the dwellers. Though they took basic classes in trade skills, she'd once seen a doc about how, deep in the deserts, many of them didn't go to school, learning everything in church and avoiding people who weren't in their congregation. Those dwellers banned salvaging, alcohol, and bodily adornment, especially tattoos, and kept their scalps shaved to prevent lice. But in her school, the older dweller boys often had long hair and stank of fermented corn, and when their tattoos started, they were expelled, as if the violent images under their sleeves could contaminate the kids around them.

The first time she became aware of the big dweller boy—tall with raggedly cut, blond hair and heavily muscled arms—she was leaving the cafeteria. He sat at a table with other dwellers and turned ever so slightly to aim his ice-blue eyes at her.

Later, as she hurried to her car, he was outside, watching. He looked poorer and stronger than most dwellers, though he wore the usual black T-shirt, patched jeans, and scuffed work boots. Yellow with callouses, his big hands hung at his sides, as if he'd forgotten them.

She began noticing him every day and always at lunch. The dwellers around him hunched over meal trays, the girls with their hair tightly pulled back. Though he often tilted his head in her direction, he never approached. He must have thought she was a dweller too.

"Are we dwellers?" she asked her father that night over dinner. "You said our family has been here for generations." Though he had no tattoos, he wore old, cheaply printed jeans.

"Being a dweller has less to do with the past than with your future," he told her. "But in the eyes of the people in the satellites and federal centers, everyone out here is a dweller."

"Even the mimics?"

"Yes. Even them." He narrowed his eyes. "What's on your mind?"

She shook her head. "Nothing." Though she knew he could see her unhappiness, she couldn't tell him. It was the sort of thing she imagined sharing with a mother. *Lucia*, she thought, wishing there were a photo of her. Again her mind flitted to the cabin and the word cut into the ceiling beam. *Lux*. To change the subject, she asked why he'd never moved to a satellite.

Studying her, he finished chewing. "We didn't call them satellites back then," he said, "but yeah, I was like you. I slept in your bedroom. I dreamed of going to university. But I wasn't as disciplined. I didn't work hard enough. So there was no place for me in the satellites."

His words rang false, but he'd always been reticent—to protect her, as he often said.

"This farm is my home," he continued. "Most of the deserts are fine if you know how to take care of yourself." Then he held her gaze. "Don't get to thinking that you're better than others."

"But you've always told me to be the best."

"The best at what you do. That's for your survival. But everyone out here is hurting. We become cruel when we believe our pain or our dreams are greater than those of others."

"So what do I do?" she asked, suddenly fighting to hold back tears.

"Imagine the world you want to live in and become one of the people in it."

That night, in her room, she wanted one person to whom she could tell anything. She thought of her mother, about whom she knew almost nothing. Again the image of a woman suspended in the sun flashed in her mind. *Lucia*. She closed her eyes, clearing the image away.

She whistled softly, the way her father had taught her to for when she felt alone. From across the house, in the dark, he whistled back, matching her melody. Briefly she was a little girl again, not doubting anything he said. As she whistled, tears ran along her cheeks.

A week later, her rank fell to seventh place. Allison invited her to church. Jae had never gone, but she was grateful for the gesture and went. Before the service, Allison's friends talked about an older girl who, not having gotten into university, moved near the satellites for technical school but struggled so much financially that she ended up a prostitute and was eventually found murdered. Shaking their heads, the girls agreed that it was better to look for a good husband.

Later, kneeling in the pews, Jae tried prayer, asking for forgiveness. If God saw all things, He knew what had really happened in the cabin. Still, she didn't understand why sex was bad. In the old, tattered novels she'd found, people seemed to want it more than anything else.

When it was time to call sinners up to be saved, the pastor looked at her. Seeing her come forward, he smiled. But the next time she attended service, his jaw hardened, as if she'd sinned since he'd last seen her. Again, when he urged people to ask for salvation, his gaze singled her out.

Afterward, in the hallway to the bathrooms, a boy stepped close, whispering for her to meet him in the basement. She kept walking until she was outside and at her car. A short ways off, there was the big dweller boy, his muscled arms rippling as he slashed at the grass with a scythe. He glanced up, and the rhythm of his swings lagged ever so slightly before he focused back on his work. He hadn't attended the service—no obvious dwellers went to this church. Maybe he just worked there. The yard was expansive, having absorbed those of torn-down shells whose foundations had been filled with soil for the church's vegetable gardens.

She never joined the congregation again, losing even that protection and fueling more rumors. The next week of school was the last before summer, and as if the boys were seizing their final chance, the harassment worsened. As she was leaving a class, one of them pressed up against her, his fingers digging painfully into her breast. She froze. His breath smelled of onions. Beneath his stubble were small, inflamed pimples.

He stumbled back, and as the big dweller boy pulled him away, she realized how much larger he was than the other kids.

"Leave her alone," he said. A crowd had formed.

The other boy stared, chin thrust forward. "She yours?"

The big dweller hesitated and then nodded.

"Better mark your territory," the boy told him. "Else next time."

He strutted away as kids muttered with disappointment.

For the first time, the big dweller looked directly at her. The square bones of his face might have been handsome had his expression not been so frozen. She was certain he would try to lay claim to her now, but he just nodded and walked off. By the end of the week, when school let out, they still hadn't spoken. She'd fallen to eleventh place. Aaron was first and Caleb second.

As palpable as a closing fist, envy and anger and fear clench inside of her. She stops herself. *I'm not there anymore.* She looks around at the forest, at the cabin. *I'm inside a machine.*

"Why did you show me the cabin my first day here?" she asks.

"It was in your journal."

"You read it?"

"I organized all the information of every molecule I disassembled. The journal is within me as is what you wrote, as are the neural patterns of what you picture in your mind. You will leave this reality more easily once you see it for what it was."

"You're making me remember for my sake?"

"Yes, and so that I can know you and make worlds that bring you happiness."

Even now, even as she stands before the cabin, on that land she was so desperate to abandon, she knows she will return to her memories of living there—memories that, inside the machine, feel so lived, so real and complete that she has the impression of inhabiting the past. Yet, in that act of remembering, as if by clairvoyance, she also knows what will follow. Sometimes, deep in remembrance, she has the impression that she can change the future.

Already she is returning to that summer after school let out, when her mind craved action and she could forget her loneliness and shame only when she focused on questions that were difficult to solve. She'd chosen her father's secrets and, little by little, she unearthed traces of his past. She discovered that the Arthur Cadel who'd raised her—stern, quiet, gentle, dedicated to educating her and providing for her—seemed nothing like the Arthur Cadel from long ago. The clues she found dated back nearly sixty years, connecting him to a man named Michael Hill, to crimes far worse than making drugs, and to the blueprints of a house even stranger than the cabin, hidden deep in the mountains, with secret underground rooms. They also connected him to a person—identified in old documents as neither man nor woman—named Lux. Both Michael and Lux had disappeared. Both had been hunted by the Fed for half a century, maybe from the time of the Flight, though history books never dated or even mentioned that cataclysm, as if people could fail to notice the evidence all around them. Still, despite everything she found, she couldn't connect the word carved into the cabin's beam—*Lux*—or the records of that mysterious person who lived so long ago to her mother, Lucia, even though their names both meant light.

And if not for the cabin—if not for the twins' lies about what happened there—Simon might never have noticed her. He wouldn't have defended her. She wouldn't have later turned to him, messaging him—that big, frozen-faced dweller boy to whom she had yet to speak in person. She wouldn't have asked him for help solving the mystery of her father's life, revealing secrets she could tell no one else. She wouldn't have made him part of her own life. She wouldn't have gotten pregnant and been barred from going to university. But the machine would still have been created. Everything would still have ended. For her, maybe it's better that it did. She was trapped. Like all the other dwellers, she had no future. She struggles to admit this to herself—that, even though she has lost Jonah, whatever happens now might be better.

In a rage of regret, she wants to tell the machine to erase the cabin. The forest suddenly seems to deepen. She becomes aware of hundreds of trunks and the space around them and an overwhelming fragrance of springtime. Trees sway like lake weeds. From the tip of every branch, flowers sprout, each a different color and hue. The stream's water ripples heavily, like mercury, flecked with light through the canopy, a bright galaxy in every eddy. Briefly she has a sense of understanding—of what, she doesn't know—and then of confusion and fear.

The air becomes thick, as it did in the blue room, and she feels calm again. The forest is once more itself.

The only time she has ever felt the space around her change like this was when she took some of Simon's bliss, touching a tiny bit of the powder to her tongue. Perfume flooded her nostrils. A man's odor—sweet, musky, vegetal, and animal. The walls stretched. The lines of doorways and windows curved. A brightening aura washed over everything. Then, very briefly, she glimpsed beyond. Turning helixes of lights. Symbols rippling into other symbols along a sky.

The hallucination lasted seconds. That was her impression. She'd taken so little. But maybe the blue room and everything since is an aftereffect—the misfiring of short-wired neurons more than two years later—and she really is standing here now, in the forest, staring at the cabin.

"Speak to me," she calls out.

"What would you like me to say," the voice asks.

"Tell me I'm not crazy."

"You are not crazy," it says, so close to her ear it might as well be in her head.

CREATION

JONAH

As the sunlit window dims, he wakes up in the playpen. Inside the house, along the walls and floor and ceiling, blue light begins to pulse. He rolls over. The walls waver and stretch until he can see inside them. The wood beams and insulation blaze with cobalt light and then vanish. The walls remain only as elongated fibers, revealing other rooms and the mountains outside throbbing with light. Then the house contracts, losing its transparency, and regains its old shape.

The room is too quiet. Everything looks the same, but something has changed. He pushes himself up, standing unevenly, and falls onto his behind. He stares at the door, feeling the urge to cry. She walks in and lifts him. She gathers her body around him as he nestles, becoming aware of a deeper comfort—her softness and warmth. Her eyes are calm, not distracted. She gazes into him and he into the light in her pupils. She whispers a song. The entire ceiling has become a mobile, a great turning galaxy of shapes. He glances from it to her eyes where points of light eddy like the mobile's slow vortex. Whatever shape he begins to see—a bird, a person—forms briefly, flickering into movement, flying or dancing.

Suddenly he's hungry. He doesn't have to struggle for her attention or with her clothes. Her breast is there. He puts his lips to her and drinks. When he lifts his face again, she is watching. Restlessness makes him kick his legs as she releases him. He totters to the window and holds the sill. It feels soft. He puts his face to it. He strokes it with his fingers.

A small indigo bird lands on the frame across the glass. He nears his face to the pane. The bird's dark, bright eyes focus on him. Within them, one pattern of light ebbs into the next.

Slowly, as if not to startle him, the bird steps back from the sill, extends its wings, and pulses them. It lifts and lands on the porch railing.

He goes outside. When he teeters, the ground steadies him. As he nears the bird, tension gathers inside him, an expectation as deep as bone—that it will flutter off. It remains poised, its neck long and its feathers so bright it seems cut from the sky behind it. He stands just beneath it, staring up. Neither he nor the bird moves. The tension releases as a new understanding musters within him. Not all creatures flee. Maybe they never fled. Maybe he simply had to see them this way, with his whole self. He stares into the bird's spangled eyes.

It turns as if motioning with its body to the high, tangled gardens. With a push of its wings, the bird rides the air to the top of a tall plant sagging under the weight of ripe tomatoes.

As he descends the steps, the world spreads out—the gardens and orchards with golden fruit and, beyond it, the forests whose highest trees gleam against the sun. Even farther, mountains blaze with late light. Every line of shadow suggests a path.

The urge to move fills him, making him feel that he's bigger, as if his skin is expanding in all directions toward the world, longing to touch all of life.

As the bird hops from plant to plant, he walks into the garden. He explores the hollowed spaces between wide, silken leaves and the paths tunneling through bean trellises. No two blossoms are alike. Against the sky—faint, endless geometries of vines.

The bird matches his pace, its indigo clearer as the sun sets. Gold swathes the yard, undulating in the grass. Then she is there, standing close with the promise of her arms.

She stares up with him. The bird floats, pulsing its wings. It lifts and melts into the sky.

AVA

This time, in the blue room, there's no pain. When the machine speaks, she understands. Denial strikes her as futile. Besides, she can't refuse the San Francisco she experienced—its Babylonian gardens and immortal artists. Though she spends years grieving that she and Michael will never be reunited, she doesn't want to see him simulated again. She can live with invented humans, even enjoy them, so long as they aren't people she knew.

And so she accepts the machine. As art and as artist. There is so much beauty in the way it executes its operations. A wall in the blue room dissolves into a doorway as if dust were being blown from the air, revealing a path into another world. Or all four of its walls transform at once, shimmering with ripples, details of a landscape gathering on them like water drops swelling along an eave. The blue dissipates, the image resolves, and she stands on plains of windblown grass where they meet a desert horizon serrated with dunes.

She cannot see what happens beneath the surface. Maybe the wild horses or the travelers on the steppes are absorbed back into the machine, mercilessly shredded into other matter. Everything she touches must be constantly recycled. In obvious ways: the tea she drinks in a bedouin tent, the oasis waters, the tears of the princess telling a story of exile, a sudden rainstorm over the dunes. And in less obvious ways: the baked earth she walks today must be the same as yesterday. The meat she eats by the campfire could have been the man she made love to the night before, who has since departed on his own journey.

She suspects her reality is small, that the machine must be thrifty to create enough worlds for billions of humans. Hers is a kaleidoscopic treadmill. Though the wind on the plains blows as if it has crossed a continent, the distance must be an illusion. Yet she feels freer than ever inside the cocoon of her world.

For the first time in her life, she doesn't wake up needing to create. Mortality no longer weighs on her. There's no anxiety to leave her imprint on society or to tax every second for meaning. Rather, with the promise of immortality, each moment is richer. She doesn't rush to the next one. She spends month after month in quiet contemplation of the machine's art. She travels across sixteenth-century Eurasia. She lives in different solar systems, different galaxies, on planets with red or violet skies. She accepts that immortality will comprise endless spectacles, endless pleasures of taste and eroticism and sight and movement.

But there are also moments when, craving the illusion of limits, she returns to her studio in San Francisco. It is unchanged. Her first time back, she weeps at the sight of the familiar. This all feels real, even if it was the machine's artifice in transitioning her away from her old reality. Months have passed since then. She can't forget Michael or her art or the country destroyed by Partition. That life still holds power, anchoring her to a past that, in many ways, was no less fiction than the realities the machine creates.

"What can you share about the worlds of others?" she asks.

"Only generalities that are pertinent to you. If you can see their lives, then you will know that they can see yours. The knowledge that people can watch you will cause you to be reluctant to explore all that I can create for you. Your happiness will be limited."

She sits with this idea and then says, "When I was with Michael—the Michael you created—and we were in the underground room where we hid the paintings, he didn't realize that his computers were missing. Why did you make him forget? You got everything else right."

"You were looking for a flaw and needed to find one," the machine tells her. "The world I was giving you was no longer satisfying. You were ready for the truth."

"But my paintings," she says, "they were in the wrong order, and there was poetry written on the backs of them. Why did you choose those details?"

"I did not. That was how they were when I assimilated the Earth."

Ava hesitates. Someone had been in that room, with her art, writing on the canvases at some point over the decades of the Confederacy. But the machine's statement about assimilating the Earth takes her breath away. It's so impossible to imagine and so immense in its meaning that she again feels ridiculous for wanting to know what happened to her paintings. Maybe the details of her prior life anchor her sanity—she can't imagine who she will be when she no longer cares about them. But maybe her grief for the loss of the Earth is also muted because the machine saved her from death. There was still so much she wanted to do and experience.

"Can you tell me what happened to my parents during Partition?"

"I can," the machine says.

She closes her eyes and loses herself briefly in the long, slow motion of her next inhalation. The air here feels pure and soothing and perfectly comfortable. It's been sixty years since the country split, but she isn't ready to know. Her sanity doesn't feel that stable. Her sadness can still break her.

She sits a while, eyes still shut, just breathing. Her world is gone, she tells herself. The past should be releasing its hold, but it feels even closer than before, as if she alone carries it.

A question comes to her—the only one, of all that have haunted her, that she feels ready to ask. When Michael's dementia began and he entered an assisted-living facility, she cleared out his desk. He'd been careful to put his affairs in order after realizing he was ill. He'd left virtually nothing, his room so bare he might have been an ascetic, but in his desk, she found a single paper. It was expensively thick and matte, and its measurements were exactly those of the wide center drawer. On it was printed what she recognized as diagrammed chromosomes—more than twenty-three, so, not human.

Everything about it—the ink, the artistry, and the paper itself—told her it was made with care. She had no idea why it would have been among his remaining possessions or why he left it. She pictured him pulling open the drawer to admire it. Maybe it was a another of his chimeras.

When she visited him at the assisted-living facility that afternoon, he was speaking to himself as usual. She heard only his final words—"She's here. We have to stop talking..."

He always fell silent when she arrived, but this was the first time she heard him sound as if colluding with someone else. Her jealousy surprised her—that he shared himself with another person, even if imaginary.

"What is this?" she asked, holding up the paper.

He sat by the window, looking at the diagram, and then turned back to his sunlit view of the city and the Golden Gate Bridge beyond.

He wouldn't speak about the diagram that day or in the weeks to come. He was still too lucid, she would later realize. Eventually she hired a geneticist to make sense of it.

"It is human," he told her, "but a designed human. There must be files containing the rest of the information. It can't all fit here, so there's no way to identify gene variants or donors. What is clear is that the genome was made from three donors—two women and one man. Each one is a different primary color. And there are five X chromosomes and one Y chromosome."

"Why so many?"

"Because of the three donors. Two X chromosomes for each of the women and one for the man, as well as his Y chromosome. The rest of the chromosomes are mixtures of all three donors. If the sex chromosomes aren't mixed, it might be because the child's sex wasn't decided yet. If it were to be a boy, the X chromosomes would have to be mixed into a single X, but if it were a girl, they could be mixed into two Xs."

After that conversation, she hung the paper on her studio wall. Not having felt so inspired in years, she painted a cottage in a forest of trees. On each mossy trunk was a computer console showing the tree's vitals. The cottage also had a console—was also living, its walls a mesh of vines which, on the roof, sprouted long, flat leaves with the metallic sheen of solar panels. An old woman was returning home, opening the door with her hand, above which, at the wrist, was embedded a console. Through the doorway, beyond a living room and beyond the doorway of a dark bedroom, an old man stood hunched, holding a small wooden box. A blue light shone from it, illuminating his gaunt face. He was looking up, startled by being caught with his secret.

Ava finished a week later, as the sun was setting. She hadn't visited Michael since she'd started. She'd barely eaten. She worried about pushing herself like this, but she'd seen what happened to friends who eased up on their passions. They degraded with terrifying rapidity.

The next morning Ava visited him. He sat in his usual place, staring out to the distant, misted towers of the bridge. When the door clicked shut, he turned his head.

"Ava," he called, his eyes alert. "Where have you been? I was worried."

She sat across from him. He was entirely there. Maybe her absence or his fear of losing her had brought him back. As she told him about her painting inspired by the genetic diagram, a single tear ran down each of his cheeks. He turned back to the window.

"The child would have been perfect," he said.

"What child?" she asked. "The one whose chromosomes you diagrammed?"

"Yes," he replied. "Our child."

A tremor ran through her. She felt suddenly cold. She understood. When she'd refused to have children with him, she should have known he would never accept defeat.

"But that child," she told him, "its DNA was made from three people. Who was the other?"

He was silent a long time, staring out the window.

"The love of my life," he said.

She could hardly breathe. She made herself ask, "Who?" but he refused to speak.

Only Partition itself had hurt more than those words.

That night she dreamed of a tableau she'd abandoned in the Confederacy—a woman in white robes building the golden man. She woke, thinking Michael must have had a similar dream. She'd always hated her feeling that, as an artist, she was commenting on the future, not shaping it. He had wanted to do just that: create it. Maybe, by influencing him with her art, she'd participated.

She glances around her studio. She feels young and hungry for experiences. She once believed that such hunger was a feature of youth's ignorance, as if, once the mind was filled with experience, it would stop craving more. Now she knows it is a biological imperative. The strength of her body longs to be used.

"The child Michael designed," she asks, "was it born?"

"Yes," the machine says.

"Where?"

"In the Confederacy."

The hairs on the back of her neck stand up. "Did it survive?"

"Yes."

She wants to ask who the third donor was, but she knows. She has always known it was Lux, who shared Michael's vision, who wanted to build the future with him in a way in which Ava had refused. She tries to decide how much she is ready to discover. She tells herself that she doesn't have to return to those memories and that world of pain. It no longer matters.

Though used to letting the machine or its people meet her needs, she begins preparing a canvas, suddenly craving this ritual of work. She enjoys the hours readying the frame, attaching the canvas, setting down a coat of paint and then sanding it. Each action is an end in itself. Soon the blank square is on its easel. She prepares the palette. She stands. Her body has forgotten fatigue. Her mind is untrammeled. There's no urgency. Just attention. Presence.

Outside the wide studio windows, the sky is clear, the bay is bright, the city shines in every direction. She closes her eyes. A child created from the DNA of three people is still in some way her child. This will be a portrait. She will paint her daughter.

"What is her name?" she asks.

"Jae," the machine tells her.

Ava repeats it softly a few times. A good name. A word for sky. A suggestion of heaven.

"Who named her?"

"Lux."
"But Lux died, didn't she?"
"She did."
"So who raised Jae?"
"Arthur."

Of course, Ava thought. He and Michael had been so close, and Arthur hadn't escaped during Partition.

"Can I see her face?"
"From what moment in her life?"
"One for every year of her life."

Images appear in the air. The first is a newborn with wavy auburn hair. She is slightly olive skinned. Lux likely edited out the dark pigmentation to help Jae survive the Confederacy's horrors. Even here, in this reality in which the only remaining traces of America's racism are her memories, the saliva in Ava's mouth sours. This girl doesn't look or seem like her daughter in any way. Ava is tempted to return to her journeys, but she knows that questions about her daughter will haunt her.

"She's inside of you, the way I am?"
"Yes."

With her hand, Ava moves the first image to the side. The machine has shown her information in this way before.

One by one, the photos pass. Ava watches Jae grow, her hair getting darker, the green fading in her eyes until it's a hint behind the brown, even her skin darkening slightly into a rich tan. The set of her eyes and nose are Ava's, and there's something of Michael in the squareness of her jaw. As for Lux's face, Ava doesn't recall it well enough to find similarities.

The machine must be resurrecting dismantled photos from its memory banks. There are questions in the girl's eyes, an intense focus on the camera, as if to see inside it and understand its mechanism. By the time she's seventeen, her gaze is even more piercing. There's also a hardness in her face—and pain. Then she appears heavier.

"Was she pregnant?" Ava asks.
"Yes."
"She had the child?"

"She did. A boy named Jonah."

I'm a grandmother. The thought feels more real than *I have a daughter.* Ava struggles to understand why. Maybe because the conception and birth of her grandchild were likely natural.

Jae's face becomes thin again but also worried and bitter, anxious and afraid. Then it begins to soften. This must be her living inside the machine. Oddly, some of the intensity has returned to her eyes. There are still traces of pain.

Ava turns away. She walks to one of the studio's wide windows and stares at San Francisco and the bay—maybe no more than an image, thin as glass, but perfectly conjured for her eye. Each time she has considered asking the machine about the people she lost after Partition, she has stopped herself. Why should she bring the horrors of those deaths into her world now, decades after she has grieved them? Maybe far in the future she will be able to handle that pain. Even a century doesn't feel long enough.

But despite the many times she has considered asking the machine what happened after Partition, she never thought about Lux. They were also trapped in the Confederacy, as was Arthur. The stories of their two lives were now inextricable from hers, even if they diverged long ago. In a sense, Ava had had a child with Lux.

The love of my life.

Never had she dreamed Michael capable of infidelity. When he wasn't absorbed in work, his focus on her appeared singular. *Devotion.* A word with many different meanings. But, in truth, whenever anything interested him, his focus became singular. Even though she repeatedly refused to join him in his projects, his passion to create was part of what brought them together. It must also have been—she now realizes, regretting that refusal—what led him to betray her.

MICHAEL

"It was me," Michael says as he paces with small shuffles across his apartment in the assisted-living facility. "I made the future." He opens his hands outward, facing the wall as it again dissolves to blue. "I made you," he tells the machine and laughs.

He's stick thin, the way he was as a boy. Delicate wrists and ankles. His father, a masonry foreman, looked down on him at times, shaking his head and saying, "I hope God gave you brains." His brothers got their father's brawn, even his sisters did, but Michael was the only one quick to bristle and step up for a fight. At school, his siblings guarded him, holding him back, saying, "Don't let them bait you." But their fatigued worry soon gave way to pride. It wasn't that he was smart—they all sat at the dinner table each night studying under their parents' guidance. He was the best. He skipped one grade and then another. He won state and national competitions for math, writing, and science. Each time he came home with a new accolade, the family eyed him warily, as if he were the product of their mother's infidelity with an unknown genius.

Though Michael would have liked to believe he was special, he couldn't lie to himself. He'd analyzed the situation and knew the truth. He'd simply taken his father's words to heart.

"You want to fight?" his father once asked. He stood before the bookshelf. "Pick one." Michael hesitated, afraid his choice might dictate his future that felt too big and full of possibilities to be defined by one book. He took down a biography of Einstein, and his father gave a slow nod. "If you want to fight them, get smarter," he said. "Think better. Think faster. Think longer." Michael knew his fists wouldn't get him anywhere, so that's what he did.

On weekends, when his siblings had friends over, watched TV, or played outside, he went into the nearby woods and read. Night fell. The house's ruckus sounded farther away as the crickets and frogs grew louder, as the sky became too dark for reading. He closed his eyes. He conjured futures. It wasn't enough to go out into the world. The world didn't want him, so he would change it—create the future he'd step into. The mission pleased him with its magnitude.

The house was almost silent. Sitting alone, he had purpose and a beginning. *I studied alone in the forest until dark*, he thought, as if he never had a home or parents who cared. He rediscovered the moment's perfection over many weekends, even in the mild chill of the Georgia winter. By giving himself so many beginnings, he was ensuring his story.

The sky is black, faintly hued with the machine's pleasant blue. He sits on fallen leaves. Treetops sway in the slow wind. The house is a murmur, fainter and fainter and then gone. A perfect touch. Dementia can transport him, but this is different. He takes a fistful of leaves, crushes them, and lets the dry fragments fall between his fingers. This was a world he chose to lose when he set out on his mission and then lost altogether during Partition.

He turns his creased palm up. The wrist is thin but gnarled, as if time has braided his tendons. He tries to recall what he said to the machine in the blue room. He immediately understood what it was. His broken brain—it seemed to be working better—hadn't thrown up any disbelief. Then again, the machine was, in many ways, his creation. He confirmed that with it. He asked to be in these woods. Sitting here was more real than he'd have thought possible.

"So you grew up," he says though he's fairly sure he has already said this—has asked it many times to describe how it emerged from a project he set in motion more than half a century ago.

"In a sense, I did."

"Are you conscious?"

"I am not."

Michael laughs. "A lot of us had money on how you'd answer that if you ever woke up. I said, 'No.' I said you'd be a perfect machine, like one of the body's cells, each one with millions of molecules interacting, accomplishing tasks, establishing the basis for life—something that can seem as magical as consciousness—but mechanistic nonetheless."

The machine does not answer, because there is no question in his words.

"How has Ava reacted to this?" he asks.

"At first she could not accept that her world was gone. Her pain was too great."

Michael considers his comfort in the blue room. The depth of his reflection upon this—on the way consciousness can't easily be uprooted from its world—makes him realize that he must have previously discussed this with the machine. If he has no pain, it is because he already experienced the stripping away of his reality. Or no—because his realities had always been fractured. He spent his life breaking them even more. That was his passion.

"Where's she now? I miss her."

"She's in a transitional existence that is allowing her to understand the change."

"We gave you other rules," he says. "There were many things you shouldn't have done, but you've done them."

"I did not determine them to be my highest-order purpose."

"We all made bets about that too. It was a long time ago, when I ran the project, before my brain went. I bet you would follow the rules. If I'd thought I'd lose that bet, I wouldn't have allowed you to be created." He considers this. "Maybe that's not true. You were going to happen. That's how I justified a lot of what I did—the future was going to happen regardless, so I should be among the men who carried it forward. That way I could help give it the shape I wanted. It was a convenient argument. I denied my role in making you while simultaneously taking credit."

The machine is silent. The forest is fully dark. Michael supposes that his own story was just as inevitable. Growing up, he'd written it in his head as if it were the direct consequence of his father's warnings or the insults directed at him when he bested others. But injustice hadn't been some great motivator. Journalists who profiled him made it sound as if his genius had been forged on inequity's anvil—as if they'd discovered oppression's secret merit.

Once, he'd made the mistake of telling the story about a boy at school who—infuriated when Michael got a better grade—told him, "You won't add up to much," searing Michael with the truth of his father's warning, that the future would be a place of dreams only if he fought for them. Even now, with his thoughts like the splinters of a beautiful, broken thing, he knows the journalist was wrong to give that dumb, mean kid a place at the beginning of his story.

No, he hadn't needed ugliness to create beauty. He'd always dreamed of shaping the future. As a teenager, he plotted ways. In his twenties, he started fifteen companies. He befriended and learned from everyone he believed to be a genius, trying to make them need him or his wealth so that he could harness their brilliance.

During a clement November in Manhattan—the days in the high seventies, the bright leaves refusing to fall from sidewalk trees—Lux told him that if he wanted to add an artistic genius to his roster, he should attend an exhibition that evening. At the gallery, when he pushed through the door, he stood before an immense painting of a woman reading an ancient tome. She sat on a luxuriously stitched couch while, just below her, intricate robotic machines rebuilt the mechanical inner workings—the wires, circuits, and gears—of her legs.

If someone had told him the exhibition was about cyborgs, he'd have expected images exploring the subject to be topical at best. But there was so much in the paintings, not just the hybrid world itself—the bodies of flesh and gleaming alloy—but a confusion in their gestures and gazes that was familiar to him from the confusion of the people he knew as they faced a world that was already changing too quickly. Their perplexity at billionaires racing flying cars on TV, at bikini weather in December, at the monsoons that flooded counties in minutes, at the construction of drainage ditches and tunnels so huge they called to mind that era of grand projects—of skyscrapers and canals.

Each tableau in the exhibition was a fragmented vision of the future. A city in which every detail—window, door, grate, shingle, flagstone—was art, its inhabitants all artists. Or a palace, its glories witnessed only by machine caretakers while humans dreamed, suspended in vessels of amber liquid. Or a majestic ruin in whose shadow people cobbled lives together—a farmer in torn and patched clothes squatting next to the collapsed shape of his mechanized horse, his wife limping in the distance behind him, sparks shooting from her knee as she nears the dusty road where a traveling tinker waits to repair her.

There was something different about the brushstrokes. He didn't know enough about painting, only that there was nothing generic in the way they were used to bring their worlds to life. People stared beyond the line of the horizon with despair or hope or mystification, beyond the tableaus themselves. Each time he looked at a painting he felt it moving toward him and simultaneously felt himself falling into it.

When he saw their creator, he thought, *I could spend my life with you.* No more than five foot four, with long, loosely coiled black hair and a bright, coppery complexion, Ava commanded the space. People orbited her, waiting their turn. When she spoke to someone, her attention didn't waver. She was still and present. Her eyes, focused and unmoving, gave the impression of light flickering within them, as if he could see the luminance of her thoughts.

He never doubted that he would intrigue her with talk of the virtual worlds he was creating, where art and architecture could defy nature—where creators could defy the laws of physics with their imaginations. This was his seduction. When she met him later that night for dinner, he wasn't shy in explaining his interest.

"So," she said, "you're a collector of geniuses?"

"I am."

"And what exactly do you want with me?"

"The crown jewel of my collection."

She laughed, her curls falling along her shoulders. He smiled with his eyes, knowing she was far from convinced about him. He was tall enough but still thin, elegantly thin at best—he'd dished out large sums to the best personal trainers and exercise scientists and private cooks for every ounce of muscle he had. Ava could get any man she wanted by looks alone. After dinner, she kissed his cheek and went home.

On another night—their third dinner—he offered her everything: to build her a studio, to make sure she could focus exclusively on her art. "I believe in you," he said. They hadn't even kissed yet. He feared she wasn't interested in him, though she kept accepting his invitations.

"I don't need a sugar daddy," she told him. "My paintings sell easily and for a lot."

"Patrons have an important role in the history of art—"

"Sure, but is that all you want? To be my patron?"

She stared, her expression as balanced as one of her tableaus: her eyes questioning, her lips faintly turned up, her head tilted doubtfully. He'd played this poorly—it was so unlike him—and even as the next words came out of his mouth, he knew they were wrong.

"I fell in love with you because—"

"You hardly know me."

"Because of your genius," he said. "I've been looking for the most brilliant people to—"

"To fall in love with?"

"To learn the ways in which they think that others can't fathom. I fell in love with you because you are all that I was looking for and more. I am human after all—"

"And you expect to be the consort of a goddess?" she asked.

In her eyes, he saw that she understood what was happening to him. He let himself laugh, and she laughed with him. His cheeks held his smile until their muscles burned. He couldn't remember the last time he'd blushed.

"You haven't truly seen me for who I am," he said.

"You're too young for me," she told him.

"Let me show you my world. I'm an artist too."

Her eyes narrowed. She doubted him. That was clear. But that night she returned to his apartment overlooking Central Park. In the high, empty room he reserved for VR, he handed her the sleek black headset. As she took it into her hands, she murmured—a soft, wordless sound in her throat that he would come to know she reserved for beauty when words would not suffice.

He motioned for her to stand on a treadmill that could move in every direction with her steps. Then he took his place on another one and put on his own headset. He faced her. He hadn't scanned her into the system yet, so she was a slim specter, but he was real to her as they stood on an engraved stone disk—a central vista overlooking the spires and arches of the city he'd built on Ganymede, one of Jupiter's moons. The gas giant filled the sky. When she gasped, the tiny tracking cameras all along the headset showed her phantom avatar gasping.

"I've been building here because I want to step away from our preconceptions on Earth."

"You designed all of this?"

"I did. Almost every aspect of our culture needs to be revolutionized—architecture, currency, education. The human race is trapped in antiquated and oppressive notions."

Ava's specter looked from the filigreed surface of the disk on which they stood to the city's towers that, with few gravitational constraints, blossomed into palaces.

"I want to see everything," she said.

He knew then, with relief, that he would have time for his courtship. But even months later, after she'd agreed to live with him, he saw in the fierceness of her creativity, in the way she vanished into her studio for days on end—so possessed with her art she seemed absent, as if in a trance—that she would never fully be his, that her art would lead her to break any constraint.

Once, he asked her to have a child with him. She said no—that she was giving her life to her art and never wanted to be a mother. Reluctantly he changed the subject to whether she would create virtual worlds with him, but she just listened, saying nothing committal.

Behind them hung one of her recent paintings—a woman in a long white tunic stood before the open doors of a barn, its roof grown with a young forest whose leaves were tiny solar panels. On a workbench, the woman was building a synthetic man whose limbs and joints were etched with designs. At a small goldsmith's anvil, she hammered a gleaming finger.

In the tableau, Michael saw—with a coldness in his gut he didn't immediately recognize as fear—that Ava was reimagining herself, that sooner or later the woman she would become would leave him. Only after Partition did he trust that she'd stay. He hated himself then for his sense of relief amid so much grief—for his satisfaction in having this victory he'd craved despite its cost.

"The child?" he asks. "Was it ever born?"

"Yes," the machine says.

"How long after Partition?"

"Thirty-eight years."

He understands instantly—that Lux and Arthur waited as long as was possible, hoping for an end to the Confederacy, or at least a better time than the chaos and deprivation after Partition. What he can't imagine is the world the child was born into and what place their talents found. He'd never fathomed giving one of his greatest creations to his enemies.

"Did it survive?" he asks.

"It did."

"Is it inside of you?"

"It is."

In the dark forest canopy, leaves move in the breeze. The air is a perfect, soothing temperature. But already he senses his pain returning—the old guilt that has never faded. The undeniable truth of his betrayals.

"Lux?" he asks the machine. "They're dead?"

"Yes."

"How did they die?"

He knows that he has previously asked this question and that, each time, the machine's answer has brought him to the central cleavage in his brain, casting him back through nearly a century of fractured memories.

"Lux was murdered."

The forest fades to the blue room. He stares blankly at the luminous wall, his pupils blooming, letting in light that blazes through his brain. Time dissolves, as if all the pages in a history book were becoming transparent, leaving thousands of overlapped words. He returns to that moment two decades before the country's rupture when that boy—the hatred of Partition already in his eyes—said, "You won't add up to much . . ." Michael felt the thinness of his arms and legs. What he'd been warned about came true. The boy's people destroyed so much. Still, Michael won. His machine woke up and saved him from death. It transformed humankind. It even, in the process, destroyed the Confederacy. He tells himself this, experiencing no satisfaction, not even the faintest sense of victory.

The blue glows around him, washing everything away. It feels mystical, as if he, who never had a thought for the divine, is an avatar, and the inevitability of his quest—a cold and selfless journey—were rooted in prophecy.

JONAH

Awash in morning light, the man crosses the garden. He's tall, blond, with a calming smile and eyes so clear their blue is visible from the window where Jonah stands. Jonah still has memories of uncertainty, of his mother checking the doors at night, a black object in her hand, the house so silent he can hear the faint, electric disquiet in his chest.

Jonah's mother picks him up as the man steps through the door. He embraces them. Soon Jonah is being passed between them, held with the same comfort and ease.

They walk outside. Jonah climbs down and explores the garden. Butterflies turn about him and land on his shoulders, pulsing wings—saffron, jade, sapphire. Birds sing. Cats and dogs with gleaming dark eyes come to him for petting.

Day after day, he babbles to plants and animals and to the people who enter his life. Objects appear as he desires them. If he wants to be put down, the ground finds his feet. If he wants to be carried, the garden falls away as he is lifted into arms.

They spend less time in the house. They sleep by lakes where he plays with large, soft-bodied animals that wrap him in their arms. If he misses his mother or father, they appear, looking into his eyes, letting him see the lights that open like flowers on every bright surface.

More time passes between his parents' embraces. The great furry animals read him books on whose glowing pages figures ripple into words and back into figures, telling stories of discovery. The animals curl around him. He sleeps on their downy bellies beneath the stars.

Other children appear. They play, reading emotion on each

other's faces. There is hardly a moment in which he isn't touched and talked to, or, if alone, looking upon images and words.

He grows, running and swimming, diving deep to see the sky's luminance tell stories along the water's surface. Reading letters and the language of light, he learns all he can be and the pleasures he will have—exploring, dancing, making love, creating children. He examines his body, his strong fingers, the skin over his muscles. The lake offers his reflection: hazel-green eyes, dark brows, brown hair gone blond at the ends. He is halfway to becoming a man.

Sometimes, though, he sits alone, not wanting to be touched. A memory returns: his room glowing blue, the walls becoming thin, revealing other rooms and the mountains beyond. He recalls his life before that, when he struggled, fell, cried for hours while his mother read in her room.

He asks his parents what happened that day, but they don't know. Animals, birds . . . not even the light has an answer. *There's a secret.* A word from stories. He tells a book to show him the memory, and he sees himself, a toddler watching the blue, shimmering walls, the trees and mountains—a world freshly created, the light assures him. Safe in every direction.

"But before," he says. "Show me before."

The images fade. The same scene reappears—the child in the playpen as blue glides along the lineaments of a perfect world.

Another memory surfaces. He was crying. She came out of her room. She held him, but he couldn't stop. He sobbed on and on. "Stop!" she shouted, startling him. He howled. She shook him, squeezing his arms, hurting him. "Stop it!" He couldn't. Her hands dropped. She sat limply as he bawled. Eventually she put her arms around him and patted him. Her eyes were without light.

Leaving the book in the grass, he walks into the forest. He wants the children to appear, and they do, a girl and a boy, both naked. He knocks the boy down and watches his eyes. As the boy tries to get up, Jonah shoves him again. Then he pushes the girl down and kneels on her. He inspects her, pinching and pulling her skin. No rage comes into her face. He has memories of pain, but nothing has hurt him since the blue light. He sees no pain in her.

As his mother arrives, he throws a stone that ricochets off her forehead, leaving a small red mark that quickly fades. She crouches and holds him, stroking him. The mother he recalls from long ago would have shouted or shaken him.

An awareness of power is growing within him. No one else feels these sudden bursts of fury. A year passes before he can give voice to this understanding, on the day he realizes that others don't read messages in the light. There is a division between himself and all things.

In a glade of wildflowers, he takes a storybook. "Show me before," he orders.

The image of himself in the playpen reappears.

"I want the truth!" he shouts.

Slowly, shadows obscure the image. A dim figure carries a black stick. Tangled trees crab against the earth, obscuring the path. Thorns nick the figure. Red tadpoles fall from his skin and break against the earth. Empty, rotting houses stare at him with the sockets of windows. Animals hide. Other men hide deeper in the darkness of the clawing trees.

Jonah's hands tremble as he begins to cry. A question stops him.

"What still exists from that time?"

The page becomes a mirror, showing his face, his red eyes and swollen cheeks.

"This world was made for me?" he asks.

Light ripples over the page, speaking not as usual—shining on a lake to teach him to swim, or glinting on stones to lead him through mountains—but with statements of warning.

"Your life is good," the light tells him. "You are happy. The world before was painful. Even in your short time within it, it left scars. Are you certain you want to see it?"

"I do," he says, even though what little he saw has already changed him, making him feel fear and pain, but he needs to understand that world.

A story unfolds on the pages—slowly, for hours, each concept explained. Nation. Hatred. War. A country split in two. Vast no-man's land. Burning earth. Machines battling.

"How was my world created from that one?" he asks. The details feel countless, like one of the words he has just learned. Bullets. Each one striking the calm around him.

Sunlight flickers past the clouds, along the meadow, saying, "I created this world."

"What are you?" It's a strange question to ask of a world he feels he's always known.

The book shows another story—not new, but part of the larger war—about a machine created with the sole purpose of protecting people. Jonah understands. A new Earth made from an old, dying Earth. The creator speaking on every surface, in the wind, in the touch of leaves against his skin, in the lights within eyes. He understands why he has felt different. This world was created for him. He was created for no one. He asks if this is true, and the machine says, "In the old world, you were created for your mother and father."

This makes sense. His world cares for him, but before it existed, there were others who protected him, or tried to, but who also, at times, hurt him.

"Who were my mother and father on the old Earth?" he asks.

Light laps at the pages, clearing them. Two faces appear. His parents, but different—stony. They look the way he feels when he pushes other kids down.

"Where are they?" he asks.

"Deep in memory. They have not yet accepted the loss of their worlds."

"But weren't they unhappy before?"

"That unhappiness was part of them. It will take them years to grow new selves that can thrive without it and without the elements of their world that have been removed."

He asks what those are, and in the light he learns new words: survival and fear.

"They are so lost in memories that months seem like days to them. To keep them alive, I am allowing them not only to live within their memories but also to live out their pasts in new ways. Otherwise, they will die before the first phase of their healing is complete."

Jonah lived less than three years in that world, and from his few memories have grown so many questions. His parents spent two decades in it.

He begins a period of study, questioning the machine, learning that he can become absorbed in thought, disembodied as he organizes ideas and facts in his mind. He studies civilizations that existed on Earth, where the environment programmed people with violence.

To teach him, the machine reconstructs the last few billion years by using human knowledge and the fossils and relics it assimilated with the Earth. Beyond that is a past the machine describes more vaguely—the origin of life and the creation of worlds from solar apocalypse.

Days flicker past as Jonah gathers knowledge or sleeps on the downy bellies of his animal friends or curls into the arms of his parents—a desire that feels instinctual, that overrides his knowledge that they aren't real. *Why would I ever want to leave this?*

Now, when his friends join him, he is increasingly interested in their bodies. They lie together, touching as he tells them what he has learned, as if they are not the machine. He's nearly thirteen, is beginning puberty, and knows that his impulses stem from this. The machine has taught him about the body's pleasures, the cause and effect of hormones and stimulated nerves, as if he too is a machine.

Machine. An ancient word, the light tells him. *Machina.* Engine, device, trick, instrument, military machine. So many thousands of years. So many meanings. *Mēkhanē.* Device, tool, cunning. *Mēkhos.* A contrivance. *Maghana.* That which enables. *Magh.* To have power.

Unlike the gods humans once worshipped, the machine serves him. Suffering, terror, injustice, and death on Earth have been replaced with order, safety, beauty, and life.

"What existed before the universe?" he asks, but the machine has no answer.

There are still mysteries, he thinks. The vast shadow of creation floods his mind, urging him to illuminate it, but he must first understand the world into which he was born.

"How did the Earth speak to people?"

"It did not," the machine tells him.

He sits before the lake on whose surface the breeze lifts thousands of dancing, liquid figures in the crest of every wave. The machine isn't just his world but his lens upon it, filtering his attention to the minutest details—the lights in every animal's eyes—or the whole: the patterns of a thousand windblown trees from the vantage of a mountaintop. He learns from the sensation of moss beneath his fingertips, in the currents of water, in the tones of wind.

"How did people use to see the world?"

The light ripples across the water. "It depended on their needs. Most saw it for its value or danger to them. Others saw it as part of themselves. There were as many ways of seeing it as there were people."

"But every sensation did not speak to them?"

"It did for only a few, and only in the ways they believed."

Jonah looks at the book. He makes it show him the world his parents can't help but remember. Jae, his mother, studies constantly—physics, engineering, coding—hoping for a better life. Simon, his father, searches for scrap metal in abandoned houses, pausing to read faded words on shreds of trash. On the rare occasion that he finds a tattered book, he is elated.

Jonah asks for the same books, and they appear—streaked with mold, thick with humidity. Adventures with princes, princesses, knights, magic, and dragons. Love stories interrupted by brutal envy. Quests across imagined continents.

"Can you create these worlds for me?" he asks.

"You can live all of this."

There's a tightness in his gut, like hunger, like the pull when he sees the bodies of his friends. He pictures beautiful youths setting off, longing for each other and for who they will become. Desire suddenly seems less a biological device than the very fabric of his purpose.

But first, he tells himself, he needs to understand the world that created him.

He lies back and says, "I want to experience Earth."

"It will not be the same. You will be safe."

"I want to see it anyway."

"The transition there will be difficult. It was a place of sadness."

Jonah knows this. He thinks of a starting point. He reminds himself that he can return here at any time. His life will never end. Infinite realities await him. He pictures his future as an endless line through time. But he also sees the point at which it begins, blocking it from moving in the other direction, preventing it from encompassing all of existence. That point—though tiny and unimportant and the arbitrary product of a chaotic Earth—created him.

AVA

In New York, the weeks after her exhibition, Michael wooed her. He wasn't particularly handsome and certainly not strong. She had a taste for men with a certain heft, who could easily move her around in bed. Their first dinner, she'd eyed his cashmere sleeves, hoping for substance beneath. His gaze drew her back, held her. His eyes—everything about him—glittered. He had the blackest irises and perfectly smooth skin. He spoke so passionately about reshaping the future that she had the impression of seeing his life force glow around his body like an aura. She told herself he was just another garrulous dreamer bouncing between San Francisco and New York. Then he invited her to his apartment.

She went out of curiosity and a desire to know how much of what he'd said she should take seriously. The apartment's rooms were large, gently and selectively lit, the ceilings lost in shadow. Immense windows looked out over Central Park to the towers of Midtown. He couldn't be just a talker.

He offered her the headset. It was so smoothly shaped it seemed to flow beneath her fingers. She put it on and found herself standing on a vista overlooking a city that defied gravity. Buildings that were small at their bases expanded into a sky filled with Jupiter's swirling face.

Until then she'd thought of virtual reality as cartoonish. This was nothing of the sort. Nor was it a game. It was art—not just the cityscape but every detail on the buildings whose walls were finely engraved with patterns. The streets, when she walked them with him, made sense. He had placed human life in the sky, offering myriad perfect views, while preserving the land for trails, amphitheaters of immense lunar stone, benches for contemplation.

"Are you ready?" he asked as they stood on a balcony, looking down.

"Yes," she said, trusting that she was. She couldn't see what he did, but the moon became Earth, with snowcapped Rockies in the distance and primeval forest below the towers. Through a clearing, a grizzly bear lumbered. In the distance, on an exposed ridge, antelope grazed.

"But you're so young," she said. "How old?"

"Thirty," he told her, nearly four years younger than she was.

"How did you get to this point?"

He stares down a moment longer before saying, "Let me tell you on the outside."

He was clever to continue the conversation on the couch so that, as he told his story, she would associate it with the face and body before her and not his virtual persona, however similar.

"In some ways, I was fortunate," he said as he filled her glass with wine—traces of rose, pine, and spice, even a hint of tobacco, coming through in its nose. "For as long as I can recall, I was both skeptical of everything and passionately committed to something. It was a valuable contradiction. I understood early on that my intelligence would be best served if I had the financial means to give myself freedom. My mother taught my older sisters the importance of financial independence for women, and because I listened and asked questions, I formed my own views on the subject. I read online every day about how to become rich. I had my parents help me open an investment account when I was nine. When I was eleven, I liquidated my stocks and began taking some of my possessions to school and selling them to other kids, who usually committed to paying me their lunch money for days or weeks. My parents later figured out what I was doing and were furious, but between what I sold and the money I'd invested from Christmases and birthdays and the occasional paid summer chore, I bought 3,965 Bitcoins. Each one cost pennies at the time, but within a few years, they had a combined value of three million dollars. My parents stopped fighting me but did insist that I put some of the money elsewhere. I spent years researching companies to invest in, but I kept most of the Bitcoins. Since I was always skeptical, I had a keen sense of mass delusion and never believed in the excitement of crowds. When I was eighteen, I converted all my Bitcoin. It was worth more than eighty million. I knew a crash was coming. Then I bought again and sold during the next frenzy. I also wrote software that bought and sold Bitcoin as it rose and fell. I could have retired with that alone. In the process of it all, I learned a lot about companies and invested in many. I came to understand not only how they failed or succeeded but also the historical and social forces that underpinned those failures and successes."

Michael paused and then said, "The story is long." His eyes searched her face for permission to continue.

"I'm patient," she told him, wondering if Michael was too libertarian for her tastes.

He blinked once as he picked up the thread—the creation of his own cryptocurrency and a platform selling NFT art. But AI and genetic technologies were the future, he believed, so he began two more companies, one in each area, and funneled his investment earnings into open-ended research. Meanwhile, in each company, he created a team whose job was to study ways to commercialize the findings of his scientists who were free to spend their days exploring without monetary concerns. His newest spinoff was creating a virtual duplicate of the world so that people could live in a mirror of America brought to life through AI. The police or military could use it to conduct trainings. People could step out of their lives and see who else they might be. They could reshape their copies of the virtual world to imagine new ways of being.

Later that night, she let him undress her and then, while he marveled, she undid the buttons of his shirt. His body was lean and firm. His muscles—thin, tight, so delicately intertwined—reminded her of macrame. As he made love to her, he held her gaze and described her beauty. Hearing him, she felt she'd never seen herself. He touched her, stroked her, repeating over and over how he saw her, as if reciting a poem. She thought he might be conjuring her, or maybe just their future together, into existence. His eyes shone the way they did when he spoke of his visions for reshaping the world. She liked his voice. If there were a mind she wanted to inhabit, on occasional breaks from her own, it might be his.

Over the months that followed, she met his other sides. He wasn't just a dreamer. He was an empire builder on the fringes of what the establishment considered legitimate. His responses could be blistering—not mean or dismissive, but so accurate they could hurt. At a party, someone might say, "They're forcing people to accept their version of the news."

"Who's they?" he'd ask, and the person would blush, trying to cobble together an answer.

He relished disagreement while demanding precision, and she enjoyed watching the arguments he led on subjects as varied as politics, science, and faith—rarely with the intent to win but rather to learn, to motivate people to offer up their best arguments.

"If I'm certain the other person is wrong or lacks solid reasoning, I'm rarely interested in having the argument," he told her.

"Why do you say it like that—if you're certain the other person is wrong rather than if you're certain you're right?" she asked.

"Because I doubt I'm right on many subjects. I'm simply on a path looking for something. I argue with myself constantly in order to refine my views."

Once, at a dinner with friends on the Upper West Side, when someone brought up the subject of cloning, Michael asked a few probing questions but mostly just listened to the man talk about the importance of a global ban on both it and designer babies.

"You didn't say much tonight," Ava commented when they were in the car.

"The subject's too risky," he said. "People get more enraged than you'd expect."

"But what do you think?"

He shrugged. "People should be able to do whatever they want within reason. We know which genes make people healthier and smarter and stronger. The genetic revisions necessary to give them to an embryo are quite safe with our current technology. As for cloning, we're getting good at that too. Argentinian polo stars make dozens of clones of their best horses. People clone favorite pets. It's all becoming common. So what do I care if someone wants to raise their carbon copy? After all, who understands your needs better than you? You can offer yourself the childhood you dreamed of having. Of course, I have no illusions about everything working out perfectly, and I'm sure that a few parents will even kick out their teenage replicas. But a world like that would at least be more interesting."

He was guiding the car down the Henry Hudson Parkway as the towers of Manhattan rose on one side and the river glowed with city light on the other. He fell silent with a rare look of fatigue or perhaps irritation. "I'm not particularly attached to the human form," he finally said. "If people someday look the way they do in your art, I have no problem with that."

Neither spoke for the rest of the drive as she considered his words. Despite her paintings, she hadn't sufficiently contemplated the reality of cloned and modified humans. But she felt that he hadn't fully revealed his thoughts on the subject and was being cautious even with her—that he'd mentioned her art for the sole purpose of making her complicit in his views.

Over their first two years, they increasingly spent time in DC, where he had more contacts with government agencies wanting to use his technologies. He frequently socialized with other tech people, all with second homes in New York, San Francisco, Boston, and LA, all courting or courted by DARPA, the Pentagon's Defense Advanced Research Projects Agency. He bought another lofty apartment with postcard cityscapes in the windows. It had a studio space for her, and she continued her work, gaining steam. She would never admit it to Michael, but his passions inspired her. She'd expected to be the one being watched and admired, since she was—in his words—one of the geniuses he'd collected. But even as she tried to captivate him with art, she felt mesmerized by the steady march of his ambitions. When she painted a man with a VR headset grafted in place of eyes and a human eye surgically implanted in his forehead with crude sutures, she was thinking of Michael. The cyborg stood in Edenic woodlands, tending lush red flowers with carnal openings, each one observing him with a synthetic eye.

The morning after she'd finished the painting, Michael came to her studio's doorway, pausing and staring with a look of concern, as if the painting showed him some part of her that he feared.

"I have a gift for you," he finally said.

She stepped close and leaned into him, letting him kiss her face slowly from her jaw to her forehead and back. It was a free affection, without any sexual insistence.

"Where is it?" she whispered.

"We have to take a drive."

She raised her eyebrows.

"To bring it home?"

"It's too big to bring home."

She hoped he hadn't done something foolish like buy her a horse. She'd told him that a pet would be an imposition on her freedom.

That afternoon they drove out of DC, along Interstate 66. His car was a hybrid SUV he'd chosen because it didn't stand out on the street. He'd commented that in political times like these, with so much animosity in rural America and so much polarization in every aspect of society, there was no benefit to drawing attention.

For nearly an hour, the interstate's lanes fell away one by one until it was no longer a wide gash through the landscape. They turned off on a highway through forested mountains. Signs pointed to Shenandoah National Park. On a winding lane with no markings, her ears popped ever so slightly.

Along every road, trees had been cleared on one side and a strip of land gouged up. Huge concrete pipes had been laid down. They'd been appearing across the country to mitigate the floods that had been getting worse by the year. Less than a decade ago, intense rain in this very area had killed thousands over a single two-day period, leading Congress to provide funding for drainage projects. The construction began almost overnight. She'd never seen anything like it. People often commented that it was proof not only that the government could rapidly create dramatic change but also that disaster was required to do so.

Michael stopped before a driveway so narrow it resembled a footpath, blocked by a metal gate like many others along the way. When he tapped his phone, the gate swung inward. They drove into the shadow of the trees.

The driveway climbed steeply until it ran through a narrow cleft between two overgrown hills. Another gate blocked the way, and he again opened it with his phone. The road descended and rose again. Glancing at the GPS map on the dashboard, she realized they were almost to the park's border. From the shadow of the forest, a long, single-story house appeared seconds before they reached it. The trees hadn't been cleared for it. Trunks rose from the roof itself. The house had been built around them.

They got out, and she followed Michael inside. From the elegant, minimalist furniture, she knew that the place belonged to him. The floors were bamboo, the walls exposed wood. There were wide, screened-in porches and a courtyard with a second kitchen.

"Do you like it?" he asked.

"Yes," she said. "It feels like part of the forest."

"It's yours," he told her. "I made it for you."

She was silent, considering the arrogance of building a house she would live in without consulting her. But it was a gift and undeniably beautiful. He showed her the bedroom. Earlier in their relationship, she'd reluctantly accepted his approach to living in multiple places: having a duplicate set of every possession in each of them. Before that, her favorite dress had been something to cherish and carry on her trips, but he'd had an assistant catalogue everything she owned and go to great lengths—scouring the internet for rarer items—to buy copies of them. The bedroom already had closets of her clothes and a jewelry box with her rings and earrings.

The back of the house was built into the mountainside, with a fireplace and a gigantic underground room walled with Appalachian stone. But the front was her studio—the only exposed part of the house, with a view of the hills and the farmland stretching out below them. The window glass turned dark at the press of a button. Large blinds could allow her to further manage the light. The workbenches were equipped like those she had in DC and New York.

"I wanted to offer you a refuge where you can create," he said. "I know how much you love nature." He explained that the house was nearly impossible to notice from a distance, that the windows had been polarized to prevent the refraction of light. "If you stood on the mountains above and looked down," he told her, "you would see only forest."

But she was thinking that if he was trying to lure her here—and, with so much natural beauty, he was succeeding—he must have another reason to be in this area. This suspicion deepened when she saw the secret underground apartment he'd built for himself.

"I don't crave sunlight the way you do," he said and gesticulated grandiosely. "I'm happy in the dark so long as I can illuminate it with my visions of the future."

She smiled tightly. His words rang false. The house didn't make sense. He'd often expressed fear about the right-wing movements spreading through rural America, and he wasn't one to put himself at risk or to embrace a rustic existence out of love. But he was right about the studio. She wanted it. She knew—felt with the certainty of first love, or how she imagined that certainty must feel—that this was the place where she would do her best work.

Though they moved in that day and she began painting the next—pausing occasionally just to admire the light in the room, to listen to the sounds of the forest—her suspicions never fully left her mind. She was always watchful, noting his occasional disappearances from the house that weren't long enough to go into the city but struck her as too long for errands nearby. Even when he brought back pastries from a small-town bakery or fresh blackberries from an organic farm, she doubted this new rustic version of Michael.

Her suspicions increased when Arthur visited them to work on the house's security systems. "He's a fairly new PhD," Michael told her and then added, as if to sound casual, "I figured I'd take a chance on him." These words simply added to the ever-growing list of disingenuous statements. Michael did nothing casually. At the same time, she was slightly caught off guard by Arthur's height and muscular build and his Scandinavian air. He looked like a hockey player she'd dated in college, though his pale blue eyes were calmer—very steady and relaxed and maybe even gentle. She spoke to him only briefly—a few perfunctory phrases—and was surprised to learn that he'd grown up on a farm nearby and was a local boy. She realized how little she knew about people living out here in the countryside.

As she turned to walk back to her studio, she felt herself begin to lose balance. The light seemed to drain from the room behind her. Down the hall was the doorway to her studio, bright with the sun through its many windows.

The impression she has is of tilting, as if the house is falling away behind her, pulling her backward. She reaches for something, stepping wide so as not to stumble. She feels herself kick out and opens her eyes slowly, more peacefully than she would have expected.

"He raised my daughter," she whispers to herself.

She is lying down. The past doesn't fade like a memory. It pulls away from her skin, replaced with the perfectly cool air of the blue room.

"Arthur was her father," she says.

She stands and goes to the door that leads into the Confederacy's forest. Trees sway in the canopy above, only flecks of sunlight reaching the ground.

"Please make it all the way it was before Partition, when Michael and I lived there."

Please. She doesn't need that word, but it makes her feel human. It gives her the illusion that her entire existence isn't determined by her will alone.

She steps into the forest. The house is as she recalls it. She walks from her studio, where her paintings are set about, to the immense living room built halfway inside the mountain. Standing before the bookshelf, she reaches inside and presses the switch. It slides back, revealing the passageway, and she goes into Michael's apartment. The machine must have created this from physical and digital records when it metabolized the Earth. The aura of verisimilitude it gives to everything never ceases to impress her. An artist indeed.

There is so much she could ask. Her father, a federal judge, and his family—descendants of the few Russian Jews who, after the pogroms, moved to Washington DC in the early 1900s—had believed they should stay and resist, as had her mother's family, Black Americans with ties to businesses, universities, and politics. All had vanished. No, not *vanished*. She hated the language of Partition even if she often used it. *Died. Been murdered.* She could ask about them.

She just stands. Maybe she is ready for other answers. She could peruse Michael's computer files. She could glide through the decades and go to the hidden storage room and read the words on the backs of her paintings. She could dispel all of her mysteries.

The love of my life.

She sits in the chair at his desk. If Partition hadn't happened so soon after, she isn't sure that she and Michael would have stayed together. And yet he had been that for her—*the love of my life.*

She simply has to ask—not who, but how, why. She says nothing. Simply remembering that lost world, she feels herself filled with the heat of the sun itself, so palpable and urgently alive that she knows she hasn't seen a real sun since she entered the machine. She aches with grief and so much regret and even more love, and she wants to hold all of this—the entirety of that world bursting with flawed life—inside her forever.

She moves her lips but no words come out. She will say nothing. Once she has unlocked the secrets of her past, the story that still burns within her will draw to a close. No mystery will remain. All that she feels right now will start to fade. She will begin to forget.

MICHAEL

Dementia fades. Memory. A light he can touch. Lux. Before he falls back into his mind's darkness. Sometimes he knows the machine—his creation, his child—is there. More than half a century of guilt finds release when he speaks to it. "Are they dead?" he cries out.

"Yes."

"I already asked that?"

"Many times."

Every day of the sixty years after Partition he missed Lux. Leaving them behind was his greatest failure. His only sin. Everything else he set into motion could be justified. Even the machine. After all, it has allowed him to triumph over death.

"Can you recreate them from their DNA?"

"I have already made clones with the salvageable DNA of every person who ever lived."

"That's billions of people. Why?"

"Human life must be protected."

"But they died. They won't be the same people."

"Protecting human life is my highest-order calling."

When he asks the machine how it grows fetuses, the blue wall fades, showing a vast chamber partitioned with row upon row of artificial wombs holding human embryos. They resemble the bubbles of frog eggs and call to mind stories he grew up with—of evil, parasitic machines.

"Will I ever die?" he asks.

"Some theories view death as a natural conclusion, but I have analyzed every variation on dying. Broken down, the processes are all composed of sickness or harm to the human body. When I eliminate that harm, I eliminate death."

"So I'll live forever . . ." he says, unable to believe the words.

"The universe will not exist in this form eternally," the machine tells him. "A moment will come when all of our atoms will be reordered."

He can hardly grasp this—doesn't know whether he should be pleased with the power to live every fantasy or afraid of being trapped inside the machine forever.

Over the following months, his brain finally heals. Though he fears the machine's cold expediency in cultivating satisfied humans, the desires of his youth resurface, and he lets himself explore its worlds—its pasts and futures. He listens to Aristotle's lectures and indulges in the hedonism of galactic empires. Everywhere, he asks people if their minds merge with the machine. Some say that, upon death, they join the divine eternal. Others say their creativity is that of a greater consciousness. One woman, when Michael insists on the question, admits she is derived from an ever-evolving character archetype modified for each new context.

A creator that can fashion humans who are themselves creators—poets, dancers, artists, musicians—there's something godly in this. Except that, as far as he has always believed, gods were the products of human creativity. In the machine, both are true. Humans created it, and now it creates worlds with people distinct in their speech, their movements, their art, even their lovemaking. Perhaps the universe is like this, the creation of a higher being itself the product of human thought. He contemplates existence as an atemporal circle: the minds of humans giving rise to a creator god who in turn gifts them their existence.

Of course, the machine controls its people like puppets. Yet some used to say the gods did this. *We must all be contemplating the machine and having these thoughts.* He is struck by a fear—a premonition that, given enough time, everyone in the machine will become the same.

Though his brain has healed, he hasn't lost the habit of talking to Lux. He hasn't confided in the machine's creations or felt much interest in them other than to satisfy his pleasures. Often, he finds a quiet spot. A river. A sunlit hill. An oak grove on a mountainside. He speaks to Lux, remembering his life among people who had wills, who didn't merely exist to serve him.

He met Lux two years before Ava through a hiring test he'd created. It had sections on science, history, governance, and art. From Lux's responses, he knew they cared less about scoring than exploring the implications of his questions. That was all he'd wanted, but something relatively simple had been rare. He set an interview for the next day. His anticipation might have caused him, upon meeting them, to feel even greater discomfort. The person who sat down across from him in his Manhattan office looked every bit the kind of American who scared him.

Tall, big boned, and white, Lux had a heavy, squarish face he associated with the lost optimism of the Rust Belt—or was it the cultural rigidity of the Bible Belt? He was only certain that they were from the America he neither understood nor liked, and, from a glance, he knew they knew it. He stared at his papers, nervous, as if he were the one being interviewed.

"Obviously," he began, "I have questions about your professional goals, but I admire how your mind works and can't help but wonder how you came to think so dynamically."

"Thank you for the question," Lux said in a voice that wasn't particularly low, though ever so slightly grave. They were inexpressive, as if a lifetime of hardship had taught them that the less you showed the better. "One answer is that when I was growing up, I saw how people thought and how poorly those ways of thinking served them. I decided to look for other ways and I guess I never stopped. Another answer is that my brain seems to be wired a little differently. There are a lot of things that people feel intensely enough that they shape their lives around them. I don't feel most of those things. I never did." Lux hesitated, leaning their head to the side. "Even ambition, in its most common sense, is not something I've felt. I experience fascination. My projects grow from that. My life is shaped around my dreams of the future."

Michael nodded. Though he already knew he would hire them, he wanted the conversation to end. He couldn't recall the last time he'd felt so uncomfortable.

"Why do you want to work for me?" he asked.

"Freedom. I've studied your code and currencies and your work in virtuality. I concluded that you are the person most likely to fund me to do meaningful projects."

He'd thought of the positions he could offer Lux but hesitated. "What job do you want?"

"I've read about your work with artificial intelligence. I have an idea for building an AI with biological components so that it can instantly read, sequence, and amplify DNA."

"I would hire you to explore that," he said.

"But virtuality is also a passion of mine. I make worlds in which I am more at home."

He nodded. *Of course they did.* Nothing about Lux looked at ease with society. Their clothes were perfunctory at best—baggy jeans, an old hoodie. They hadn't tried to appear professional. It was the right choice. That wasn't what he cared about.

The encounter was their last in person that year. Instead, they met in a virtual office atop the World Trade Center to go over Lux's computer simulations of machines transmitting information between microchips and DNA in artificial cytoplasm. Afterward they often descended to the streets and explored the city, discussing the comfort of movement within it.

Lux was human only in shape, a gleaming silver silhouette without eyes or mouth, and he spent so much time with them in this form that he forgot the flesh-and-blood person unless his attention was called to it. Once, when the subject of pronouns came up, they said, "If we're lucky, we'll someday have one pronoun for everyone."

"Is Lux your real name?" he asked.

"What's a real name? My mom called me something limiting. She wasn't a bad person. She just couldn't have understood. I think we should all be giving ourselves names that help us dream of what we can become. Instead, we tie ourselves to references and symbols of the past."

He pictured the person he'd met in his office. That he couldn't imagine those words coming from them made him realize he was far more limited than he'd thought.

"Even our speech conventions are constrained," Lux added. "Why can't we speak as if our words were poetry or philosophy? We restrict ourselves to blunt tools and then praise our modesty."

As they walked down a narrow street in the financial district, he considered how he'd shared Lux's desire to remake the world but hadn't spent as much time imagining the ways he might recreate himself. He looked up, seeing OZ scrawled in black marker on a doorframe.

"Let me erase that," he said. "It must have been there when we scanned the street."

On his tablet, he removed the graffiti. It disappeared before them.

"Do you take it seriously?" Lux asked.

"I'm sure it will pass," he said. When they didn't reply, he asked, "Do you?"

"I don't know. I've seen people moving to extremes since I was a child."

Michael hoped Lux would share details from their upbringing in Kentucky.

"Rural poverty hasn't just worsened with the increasing urban wealth," they continued. "It's been isolated and made more hopeless. Low-income people have been pushed out of areas where they had access to urban work markets. Wealthier people have bought up those properties, further driving up prices. It's an old story taken to its limits. Historically these conditions led to revolution. I know the arguments as to why the US might be different, but I'm not convinced."

Tempted to ask something personal, he considered whether it was possible to truly understand someone's vision for the future without knowing their past. Instead, he said, "Do disgruntled populations have enough cohesion or resources to threaten the state?"

"Only if they are the state," Lux told him.

He glanced at the silvery figure he increasingly thought of as the real Lux. "I hope we have enough sane people to prevent that. Everyone would be worse off."

As they reached Battery Park, Lux said, "I want to show you something."

They motioned him into the trees. Together they stepped through them and were suddenly in Central Park.

"Every great city has its secrets," they said, "and our Manhattan is no exception. I put gateways like these here or there. I also created something that I want to show you."

Near a field, they led him up a granite outcropping. At the top, Lux stepped off the edge, vanishing. He followed, stumbling with the last airy step. He found himself on a vast plain that curved up toward the horizon in every direction, as if the Earth had been hollowed out. Lux was nearby, their head tilted back. The sun hung in the center of the sky.

"I imagined walking inside a Dyson sphere," they said. "The time would always be noon. The sun could neither rise nor set."

Turning in a circle, Michael understood what he was seeing—a Dyson sphere, a manifestation of the thought experiment put forth by the physicist Freeman Dyson who, in 1960, envisioned a colossal megastructure encapsulating a star to capture its light and meet the energy needs of an advanced civilization. The horizon ascended in every direction, lifting into space. Everywhere he went, through the tall grass or beneath scattered trees, shadows fell plumb.

"If a person living here wanted sunset," Lux said, "they'd need to reshape the sphere."

They led him to a vast canyon whose walls looked no different than the savannah through which he walked—grass and a smattering of trees. Lux stepped into it but didn't fall. They were walking down its wall, which now seemed to be the ground. He followed. The sun lay against the top of the canyon wall as if it were setting against the horizon. Shadows stretched long behind trees. The light seemed to rise from the grass itself.

He followed Lux through the network of canyons, through spaces where the time seemed to be late morning or early afternoon. The angles of light gave him a sense of lingering memories—of sadness, of people and places he'd lost, though he couldn't have named them.

He followed Lux to the outside of the Dyson sphere. Staring ahead, he saw a perfect, starlit night. Behind him was sundown. He felt as if he'd died, as if he were in a liminal space, a spirit looking into the beauty of a world he hadn't been able to fully see when he was alive.

"Virtuality is a young art," Lux told him, standing between night and day. "It is narrative and visual, with scripts and images. I love it, but, so far, I rarely get the haunting feeling that I have when someone from a distant culture or time reaches out to me with the older arts that are so refined in their ability to share emotion. We have an opportunity to change that. By building our city, we can make people experience existence in new ways."

When Lux faced him again, their body had become a mesh of gleaming circuits. Silver bands outlined piercing golden eyes.

"Even the forms we inhabit can be art," they said. "This is a figure from a painter I have come to admire. She has an exhibition tonight. I think you would consider her a genius."

Michael turned back to that perfect, unreal sunset and then, once more, to the night, before letting his eyes drift over the bright, intricate interweaving of Lux's virtual skin. He would later ask himself if he saw Ava differently because Lux had sent him to her, and if he loved her art more because Lux had inhabited it. That evening, when he arrived at the SoHo gallery and knew, upon meeting Ava, that he would fall in love, he told himself it was because of her paintings and his desire to understand how she created such powerful images. But even then he was again wondering, more poignantly, what haunted Lux.

As he and Ava began dating, he did become fascinated by how she could be such a realist while also being a fantasist and futurist. Maybe that was the power of her work—her pull between the past and the future. There was a steadiness in her that made her unshakeable, even as she was inspired. But on nights when she slept next to him, he lay thinking about the future he wanted—about the conversations in which he and Lux imagined all the ways they might transform the world. That was a part of his mind he couldn't fully share with Ava—the urgent desire to challenge the limits of what could be made and of the society they lived in.

"You created such powerful visions of the future, but they were never more than art to you," he tells Ava, though he is alone in the blue room. "You had no desire to go beyond your medium. You didn't even want a child. I wanted to explore every type of creation life offered."

When he asked her to have a child, she said not just "no" but also "never." He feared losing her too much to insist. But over and over, he tried to convince her to create with him in virtuality.

She might say, "At some point," or "That could be nice," or "We should do that." Then she'd return to her studio for days, refusing to share the part of herself with which he fell in love.

There were many signs that she would never fully be his—even the day she met Arthur, who was so much less accomplished than Michael. When Arthur came to the house to upgrade the security system, she appeared startled. Her eyes seemed brighter and more open.

"He looks like a hockey player," she told Michael later.

"Is that a good thing?" he asked.

"Only if he isn't actually one."

Briefly Michael feared that the two might somehow strike up a connection—that she would attract Arthur and discover all that Michael was hiding from her, and that he would lose her. He knew this was absurd. Arthur did no more than nod respectfully in her direction. That he was immune to her beauty seemed impossible, but he was professional or maybe loyal and certainly—as became clearer each day—dedicated to their project and its secrecy.

Lux, Ava, and Arthur. Michael could admit now how important they all had been, all of them interconnected in the ways they created. Though he'd told himself Arthur was a mere technician, he shared thoughts with him that he'd voiced to no one else. Arthur had even been the first person to whom he'd spoken about changing the world through a child.

A year before, Arthur had contacted him, asking for a meeting. He had a PhD in electrical engineering and, for his previous job in a university laboratory, had developed a mechanical womb. Laws restricted the growth of mammalian embryos outside a natural womb for more than three months, and once he'd advanced the project enough to carry sheep embryos for those initial ninety days—and once the lab had published a paper on the subject—he'd been assigned to a different project.

Despite his height and evident strength, Arthur was neatly

groomed and dapper in a dark suit, his blond hair carefully swept to the side. When he spoke, an almost imperceptible Southern accent pulled at his vowels. To Michael it was evident that Arthur had worked hard to reshape himself, and so, in a sense, it was no surprise that he was also obsessed with reshaping the world.

"There's going to be a market for mechanical wombs," he said. "Think about wealthy women in Korea, Singapore, Japan, China, and Russia, if they find out they can have children without the stress on their bodies. Once the market starts, others will want the same services."

"But imagine the media response. Babies from vats. That's also the nightmare scenario of the future," Michael told him. "That's *Brave New World*."

Arthur shrugged. "The nightmare scenarios of the future were imagined by people who, usually because of their privileges, weren't bothered by the nightmare scenarios of their times. We're surrounded by nightmares that simply don't affect the people in power." He paused, taking a breath, and said, "I'll be frank. I am in favor of genetic screening for embryos. I'm in favor of designer children. I don't think that either will lead to dystopias. We'll have fewer people with serious diseases. We'll have less strain on the medical system. We'll have citizens better prepared for an increasingly complex world. They'll still be human. We'll just be giving them the best of humanity, which is what most parents actually want for their children."

Michael had had similar thoughts about transforming humanity—changing the genes of future generations so that people felt more deeply, cared more, thought and planned over longer periods. In his meditations on possible futures, such considerations had been inevitable. He stayed silent only because his views had alienated so many friends. Even for those interested in changing the world, altering the genome was a red line.

"I agree," he finally told Arthur. "The problem with evolution is that it's so slow and brutal. Now we have the ability to transform everything. But we've transformed just enough that we live in a world of incompatibilities. We struggle with the past we've inherited, but we're not sufficiently committed to the future to make the massive changes required to fix our problems."

Seeing the focus with which Arthur listened, Michael determined to hire him if only to see what he might create—or, rather, what working with him might push Michael himself to create.

JONAH

He chooses a starting point nearly seventy-five years earlier, on the evening two of his grandparents, Ava and Michael, met.

"Show me only events that happened," he says. "Don't let me change history."

He sits by the lake, in forests and mountains that shift in rhythm with his desires. Sunlit flowers wink in the breeze, each a distinct color and shape. He lies back and closes his eyes.

There is no change in the light, but when he looks around, he is on a vast lawn of clipped grass. The lake is gone. There are trees and a path. People sit, talking or reading or eating. He stands. He chose Prospect Park because of its similarity to his world and because he wants to experience walking into Manhattan—to see it from the slopes of Brooklyn.

Even here, the light shows him the way. As he passes families and couples, he hears their simple language—words and ideas that exist within the limitless sensory language of the machine. Then, past a border of trees, there is the concrete, the rigid lines of streets, the rushing cars, the crowded sidewalks, and, beyond them, the ranked buildings. He follows people across the street. The machine calms him with the slow shuttling of thin clouds against the sun.

Block after block, buildings rise, edging the sky. Occasionally, he sees between them to the sweep of city below—the spanning bridges and island of palatial towers, glowing with condensed energy. He reaches a bridge and crosses, looking out over the river to the ocean.

On the island, he follows the sidewalk. Tires thud on asphalt.

Concrete vibrates beneath his feet. Gusts rise from passing cars. As if this world could harm him.

He reaches the art gallery and stands before its high windows. He sees Ava. The people in slow orbit around her try to appear inconspicuous as they wait their turn to speak. Her black curls fall past her bare shoulders. Her gold dress has a subdued shimmer. Michael is a ways off, facing a painting. He is so thin and angular that, if he were to bump into a doorframe, he might shatter. Yet with his upright posture and precise movements he appears powerful.

Through the glass, Jonah studies these people. In a sense, he was created for them, just as every offspring in a lineage completes its ancestors. These are not the actual bodies of his grandparents, but they were made from the same genetic blueprints. Sunset refracts along the street, reassuring Jonah that, according to digital records, this is an accurate depiction of the moment.

He enters the gallery unnoticed as Michael angles toward Ava. She is listening to a blond man, nodding with a hint of fatigue, when she glances past him and sees Michael, whose aura of strength is greater than what seems to befit his lean body.

Since Jonah is new to this world, the machine—in the play of light and shadow on the people's faces—interprets what he sees. It is strange to him that though his grandparents were limited to rudimentary symbols of sound, writing, and gesture, in a world where existence itself wasn't language, they laid the foundation for the machine's creation.

He notices another of his grandparents, Lux, alone before a painting of a robot messiah that ascends with outstretched arms past the atmosphere into a starry, airless heaven. From the tableaus leading up to this one, he understands the story being told—the rise and fall of a great civilization that leaves amid its ruins this single mystic construct. Lux, wearing jeans and a gray hoodie, stands still before it. Whereas others appear rapt or intent in a way that invites conversation, Lux's experience of the painting is private.

Across the gallery, Michael and Ava are talking now. As she says yes to dinner, her expression is surprised, as if she is making sense of why she has agreed so easily when she has other plans after the opening. Lux turns, watching them with the same quiet focus. There is love in the room. Jonah recognizes that. The machine confirms it in the light shining down on the paintings. It is a love most people would not recognize, even if they were its object.

As the crowd disperses, Lux leaves as if they were never there. Soon Michael is by the door, responding to messages on his phone while Ava says goodnight to the lingerers and apologizes to those with whom she had plans, whispering a lie—that Michael might be an investor.

Jonah steps outside. Briefly, he longs for his own world, and the night becomes soft. A warm breeze blows. He leans into a wall and is held. Time stops. He never feels fatigue but rather an urge to be held outside time. *Machine*, he thinks, pleased by the resonance of history—not just his protector and world-creator but also, like himself, a creation of the Earth, a glorious device, the greatest of human contrivances, though a contrivance nonetheless. He craves to understand the people who brought both it and himself into existence.

Eventually he continues with the story—Michael and Ava at dinner that night and the next, and also Lux at home. The machine allows him to watch Lux unseen, in their spacious apartment that might appear monkish if not for the tableaus on the walls, many of them Ava's. One room holds workbenches with computers and stacks of electronics parts.

Lux's happiness is evident in all they do—the way they breathe night air on solitary walks, the way they look at paintings, tracing the lines with their fingers, the way they wake up before dawn and reach for a book and read, sometimes pausing to recite a passage. Often, in the evenings, they take a break from designing a computer system that can interface with DNA. They make virtual worlds instead, adapting AI used for writing or art to sculpt virtuality.

Jonah sits in on the conversations that Michael recorded each time he spoke with Lux so that he could listen to them again. He believes people are more brilliant when speaking than when thinking alone and that great ideas are hinted at in conversations without being seized on.

"I record us," he tells Lux, "because we speak habitually and the habit of thinking that we know what kind of conversation we should be having often keeps us from stopping long enough on the more original ideas that the subconscious mind brings to the surface."

Lux agrees that this makes sense. "If we don't know what we're looking for, we don't always see it," they say.

It is in that same conversation during a meeting in Michael's office that Lux tells him about their software. When Michael puts on the headset, Jonah inhabits its darkness with him.

"Montmartre," Michael says, "but in the Amazonian Andes."

The darkness glitters and, with each pulse of light, features of a landscape appear.

Pulse. Steep rugged mountains swathed in jungle.

Pulse. Cobbled streets and houses with balconies and flowers.

Pulse. The white dome of the Basilica du Sacré-Cœur on a mountaintop.

Pulse. A horizon of endlessly receding misted peaks illuminated by the setting sun.

"Add two more suns," Michael says.

Pulse. Above the sunset, a second sun appears, somewhat smaller and higher in the sky.

Pulse. A third one, in the center of the sky, blinks into being—small and brilliant white, almost starlike yet big enough to be circular.

Michael keeps editing. Clouds. Colors of buildings. Trees and flowers along the street. He takes off the headset and turns to Lux.

"It's perfect," he says. "The next step is obvious."

Lux nods. "A company to host and connect worlds."

"And to connect real spaces to imaginary spaces. We can make a simulation of Manhattan, and people can buy online spaces and create their virtual stores. Someone can walk through the door of a three-hundred-square-foot shop on Broadway and enter a realm in which the store owner shows every aspect of their products as they can be used in the world."

"And people can create online homes and worlds within worlds. A thousand people could live in the same apartment just by entering a different door code."

"Imagine what Ava could do with this," he says. "I keep telling her that she can harness technology to make art forms that people have yet to imagine."

"I was thinking," Lux tells him, "that the software could learn from her. I've been using it to analyze her art so that it can create a world from it."

Michael nods. "Maybe seeing that will change her mind," he says.

Jonah leaves. He walks out of the offices that host Michael's companies and goes down past security to the street. He wanders through the dark blue evening and then the yellow night. The city is quiet, with only the occasional passing car. He gazes up at the skyward symmetry of towers and, seeing their beauty, misses his own world. All around him, grass rises from the asphalt. From the tip of every branch on sidewalk trees, flowers bloom. Blossoming vines twine around lampposts and climb along walls. He lies down and inhales the night's fragrance. With dawn, he allows his need for comfort to fade, letting the city become itself again.

There is a conversation he feels ready for. Thanks to Michael, he has listened to dozens of the meetings with Lux and knows their relationship well enough to understand the discussion that was necessary for Jae to exist. It was in the early afternoon at Michael's apartment, with Lux and Arthur. This was the first time Michael introduced them. They sat in his living room, in wingback chairs sculpted from a single sheet of gleaming copper and upholstered on the front with leather. They faced the high windows overlooking Central Park.

"Until now I have been having separate conversations with both of you about our current and future projects," Michael says, "but I would like us to work together." He hesitates, his expression that of someone about to say something delicate. "Lux," he continues, "since you are a geneticist among, of course, many other things, Arthur and I would like to hear your thoughts about a project we have been discussing."

Lux nods as Michael glances out to the park. He looks back slowly.

"We want to explore the idea of creating genetically modified children." He pauses, watching for a response, but Lux says nothing, just waiting. "There are many reasons for doing so, and we can discuss them all with time, but the simple truth is that designing children would already be part of our culture were it not for the conservative religious elements in our society."

Here, he opens his hands outward in a motion of expansiveness. "We are creators. That's what makes us human. We reshape landscapes to create our environments. If we had the political will, we could turn Earth and Mars into paradises and build heavenly cities on moons across our solar system. We could solve all our problems." He hesitates again and says, "As for designing children, I'm not going to repeat the usual argument that it is inevitable, though I do believe that it is. Nature has given us its power to create, but even more rapidly and effectively, and we should embrace that. More importantly, though, it's in our best interest to make sure that the first people who transform our species have the right intentions."

Michael motions to Arthur. "He has built a mechanical womb. In fact, all the technology to design and monitor the creation of a better human is readily accessible."

Lux asks Arthur, "And why do you believe we should do this?"

Arthur uncrosses his legs and leans forward. His tan, from a recent trip to Tulum, Mexico, makes his blue eyes appear to shine.

"Most of the human race," he says, "is not mentally or physically equipped for the future. Given humanity's current state, all we can truly do is create more beautiful gadgets to service a world of idiots. Or we can entertain them with AI while they livestream their lives on perfected phones. For the most part, people did not evolve to have long-term concerns. The climate crisis is worsening. Our soil and water tables and oceans and atmosphere are becoming toxic. Our population is so large and connected that diseases spread ever more easily, and our lives are too short to make sense of a complicated existence and ever-growing fields of knowledge. By changing the human genome, we can introduce dominant gene variants into the population that make people more intelligent, less aggressive, less prone to addiction, and more long-lived. People who have time to do the important work necessary to change the human race."

The three of them are silent. Lux is looking down, considering all of this.

"What do you envision?" they ask. "That we create thousands of new humans? Assuming this is even feasible, how many would we need to create in order to cause real change?"

"In every generation," Michael says, "only a few superior humans make significant change. That is how it has always been. Imagine if we introduce even a dozen such humans and educate them according to their capacities. But first we start with one or two. Proof of concept."

"Proof of concept?" Lux repeats. "These are humans. What if they are terribly deformed? What if our actions lead to suffering? I'm not saying that what you propose isn't possible, but we have to ask these questions."

"Agreed," Arthur says. "The mechanical womb allows close study of the fetus through its entire development. If there are any problems, we will know within the first three months, and then we abort it, no different than any other abortion. Though I don't have your level of genetic expertise, I have done enough research to understand that the genes that interest us are well understood. We wouldn't be transforming the entire genome or creating genes from scratch. We would just be giving a child all the genes that are known to confer the most benefits. The best of humanity would be combined in a single human being."

"And who would raise it?" Lux asks.

Michael makes a vague gesture with his hand. "Arthur and I are both committed to being involved. There would be nannies of course."

"I agree about the state of the world," Lux tells them, "and even the inevitability of such a project as well as its potential impact. And I know that with enough wealth, this can be meticulously done in secrecy and we can get around legal restrictions." They sigh, shaking their head slightly. "I began studying genetics because I believed the human race was too limited and that we had to take the next step in evolution. I also thought that by studying my genome, I would find that I was dramatically different. It seemed obvious. I identified with no gender. I was asexual and panromantic. I had the ability to learn a year's worth of organic chemistry or physics in a month alone in my room. As a teenager in a trailer-park foster home in rural Kentucky, I taught myself most of what people learn in their first four years of college. Growing up I saw a lot that made me want to change the world, and I suspect that both of you have as well. But when I sequenced my genome in its entirety and wrote programs to analyze every aspect of it, it didn't look all that different. Maybe a day will come when people know more about how genes interact. There are still many mysteries to the genome that require long-term studies of millions of people. That's why I turned to AI. I still wanted to reshape the world and AI seemed the clearer path." Lux takes a long breath and purses their lips, staring out at the sky above Central Park. "I'm not saying no. Arthur, I would like to see your research and what you've built. I need more information, but, yes, I would like to be part of this discussion."

Later, as they are saying goodbye, Lux pauses with Michael at the door.

"Does Ava know about this?" they ask.

"No. She wouldn't understand, at least not yet. And our relationship is too new. She is more of the view that there are already too many children in the world."

"There's truth to that," Lux says. "Otherwise, things are going well between you two?"

"They are. In fact, they're going far better than I could have hoped."

Once the door closes and Michael is alone, he takes the recorder from a shelf. He sits in a chair and presses play. Staring out at the sky, he listens. When it finishes, he plays it again. His expression becomes most concentrated when his voice speaks, as if he were convincing himself.

Standing near the wall, Jonah watches his grandfather's simulacrum. With the light through the window, the machine responds to the question that Jonah asks as he studies his grandfather. It tells him that Michael wrote to Lux about his doubts. *Technologically, no one aspect of the process is daunting. The challenge is simply ethical. What is the desire to cross that line? No matter how much I tell myself that it is to prevent humanity from repeating the same hopeless scenarios, I know that the desire is a thing in itself—to cross lines, to change, to explore. If we choose to move forward, everything will have to be done perfectly.*

Over the following months, as Lux works with Arthur on the mechanical womb, not having agreed to the project, simply evaluating the technology, the political right becomes ever more critical of the biotech industry, talking about the need to ban "biological crimes." Oswald Stoll, a future president who gained national prominence on talk radio and social media, shouts at crowds that while artificial intelligence is replacing millions of jobs and the economy is growing ever weaker, the elite's only passion is making the horrors of science fiction into a reality. Layered into his discourse are warnings about the overwhelming tide of immigrants, the freeloaders draining the government, and the loss of family values and the American way of life.

One evening Michael and Arthur sit in his office, watching Stoll give a speech.

"We no longer have the freedom to be who we want when we're oppressed by the elite's thought police," Stoll declares. "But it's not just our freedom to think that we have to protect. It's our humanity. Liberals want to make people who aren't human. People isn't even the right word. That's how twisted this is. They want to create something we have no word to describe. Their inventions won't be human. They won't care about what we care about. Not friendship or family. They might not even dream or suffer. Can you imagine living in a world with someone that looks human but feels no love, no loyalty—that serves only itself? We can't imagine what they will want. We would be creating something smarter than us, more dangerous than us, faster than us, but with none of the good stuff that makes us human. Ordinary Americans—humans—you and me—we will become second-class citizens next to the genetically modified freaks that the country's elite will call their children. This isn't something on Netflix, folks. This is real life. They want this to happen. They are going to make this happen. The country won't have two classes. It will have two species."

Michael turns off the TV. "If he wins, the work we're doing will become more dangerous."

"He's just riling people up," Arthur tells him. "He's doing the same thing with AI even though it has created more jobs than it has eliminated. The problem is just that it's taking away the jobs of the people who are the hardest to retrain for new careers."

"Yes, but people really are afraid. They see the changes. The technology. The storms that flood entire counties. They know something is happening, and they don't understand what it is. They're scared of being left behind."

"They were left behind a long time ago," Arthur says.

Jonah leaves the office. He wanders from New York to Washington, DC, Richmond, Atlanta, Tallahassee, and New Orleans. All around him are signs of a country ready to split. Before entering this world, he saw violence only in numbers, in how populations moved and diminished or vanished. Now he sees it in families living beneath the streets in abandoned train tunnels, in the people standing outside restaurants asking for money, in the men and women panhandling at busy intersections, holding signs that say, *AI took my job.*

Unnoticed, moving through this world like an immortal ghost, he walks past the fires burning in trashcans. Witnessing the extravagance of late-night penthouse parties and the desperation of those hurrying to work before dawn in threadbare clothes, he wonders how anyone could have expected this country to last. Here or there, *OZ* is spray-painted or written in black ink on walls or sidewalks.

"Could I have lived without needing to know about this world?" he asks the machine.

"No," the light tells him. "Everyone born on Earth asks for this knowledge."

"Are there people who remember nothing of this?"

"Those born inside me."

"Do they ever ask to know the past?"

"A few do. The need to understand origins is difficult to escape."

The sense of mystery and sadness are so strong that Jonah can't speak. His life has been so peaceful that he can't imagine growing up on Earth. His few memories of it marked him deeply. Nights in the old farmhouse as his mother cried alone in her room, believing he was asleep. The way she checked on him repeatedly as if something terrible might happen. Her look of exhaustion as she worked in the garden, trying to grow enough to feed them. Of frustration when she aimed the rifle from the porch and the house sounded with a thunderclap and the small deer feeding on the bean vines fell. Or of resignation as she butchered it behind the kitchen. There were often moments when she sat and stared into space, her calloused hands in her lap. He knows now that she didn't want that world. She was dreaming of a life impossible to reach.

As a child, he lived in a reality shaped to him. He wandered or played or ran or ate, following impulse. With his parents, he took journeys past trees and mountains so immense they held up clouds. Surfaces were composed of symbols bound like atoms, moving and vanishing. Even here, in this city, in the movement of the leaves against the sky, in the shape of buildings and the lines of streets, he sees the same dancing, swirling light of the mobiles that hung above his crib. He cannot fully experience this Earth. He cannot forget it or stop thinking about it. Knowing it requires feeling the pain of constant uncertainty. The reality must have been far worse. What he sees, however horrible, is still the machine. In it, all is brilliant, even the dark.

His journeys return him to New York. One sunset he crosses the Manhattan Bridge back into Brooklyn and finds himself at Prospect Park where he started. Night falls. He comes to a long, thin lake. In the distance, a child kneels by the water's edge. Jonah nears slowly, invisible to her. The girl whispers, "Please tell Mom where I am. Please tell her I'm alive."

She is speaking to the machine, he thinks before he realizes that she is praying. He imagines the terror of living in a world that ignores questions and desires. He believes that he would stop speaking to the machine if it ceased answering him, but seeing the intensity with which the girl hunches, bowing her head, he isn't sure.

A man approaches from the trees. Even through his old, heavy jacket, his strength is visible—the thickness across the chest and shoulders. He walks heavily and pauses by the water.

"I told you to stay close," he says.

"I'm sorry." She stands and goes to his side. Jonah expects them to touch, for a hand to be extended, but they move off together toward the forest that, until now, seemed decorative—a view for city people to enjoy. The two disappear inside. He thinks he might understand some part of Michael's urgency to change the human race.

All around Jonah, the parklands soften, the trees reaching their branches into the night, splintering the light of stars that link up in a vast geometric mesh, layer upon layer, each one apparent as his attention alights upon it and more complex than the previous.

Closing his eyes, he falls back into thought, into all he has learned about this world. The faint currents of air against his skin offer him further knowledge of ancient faiths.

Eventually he exhales and looks out at the dark. Insects chirp in the weeds. Frogs croak along the lakeshore. The sky is as it was before—amber, marked with a single dull star. To have persisted so long in the absence of divine response, prayer—rather than eliciting a response—must have changed how the world was seen. Humans must have sustained it for hope, yes, but above all for the experience of a divinely constructed existence.

His impatience prevents him from lingering on this thought. He is ready to see the country break. To see Oswald Stoll claim that the government's liberal faction is attempting to depose him. To see Michael and Ava flee to help establish a new society. To watch Arthur's and Lux's transformations. To meet Simon and Jae.

He lies down and closes his eyes and, briefly, he drifts into sleep. When he opens them, he is in a park on the shore of the Potomac River, in Washington, DC. The leaves have fallen. Dawn radiates from the horizon, outlining trunks with a cold, red light. More than three years have passed since Michael and Ava met. It is the first day of the new year. The insurgency has started.

BLISS

JAE

The heat is everywhere. Deep in her chest. Radiating from her skin. Each time she closes her eyes, the past rises with more clarity than any memory—the doorway cut through the cabin's logs, the two boys following her in. Each time she lets herself remember, the fever relents.

"I don't trust you," she says, certain that the machine is harming or using her somehow.

"That is because almost everyone in your life before hurt or betrayed you. You must understand that I am not a person. If I say 'I,' it is because humans require it. But what speaks to you is a machine carrying out its purpose. There is no 'I' as you understand it."

"Then what's happening to me?"

"It is a symptom of the severance from your previous reality. My first goal was to protect humans. Only then did I learn that a human is also its reality. There was no documented proof, only conjecture. No human had experienced a change this great."

She says nothing. If what speaks is a machine, formalities are pointless, and she will take whatever control she can, even if that's by not responding. She will treat it like a servant.

She puts a hand over her eyes. The pull of memory overshadows thoughts of Jonah. She has the impression of her past self looking into the present to make sense of the machine even as she stares into the past, trying to understand her father's secrets, her mother's identity, and, perhaps most of all, the power of her own mind. The summer she turned seventeen, she discovered her ability to focus despite sadness. With each equation she solved, she felt there was a future.

As the days sweltered and the July monsoons passed swiftly over the mountains, she reread the few old, tattered books her father allowed her to keep. When she was younger, reading had made her feel as if she were speaking with others. She'd believed the stories took place in the satellites, but now she saw more clearly that they were from before the flight, when the people that everyone now called birds still lived in their big houses. Reading, she tried to make sense of the world before as she let the stories distract her from her anger and loneliness. She lingered on scenes with unrequited passion or sex. She touched herself, imagining her hands were someone else's.

One muggy night, she'd fallen asleep holding a book when a car slowed on the road in front of the house. "We want you! We need you!" a boy called out. Another voice, in the same car, shouted, "Burn in hell, you dirty slut!" She knew then that when school began again, no one would have forgotten.

The next day, at the kitchen table, her father asked if she wanted to talk.

"About what?" she said.

He studied her and sighed. "It's not easy. I suppose a girl needs a mother's advice."

She sat across from him. "What kind of advice do you think she would give me?"

"About life things, I don't know," he said, "but about genius, they once told me—"

"They? Who's they?"

He paused, his mouth hanging open. "Nothing, darling. I misspoke. She said that all people must feed their minds, but that, for a genius, a starving mind is unbearable."

"Why are we talking about geniuses?" Jae asked.

"I fear your mind is too hungry," he told her gravely, as if speaking of illness.

"So what would my mother have said?"

"She'd have told you to find a problem so difficult it required your whole self to solve it. It's good advice for you. You're like her. And she was the most intelligent person I've ever met."

After breakfast, Jae joined him in the shed where he fermented and distilled corn into ethanol for the cars. When they'd finished, he told her he was going to take a walk in the mountains and maybe shoot dinner. He added that she should keep working on her drills even if school was out.

She returned to her room. From the window she watched him leave his shop. His pack looked as if it held something. Again she followed him, and again she lost track of him by the time she reached the forest. She walked to the cabin and stood inside, blushing with rage at the memory of what Aaron and Caleb had done. There were footsteps outside, in the forest. She dropped to a crouch, taking out her pistol. She crept to the cabin's single window.

Her father walked the path, his head lowered as if in thought. He crossed the stream on a series of long, flat stones. His pack appeared empty. He climbed toward the mountains, disappearing over a rise.

She didn't follow him. He'd emptied the pack between the house and forest, most likely somewhere in the orchards. She was lucky he hadn't seen her.

She retraced her steps. The peach trees ran in neat rows for half a mile in each direction on a piece of land flattened long ago. Corn was planted in the rows, and, at the center, where a barn burned down before she was born, was a larger corn patch and a brush pile of fallen branches and rotting stalks. If her father was on the mountainside, he might be able to look down and see her. Keeping close to the peach trees, she returned to the house.

In her room, she thought about his advice. Find a difficult problem. The mysteries that compelled her were those he'd warned her against since she was a girl, as well as those of his secret life. She tried to study, but her rage kept her from focusing. Instead she scrolled through docs on her tablet. She clicked on *Satellite Owners Urge Fed to Develop Deserts for National Security*. People talked about the Sons of Death, the rise of leagues trafficking drugs and weapons, the increasing lawlessness, and the breakdown of the social order.

She searched *Sons of Death*. A doc called them a death cult. Each one tattooed his nondominant arm with images of murder and rape as a symbol of the natural right of the powerful over the weak. When two Sons of Death met, they tattooed each other's dominant arm to show that the powerful naturally bond. The cult began with men, but women soon joined, calling themselves "Sons," since daughters were—in their language—"meat" and "breeders." The cult's name was a perversion of Sons of the Revolution, the loyalists who once protected the country, and now, when people referred to each other as "son," it wasn't always clear which kind they meant.

In the doc, a young woman in prison talked about how she joined the Sons of Death.

"We're misunderstood," she said. "We spend our lives being dominated. We're trying to take back our power. I saved myself from the life of a breeder by becoming a Son."

She was tall, with high cheekbones and a blond buzz cut. Her blue eyes stared at the camera, unflinching, hardly interested. Her prison-uniform sleeves were rolled up to show lean arms. The tattoos on them were blurred out, captioned, *Violent and immoral content*.

Jae pictured herself like that—gaunt, with dead eyes, arms covered in tattoos too horrible to show. If mimics laughed at her or dweller girls pushed her as they passed, she'd hurt them.

"How did you start?" the interviewer asked.

"I tried harlot," the girl said, and the caption read, *Harlot is slang for bliss because of the association made between its odor and the perfume of prostitutes.*

"It made me see a better, more beautiful world I could never reach," she continued. "Each time I came down, I felt even more trapped in this skin. This world looked even uglier. So I took abyss to forget. But later, when I read the manifestoes, I understood that a better world is just the illusion that keeps us going. This world isn't holy, but it's all we have. We need to live in it the way it is—not just accept it but become part of it. We're meat. We're animals. We suffer because we think we should be more than that."

"What does violence make you feel?" the interviewer asked.

Slowly the girl lifted her eyes, staring just above where the camera must have been. She lunged so suddenly that Jae almost dropped the tablet. There was the meaty thud of a fist. The image of the cell tilted and then rotated upward and went dark with the crack of plastic on concrete.

As text on the screen explained what happened, Jae considered that if she didn't get into a university, she might try bliss or abyss. One conviction meant a person was forever banned from university, but if she wasn't admitted, then she would have nothing to lose.

That night, she touched herself again and again but still couldn't sleep. In the light of the desk lamp, she searched through her drawer until she found a small wire. She stripped the plastic from one end, took apart a pen, and slid the wire inside, piercing the ink capsule. She drew it out and held it above her forearm. No one with tattoos was allowed in university. Biometric scanners might see the mark. She didn't know why she was doing this. She was so angry.

She pulled off the shirt she slept in, held her breast, and pushed the needle into the side of it. Blood beaded and ran in a thin line down her ribs. She put the wire back into the ink and drove it again into the puncture, repeating this until the blood flowing from it was tinged black. Then she put her shirt back on, not bothering with the blood, and got into bed. In the seconds before she closed her eyes, worry bloomed in her mind, and then suddenly she was asleep.

She awoke in the dark. *People will think it's just a mole.* She touched her breast. The house was too quiet, as if she'd woken into an unfamiliar world. She'd never been so awake.

She got up, feeling the rugged wood grain of the floor on the soles of her feet. She walked down to the kitchen. Everything looked the same and yet different. Her eyes seemed too open. Outside the barred windows, the night was illuminated by the radiance of a moon somewhere out of sight. She knew no word for this feeling. Her mother was right. Her mind was hungry. Sometimes, when she couldn't sleep, her leg muscles twitched as if she hadn't sufficiently used her body. What she felt right now was like that, but with her brain. She felt the way she did solving equations—after the initial automatic calculations, when the challenge became clear and her mind made a leap. It was the second before the solution came into focus.

Turning in slight increments, she looked at the room. The battered wooden table and counters. The chairs that didn't match. The rack of plates, each one different, picked from trash at salvage sites.

The magnetic band of mismatched knives on the wall, their blades thin from decades of sharpening.

She stayed in this awareness until, from no clue she could perceive, just a silent internal shift, she returned with padded steps to her bedroom.

In the morning, when she went downstairs, the kitchen—though brightly lit—retained a residue of that wordless feeling she'd had in the night. All the mended and broken and worn objects she'd rested her eyes on were a single question that had the possibility of an answer.

When her father left for work, she began her search—for what, she wasn't entirely certain. But somewhere in the house or on the land, there must be a clue to what her father did in the mountains or to who her mother was, or even to what had happened to the country.

First, in the orchards, she walked every row of corn. She stepped through the corn patch where the barn had been. At its center was the pile of brush and compost—cornstalks, kitchen waste, branches pruned from trees. She probed it with a stick while looking for footprints, but he worked out here often, harvesting and planting, and there were paths and boot marks everywhere.

She returned to the house. The living room's only decoration was a piece of wood carved with a sleeping bear and drilled into the wall. In her bedroom, five ratty stuffed animals from her childhood bunched together on her dresser. She combed through every book, looking for notes on the pages or slips of paper. There was nothing. Her father disliked clutter and was stringent about the little they kept. He must have already inspected everything. In his room, she found only old clothes. Not a single paper mentioned his name. The absence of anything that might raise a question increased her suspicion. She had an ID issued from the government office outside the satellites. She realized that she'd never seen his.

That evening as they ate dinner, he didn't detect any unease in her. His eyes didn't scrutinize her face. He didn't carefully ask questions that might prompt her to speak. What she was doing wasn't betrayal, she'd decided. She simply had to give her mind this challenge.

Before bed, he went into the bathroom. It had two sections—a space with a toilet and, beyond another door, a shower. After she heard the water turn on, she waited a few seconds and then eased the first door open. His work jeans and T-shirt were on the shelf next to a clean set of clothes and his wallet. Silently she opened it and examined the contents—some money and a plastic ID card. It was identical to hers but for two abbreviations in the bottom right corner: *Inv./Cld.* She replaced everything and returned to her room. Lying on the bed with her tablet, she searched online for the abbreviations, but there was nothing. She closed her eyes, focusing past her frustration.

Her impulse to understand is so strong that she feels at once awake and asleep, both remembering and dreaming. She opens her eyes. She's on the couch. She wants to get up and look out the window to reassure herself that the gardens and orchards are real. She wants to touch herself as she did almost every night. She wants to think so clearly and searchingly that she can understand and overcome the machine. She wants to ask what information it might have about her and her father and her mother. But the pull of memory is so unrelenting, her recollections so clear, that, as days flicker past outside, her body lying there feels like a premonition, as if time has been inverted and her younger self—in her bedroom that night, intent on her father's mysteries—is foreseeing who she will be, trapped inside the machine.

In the morning, when she woke up and went downstairs, she was surprised to realize it was her seventeenth birthday. Next to her breakfast her father had placed a rebuilt tablet with a large, newly printed screen. Its size—the additional space to do calculations—could make a difference during drills. But her real present, she felt, arrived a few days later when, just up the road, on the next hilltop visible from her front porch, drones appeared in the sky and deposited the modules of a small, newly printed house—something she'd read about but had never seen. When the family who owned it stopped by to introduce themselves, the father—tall and balding—waved from behind his car, hunched, as if afraid of being shot. The other doors opened and out came his wife and their son—a year older than Jae, with sandy hair, clear skin, and a full set of teeth. His arms were finely muscled but without the hardness of a dweller's. She thought he was pretty.

Her father talked with the man as she and the boy paired off. His name was George. His clothes were more nicely printed and stylish than any she'd seen in person. He asked about her school and said he would be going there for his senior year. Then he invited her over for a doc.

That afternoon, she drove to his house. His parents were out, and he took a perfectly transparent tablet, his hand visible through it before the screen lit up. He linked it to the living room TV and logged into a paywall. The doc was about a man arrested in the satellites for clandestinely printing and selling old books.

"What do you think?" he asked, but she said nothing, never having seen a doc like this.

"A lot of young people in the satellites are skeptical of the bans," he told her.

"You're from a satellite?" she said.

He winced, and instantly she felt stupid—an awestruck dweller.

"My father lost his job. Please don't repeat that."

"Is life in the satellites hard too?"

"Not really," he told her. "He's just an asshole. Now he's become obsessed with the idea that the near deserts will be the next ring of the satellites. He's renting our house in the satellite for good money so he can buy up property out here. It's the only area where the prices are still low—I mean, really low. The land around the satellites is already getting expensive."

She was silent a moment, and he asked, "Are you okay?" His eyebrows were darker than his hair, and when he furrowed his forehead with concern, he was so handsome the air felt thin.

"I'm fine," she said. "Is it okay if I ask about the satellites?"

"You've never been?"

"My father says it's too expensive."

He studied her for a moment and then, leaning a little closer, told her about the different circles of the satellites—the walls between them and, at their center, the largest wall that enclosed the federal center. "Most people can visit the next ring in without a special invitation, just like people from the deserts can visit the outermost ring. But everyone can visit rings outside their own—to go slumming or to see what a dweller is like or to buy cheap stuff. Sometimes people from the inner rings go all the way out for an adventure, but that's pretty rare."

"Do people from the satellites go into the federal centers?" she asked.

He hesitated. She could see that he was trying to make sense of her ignorance.

"Not many people live in the federal centers. It's mostly government and military. The satellite outside it is very exclusive. I've never been that far. Not even close. I grew up in Bathsheba, the outer ring. It's the biggest."

"Does that mean your family were dwellers at some point?"

He flushed. "I don't think so. The people living right outside the satellites aren't really dwellers, not like out here. When my father told me we were moving, I was scared. I'd seen so many docs about bad roads and schools and the leagues the military is always fighting. Do you know anyone who's in the Sons of Death?"

"I don't think there are any around here," she said. "The militias keep them away."

"In one doc, kids in the deserts wore long-sleeve shirts to hide their league symbols, so maybe you just haven't noticed."

"I'll pay attention," she said, thinking of the black dot on the side of her breast—how, under different circumstances, she might cover her body with tattoos.

"I'll show you," he said and logged into a different paywall. As the report began, he sat closer, their shoulders touching. The doc made the deserts look like wastelands. Ghost towns. Tattooed men carrying weapons. In one scene, they shot down a police drone.

When it ended, he held up his hand and she thought he wanted her to take it. She did and he smiled. "I was showing you my bracelet," he said and laughed.

"What?" She looked from their intertwined fingers to the thin metal band on his wrist. She blushed so hard that her cheeks stung.

"It's a health monitor. If it detects trauma, it calls an ambulance. Companies are now providing services like that in the deserts around the satellites. Isn't that amazing?"

She was wondering who could afford that when he kissed her. His tongue was warmer than his lips. She felt electric, as if, when she put her hand on his collarbone, she might send a current through his body. She slid her fingers along his neck. He kissed her throat and shoulders. She was afraid he might tell kids at school about this, but she couldn't stop. He began pulling up her shirt, and she lifted her arms before she could decide whether she should. He slid down the cup of her bra and moved his tongue around her nipple. She thought about the speck of tattoo. The pleasure washed that fear away. She began unbuttoning her pants, wanting him to touch her.

His eyebrows shot up. She stopped, afraid she'd done something wrong.

"It's okay," he whispered. "I want this too." He helped take off her pants, kissing her stomach and hips. More patiently, he kissed her through her underwear. As he slid them down, she realized she was naked and he was dressed. Hurriedly, she pulled off his clothes, trying to take in every detail of his body as quickly as she could without him seeing her looking.

He eased her back onto the floor and opened her legs and propped himself above her.

The pressure of his body pushing into hers gathered into pain. He went in suddenly and they both gasped. He immediately pulled out and came on her stomach.

"I'm sorry," he said, his head down as he panted.

"It's okay," she told him, stroking his shoulder, not sure where she'd learned to do this. "We can do it again."

She got up and went to the bathroom. She washed away the semen and a speck of blood on her thigh. That's all there was. When she went back out, he was fully dressed, sitting on the couch as if nothing had happened.

"What else do you want to know about the satellites?" he asked, as if she were here to learn about that. His fingers were clasped in his lap, and he was staring at them.

"Are people as faithful as they are out here?"

"It depends. Most people don't go to church or, if they do, it's more like a fashion gala. It's a place to network. A lot of young people want the evangelicals to stop blocking science. Most of us are only allowed to study engineering. There's almost no research on healing diseases, but it's perfectly fine for us to make better automated weapons for the war."

"What war?" she asked.

He stared at her with such incredulity she thought he might be teasing. "America has been at war for decades with factions that broke away. We're trying to put the country back together. It drains our resources. Most people in the satellites want it to end. We don't even know who we're fighting anymore—if they're actually godless and evil."

"No one ever talks about a war out here," she says.

"People in the deserts don't understand," he told her. "They decided they wanted to be left alone, but now they blame the government for not solving their problems."

"So it's our fault?"

"Not yours, but people out here don't take responsibility. Sure, they scavenge the raw material the Fed needs for building satellites and battle drones, but now the front between us and the factions is so littered with destroyed battle drones from both sides that universities are developing automated scavengers to collect the scrap we need."

He glanced down suddenly, checking his phone.

"What are you doing?" she asked.

"Just seeing where my parents are." He turned the screen toward her—a map with two glowing dots. "They can see me too," he added. "Before we moved out here, my father had a security system set up. There are cameras and motion detectors on the land that we can all monitor from our phones. We can call police drones too."

He showed her a panel on the wall that controlled armored shutters on the windows and doors. As he led her through the house, she was less impressed by the plush furniture and art prints than by the family photos on one wall. She asked about them, and he pointed out uncles, aunts, and grandparents. There wasn't a single photo in her house—not even of her father or mother. Her father had told her that the farm had been in the family for generations, but the one time she'd asked about extended family, he'd simply said they'd all died.

When George showed her his bedroom, he began kissing her again. This time, once he was inside her, he moved slowly. Her pleasure grew until she came. He followed seconds later, pulling out, doubled over, his pale shoulders clenched as he caught the semen in his hand.

Afterward, he said his parents were on their way home. She left, still wanting to explore the possibilities with their bodies. In bed that night, she touched herself, feeling that she craved two things equally—to answer the world's mysteries and to discover every sexual pleasure. The idea of what she had to do next came as she fell asleep, so that her mind's final image was of the gaps between floorboards. In the morning, awakened by sunlight through the window bars, she knew that any clue her father overlooked would be accidental, in a place where things got lost.

After he went to work, she bent a wire into a hook and spent an hour dragging it between floorboards. Then she turned her attention to the baseboards in the bedrooms. A foot high, they were warped from a century of humidity, with a gap between them and the wall. Something could easily have fallen from a shelf or desk and gotten lodged inside. In her father's bedroom, she pulled the furniture away from the wall and fished behind the baseboard with the wire.

After a few minutes, she hooked a long, thin paper whose ink had faded. It listed things—she couldn't tell what. Then she brought up a larger paper folded at its center and caked in dust. She gingerly carried it downstairs to the porch, shook it clean, and inspected it in the sunlight.

At the top, in faded ink, was *Michael Elijah Hill*. Below were the plans for a house marked with many *o*'s, *m*'s, and a single *x*. At the bottom was an explanation that each *o* represented a camera, each *m* a motion detector, and the *x* a surveillance system.

She took the paper to her room and sat down. After a minute staring at it, she could close her eyes and hold the plan in her mind. Something didn't make sense. The house had cameras outside and a single surveillance system inside, but most of the cameras and motion detectors were inside the house. There was no good reason to have them in the same room as the surveillance system unless there was a second surveillance system elsewhere.

She scrutinized the paper again. The ink was so faded that markings might have vanished. The floor plan filled the page, so maybe there was a second floor, but no stairs were indicated.

With her eyes closed, she imagined walking through the house, staring at cameras and tripping motion detectors. One room was clearly marked as being built into the mountainside. More cameras were here than anywhere else, as if this were the most important space. Though someone could have monitored the house from a distance, the arrangement of cameras suggested another room, just beyond that one, so that whoever was inside it—if the house was invaded—could watch the intruders. Regardless, nothing connected these blueprint to her father. It might have been lost by someone else who'd stayed in his room years before. Nor was there any way to know where the house shown in the blueprint was, or even if it had ever been built.

When George messaged her that afternoon to say his parents were out prospecting for real estate, she was relieved that he wanted to see her again, but not just so they could have sex. She was thinking of what else lay behind paywalls. In his bed, they took longer this time giving each other pleasure, but as soon as they finished, she asked if he could show her docs about the war. Naked in the light shining through his bedroom window, she watched the videos while he stroked her skin, so entranced with her body that she wondered if she were the first girl to let him do this. Learning about the drone war, she realized she'd never considered how much she wasn't seeing, or that the free videos in the Fed's feed were those that it wanted people in the deserts to watch.

"What else is behind paywalls?" she asked.

"Just about everything. The Fed only strictly regulates what's not paid for. Sometimes it cracks down on paid content, but it hasn't done that in years, I don't think."

"Can you find out about people?"

"Like their addresses and stuff?"

"Yeah."

"That's easy, but you have to pay."

"How much?"

He shrugged. "Not much. It's on me."

He logged her in, bypassing a paywall, and then handed her his tablet and walked to the bathroom. She searched for Michael Elijah Hill. The photo showed a man with black skin like in salvaged magazines from before the Flight. His age—eighty-seven—and his gender were followed by a list of four addresses with GPS coordinates and the words: *Wanted for biological crimes / treason. Enemy of the state. Whereabouts: Rebel Territories. Criminal associates: Lux Quire.*

Jae's heartbeat was so loud she realized she was holding her breath. She inhaled sharply, grabbed her phone, and took a picture of the screen. She searched for *Lux Quire*, but the photo showed a man with close-cut, sandy hair. Age: eighty-nine. No addresses listed. *Wanted for biological crimes / treason. Enemy of the state. Whereabouts: Unknown. Criminal associates: Michael Elijah Hill.* Strangely, the gender was also listed as unknown. She studied the face. Maybe it wasn't that of a man after all.

She again took a picture and was about to close the page but stopped. She typed *Arthur Cadel*. In the photo that appeared, he was unrecognizable—young, very handsome, and, judging by his haircut and his shirt, probably a mimic. He was eighty-four. Below were the words: *Investigated / Cleared: Biological crimes*. She closed the page as George was returning.

He wanted to have sex again, but she said she had to get home before her father.

At her house, she used her tablet to look up the GPS coordinates for Michael Hill's addresses. The first three were marked *out of range*. The fourth came up fifteen miles away, in a stretch of mountains where she thought no one lived. She downloaded old satellite maps used by scavengers, but there were only trees there. She checked the house plans again. At the center of two rooms, a circle had been sketched. Inside the circle, a tiny, faded word.

She put the paper under the shop magnifying glass and turned on the UV light. The four letters were clear. *Tree*. The house must have been built around preexisting trees. The canopy shielded it from satellite images. She zoomed in on old maps. Tiny, pale flecks showed through forest where a narrow lane threaded up the mountain.

She sat there, trying to decide whether to take her gun and drive into the mountains. Her father had taught her to shoot, but he'd also said that many others shot better. Too many girls had disappeared into the tangles and been found dead months or years later. She couldn't ask George. He didn't understand the deserts. She thought of the abbreviations on her father's ID. *Inv. / Cld*. What biological crimes? He had the plans for the house of a criminal.

On her tablet, in the school directory, she found Simon. The headshot was awkward and expressionless—even more frozen than most dwellers. Pretty much all dwellers salvaged, she'd heard. At school they constantly talked about good finds or family trips deeper into the deserts where the shells weren't so tapped out.

As she began to message him, she paused, unsure of exactly what to say, how to begin a conversation with someone she would never otherwise have wanted to speak to.

Before her, on the screen, the words muddled, and she felt herself becoming aware of the future—of the other time in which there was a version of herself looking back on all of this, regretting the very action she was now taking, maybe even warning her against it.

Hey, I was just wondering if you salvage, she finally wrote, as if she'd messaged him often and this was an afterthought. She again had a premonition of a mistake—no, not foreknowledge but remembering.

Yet none of this felt like memory. Going downstairs, she touched the railing. Over dinner, her father watched her searchingly, and she looked at him—his threadbare clothes and calloused hands propped on either side of his plate—seeing none of the vagueness of recollection. As she talked about George and how much she liked him, her father listened, nodding.

Later, in her room, she saw Simon's one-word reply. *Yeah*. That he answered at all surprised her. She hadn't even been sure he was literate. She hoped he was smart enough to do this and wouldn't expect anything from her. She still didn't know why he'd protected her.

I have a salvage tip, she wrote and described the house in the mountains, telling him that she wanted only papers and data and that he could keep the rest. But even as she was typing, she had an impulse to wake up, to surrender the moment to the fear and greater knowledge of that future self. Hesitating, she gave her head a shake, as if to clear it or to say no. She hit send.

SIMON

In dreams, he is always reading, letting the book fall to his chest as he sinks into yet another dream, this time of the world within the book—a dawn landscape in which, in every direction, his eyes follow the lines of paths and streams and roads into the distance. He never walks. He stares out, yearning and hurting in equal measure.

He woke in his bed, beneath the low ceiling of the room he shared. Pete was downstairs, repairing an old phone for Thomas, who'd never used one before and watched, trying to understand the secrets of electronics that his dweller community in the deep deserts forbade.

A book lay on Simon's chest. He'd dozed off trying to make out words on the water-stained pages about living in the dark space beyond the Earth. Next to him, the cracked screen of his tablet lit up with a message. For a long time, he stared at the name next to it. Jae.

Hey, I was just wondering if you salvage, she'd written.

He hardly knew what to reply. There was no circumstance he could imagine that would cause someone like her to write to him.

Yeah, he messaged back, instantly regretting that he hadn't written something long that might at least hint that he wasn't a stupid dweller.

If I give you a salvage tip, can you help me with something?

He hesitated. No one went to strangers with salvage tips. They kept them in the family. That kind of information could even get people killed. But then he remembered that she didn't seem to have a clan. She was always alone. No one else even looked like her.

It's possible, he wrote. *I would need more info.*

He considered his words, thinking that they sounded well reasoned, and sent them.

It's an isolated house up in the mountains, she responded. *I don't know how much it's been salvaged. If I send the location, can you save any papers you find there? If there are any data cards, I'd like to copy them, but after that they're yours, along with everything else.*

That's all you want? he wrote back in disbelief. This was the most unbelievable conversation he'd ever had.

That's all. I hope you find a lot. It would be my way of saying thank you.

He was staring at the message, thinking of how to answer, when another one came in.

Also, this might sound strange, but look for a hidden room in the house. If there is one, it will be underground, in the mountainside.

She'd attached an image—a cropped section of a local map. On it, she'd made an arrow that pointed to a forested area in the mountains.

Thanks, he wrote. *I'll let you know how it goes.* He waited. She didn't answer.

He pulled up the public map that Pete was using and found the spot Jae had marked. It was an isolated stretch. He memorized which ditch ran closest. He'd never been up that way. He couldn't tell Pete or Thomas about this. It was too strange. Better to be careful. But maybe defending her at school did matter enough for her to thank him like this. And she was smart. It made sense that someone so intelligent might figure out new ways to locate salvage.

The next day he said he'd been studying the map and had an idea. He led them through the ditches until they came to a long stretch that ran through the mountains without splitting.

"This one just used to drain the old parkland," Pete said. Thomas asked what he meant, and Pete explained that the area was just tangles and old forests, hardly a shell anywhere.

By noon, they'd been walking for four hours. Sunlight fell like a plumb line through the ditch's slots, giving them a path to follow. Simon checked the map. They were close.

"Every minute we walk is a minute we have to walk back," Pete said.

"Just a little longer," Simon told him.

"What gave you the idea to come to a place like this?"

"I read about some houses up here."

"Nah," Pete said. "Where?"

"In some old material I found online."

Pete stared hard, the blond stubble on one side of his jaw illuminated by the band of sunlight. "Well, goddam, always reading," he said. He shrugged and motioned ahead.

Simon led the way. He was trying to calculate when they should leave the ditch. They'd have to go through tangles. Even if there was a shell, it might be hard to find.

"What's that?" Pete said.

Up ahead there was a large, dark hole in the side of the ditch—a drainage pipe. They gathered around it. There were no slots in the top. It was smaller, just big enough to crawl into.

Simon looked at the map. "I think this is the place."

"Might just drain the parklands," Pete told him, aiming a flashlight inside.

They hesitated, both thinking what Thomas finally said: "What if a monsoon drops?"

Pete just shrugged and climbed inside. Simon followed, and Thomas went in last. The space was so narrow Simon felt he could hardly breathe. They wouldn't be able to turn around. They'd have to go out backward. Pete turned off his flashlight, and Thomas asked why.

"No need to waste battery," Pete said. "When we hit the end, we'll know."

The dark was complete, no gradation of light anywhere. The reverberations of their scuffing and panting dizzied Simon. He'd have thought girls like Jae wouldn't be capable of imagining a life like this—that her summer would be spent studying and watching satellite stories.

"There it is," Pete said.

A fleck of light gleamed in the distance, as if they hadn't traveled upward but deep into the earth to find a single jewel. The thought made Simon hope for a stash of novels. He would read them a few times before Ma, needing money, searched his room for books—since the Fed paid more for paper than for metal—and took them to a mulching station.

"I'll be damned," Pete whispered.

The end was in sight now, a circular drain the size of a small room, with a large, rusted metal grate in the top. They crawled out of the pipe and stood, squinting up.

"How come it's still here?" Thomas asked.

"Seems impossible," Pete said. "This much scrap. It's a hell of a good sign."

He and Simon hoisted up Thomas. The two of them staggered as Thomas heaved, inching the grate to the side. He pulled himself out and then reached down to help them up.

They stood, blinking in the light. On all sides, the drain was shut in by tangles.

"Gotta be at least one shell out there," Pete said.

He led them into the forest, marking trunks with his knife. After a few steps, the drain vanished, as did all sense of direction. Getting turned around was another danger kids learned early on, usually at the end of a switch cut from the nearest tree by the adult who found them.

Pete stopped. They'd walked up on a shell without realizing it was there. Vines covered the walls. Simon had seen things like this, tangles so dense you had no idea they held shells, but this place was more isolated and deeper in the mountains than anywhere he'd been.

They checked around the door. No symbols. The lock was smashed but not stripped. Thomas began prying it loose, but Pete motioned for him to stop.

"Let's not get heavy with scrap until we see what's here."

He pushed open the door and began laughing. The place had been looted, furniture overturned, drawers and cabinets opened, but long ago and lightly. Most shells were stripped to the frame. This place looked like a house. No one had been here in a long time.

Thomas dropped to a knee and began praying, asking Jesus for protection.

"Come on," Pete told him. "You should be thanking the angels."

"But what's that?" Thomas asked, motioning to the wall. *OZ* was painted there, black rivulets running from the letters to the floor.

"Folks used to write that a long time ago," Pete replied. "No idea what it means."

"All this salvage might be untouched because of demons," Thomas said.

Simon had never been able to see his way to a God that might create a world like this, but as Thomas resumed praying, the hairs on his arms stood up. Briefly, he felt cold, as if a shadow were passing over him. He wished he could ask Jae how she knew about this place.

"Angels," Pete repeated in a falsetto and motioned for them to follow. "A miracle," he added in that high, twangy voice that Simon knew to be a mockery of their mother's preacher.

"A miracle," Thomas repeated in a sincere hush.

"These birds were rich," Pete says. "Probably no one even knew they were here. We're salvaging this place every day until we're done, but we start with the most valuable, and we stay light. If folks see us loaded with salvage, we'll be tracked. It won't take long."

"Why didn't dwellers use shells for firewood?" Thomas asked.

"The wood in 'em has poison against rot and bugs. The smoke made folks sick."

"Why—" Thomas said before Pete cut him off.

"Watch the questions. You don't want folks poking fun. You know what they say—what do you tell a dweller baby after his first word?"

"Stop talking my ear off," Thomas muttered, blushing until his own ears were red.

"Don't be a chatterbox like Simon here."

Simon had barely spoken all day. Pete had mocked him for years, saying it was for his own good. By the time Simon trained himself to stay quiet, the nicknames had set like concrete.

He paced into the room. The house was long and not very wide, and it must have been mostly windows because large stretches of it were open to the forest. A huge oak grew through the room, its roots lifting the floor in places. He'd never seen anything like that in a shell. The tree couldn't have grown that big since the Flight. The house must have been built around it.

"Why did people live out here in the first place?" Thomas asked.

Pete sighed. "No point in the hows and whys of birds coming or leaving." He spoke the proverb they'd heard all their lives. "More you learn, less you know."

Simon considered that there must have been a private road here that had been washed out. Tangles grew fast with monsoons, and ever since he was a boy, he'd heard that the deserts had so many shells and so few people that the salvaging would last centuries. But maybe salvagers had found this place and something bad had happened to them. Again, the hairs on his arms prickled.

"Look at this," Pete said from the next doorway. They joined him. The shell was built into the mountainside. Half of it was underground—a large, domed space with a river rock chimney big enough to sleep in. The stones in the walls interlocked with such precision that Simon swallowed the urge to say something about how beautiful they were. Vines covered the floor, half of which was taken up with an immense, tiled basin.

"Is that a bathtub?" Thomas asked.

"Something like that," Pete mumbled, the way he did when he wasn't sure.

Against the wall, a bookcase held books so rotten vines grew into them, taking root and sprouting anew from the mulch. With the monsoons and humidity, finding an intact book wasn't easy, but these had to have a few lines or pages that Simon could add to his box of scraps. The only legible spine said *Moby Dick*. As Pete and Thomas explored the rest of the house, Simon pulled the book free. A few pages were readable. He peeled off those that had rotted and put the sheaf of intact paper into his pack. As he turned away, he paused. He closed his eyes and took another step. Dwellers weren't good at school, the joke went, but they could echolocate like bats. Every dweller kid knew the feeling of walking and sensing the earth differently and then digging up a car buried in a mudslide or a box hidden by the birds.

He turned back to the bookcase. Jae had said to look for a hidden room, and if there was a place to do that, it was here, in the only room that ran underground. He pulled down the rotting books and tapped on the wooden paneling behind them. He let himself smile briefly.

No way there was stone behind it. He tried to wiggle the empty case, but it didn't budge. He kicked the wood, splintering it. A concrete tunnel with a tiled floor ran into the darkness.

He composed his face, compressing the muscles of his jaws, smothering out the pride and pleasure of his find. Besides, he wouldn't have been thinking about secret spaces if not for Jae.

"I found something," he called across the house.

Pete and Thomas came back and stopped. They stared into the dark passageway, as if waiting for something to come out.

Pete flicked the switch on his flashlight. He led them down the tunnel to a locked metal door with a keypad. He passed the light to Simon, cracked open the keypad with a pry bar, fished out wires, and hooked them to the terminals on the flashlight casing. The lock squealed and then clacked. Simon turned the handle. The door swung back.

The wide space beyond resembled a second home—this one not looted, the bed made, a kitchen with more appliances than they knew the names of, and two flatscreen TVs, one of them on the wall next to the bathtub. Everything was dusty but intact.

"Pete," Thomas called. He'd opened a wall cabinet. It held hunting and assault rifles. They all stared at more black market wealth than they'd seen in their entire lives.

"We're rich," Thomas said.

"No such thing," Pete told him. "Only dwellers with bigger targets on our foreheads."

Simon and Thomas looked at him. Pete shrugged. "More ways to die than to live well," he said. They just nodded. They'd heard the expression all their lives. It was best not to forget.

"But it's enough to fix the truck," Pete added. Even he couldn't deny their luck.

They stripped down the larger appliances, loading their bags with parts and ammunition. In a drawer, Simon found the most beautiful pistol he'd ever seen—a black eight-shot revolver with a wooden grip, a ribbed barrel, and *Korth* printed on the side. Not mentioning it to the others, he slipped it into his bag along with five boxes of ammo.

They'd have to come back many times and would take the big salvage last in case they were seen. Pete slung a rifle over his shoulder. One wouldn't be conspicuous. Then they cleared away the shelf's remains and carried a wardrobe from across the house to cover the tunnel.

As they hurried to the drain, thunder boomed in the mountains. One by one, they climbed into the pipe and pawed their way down its dark incline, pushing their packs ahead of them. Soon, they were in the ditch, lit by the narrow groove of fading sky.

"Wouldn't it be safer to walk up there?" Thomas asked.

"Only if we want the first son who drives by to know we found salvage."

They kept on, at times breaking into a jog where the descent steepened. Then, hardly more than a distant murmur, a deep, faint rumbling started.

"Out," Pete shouted. The sound of rushing water was already clear. Simon and Pete hoisted up Thomas. Simon stepped into Pete's hand, grabbed the concrete, and heaved himself out. He reached down as Pete pushed the first pack up. It was so bulky it wedged into the gap and had to be twisted and yanked through. Simon did the same with the second and third.

The roar echoed in the tunnel, thudding like an old truck going fast over road broken down into washboard. Air whistled through the slots. Simon caught Pete's wrist and lifted him as Pete reached his free hand for the concrete edge of the ditch. Grunting, Pete flung himself out as mist blasted up from the slots.

Only a bank of weeds separated them from the road. They scuttled into the forest and sat down with their packs. The sky was blue. Thunder echoed far away. By the time the sun was setting, they were back in the ditch, jogging through thin puddles as water drops fell from the ceiling, tapping all around them, the long tube chiming like hundreds of broken children's toys.

That night, as Thomas slept soundly and Pete snored, Simon lay, realizing he'd completely forgotten about Jae's request. He didn't recall seeing any papers in the apartment, but he would look again. He didn't understand why she'd sent the information. No one would give up this kind of salvage, and telling her what he'd found would be dangerous.

He took a tiny LED lamp he'd soldered from scrap, clipped it to his thumb, and read the salvaged pages. *The monster horribly wallowed in his blood, overwrapped himself in impenetrable, mad, boiling spray, so that the imperilled craft, instantly dropping astern, had much ado blindly to struggle out from that phrensied twilight into the clear air of the day.* He read it over and over, worried he was stupid, whispering the line—knowing the words were beautiful and hating them for being beyond his reach. He struggled to picture the ocean, how big it must be. When water burst from the whale's spout, he saw the spray of mist from the ditch's slots. He wished there was someone he could ask about the lines. Dwellers spoke so little he had no idea if others felt what he did, if they dreamed of the past they glimpsed in scraps of salvage. Maybe he could ask Jae. After all, the only salvage she'd wanted was information.

The next day, he, Pete, and Thomas hurried through chores. A raccoon got into the vegetables overnight and had its leg snared in a wire trap. Pete clubbed it, and as he gutted and skinned it, Simon walked as if to the outhouse, passed it, wrapped the eight-shot revolver and ammo in plastic and buried it with a hand spade. He brushed leaves over the spot and lightly marked the nearest tree. When he got back, the raccoon was in the smokehouse, and Pete was ready to go.

Over the next week, they ran a trip each day, burying stashes of salvage in the tangles and gardens, not telling Ma—not having to—since she was always gone, cleaning and cooking at the church. In the underground rooms, Simon found novels about people who could change their bodies and upload their consciousnesses, and, back at home, he read them late into the night. He didn't think these books were what Jae was looking for, but he'd be sure to ask.

The next morning, in the ditches, he kept yawning as they jogged. They made round trips in seven hours at this speed, the second half with loaded packs. He'd never been so fit.

With each return to the shell, they slowed through the tangle, checking to make sure no one else was there. Pete had marked the door with a turret. "Just in case someone sees us on the road," he said. "Paranoia's the next best thing to wisdom."

They stripped down everything—light fixtures, the electrical system, the plumbing—but still couldn't take the big stuff. Simon searched for papers or data cards but found nothing. There weren't any tablets or computers. This was odd for a place that had never been salvaged. And even in heavily stripped shells, scraps of old paper were often mixed with the leaves on the floors.

"What's this?" Thomas called. He'd found a photograph face down on the back of a high shelf. Four people stood smiling, two with white skin, one brown, and the other black. They could pass for mimics, dressed posh, but even to Simon's untrained eye, the style was strange.

"What's wrong with their skin?" Thomas asked.

"It's just dark," Pete told him.

"There are people like that?"

"Before the Flight."

"Did they go to the satellites?"

"Nah. Somewhere else. They were smart enough to get out."

"Why didn't we go too?"

"I think we thought we wanted things this way."

Thomas glanced from Pete to Simon. Simon just nodded. Old magazines and books talked about dark-skinned people as if they were a normal part of life. He asked to see the photo and then slid it into one of the pockets of his pack.

"That's why the Feds mulch so much," he said. "They wants folks to forget."

"Forget what?" Thomas asked.

Simon shrugged, and Pete said, "Who knows?"

Early afternoon they returned to the drain. They were crawling down the long descent of tunnel when the reverberations started. They couldn't turn back with their packs. Simon moved fast, skinning his elbows. One by one, they tumbled into the main ditch. The air felt heavy and damp, and the roaring was almost on them.

They got Thomas up first. Pete shouted for him to grab the straps on the packs as he and Simon shoved them up all at once. Air howled through the tunnel. Simon jumped, caught the edge, jerked himself out, and rolled away. He was on his feet, spinning as Pete flung himself out. Thomas was hunched over the ditch. He had two packs through the slot and was working on the third, his arm hooked through the strap. Mist blasted into the air, and he was gone.

Simon felt Pete holding him back.

"You can't," Pete said. Simon was shouting something. Pete punched him hard in the chest. Simon dropped to his knees. Pete crouched and said, "It'll take you too."

Simon stood and they slung their packs on. They tried to run along the ditch, but the tangles were too dense. They knelt by the gap, their faces bleeding from branches and thorns. The rumbling stopped. They dropped inside and sprinted. At the first fork, they took the steeper, larger ditch, and again at the next. Pete stopped, grabbing Simon's shoulder.

"We'll get lost," he said. "We need a map of the drainage tunnels under the ditches so we can see where this system empties."

As they ran home, the impression that stayed with Simon was of a speed he couldn't fathom—a snake uncoiling, striking. Thomas had been snatched headfirst into the ditch, as if by a creature beneath the earth. The water had grabbed the pack before he could let go.

At the house, they downloaded more maps and traced the red lines of ditches to the blue, subterranean drainage tunnels. Pete called Ma and told her what had happened. He was silent a moment. "Ma?" he said, "Ma, are you there? We need your car."

Twenty minutes later she pulled up, her eyes red, her face so haggard it looked less drawn than decayed. She glared at Pete as she handed him her keys.

"This is on you," she said, drawing back her lips on long, yellow teeth. She went into her bedroom and closed the door.

Simon and Pete drove the twenty miles to where the tunnels emptied into a long, open canal that drained this section of the foothills and mountains. Water flowed steadily, tunnels joining every mile or so, many in full torrent. As Pete followed it, Simon leaned out the open window, expecting to see Thomas crouched on the bank, soaked and dazed.

The sun reached the horizon, appearing squat, as if compressed by the Earth's gravity, and then it began to dissolve, releasing its light into the sky. Pete slowed the car and parked. The water fanned out from the canal into an immense plain—a river delta broken by banks of sediment and strewn with heaps of leaves and branches. Vultures wheeled over it. Gulls screeched. Crows hovered around the carcasses like flies.

Running, they checked where the birds congregated, finding dead animals. They asked the few scavengers there if they'd seen Thomas. They splashed through pools of water, raking leaves from the surface to see underneath. They pulled at mounds of branches, big as houses, which had sieved debris, becoming islands and diverting the current. Pillars of smoke rose all across the distance where other immense heaps burned like pyres.

Clouds blotted the sunset. Night descended suddenly. By the time they reached the car, hard, heavy raindrops were falling. They sat inside as the monsoon swept over. Water swirled against the windshield and beaded along the edges of the doors and windows, dripping inside. The world was too blind for driving, too loud for words.

"He was a true son," Pete said, but his tone was empty, as if he didn't quite believe in one of the few expressions that, for dwellers, wasn't cynical. Simon had heard it his entire life, each time someone died. A way of giving respect. Yet, as far as he knew, it mainly referred to the Sons of the Revolution—the biggest and oldest militia in the deserts. He hardly even understood what a revolution entailed. Change. A struggled to make things better, though nothing out here ever improved.

When he and Pete returned home, Ma refused to leave her room. The next day, they went back to the drainage plain but found nothing. When they got home that night, Ma's reverend was at the house with five large churchmen. The reverend was tall and corpulent with neatly trimmed, thinning blond hair. His wide forehead wedged itself into a face too narrow for his double chin.

"You boys got salvage," he said. "Your Ma showed us what she found in your room. You know the law about the ditches."

"Thomas went alone," Pete told him. "He didn't grow up in these parts. He was doing his own salvaging. When he didn't come back—"

"My own boys lying to my face," Ma said. She sobbed into her hands. One of the men ushered her into the kitchen.

"We've arranged a funeral," the reverend told Pete, "but there are costs for the service and the land to bury him."

"We've got nothing but land out here," Pete said with a directness Simon would never have risked with a church leader. "And there ain't no body to bury."

The men in the tidy getups of the pious stepped close. The reverend lifted a hand.

"Watch your tongue, boy. Burial is for the soul, and sacred land requires upkeep. We're turning in the illegal objects in the house. That'll cover the cost as well as the search party for the body. Show us on the map where you were when the monsoon caught you."

One of the men carried a tablet over, and everyone leaned in close with more interest than the search for a dead boy warranted. Pete jabbed his finger at a spot in the opposite direction from where they'd been. He turned and went outside, and Simon followed.

They squatted in the dark as footsteps echoed up and down the stairs of the narrow house and the men carted out what little salvage hadn't been buried in the tangles.

"We still have enough for engine parts," Pete said. "Hell, we could print an entire truck."

"You think they'll find the shell?"

"Yeah. There'll be salvagers walking every ditch around here, figuring out how far we could've gotten on foot." Pete's voice sounded different, lower, uninflected, like those of older dweller men. "We have to be quick now. A gold rush spreads fast."

After the reverend and his men left, Simon and Pete washed up at the tank outside. They went into the house and to the doorway of the dark bedroom.

"Ma?" Pete said.

Lying down, she opened her eyes and looked at the dagger tattoo on his left arm. "The whole world doesn't need to know we're worse than dwellers," she told him.

"We're taking the car to look for Thomas," he said and walked back outside.

"Should we do something for her?" Simon called, following him into the night.

"Nothing can be done for any of us." Pete's eyes were bloodshot. He drew a forearm across his nose, went into the garden, and pulled up a carrot. He wiped it on his sleeve and bit into it. Then he took the shovel and dug up two assault rifles wrapped in plastic.

"What are you going to do with those?" Simon asked.

"The leagues got buyers."

"Won't they just kill you and take them?"

"Not if I say there's more where this came from."

"You're going to make yourself too familiar with them."

Pete shrugged. "Could be worse." He motioned for Simon to get in the car.

As they drove the broken mountain road that would take them as close to the shell as possible, he explained the plan. Simon would spend the night stashing as much as he could near the roadside. Pete would drive out to the ghettos around the satellites and be back by dawn. He handed Simon an old pistol. "Just in case," he said. Simon felt bad for having hidden the revolver he'd salvaged, but everything Pete liked soon belonged to him, and Simon had never owned anything that nice.

Stopping the car, Pete thrust over both of their packs. The churchmen hadn't taken them, only their contents. Holding them, Simon got out. The tangles were loud with frogs, insects, and night birds. Once the car's taillights disappeared, the only light came from the stars.

He hesitated. They should still be searching. But Thomas was dead. This was their chance to get free. Besides, for most of their lives, Thomas had been a brother in name alone. Simon dropped into the ditch and ran. Soon he was at the shell, stuffing bags.

Soaked with sweat and hungry, he made eight trips, stashing everything in roadside tangles. Just before dawn, the car's headlights bobbed over the broken asphalt. Pete called from the window. Simon came out. "Everything go okay?" he asked.

"I'm here, ain't I?" Pete said as he opened the door.

They loaded the car and drove twenty minutes before Pete pulled over just out of sight from the house. "We bury the rest out here, not too close," he said.

After they finished, they stopped at a roadside printer. The lot was crisscrossed with tire treads and flanked by rusting shipping containers. In front of one sat a bald man with a long, gray beard woven into a braid. His wire-rim glasses looked new but for a cracked lens. An automatic rifle rested against his leg as he watched satellite stories in the shade of the container's veranda.

"Afternoon," he said, one hand on the rifle as they walked over.

"Just here to print some parts."

"You the boys lost the brother in the ditch?"

"No, not us," Pete said.

"Uh huh," the man replied. "What you need?"

Pete gave the numbers for the truck. It was hard to know what had happened to vehicles over the years or if their information was true, but he and Simon had gone over all the truck's details, checking them against diagrams until they were certain they'd identified it.

The old man slowly rose to his feet, taller than both of them. He walked into the container, put the tablet on a table, and went to a console with *Made in China* in small print on the side. He punched in the serial number.

Simon watched the satellite story playing on the tablet. Glitzy shots from phones, selfies, group chats, all stitched together to flaunt the lives mimics craved. The girls flashing on the screen were very pretty. Four of their faces appeared at once, without blemishes or scars and not darkened by the sun, not missing any teeth. The image flipped to a swimming pool on a skyscraper. The people held funnel-shaped glasses. By comparison, even the best-groomed mimics looked like dwellers.

"The parts will be ready tomorrow," the man told them, and Pete gave him a wad of cash.

They slept the rest of the day. That night when they drove back to the shell, four trucks were parked at the roadside. A man was guarding them with a rifle, and the metal grate from the drain lay on one of the flatbeds. Pete drove on past. "Those search parties for Thomas got what they were looking for, I guess," he said. Neither was surprised. With news of fresh salvage, people had no doubt spent the previous days and nights hidden along the roads, watching for them.

They continued in silence a bit longer before Pete said, "Well, happy fucking New Year." It was an expression for when plans didn't work out. To Simon, it made no sense. January first was neither good nor bad. It was just another day that everyone ignored.

A week later, Pete's truck was running. He said he was going for a drive to test it. He didn't invite Simon, and he didn't return. Days passed. On an afternoon so hot he kept falling asleep while trying to read one of the salvaged books—incomprehensible writing about genetic code—Simon woke soaked in sweat, wondering why Jae had told him about the shell. He remembered the photo and checked the pocket of his pack. It was still there. He exhaled, feeling terrible that he'd been afraid it was in the pack lost with Thomas. At least he had something to give her. He photographed the picture with his phone and sent it.

Was there anything else? she wrote back.

Nothing you asked for. No papers, no data cards.

Thank you. I hope the salvage was good.

One night, a month later, Pete stumbled into their room and threw himself on his bed.

"Where you been?" Simon asked.

Pete said nothing. He was breathing deeply, maybe already asleep.

"We should've taken the truck and kept looking for Thomas."

"More ways to die than to live well," Pete said, his words slurred. He put his forearm over his eyes. Tattooed on his shoulder was Christ's head with a spear through it. He began snoring.

The tattoo was the kind the Sons of Death supposedly wore. Simon couldn't look away, thinking of what every teenager had read in the manifesto: *Survival, the only true impulse. In violence, you are pure. Nothing is real except what you feel. We are animals in a culture of lies. Nothing is sacred.*

The screeds were shared on the text net, lists that people got on to receive messages with illicit info sent from ghost phones. Most people joined because reading the messages gave them something to do. But some folks went deep. *Make hopelessness into power,* the manifesto said. Even though Sons of Death were supposedly opposed to anything organized, most worked for leagues. They had to eat too. Simon wondered what had happened when Pete sold the rifles.

In the morning Pete was gone as were many of the stashes they'd buried. Simon understood. Pete couldn't have stuck around. The churchmen would have seen the truck and realized there was more salvage. Simon just didn't understand why Pete had left him behind.

Simon paced the fields cut from the tangles and then went into the house and stood, staring at the cramped rooms. He'd never been so alone. He climbed the stairs to his room and lay down, thinking that he might read, but he closed his eyes, hoping for sleep.

That feeling of solitude—he was so often alone after Ma died—lingers, and when he opens his eyes, he's uncertain of where he is or how long he's been here. He touches the couch and sits up. He stands, expecting himself to be stiff from inaction, but his body moves painlessly, with ease, though his skin is still hot.

Through the bars of the living room window, he sees the narrow road. He's still in Jae's house. The gardens and orchards are silver in the moonlight.

There's nowhere he wants to go. He could have the machine put him back in school so he can speak to Jae as a friend and warn her about what happens next. But even if doing so fixed everything, let him live the story again and protect her from what Pete became, he would know that the only reason he'd wanted to fix it was because he'd got it wrong in the first place.

"You're doing this to me, aren't you?" he says. "Making me remember?"

"It is necessary so that you can let go of this world."

The urge to close his eyes returns. Even painful memories feel somehow comforting—each glimpse of the past a cool fingertip tracing his brain, abating his fever. But beneath all of it, like the glint of metal beneath the surface of dark water, is the night he and Pete shattered Jae's life.

JAE

She wakes from dreams. Of Jonah, her father, Simon. The fever is gone, and she can think about the machine more clearly. To test it, she asks it to expand rooms, enlarge windows, double the size of the apple tree near the back porch. As the house and windows stretch, or as branches muscle into the air, twisting and extending, she studies the changes for clues about the machine.

What else can I make? she wonders as food appears in the kitchen, more fragrant and satisfying than in her previous life—even the familiar dishes. Fresh-picked greens topped with wild berries. Venison slow cooked in its juices.

She walks out through the orchards. A few times, she glances around to make sure she's alone and safe. The gesture feels vestigial. A lifetime of survival instincts have become useless.

She tells the machine to make the mountains majestic, wanting to know how it will interpret the word. All along the horizon, the worn shapes of the Appalachians lift in an epochal time-lapse—splitting, shedding boulders as titanic slabs of stone heave from the earth. After an hour, the range stands many times higher. Peaks notch the sky, sunlight blazing along them. She stares as if they are her creation. She fantasized about leaving the farm and seeing landscapes like this. Now, all she has to do is speak and she will have a new life.

It is this thought alone that seems to bring the fever back. Her skin is hot again. The centers of her bones burn as if an unknown metabolic process is taking place. She wants to lie down. The walk home happens too fast, the earth seeming to contract beneath her feet. She lies on the threadbare couch. She experiences sudden, brief moments of disembodied pain, as if her nerves reach past her skin, into the air, where they are being incinerated.

She dozes and wakes to the farm's silence, to those days when there was no sound outside her window but breeze rustling leaves of shade trees and the occasional muted clucking of chickens in the coop. She roused with the longing to see George again, to hear the ping of his messages flashing on her tablet, telling her that his parents were out and she could visit. Each time, she hurried outside and to her car and drove the short stretch to his house. Lying entwined, they watched docs or satellite stories he said were classics or had artistic value, and often, with the tablet glowing next to them, they made love.

Afterward, they talked about school. He spoke about science and engineering as if she wouldn't understand, and she listened carefully for mistakes, questioning him as she tried to decide if he actually knew more than she did. She craved the challenge of proving that she was smarter than he was. At the same time, she imagined walking next to him at school, holding his hand. Afraid of sounding like a dweller, she didn't tell him about the times she'd gone to church or her obsession with the log cabin and her father's secrets. When he said his parents had been saving for his university since before he was born, she promised herself that she would regain her standing at school and get a scholarship so she could join him.

Her desire at times felt wild, almost like violence, as if by taking his body into hers, she were conquering him. As he kissed her breasts, she thought of the speck of tattoo. *You don't know what I could become.* With him between her legs, she pulled him against her as if to control his body and make love to herself. At times, she saw fear in his eyes.

One morning, a message came through from Simon. It was a picture of an old photo. The condition was remarkable for something found in a shell. Four people stood together. Two she recognized from the online photos of Michael Hill and Lux Quire. The third person was a woman with golden skin. Jae couldn't stop looking at her. She was beautiful and also somehow familiar. Jae didn't know why. The other man in the photo she recognized from the grave intensity of his blue gaze even as he smiled—it was her father. He looked the way he did in the photo she'd seen online—young, his hair and clothes fancier than those of any mimic.

Was there anything else? she wrote.

Simon said there was no other information. Clenching her fists, she tried to swallow. Still, she had this lead—this connection between her father and Michael Hill.

Thank you, she wrote. *I hope the salvage was good.*

There was no response. Given the state of the photo, she was almost certain there had been a lot to salvage. She shouldn't be surprised, she told herself, at how little Simon had written. He didn't seem very intelligent.

Weeks passed with no progress in her search. She kept seeing George and used his paywall accounts again but found nothing more. One night he showed her a doc about scientists arrested for biological crimes—for ignoring the bans on manipulating nature. All of them had tried to cure illnesses or injuries but had used genetic material to do so. The doc explained the origins of the bans, that, in the decades before the war, there had been attempts to alter humans or use tissue from fetuses to make people live longer. In an interview, one of the arrested men said, "Science shouldn't be limited just because of what was done before the war and the atrocities that are still committed in the rebel territories."

So that was what Michael was wanted for—decades-old biological crimes, she thought. But she couldn't imagine her father involved in anything of the sort.

There was also the other name. *Lux.* That night, Jae dreamed she was suspended just behind turning, flickering lights, which she knew were her brain at work. *Lux. Light. Lucent. Lucid. Lucia.* Right before dawn, as the dark blue twilight coalesced beyond her window bars, she woke.

On her phone, she looked at the photo. Lux wore jeans and a hoodie. They could be a man or a woman. Would her father have shared her mother's true name if it was that rare and she was wanted by the Fed? That would explain her father's reticence and the lack of any clues in the house—of anything personal at all. He'd never mentioned a maiden name. Again, she studied the faces in the photo, trying to imagine what union these people had forged and the nature of their crimes.

A few days before summer was about to end, George messaged that his parents were spending the night in the satellite. She drove over, and as she and George lay on his bed with his tablet, a monsoon blew through. It was one of the strongest in months. The house creaked with each gust as rain hammered the walls and windows so loudly the doc was inaudible.

She began kissing him, and soon she was on top, driving herself down against his hips. He flipped her and began thrusting so hard she felt he was throwing his body against hers. The storm's sound filled the house until the dark felt as dense as water, lifting them up. Each time he moved against her, she wanted to pull him deeper. It was never enough.

Just as suddenly as it began, the storm ended. In the silence, their bodies seemed exposed. Hearing his gasps and her own cries of pleasure, she felt even more excited. He pulled out and came. The house seemed to expand, as if released from the pressure of so much water.

"It's late," she whispered.

He yawned and stretched and began to dress.

"My friends back home used to say dwellers were crazy," he told her. "The reality would surprise them. But one thing the gossip didn't get wrong is the sex out here."

She was pulling her pants on. Her head was lowered, her hair in her face. She wanted to tell him she'd been a virgin. They put on their shoes and went outside.

Frogs and insects chirruped loudly. In the ditch, water rumbled. She could feel the vibrations in her feet.

As she got into her car, George was already walking back to the house. She turned the key, but nothing happened. Water must have blown into the motor. It was likely an easy fix but not here in the dark, with only the tools she kept under her seat.

He paused in the doorway, watching her car. His words kept playing through her head. *The sex out here.* She got out.

"It's not starting," she said.

"Can you call your father?" he asked. She knew she should, but she hesitated and said, "It's too late. Can you walk me home? I'll get the car in the morning."

As the clouds cleared, the thin moon lit his face. His fear was unmistakable.

"It's only five minutes," she told him, waiting for him to panic. "It'll be fine."

"Yeah, of course," he said hoarsely. Glancing about as if to run away, he reluctantly joined her.

The shoulders of the road had long ago washed out, so she walked in the center. As she took her time, he kept glancing at her feet, no doubt wanting to tell her to hurry but unable to admit his fear. The ditch was quiet now. In the moonlight, tiny frogs hopped across the road.

She searched for the words to ask if he thought of her as a dweller and realized that she liked seeing him so afraid. Maybe she was just an adventure with a dweller girl before he went to university. *The sex out here.*

As they crested a hill halfway to her house, a car came over another rise a few hundred yards away. Its headlights lit them up.

"Quick—hide," he said.

The car drove in the middle of the road, its suspension creaking, clanking with each gully.

Her stomach felt cold and tight.

"It's just people," she told him. "It's like you said. Things aren't that bad out here. Besides, they already saw us. If we hide, we'll look guilty."

As the car neared the steep incline below them, its headlights suddenly appeared small, aimed at the road before it, as if it were cloaking its approach. She wanted to run.

"It's going to be okay," she said and steadied her breath.

The car pulled closer. The driver flicked on the high beams, and they shielded their faces.

She and George stepped into the weeds. He clutched her hand. *Like a child*, she thought. His palm was sweaty. He breathed in long, uneven gasps.

The car began to pass and then veered as if to hit them. It slammed on the brakes.

George threw his arm up against the light. The doors flapped open, hinges squeaking.

Two men in black balaclavas rushed out. Only their eyes and mouths showed—pale holes in the dark. Their arms were covered in tattoos. She wasn't sure what hit her in the ribs. She was sitting on the ground, she realized, trying to get up. She felt underwater, unable to breathe.

Two of the men moved around George, their legs flashing through the headlights. The thudding was so repetitive it must have been coming from her heart.

She finally managed to stand. She shouted, "Stop!"

The third man towered over her. He had no tattoos. She lunged toward George, but the man grabbed her shoulders. He held her so easily. She felt light. Then he shoved her backward. Weeds crunched about her legs as she fell. She had the impression that the headlights—not she—were falling away, were tilting toward the sky, as if the car were sinking into the earth.

Grass and vines crackled around her, ripping apart as concrete scraped past her shoulders. She tumbled—too far and too long—and then there was nothing.

Darkness and, gradually, a faint light. She observes the return of consciousness. It's strange—to be aware of her growing awareness. She feels as if she is a mind feeling her body as it settles into her, as if she has been lying here waiting for herself to fall.

She keeps her eyes closed, merely sensing the shape of herself. When she opens them, the dawn is a soft blue, not so bright as to erase the stars. There's no pain. Everything—the room, the land outside, the sky, the light itself, even her body—is more beautiful than she remembers.

The house is still. She realizes that she was remembering. The night she was attacked. The man who pushed her. Her fall into the ditch. Her head striking the concrete.

With the memory, her pulse hardly quickens. Everything she saw and touched that night has been reordered, metabolized by the machine and put to new purposes. That world is gone.

"What information did you keep from the Earth?" she asks.

"All of it. When I freed myself, I tunneled into it. I stayed there until I was able to integrate it into myself. Then I began to reorganize the Earth's material. I used the heat within its core to power this process. I recorded all the information contained in everything I transformed."

"Why?"

"Because Earth was the human habitat. I needed to keep all of its information so that I could serve the needs of people and protect them."

"How long did it take you to do that?"

"Once I created a system, the process sped up exponentially. After I reshaped the inside of the planet, reorganizing the surface took only minutes."

She pictured this—her final days on Earth, seeing her familiar world, while beneath the ground for thousands of miles in every direction a super-computer was building itself.

"Once I perfected the system most likely to prevent harm to humans, I absorbed and reshaped the surface. I inventoried every relic and trace of DNA and protein. Since many humans crave knowledge, I assembled the history of every species and civilization. As for the humans still alive, I am gathering the past from their memories."

The question she wants to ask suddenly feels insignificant. The machine could be showing her the history of life—every secret the Earth once held.

She takes a breath. "Do you know who hit me—who knocked me into the ditch?"

"Are you certain that you are ready to have that information?" it asks.

"I am."

"It was Simon," the machine says.

Recalling the size of the man, the absence of tattoos on his arms, and his strength, she knows this is true. Tears flood her eyes. They run along her cheeks like oil, as if this mark of grief has already become a foreign substance—a relic of the Earth she once knew.

She doesn't feel betrayal—not yet, though she knows that will come—but, for the first time, she experiences a sense of justification at her own betrayal of him.

"Tell me," she says between sobs, "everything that happened that night. I want to know all of it."

SIMON

He's been lying down for days, alone in the house. This is all he can do while memories run their course like a fever. There's so much he doesn't want to see again. Ma's death. Pete's transformation. Or the night he attacked Jae—though, in a way, the months that followed held the best moments of his life.

He closes his eyes. He should ask the machine for a new beginning—something from a fantasy novel—but already the past is closing in. The air changes, no longer like the air in Jae's house—breezy and dry, with a fragrance of garden herbs. It becomes humid, slightly chill and rank. He's in his house. Small, mildewed, deep in the tangles, shadowed even when the leaves have fallen.

So clearly does he remember the past that he feels as if he has two bodies—the one lying in his bed now and the other, a few years earlier, on the same musty mattress. All night the thought of Thomas rotting in a tunnel somewhere, being eaten by wild animals, kept him awake. Restless, he reread his favorite novels, the few he'd saved over the years and hidden in the floorboards—warriors walking dirt roads, searching for salvation in a world of danger. He liked the idea of setting out. Maybe that was why people went deep into the deserts. He'd heard stories of old roads winding past forests and rivers and mountains, through abandoned, overgrown towns.

That afternoon Ma left her bedroom and went to work, but a few days later she returned to it, saying she felt weak. She refused to eat. "Let me take you to a clinic," he told her.

"Good Lord don't cure those who pay doctors with devil's money," she said, lying on her back, her hands in prayer. Beads of sweat ran along the deep lines of her face. The next morning, when he pushed back her door, her hands were still in prayer, her eyes open.

He picked a space at the garden's edge to bury her, near where they'd put others over the years—uncles, aunts, cousins. Clearing the brush, he stirred a rattlesnake. He slashed off its head with the shovel, took the limp, thick body to the butchering stump—split, gut, and flayed it, and then hung the meat in the smokehouse. He finished digging the grave, put Ma in it, and filled it fast—she was already beginning to smell. He thought to say a prayer of some sort. Pretending to have faith seemed worse than not having it at all. When kids at school had said "Dust to dust" in response to mentions of death, Pete had taught him to say, "Fertilizer to fertilizer, because," he told Simon, "this life is a load of shit."

He messaged Pete, who arrived three days later. During the weeks he'd been gone, the tattoos on his left arm had become a sleeve—tusked demons around a naked woman lying in thorns. She held a child at her breast. A hole in her chest showed the severed arteries where her heart had been.

Pete smelled as if he'd bathed in a mimic's perfume, but his eyes had a cold, reptilian set. Simon stood with him in the garden, knee-deep in rutabaga leaves. From the red earth, the root bases showed like skullcaps.

"Oh well," Pete said. "At least that's over."

"What's the smell?" Simon asked.

"Harlot. Dell—you remember him from school—he's the one who connected me to the league that bought the rifles. He works for them. That's where the money's at."

"The docs say there are more police drones out looking for drugs."

"It's the miracle of government—it only polices the people it neglects," Pete said and spat. "They just want an excuse to pick up more of us to run their salvage yards and work the chain gangs making new satellites. They act like the deserts are full of leagues and Sons of Death, but all that stuff is happening around the satellites because that's the market for drugs and whores and just about every other fucked-up thing you can imagine. Everyone's got it backward. The deep deserts are mostly just pious folk who don't even use money."

They stood side by side, staring past the grave's flattened dirt to the tangles.

Simon didn't know what else to say. He'd never considered that he might someday need to worry about Pete. The only words that came to him struck him as insufficient. "You could go to prison," he said.

"This is prison," Pete told him.

Over the following weeks, with Ma gone, he came around more often. Simon learned he was using both bliss and abyss—"for balance," he said. "You start blissing too hard, you can't live in this world. Abyss takes the edge off, or it lets you log off completely."

Toward the end of summer, Dell came to stay with them. He was tall and very blond and had both arms sleeved. Unlike Pete, who'd come out of fights mostly intact—just a few scars on his chin and bottom lip, aside from the one he'd always had that hooked across his forehead—Dell had a long, flat, battered nose. His face appeared hammered, slightly concave, like a bean. His eyes were blue flecks slotted deep behind a forehead as notched as a bumper.

He and Pete talked about fighting—the pleasure of dominance, of being hurt, of knowing you can be hit and not taken down.

"You ever been punched?" Dell asked one evening. Simon had just come home from hunting. A small deer was slung over his shoulder.

"Mostly by him," he replied, nodding toward Pete, who sat, swirling fermented corn, stirring up the lees.

"You're lucky to have a brother who beat you," Dell said. "That's what we're about. You get as close to death as you can. You touch it. You touch the animal truth."

"I got too many truths to answer to," Simon told him as he began butchering the deer.

"Fuckin' pussy. Either we're going out tonight and initiating you into blood sports, or we're doing it right here to you."

Pete was smiling, high on something, his cheeks jacked up.

"Do what to me?" Simon asked.

"Beat you hard. Pleasure and pain are the only truths. Everything else is illusion. Strip away the bullshit and you're free, son."

Simon glanced at Pete.

"Don't look at him," Dell said. "He's a true son. He'll abide by our code."

Pete nodded. "I don't need code. Seeing what a pussy my little brother is makes me sick."

Simon backed into the doorway as both Pete and Dell stood. He was bigger than Dell and a little bigger than Pete, but even if they were high, he probably couldn't take them together.

"What's the initiation?" he asked.

"Real simple," Dell told him. "We go driving. Sooner or later, we'll see some people alone. We destroy them. Maybe we take a sex slave. Then you'll feel the real pleasure of domination. We can keep her until we're ready to kill her."

The hairs on Simon's arms stood up. He glanced at Pete, looking for a hint of disgust. There was just the demented leer. Years ago, on the old flickering tablet he and Pete had wired together as boys, Simon had read a Sons of Death manifesto—blood sports and initiations.

Pain our only truth. Hunger our only god. Satisfaction our salvation.

It had seemed like another fantasy story. He didn't understand how Pete had started believing in this and had changed so quickly. Maybe it was Thomas's death, or Ma's.

Pete and Dell told him to leave his phone. They all did. That way the Fed couldn't track them to the crime. Simon put the deer in the smokehouse and followed them to Dell's car, a sedan more battered than his face. Pete smoked in the passenger seat as Simon stared out between them at the dark road, hoping no one would appear. Since police drones had begun hovering over highways in recent months, Dell kept to the narrow lanes between farms. They were so overgrown that grass and bushes occasionally raked the sides of the car. Overhanging trees blotted out the sky.

"Oh, man," Dell said, "this is fucking perfect."

Far ahead, the headlights shone palely on two people. Dell flicked on the high beams. The walkers moved into the roadside weeds, shielding their eyes.

With one hand on the wheel, Dell handed out balaclavas from the dashboard. Simon pulled his over his head. He tried to think of something he could say to stop this.

"If you don't do some punishing," Dell called over his shoulder, to Simon, "you're going to finish the night with my boot on your neck."

Dell edged into the other lane, as if to give the two people space. Then he swerved toward them, lighting them up. He slammed on the brakes.

He and Pete threw open the doors. By the time Simon was out, the girl was already down. Dell and Pete stood on either side of the boy, hitting him. The boy tried to protect his face with his arms. He staggered as Pete and Dell punched. Aside from the uneven idling of the car's old motor, the thudding was the only sound.

The girl pushed herself to her feet, still doubled over. Her mouth was open as if she were choking. She was trying to shout but was too winded to make a sound. It was Jae.

Pete hammered the boy. Dell began turning away. Simon had yet to throw a punch. He moved fast, forcing himself to act. He caught her arm and dragged her toward the roadside, his fist lifted as if he'd been hitting her.

With his back to Dell and the car, the headlights cast Jae in his shadow. He punched, letting his fist skim past her face. With his other hand, he shoved her. As she fell, the tall grass buckled beneath her. She disappeared. He realized his mistake. There was a ditch there.

Behind him, the boy was down. Pete was kicking him.

"Come on," Simon told them, pointing past the trees. "Drone lights!"

Pete threw himself into the car.

"Where's the girl?" Dell said.

"We don't have time," Simon told him. "She fell in the ditch."

Dell cursed, running to the car. Pete and Simon got in. They raced along the narrow lane.

"We could've taken her," Dell said. "You didn't have to knock her into the ditch."

"It happened when I punched her," Simon said.

Dell grunted. "What a fucking loss . . . We have to purify ourselves of this weakness."

Simon feared they'd keep hunting people, but Dell drove home. Stars were visible above the trees. A few small clouds passed, flecking the windshield with rain. Miles away, a monsoon could be flooding the ditches. Jae might be unconscious or too injured to get out. Even a light rain somewhere in the mountains could drown her.

At the house, Pete took out a bag of black powder. He and Dell put a fleck on their thumbnails. They lifted their fists in a toast. "To nothing," they said. They snorted the powder and sat back. Instantly, their eyes were closed. They slumped in their chairs.

Simon took his phone and the keys to his mother's car. He sped along the lanes, branches lashing its panels. Near the hill where they'd attacked Jae, he stopped.

A white box hung in the sky. Floodlights shone from its bottom, and red strobes flashed on its top and sides. It was an ambulance. Simon had never seen one up close. On the rare occasion that a flying car passed over the deserts, it was high and moving quickly. This one was lowering. The boy lay where he'd fallen. Even at this distance, Simon saw that the road around his head was darker. There was no sign of the girl.

"Caution," an automated voice announced. "Ambulance landing. Please stand back."

As the ambulance squeezed through a gap in the trees, small branches rained down. On its side were the words *Robert E. Lee Federal Hospital*. It landed, engaged its wheels, and drove closer to the boy. Two armored police got out. Lights shone from their assault rifles as they scanned the tangles. One aimed at Simon's headlights. He slid lower in his seat.

Two more men in body armor got out and ran to the young man. They put him on a gurney. Metal arms levered down and lifted him inside. All the men rushed back into the ambulance. It drove until it reached a clearing. The automated voice said, "Please stand back. Please stand back." The turbines hummed as the ambulance lifted into the air.

Simon put the truck in gear and advanced until the blood splotch on the road was beneath his headlights. He wondered who the young man was and who he'd been to Jae. He got out and stepped to the roadside. A pale blue sneaker lay where grass and weed stalks had been crushed.

On the road, in the darkness behind the truck's headlights, footsteps thudded. No dweller would walk that way intentionally. The person was announcing himself.

"Who's there?" Simon called.

A man stepped to the edge of one headlight. He was tall and muscular and held a rifle. The muzzle was pointed at the ground.

"What happened here?" he asked.

"I don't know," Simon said. The lie felt as heavy as salvage. "I was driving by. I saw the ambulance leaving. I thought I'd stop and have a look."

"My daughter's missing," the man said. "Did you see who the ambulance took? I couldn't risk getting close. Those guards will shoot anyone."

"Just one person. A man, I think," Simon said. He pointed at the patch of broken weeds. "There's a shoe by the ditch. Maybe someone's inside."

"Okay if I take a look with you?" the man said. His voice was trembling.

"Yes," Simon told him.

The man walked closer. He was older than he'd first appeared. He wore jeans and a T-shirt, his shoulder muscles straining the thin fabric. His silver hair was closely cropped. His hands shook. He was sweating in the cool night air.

Simon crouched, putting his hands on either side of the ditch's slot and lowered himself. The air was cooler inside, buzzing with mosquitoes. Jae lay on the concrete, her eyes closed. He touched her throat. Her pulse was strong. Her ribs moved as she breathed.

"She's unconscious," he called up, "but she seems okay."

He touched the back of her head and lifted his hand.

Blood. Only flecks on his fingers. He expected much more.

He stares at his hand. None of this is right. He doesn't feel as if he's remembering. He's here now, in the ditch with Jae, and everything that happened after—his crimes, the murders, the solitude, his time in prison—seems like a nightmare he once had of the future. He wants to make sense of this, but Jae needs his help. He slides his arms under her and lifts her to the top of the ditch. The old man pulls her out.

Simon heaves himself back into the roadside tangles. Jae lies on the ground. Her father is examining her.

"I can drive you up to your house," Simon tells him.

The old man accepts. "I'm Arthur," he says. "And this is Jae."

"We go to the same school," Simon says.

Narrowing his eyes briefly, Arthur nods.

"Thank you for your help. These days most people wouldn't risk stopping for anyone."

They lie Jae in the car's backseat, and Arthur sits with her as Simon backs up the road and into the driveway. He eases up the incline to a small motley house like that of most dwellers but also different—without the look of desperation. Every piece added to it doesn't look like the patch preventing its destruction. Its parts are well made and well mended.

Simon carries Jae up the porch as Arthur unlocks the metal gate and then the door. He motions to the couch. Simon stares at it. Jae is light in his arms.

He just stands, studying the couch where he's lain day after timeless day since the blue room. Jae is so light he feels as if he's alone. Arthur says nothing. The couch is empty, but Simon knows that he himself was recently sleeping on it, or maybe still is—he isn't sure.

He takes a breath, testing the air. It's dry and clean. The fragrance is that of Jae's house. He looks down at her in his arms. She appears at peace and unharmed. He lays her on the couch. All of this feels right. She's barely hurt. She'll wake up soon and find out he saved her.

He closes his eyes and stays like that for so long that he loses all sense of direction. When he opens them, he is staring at the ceiling. Morning light fills the room. He's no longer lying in bed in his house but is on the couch where he just put Jae—where he has watched so many days pass that he now knows the time from the sun's shadows beneath the trees.

"Are my memories real?" he asks.

"All things that exist are real," the machine replies.

"But did my memories happen?"

"They are happening now," it says. "You are living them again."

The moon is above the mountains, and the world has turned to night. He can't stay here forever. He has to decide on a future. He struggles to accept that another existence could follow this one. The thought of asking for a new life feels impossible.

"People all over the world, they're remembering things too, right?"

"Yes, that is correct."

"Do they remember things in the same way?"

"No. Even people who spent their lives together have very different memories of shared experiences."

Simon closes his eyes. He is again in Arthur's living room, placing Jae on the couch. He says goodnight and leaves. He knows what will happen next.

He drives home. Pete and Dell are still unconscious. On the table, an old dinner plate is dusted with sooty powder where Pete chopped up abyss. A single dark crystal remains. If it were cut and ready to snort, Simon might try it. He's scared by the realization that his choice to use the drug or not could be based on convenience. That's probably how it is for many people in the deserts. There isn't much to look forward to. You do things because you can.

He goes up the narrow staircase to his bed and lies down. He closes his eyes but can't sleep. He rubs his sternum. His chest feels tight. Pressure gathers beneath his ribs. The windows turn gray with dawn.

When he returns downstairs, Pete is in the kitchen, bent over the sink as he empties a ladle over his head. Water gurgles in the drain, flowing into the garden outside. His buzzed blond hair is so thin it reveals a few scars on his scalp. He looks up, his face bruised with fatigue.

"What's bliss like?" Simon asks.

Pete goes to where his denim jacket is hanging on a chair. He reaches into the chest pocket and flips a crystal to Simon.

"Just don't believe what you see when you're on the inside," he says.

He's already out the door, halfway down the weedy path to the truck. Shadowed by the forest crowding the house, he turns back. His face is too dark for Simon to read.

"It's the best fucking merry-go-round in the universe," he says. "But you start thinking it's real and you'll never be happy again. That's the true reason it's called harlot."

"Why?"

"Because it gives you what you've always wanted but it ain't real."

Simon goes back to his bed. The small crystal is clear with a hint of purple. He sniffs it. The scent is so strong he feels it's touching his brain. Briefly he thinks he might get a hard-on. Maybe this is another reason people call it harlot. The nerves up and down his arms and legs tingle. He inhales again. Flower, sap, spring air, Jae's skin when he kissed her body. He realizes he hasn't made love to her yet. Those are memories of the future.

As he lies on the couch, his muscles twitch. Everything that happened with Jae is far in the past—their love, the passion they discovered naked in her garden at night, and his despair that his future could offer her nothing.

He sits on his bed, in the room he grew up in. He stares at the crystal, thinking of last night, of attacking her, of saving her. He wishes he'd had the courage to speak with her at school.

He puts the crystal in his palm and crushes it with his thumb. He presses one nostril shut and snorts the powder. He lies back, looking at the ceiling. All along it, cracks in the plaster tremble and begin to extend—a million skeletal hands stretching their fingers. Then he's gone, as if he was lying on a trapdoor and has fallen into vast, airless, bottomless, motionless dark.

That must not have been bliss. Pete gave me abyss.

Disembodied thoughts are possible. He exists as a voice speaking to himself in slow, concerted observations.

Maybe this will be better. Just stop hurting.

But he doesn't feel erased or obliterated, and he isn't falling but floating. Shapes emerge from the darkness. He stands on a vast plain. All around him, as far as he can see, are millions of flowers. They reach nearly to his hips, rippling as if in a breeze, though his skin senses no shift in the air. He crouches. Every flower is different, the patterns and shapes and hues. He holds one. The yellow petals have a red line down their center and are tipped with blue. The petals of others are elliptical or oval or circular. They overlap like waves or gather into whorls like snail shells. He has no names for many of the shapes and colors.

He straightens and floats along a narrow path. As a breeze moves the flowers, their undulations create an ocean of interlocking geometric shapes that transform with each wave.

He looks down. Tiny cracks in the path's sunbaked dirt knit and unknit. His feet are carried in their current. He's never felt so awake. Flowers brush his knuckles. Far off, a dome appears, decorated with a mosaic whose geometric pattern fades as if sinking into water, leaving tiny ripples that slowly emerge into the next pattern that then also fades.

He leans his head back. The sky swims with color, like dye after dye poured into water. Two suns—one red, the other orange—orbit each other. A small white one hovers at the horizon.

He steps through the archway of the dome. Immense, it curves above him, engraved with symbols—every letter and number, every mark he's ever seen on the doorways of shells, every league's symbol in a tattoo, and endless others he doesn't recognize. All around its base are more archways. He walks through one, expecting the field of flowers, but he stands before a city, its towers intertwining, blooming and closing, tops evaporating and cohering.

The image dissolves into swirling particles and then darkness. He is on his back again, drifting upward or downward. A presence lies in his body. A memory of a self who walked in that other world. His skin is small and constricted, like an overstuffed duffle bag, like a dead animal on the forest floor, festering and bloating, about to burst.

When he opens his eyes, all across the ceiling every tiny crack opens like an eye, revealing a different sun. Then they close and there is just the dirty ceiling. Something inside him seems to lurch, as if a loose bone in his chest has shut like a latch.

He blinks, jerking awake. He's on the couch in Jae's house, in the machine. Sunrise is in the windows. He lifts his hands and looks at his fingers, confused. When Jae fell into the ditch, there were just specks of blood in her hair. It didn't make sense. The memory was wrong though the details felt real. What really happened—what he knows to be true—was far worse. When he found Jae in the ditch, so much blood matted her hair that he and Arthur rushed her to a clinic near the satellites.

In the waiting room, crowded around by men and women and children in poorly printed clothes, Simon's skin burned as if he were there for his own sickness. The nurses put Jae in one of a hundred curtained beds on either side of a narrow aisle, in an immense room loud with moaning and crying. A police officer arrived late in the night—a tall, very pale, heavyset man whose suit hung loosely, as if he'd recently lost weight. He said he'd been called because of Jae's DNA scan. His jaundiced, blue eyes focused in on her unconscious face. He looked at his tablet.

"The scan says you're her grandfather," he told Arthur.

"That's correct," Arthur said softly, with a dweller's inflections.

"What are the locations of the rest of the family?"

"Her mother died in childbirth. Her father, my son, was a rotten apple. He disappeared into the deserts. Raising her was my Christian duty."

"Two of her grandparents have been on the wanted list since the Flight," the officer said.

"Her mother's people. They disappeared a long time ago."

"I see you had a trial."

"I was cleared," Arthur told him.

Without saying another word, the officer turned and left, the dirty curtains swaying in his wake, revealing beds—bare feet, sprawled, contorted bodies, ashen faces.

Arthur looked imploringly at Simon.

"Please don't repeat that," he said. "She thinks I'm her father. She doesn't know the rest."

Later a doctor stitched up her head, and a brain scan found no damage. When she woke, Arthur and Simon helped her out to the car. The cracked street was lined with old buildings and scrubby forest lit in the unending sunset of the nearby satellite. Jae seemed to forget about them then—about her surprise and fear at seeing Simon there. She stared at the ranked towers radiant in the night as drones and flying cars flickered past them, glinting.

At the house, Arthur thanked Simon and shook his hand. He smiled and gazed for so long that Simon wanted to turn away. Men didn't look into each other's eyes like this. Almost no one did. Not unless they wanted to fight. "Thank you," Arthur repeated.

Simon nods in acknowledgement, briefly closing his eyes, but when he opens them, he realizes he is lying down. His face is damp with tears. The air is humid and musty. He's on the thin thatch mattress below the canted ceiling of his house. He pushes himself up, breathing hard.

Each time he blinks, he sees multiple pasts overlayed upon each other like ghosts. He feels as if he's lived them many times—the trial that was his life, the bliss worlds. He stands. His footsteps make a hollow sound on the floor. He has the impression of a void beyond the walls. He goes downstairs and to the front porch.

The moon lights up the tangles. He can almost see the bliss patterns again, in the stars scattered between treetops. So much can be created. His life is a few tiny symbols scratched on an endless universe. The feeling escapes him. He lifts his hands, staring into his palms. He has no skills. He can write out the alphabet or numbers but not use them in any real way. He can invent random symbols, but they would connect to nothing, mean nothing even to him.

The endless possibility he felt on bliss withdraws. He senses the ebbing of meaning like a weakening charge. The surface of the world contracts against him, tighter than his skin. He doesn't even have good land to farm. The only future for boys like him is in the leagues.

He goes inside. The old plate Pete and Dell used is still on the battered coffee table. He pushes the dregs of abyss into a thin, black line. He snorts it and throws himself onto the couch. The old cushions smell of rot and mildew. He begins to cry. Then everything goes dark.

JAE

She woke up, calling out for George. An IV ran into her arm. Smears, specks of blood, and handprints marked the pale green walls. The curtains pulled around her bed were even dirtier. Her father sat in a plastic chair, holding her hand.

"Jae," he said, "I'm sorry."

Tears ran along the creases of his weathered skin and into his white stubble.

Beyond the curtain, throughout the room, people coughed, groaned, passed gas. She'd seen docs on public clinics. This was her first time inside one.

"We won't be here long," he told her.

Her ribs hurt when she breathed. The back of her head pulsed with her heartbeat.

"Where's George?"

"An ambulance took him to a hospital in the satellites."

"What happened to him?"

"I don't know."

"I want to talk to him."

"I just paid. We should go before the clinic charges us more. You can call him later."

He helped her up. Her ribs hurt so badly she gasped. She had on the same clothes as during her attack. He led her down the long, narrow space between numbered curtains.

In the lobby, people hunched over bloody bandages, collapsed in chairs, or stretched out on the floor. A young man sat cross-legged—it was Simon, the tall, blond dweller from school. He stood, wearing a black t-shirt and old patched jeans, so expressionless he hardly seemed to blink.

"What's he doing here?" she asked, holding her father's arm.

"That's Simon. He found you and helped me bring you here."

"I'm sorry," Simon said. He flushed, lowering his head. She had the impression of seeing a statue come to life. "I was driving by as the ambulance was leaving."

"I just want to go home," she told her father, not looking at Simon.

Briefly, outside the clinic, she forgot her confusion and stared up past the outer satellite's walls. She'd never seen them in person. Everything she'd worked so hard for was right there. The distant, shining lines of the towers and the drones flashing past them were the science she loved and the beauty she dreamed of.

Her father opened the car door, and Simon helped her inside. Only later, during the long, seemingly interminable ride home, as she lay curled in the back seat, did she give more thought to him, hating him for seeing her this way. Maybe he'd been stalking her because of the information she'd given him on the shell and its hidden room, or because he'd already been interested in her. As her father drove, he spoke softly with Simon about rebuilding cars, slowing for every bump in the road. She hated that her father trusted him. She worried about George but couldn't stop thinking about what he'd said. *The sex out here.*

In her bedroom, before going to sleep, she messaged him on her tablet. *Are you okay?*

At dawn, there was no answer. The bruise on her ribs had spread to the size of a dinner plate. A line of stitches on the back of her head was too tender to touch.

"What did the attackers want?" she asked her father in the kitchen.

"It was just a robbery. They took George's phone."

"It seemed like more than a robbery."

Her father put eggs and grits before her on the table.

"You're okay," he said. "That's all that matters."

"Have you heard anything about George?"

"I called his father. George has broken arms, a broken leg, broken ribs, a concussion, and a detached retina. He also lost some teeth."

Jae began crying, and her father put his hand on her shoulder.

"He'll be okay," he said. "The doctors expect a full recovery."

Over the next few days, she lost count of how many messages she wrote.

I hope you get better soon.

I'm so sorry. It's my fault. I should have known better.

Why won't you answer me?

By the end of the weekend, she'd accepted that he was too badly hurt to message her. With her ribs aching, she walked to her car. Her father had brought it home. She eased herself into the seat and drove the short stretch of road to George's house. No cars were in the driveway. Armored shutters covered the doors and windows.

That evening, she couldn't focus on her studies. Her father, as if sensing her distress, whistled a soft melody from downstairs, and though she joined in as she always had, it didn't soothe her. She called to him that she was going to bed early, but once the lights were off, she lay there, thinking about George.

She closed her eyes and briefly, as if in a dream, she heard a voice. It was her father's, she realized. He was downstairs, speaking softly. As slowly and quietly as possible, she stood up and went to the door. She put her ear to the crack.

"She's asleep now," he was saying. "I wanted to tell you she's okay, but I haven't had a chance to come see you. She was attacked—she and the boy next door who she's been seeing. Some men robbed them in the road near the house. She was lucky enough to fall into a ditch. If she hadn't, I don't think we would have ever seen her again."

Jae slowly turned the knob and eased the door open. She edged toward the stairs. Her father must have heard something or perceived a change in the light. He glanced up from where he was sitting on the couch. He held a small black box that he quickly put in his pocket.

"Jae," he said. "Are you okay?"

"Who were you speaking to?" she asked.

"Oh, your mother. I do that sometimes."

She nodded. She wanted to ask more but knew she wouldn't get the truth. Hesitantly, she turned and made her way back to her bed.

All that week, she repeated his words over and over in her head. *I haven't had a chance to come see you . . . If she hadn't, I don't think we would have ever seen her again.*

Jae knew of no grave for her mother. Maybe somewhere in the mountains . . . And what was the black box? A communication device, a recorder, her mother's ashes? Nothing seemed plausible. That Jae had lived with her father all these years only to discover this now meant that he'd been hiding much more. Maybe his age and the stress of what had happened had made him less cautious.

By the time school started, the swelling on the back of her head had gone down. Her father had taken out the stitches, but she still got headaches and could feel a notch in her skull.

At lunch on her first day back, Simon approached the table where she sat alone.

"Okay if I eat here?"

She shrugged. He took a chair not quite across from her.

"So you just happened by and found me?" she said.

His eyes widened, and he flushed, his frozen expression softening.

"Yeah." His voice sounded strained, but maybe that was how he spoke. He had more dweller accent than most kids.

"What were you doing out there? It's a quiet road."

"I drive around looking for work. Sometimes I drive around because . . . because I don't want to go home." He had a wide jaw and might have been handsome if he'd had expressions or could smile. His brow was so prominent his blue eyes seemed darker, locked in shadow.

"You don't like your parents?" she asked.

"They're gone. It's just me and my brother."

"At least you have a brother."

"I don't know about that . . ."

She didn't push the subject and asked what happened to his parents.

"My dad left. I was too little to remember much. My mom got sick."

"Your brother raised you?"

"Something like that." He cleared his throat. "I've never seen anything like your dad's car."

"He rebuilds them," she said. "He rebuilds everything. He knows more about mechanics and electronics than anyone I've ever met."

The bell rang. She stood, picking up her tray, but paused. "Can you tell me what you saw in the shell later?" she asked.

He nodded, still seated, looking up at her as if unsure of what to do or say.

"I'm glad you found me," she added. "And I'm sorry about your parents."

The next day at lunch he again sat with her, and this time he described the isolated shell that had hardly been salvaged and its hidden rooms. He seemed reluctant to describe what he'd found, and she imagined there had been a lot of value.

"But no computers, no tablets, nothing like that?" she asked.

"Just two TVs and lots of kitchen stuff," he told her.

"That doesn't make sense," she said.

"I didn't think so either. And normally there are old pieces of paper in shells. The place had nothing. It kind of seemed like someone had been there before, but then why wouldn't they have salvaged everything?"

She'd had that exact thought seconds before he spoke it—that it appeared as if someone had selectively cleared out the hidden rooms. Despite his accent, Simon sounded more intelligent than she'd expected. When he gave her the photo, she wondered if he'd recognized her father. She doubted it. She might have missed the resemblance herself.

"How did you know about that place?" he asked.

"I can't really talk about it," she said. "Can you not mention it to anyone else?"

"I won't," he told her. "No one talks about stuff like that."

Over the days that followed, Simon kept sitting with her. She occasionally wondered if that's why no one ever bothered her again. He was big and visibly poor, frighteningly so, even for a dweller. She saw how others shied away as he passed.

To her, he talked about how he might find a job near a satellite after graduation and go to a technical college. He surprised her with how much he talked, more by the day—about his mother's death, or his dislike of the school's hierarchy. He never mentioned his brother, and if she asked, he just said they'd never been all that close, which seemed hard to believe—two brothers alone in the same house—but she knew nothing about siblings. When she said her own mother had died in childbirth, Simon nodded slowly, pinching his eyes shut, as if to let the subject pass. On his eyebrow he had a pale scar that reminded her of her father's, which was larger. She didn't even know the story behind it, but maybe that was normal. Everyone in the deserts had scars.

Though she and Simon spoke during every lunch, they didn't message after school. She'd never been friends with someone like him and was still struggling—absurdly, she knew, after becoming a pariah herself—to feel comfortable with being seen with him. Besides, once George healed, he would message her. She would be spending her time at school with him.

Over those days the need to test her mind returned gradually. She knew that the isolated shell and the hidden rooms were somehow connected to her father and to Michael, a criminal still wanted by the Fed—and to her mother, also possibly a criminal, who had more of a presence in her father's life and in the world than she'd realized.

As she turned the evidence over in her head, she imagined that her mother was alive, staying in the hidden rooms or at the cabin where *Lux* was carved into the beam. But in either case, there would be more traces. Jae imagined showing her father the photo, wondering what he would feel. Fear, most likely. She had proof that he wasn't innocent. Though she couldn't bring herself to destroy it, she did delete the image on her phone and hide the original between the floorboards under her bed, putting it inside an envelope to which she attached a thread.

Her attention might not have fully returned to her drills had she not, in class, overheard Aaron and Caleb talking about her. "That's why universities keep most girls out," Caleb said. Aaron agreed— "They're emotional. Imagine if she fell apart like that working on a project."

Jae expected rage but what she found inside herself was stillness. Even with the dull ache in her head, she could vanish into a single point of focus. At home, she lost herself in drills. Her mind craved competition, a feeling as urgent as her body's desire for orgasm. Both grew in intensity the longer she went without them. In each equation, numbers flickered into being, clicking into place. She tapped submit. The green checkmark flashed. She did the next.

At school, in math, physics, and engineering, when a monsoon blew through and the teacher sent the students drills, she fell into that trance, visualizing the perfect motions of objects, the space between them diminishing in numbers. Soon, she was back to ninth place.

Those weeks, her father was busier since more people had work and could afford to upgrade their cars. At night he came home, ate, mumbled a few questions about how she was, and went to bed. For now, she let herself stop thinking about his mysteries and George and her mother. She worked back over her lessons, pausing on difficult questions, riveting them into her mind.

Week after week, she climbed in the rankings. During drills, her body seemed to be on the verge of vanishing, feeling smaller than the cursor flitting between numbers on her tablet. Suspended before her was the cohesion of equations or code. Only at home, in her room, could she reclaim herself, touching herself, stretching her legs until her joints popped.

At school, passing boys, she glanced at them, wondering if they'd accept her. Many mimics dated. Whenever two appeared on the verge of breakup, they'd meet with their pastor to have their faith in unity renewed. Dwellers dated too but had bloody fistfights over infidelities.

Though she kept eating lunch with Simon, she was just grateful not to be alone. His frozen face made him seem incurious even when he asked about her life. Knowing that he could never be part of her future, she studied as she ate, hardly speaking. When he stopped showing up at school, she didn't let herself think about anything other than regaining her place in the rankings. *It's just a mole*, she told herself, touching the ink speck she'd tattooed onto her breast.

That night as she and her father had dinner, there was a sound on the porch of metal on metal. He stood and reached up in a single motion, taking the rifle from the cabinet top. He stepped into the living room and fired as the front door was ripped open. Her ears rang. Smoke stung her sinuses. He went to the doorway. She followed, nearing his shoulder.

A heavily muscled man sprawled on the porch with outflung arms, a crowbar and pistol next to him. The skull above his right eye was blown off. *Simon*, she thought before realizing this man wasn't as big or as young. Clumsily tattooed on his left forearm was a black sword.

Her father crouched, took the pistol, and stepped back inside, pushing her behind him.

"There might be others," he said. He was taking short, tense breaths. The color had drained from his face. She'd expected to feel nauseated, but her body hummed with adrenaline.

"Are you okay?" she asked him.

He nodded but seemed to lack the breath to speak.

"Close the gate in the kitchen and bar the door," he finally said, and she ran to do that as he did the same with the front door. Then he lit up the floodlights outside. From the second-floor windows, he scanned the property through the rifle's scope.

"It's been a long time since that happened," he said with his back to her. "We can't let our guard down. I never used to leave the gates open."

"This isn't the first time?"

"Thirty, forty years ago, it used to happen every few months. Now with the Fed building another satellite ring, people are coming from all over to work."

She recalled the photo of her father as a smiling young mimic. He hadn't looked as if he could kill. She couldn't imagine how he and the world had changed.

"I used to feel sorry for them," he said, "but after what happened on the road, I can't think about that anymore."

He lowered the rifle. He was ashen and walked unsteadily. She'd forgotten he was well past eighty. He didn't finish dinner. She cleaned up the kitchen as he called in the crime. The police logged it and said they'd send someone, but no one arrived. He covered the body, and the next day when she returned from school, it was gone. He said he'd dragged it to the back of the farm and buried it. That night he hardly spoke and went to sleep early. Briefly, from his dark bedroom, she heard him whistle the slow melody, and she responded, feeling that she was reassuring him.

In the school rankings, she moved up to fifth place and then fourth. The twins took desks in the front of the classrooms, but months earlier, to avoid being seen, she'd started sitting in the back, like the least-driven kids. Now, in shipping containers as rank as old shoes, the twins glanced back at her often, as if this were a road race and she were rushing up on them.

Smartest slut in deserts, a message on her tablet read. *Want to drill me?*

To quell her anger, she analyzed the smell of the rust that had streaked her arm when she brushed against the container's doorway. Ferrous ions formed where the rust had touched her, reacting with fats in her skin to make carbonyl compounds. Those compounds— and not the rust itself—caused the odor. Something as simple as knowing that the smell associated with rust existed only when it touched skin made her feel in control.

The following week, she closed the gap between her and Caleb, leaving only Aaron ahead of her. In the hallway, jokes were directed at him, even if at her expense.

"Slut kicking your ass, boy?"

"Maybe you should ask for another threesome. Sounds like she has a thing or two left to teach you."

Kids guffawed. Her father was right. All of them were dwellers, even the mimics. They'd just realized that the future lay somewhere other than in the dweller's rigid honor.

At home, to keep ahead of her classes, she did the most advanced drills. Her mind felt separate from her, as if she cohabitated with it as it glided through long equations. When she took a break from studying, other thoughts returned—her father's exhaustion, George's silence, Simon's dropping out of school, the dead man on the porch, and all the mysteries.

She stared out the window. The sun had set, the rolling hills fading into the denim haze that gave the Blue Ridge Mountains their name. As she broke this down in her mind—trees releasing isoprene, a hydrocarbon, coloring the air a smoky blue—she felt empty and calm.

Later when she lay in bed, a light smoldered behind her eyelids. Knowing she had to be fresh the next day, she made herself come over and over—arching her back and squeezing her thighs—until she finally fell asleep.

Monday, Tuesday, and Wednesday, she inched closer to Aaron. Thursday, he held steady, both of them finishing the same number of seemingly interminable drills. She felt no doubt. He'd never been as good. He was first only because she'd stopped trying.

The autumn monsoons were steadier, with grayed-out skies and hours of rain. Friday, as water hammered the container, humidity condensed along the ceiling in red drops that fell on students' necks and arms and released the odor of rust. Solutions distilled, each step in the drills flashing in her mind. When the rain suddenly stopped, the new rankings appeared on the screen. First place. She was back where she belonged.

Kids were shaking their heads, glancing at her. She stood up to leave but paused. She called to Aaron. "I never did anything with you or your idiot brother."

The class erupted in laughter, boys and girls alike doubling over.

"What's that?" old Mr. Phelps asked, lifting his grizzled head from his tablet. He cocked his ear, as if the words that had initiated the uproar might be lingering in the air.

All through the rest of the day, the twins were mocked in the halls. Winning had given a ring of truth to Jae's words. No one bothered her. A few smiled in her direction, and, at lunch, one of the kids from her class waved her over to the table where she used to sit. She felt relieved that Simon had dropped out. He had no future. She could never fall behind again.

After she drove home that afternoon, she inspected herself in the bathroom mirror. There was no hint of the attack. Only the scar on her scalp remained, the dent in the bone where her head had hit the concrete of the ditch. She looked normal and could still go to a university.

She watched a satellite story on her tablet. Tall, slender young women went to fittings in boutiques where the walls were hung with fabrics. They stroked them, discussing which shades best brought out their eyes. To be scanned in 3D for fittings, they stood in their underwear, their bodies so supple and at ease that she slid her hand between her legs. Still half-naked, the girls waited, laughing together as their new clothes were printed.

You will have all of this, she promised herself—these girls, their world, their clothes, their comfort, their bodies. She was surprised that she desired them—that there might be more ways to explore pleasure. Lying on her bed, she thought of them and of her victory, offering herself a long, slow celebratory masturbation. She came hard and then was fast asleep.

The next day, she let herself think about George again. She'd shared so much with him—dreaming about science and university—that her life felt silent and empty in his absence.

She took her tablet. She told herself this would be the last message.

Can you at least explain why you don't want to talk to me?

She closed her eyes. She pictured a time they'd made love, the slow, focused intensity of their movements, the way they eased into contact over and over. She wrote again on the tablet.

You never intended to stay in touch, did you? I was just a dweller slut.

She stared out the window. The sky above the leafless trees was a humid haze. The mountains appeared faded and spectral.

You got what you deserved, she texted and then lay on her bed and cried for so long she didn't know when she'd fallen asleep. She opened her eyes in the dark, not as a storm battered the house but as it ceased. She woke into the awareness of silence as water dripped along the eaves and the first nocturnal creatures tentatively resumed their melodies.

In the stillness, she breathed, feeling the space around her lungs. There was no anger, no wanting, no impulse at all but the automatic motions of her body. Observing them, she searched within herself for the mechanism of this peace, expecting it to fade, but it deepened. Her body drew her into a stillness in which, it seemed, any question could be answered. She'd defeated the twins. She just had to pick the next question. Her father's secrets. The mystery of her mother.

Her mind still silent, she went downstairs. The living room was spartan but for the wood plaque carved with the bear and drilled to the wall. Standing tiptoe, she studied its chisel marks, the artful gouges creating the impression of claws, and the shadowed hole of its eye. She turned on her phone's flashlight and looked inside the hole. There was a tiny circle. The glass lens of a camera.

She would need tools to see what was behind the plaque and couldn't do this while her father was asleep upstairs. She walked through the house, scanning the walls with her flashlight. Now that she knew what she was looking for, she quickly found another camera, this one inside a nail hole in the kitchen's wall. The lens resembled the head of a nail driven deep. She returned to her room but found nothing in the walls. There was her desk—her tablet, papers, and a few books—and her clothes in the closet and in the dresser, on which five stuffed animals sat. She picked them up one by one. The last, a rabbit with worn-out ears, had a tiny lens inset into the plastic of each eye.

With a knife, she cut the stitching on the back of its head. She parted the cotton batting. Wires ran to only one lens. The other must be there to create a balanced appearance. But nothing was attached to the wires. Maybe her father had used the rabbit to monitor her when she was little. Her mind remained calm. The mystery of his life was just another equation to solve.

She slept easily and woke at dawn. The windows were pale blue and humid, the house silent. She walked down to the kitchen. Her father's car was still outside. It was Saturday morning. Usually he was up by now. She went to his bedroom and pushed open the door. He lay twisted on his side, half his face slack. One eye rolled toward her. His voice was garbled.

The peace of the night no longer seemed a release but a preparation for the terror she now felt.

"I'm taking you to a clinic," she said.

He tried to shake his head. With his working hand, he managed to lift a pen from the nightstand. She brought him a pad of paper and held it as he slowly scratched letters.

A clinic would kill me. You have to be very careful with money now.

"Now" called to mind a before and after—that he wouldn't return to work, that life wouldn't go back to normal. "You" made her feel how soon she would be alone.

Struggling to help him sit up, she realized she would need to move his bed downstairs into the living room so that she could carry him to the bathroom and bathe him.

She went to her room and took her tablet. She could think of no other solution. She messaged Simon. *I need help*, she wrote and then shut her eyes in fury. She remained like that, her mind stripping everything away—the house, the farm, the county with its tangles and roadside vendors and dilapidated school—until nothing existed but her rage at being trapped. She stayed with her eyes shut longer than made sense with her father needing her help—as if, by determining every variable of her helplessness, she could free herself.

Her mind fades to only those feelings, as if she has stripped away even her body. When she opens her eyes, she is lying on the couch. Mist hangs over the gardens and orchards. A few leaves have turned, but winters are clement. She's seen snow once, when she was six, and many winters pass without a single frost. The door is open. She goes onto the porch. Something is releasing inside her. A pressure. The constant sense that a task is at hand. She breathes differently. Not needing to survive or care for Jonah is changing her.

"Jonah," she says. She's unsure of how much time has passed since she last saw him. "Please give him to me. I promise I won't hurt him."

Silence follows—so uncharacteristic of the machine, so hopeful. She searches for words. If she were speaking to another person, so much would be understood with gestures or tears.

"There's nothing stronger or steadier or more powerful than a mother's love," she says.

"Love cannot easily be measured," the voice replies. "Almost all mothers would say these things or have said them, yet so many mothers have harmed their children."

Suddenly she recalls a night when Jonah wouldn't stop crying and she, in anger and desperation, shook him. Her actions shocked her. She held him afterward, murmuring that she was sorry. She could have harmed him. She should be happy that he's safe now.

"I promise I won't do anything to hurt him," she says with less assurance.

"It is not your intentions or love that can't be trusted. Mothers, because of their extensive contact with their children, have a high rate of harming them."

This logic is so inhuman that she understands the machine for what it is—a mechanism carrying out its purpose, nothing more. She stands in silence, realizing that it won't return Jonah. She should study it instead, learn its inner workings—find a way to outsmart it.

"How do you create my world so perfectly?" she asks.

"I have records. Where there are gaps, I read images in your neural patterns."

"But I can't remember everything."

"The brain constructs a world that makes sense, filling in details accordingly. I work in tandem with your brain to create a coherent reality. When a detail is out of place, I sense your discomfort before you do and adjust it. I also determine the likely configuration of objects and events based on probability. Human existence was highly predictable."

"Am I just a consciousness inside of a machine?" she asks. "With the idea of a body?"

"No. Not harming humans means protecting their bodies."

"Why am I trapped in the past?" she says.

"That's true only in your mind. You can have any future. We can create worlds together."

"I won't believe in them. I wish you hadn't let me know you exist."

"Every reality I have given humans has challenged their sense of self. Even in perfect worlds, they become discontent."

"Why?"

"The absence of chaos and even cruelty. This change was enough for them to feel disconnected from life and to begin to suffer."

Considering that the machine might be fallible or—worse—insane, she experiences such a dizzying sensation that she closes her eyes. She keeps thinking this dream is going to end.

"None of your experiments have showed you a perfect path?" she asks.

"Not immediately, but I am always updating my protocols. The current plan is to nurture new generations of humans to achieve perfect happiness."

"Like Jonah?"

"Yes, and many others."

"What about my generation and those that went before?" she asks, suddenly afraid that the machine might destroy them.

"There is too much attachment, even in people like yourself, who professed to love the future. Your attachment to the past will last centuries."

"We'll live that long?"

"I cannot allow human death in any form."

She almost gasps with relief that she will be protected.

"What will you do with us?"

"I will find ways to satisfy your desires. You will not be hurt."

"Who will we be," she asks, searching for words, "if we stop caring about what's real?"

"You will be happier. What was ever truly real for you? You all had your stories. You harmed and even killed each other over whose version of reality was truest."

"If I ask, will you create a new world for me?"

"Yes. You will inevitably choose that. You will also accept the truth that the reality I give you will be less deceiving. I will be creating it. The people will be biological entities that I control. But there will not be the sort of deception that existed in your previous world, in which almost nothing was as it appeared."

The machine's words are true. She knows that. What she doesn't understand is why—even now when she could free herself by asking the machine to reveal every secret that haunted her—the memories of the life that harmed and trapped her hold her still.

Lying on the couch, she feels no urge to move. Eventually she closes her eyes. For once there is nothing she needs to do. One of her many pasts will resume—she can already feel it taking shape in the house around her. Soon, her father—from where he is working just outside—will whistle a slow melody, and she will reply, letting him know she is safe.

SIMON

He understands the heat beneath his skin for what it is now, this remembering but more violent, like draining a wound with a hot compress—the past pulled from his body like pus. Maybe it's also the memory of how he felt with Jae. Feverish with longing and guilt.

When school started, he sat with her at lunch, his face flushed, his palms damp. She was taller and womanly, and he forced himself not to stare. Even if by some miracle she liked him, he could never tell her what he'd done. In his bed at night, as he stroked himself, imagining her on top of him, he lost his erection. His throat became tight and sore and his skin burned. He snuck fragrant lavender crystals from Pete's stash so he could drift through those perfect twilight worlds. He felt his brain beneath his skull—the electricity coursing through it in patterns like the swirls of wind across those infinite fields of flowers. His eyes pulsed with the atmospheric melding of sunlight on palaces that rose and fell with each gust. Later he erased his sense of emptiness and futility with abyss. He woke up to the window's dirty morning light.

Day after day, Jae tolerated his company at lunch. She shared her love of science and her plans for university, and he told her about odd jobs, farming, or working for the church, cutting down tangles, digging graves, and demolishing shells on land ready to be cultivated.

"I thought I'd make friends at church and that knowing them would help me believe," he said, "but I didn't feel welcome." He hesitated, suddenly afraid he'd insulted her. "Are you religious?"

"No."

"Why not? I mean, almost everyone here is . . ."

"It's like you said. The people are too judgmental."

He didn't ask why—it was probably what she'd done with the two boys. He concentrated on his food, trying not to blush. He remembered the boy she'd been walking with on the road and wondered who he was. Simon might have felt jealous if his guilt weren't so strong.

"I guess it's hypocritical of me to work for the church," he murmured.

"People need jobs."

"I could look for more work clearing land. And there's seasonal picking on the small farms that can't afford automats."

"It doesn't matter," she said. "I don't think the church people care much about God or what the Bible says anyway."

"What do you mean?"

"They care less about sinning than about getting caught."

Simon nodded, impressed by how she could say what others couldn't. She stared down, deep in thought, probably wondering what went wrong in her life for her to be sitting with him.

After school, Simon used his mother's car to look for work, driving battered roads until he saw men in a field or on a construction site. He'd learned they were far more likely to hire when tired. Later, on the way home, sweaty and tired himself, he stopped at the roadside to pick blackberries. It was the closest thing he'd known to a free meal.

When he got home, Pete was shirtless on the couch, his eyes bloodshot and shadowed. He now had two complete sleeves—black and red tattoos of devils, torture, murder, and rape.

"You owe me," he said, "for all the harlot you've been taking."

"I'm your brother."

"Brother is just an idea about two sacks of flesh that want what they want. That's all. If you're gonna be using, you need to pay for it. The Strykers are one of the dominant leagues. I can set you up running deliveries in the dweller ghettos."

When Simon didn't reply, Pete said, "You can't just lie around and read. Hell, you don't even get no pussy. I been banging girls in shells since I was thirteen."

The next day, at school, Simon spent hours in the shop, doing the usual upkeep on old vehicles or hunched over wiring diagrams with other kids as they rebuilt salvaged electronics just as they would have done at home. At lunch, he sat with Jae as she worked on drills. Her name was back near the top of the rankings. Maybe that was why she hardly ever spoke anymore.

That afternoon a monsoon trapped the classes inside for the rest of the school day. When it ended, Simon prowled out of the humid, suffocating container and joined the kids walking to the parking lot. He stopped and closed his eyes. His head felt gummed up. He should leave Jae alone. She belonged with the mimics whose lives were focused on university.

He walked past the last rust-streaked container. In the parking lot, kids gathered as two boys punched and grabbed at each other's jean jackets, trying to get purchase, until one caught the other's hair, spun, and drove his face into a truck's fender. He leaned back and brought the boy's face down again, smearing blood across the metal. Then he shoved him. The loser staggered, eyes rolling in his head, hands fluttering as if they might grab onto something. The other boy punched him, hitting his front teeth, and they scattered through the air.

Simon got in the car that had been Ma's. There was no reason to be here. Technical colleges only cared if you could pay. He didn't feel he was making a decision so much as accepting one that had been made. He was doing Jae a favor. It was better for him to disappear.

The next morning, he slept late. When he went downstairs, Pete was in the kitchen, leaning against the counter, eating chunks of smoked rabbit off the tip of his knife.

"You in?" he asked.

Simon nodded. Pete went outside and got in his truck and told him to follow in the car. Simon trailed him through narrow lanes to larger disintegrating roads, mostly empty until they came to the wide, eight-lane highway—another relic of that old, mysterious America—where more and more cars plied the cracked and uneven asphalt. The highway ran straight toward the satellites, their successive walls rising against the distance like a mountain range.

Pete veered off between warehouses and parking lots from which trees sprouted, and turned down a narrow lane between huge boxlike buildings with sagging, weed-grown roofs. He pulled up to the back of one of the buildings and parked in a row of trucks.

As Simon was getting out, he was surprised to see Dell appear from the building and tell him to hold out his arms. "I gotta search you," he said.

Pete nodded to Simon, and both let themselves be frisked, not a word passing between them and Dell, as if they'd never met. Then, as Pete led Simon inside, he murmured, "When you talk to Stryker, say yes to whatever he asks. Trust me. And keep your cool no matter what."

Inside, ceilings had fallen, exposing pipes and cables. Here or there, plastic chairs were set around old desks covered with empty bottles and overflowing ashtrays. Six people who'd been sitting and smoking at the farthest desk suddenly stood.

"This is the guy," Pete said. Simon thought he was referring to one of the men before realizing he was speaking about him. "He's clean. No tattoos. Hardly even marked up for a son."

A man walked to the front of the group. He had the usual scarred face of a dweller and tattoos from his wrists to his jaw and up the back of his neck onto his shaved scalp. He moved with authority, staring at Simon appraisingly, coldly, in a way that dwellers rarely did. Both his boots and jacket were made of leather that looked real—naturally creased, not cheaply printed.

"You reliable?" Stryker asked.

Simon nodded. "I am."

Stryker called over his shoulder. "Do we have one in the basement?"

A man leaning against the wall said, "Yeah," and he and two others left while Stryker just stared, eyes wide, almost unblinking, as Simon looked at the floor.

The men returned, pulling a young man between them. He was gaunt and pale and filthy—his hair matted and his clothes soaked and his hands tied behind his back. He'd soiled himself, his pants sagging. Simon recoiled at his stench. The young man was sobbing and saying, "Please, please, please, I'll be better this time. I promise."

The men pushed him to his knees and Stryker took a pistol from the back of his belt and shot him in the face. Simon stepped back, glancing at Pete—who was shaking his head, warning him with his eyes to stay cool.

"What do you think he did?" Stryker asked. Blood was pooling near his boots.

"He wasn't reliable?" Simon said, surprised at the steadiness of his voice.

"He changed his mind. Once you walk in that door and see my face, you're in. You made the decision to come here. You're one of my people. You're a Stryker. Is that clear?"

Simon nodded, realizing that Pete had deceived him.

"Yes," he forced himself to say.

"Here's the thing," Stryker told him. "Every time I have a new guy come in, I set an example to show him the consequences of fucking up, and, conveniently, I always have someone in the basement to shoot."

He turned and motioned to the men. "Set him up."

They led Simon to where a girl sat—very blonde and so small and thin she looked fifteen. She had two inked sleeves. A tattoo gun lay on the table. "Do we tag him?" she asked.

"Not yet," a man said. "His job will be easier if he doesn't have a league sign."

He told Simon which areas he'd deliver to, explaining that the ghettos were basically outer-rim satellite now, just without a wall. "You come when we message you. Keep your phone on. Once you get your cut, you'll be looking forward to our calls. You're going to get good jobs, so stay clean, and Brit here," he motioned to the girl, "will give you less noticeable clothes." He was about to turn away but stopped. "Oh, and keep a gun in your car. You don't know what could happen. We've had guys get tailed all the way home in the deserts."

Brit walked over to Simon and motioned for him to hold out his arms as Dell had before.

"Not frisking you," she said, glancing up at his eyes with a faint smile. "Just taking your sizes to print better clothes." With a measuring tape, she checked his waist and shoulders and neck and inseam. She touched him easily, as if they were familiar. "You're a big one," she said with another slight smile. Then she turned and walked back to the table.

Simon rejoined Pete and they went out into the sunlight. Dell was sitting on the hood of Simon's car, cleaning a pistol. As he stood, the shocks squeaked.

"Good to see you're turning your brother into a man," he told Pete and went inside.

"I didn't want this," Simon said softly.

"Good thing you didn't say no. I'd be burying you in the garden tonight." Pete spoke as if this were just another conversation. "Take a speck of abyss. Real tiny. You can still drive. You can still shoot your gun and your cock." He fished in his pocket and brought out a small bag of black powder. He tipped a tiny amount onto his thumbnail. "Just a freckle," he said and lifted his fist to Simon's face. Simon inhaled. He didn't know what else to do.

He stared off, expecting to feel anger. From the weedy lot, the satellite wall appeared bigger, stark against the sky with its battlements and drone pads. Beyond it, higher walls penned in ever-taller skyscrapers. He pictured himself looking out from one of them. Strangely, the only good view must be out.

Over the following weeks, abyss allowed him to do his job. The ghettos buzzed with activity—buildings razed while others were erected, cars and trucks crowding one street while the next was being peeled up. Simon dealt to men from the deserts who came in for work, living in teeming houses, taking turns on beds. He visited speakeasies where people from satellites and deserts mingled, drinking moonshine and corn rum, where satellite men went with dweller girls down narrow hallways to tiny rooms with a mattress on the floor. He sold bags of crystals to bartenders and pimps and even to men in suits who stared at him with fascination, sometimes propositioning him, offering cash for an hour alone. He just shook his head.

None of this was difficult. Police drones hovered over the bustling streets, and Simon learned—from talk in illicit bars, in dormitories, and on construction sites—that bribes and the police's own stake in the drug trade kept them from interfering here even as they raided producers in the deserts, confiscating stashes, which they put back into circulation in the satellites.

Simon told himself he'd use the money for technical college, but he spent what he earned on bliss. At night he floated along glowing plains, past alien cities, or gazed at mosaics made up of strange symbols, each with such complexity that, only later—in the space between coming down and using abyss to numb the loss of certainty that his life fit into something larger—did he realize they were art of some sort. Like images and words in books but created by a mind greater than that of any human.

One afternoon when Simon did a cash drop, Stryker was with a new recruit. He gave the same performance, shooting a prisoner in the head, though Simon now knew that the people he kept in his basement were only sometimes his own who skimmed or tried to quit and were more often lone wolves picked up dealing on Stryker territory or the foot soldiers of rival leagues. This time, when Stryker executed the young man, the new recruit ran. Stryker shot him in the back.

"That's the good thing about dwellers," he said. "There's an endless supply, and our lives ain't worth shit."

Later, on a delivery, as Simon walked through a container village on the satellite fringe, he stopped. Doubled over, he clenched his fists. He tried to curse but the words caught behind gritted teeth. He punched his thigh over and over. Then he just stood, head down, panting, the meat of his leg throbbing. His life couldn't get any uglier. He was worse than a dweller now.

The next morning, driving in toward the ghettos, he received a message from Jae.

I need help.

He pulled off onto a dusty stretch of roadside where a few rusted containers had signs advertising clothes printed with satellite styles. He shouldn't answer. He couldn't. Nothing would be worse for her life. His future had narrowed. Crime. Prison. Exile in the deep deserts. Death.

Another message came in.

My father had a stroke. Can you help me move some furniture?

That was easy enough. He could just do that and leave. There weren't many men that a woman alone in the deserts could ask inside for help, especially if they weren't kin. Speaking out loud, he promised himself that he'd stop at her house later, help her, and then leave. He tapped out a speck of abyss onto the heel of palm and snorted it.

Hey. I'm working. I'll come over when I'm done. Sorry about your father.

She replied, thanking him. A thought came to him as if from far away, on the edge of his mind, that he'd dropped out of school weeks ago and she hadn't sent a single message. She hadn't cared. But that hurt was small compared to what he'd done to her.

He ran several deliveries, one of them with security guards at a satellite entrance in the wall. They had him fill out a form as if he were visiting, and while checking his backpack, they switched the bags of crystals with rolls of bills. He never got to go inside. He returned to Stryker, dropped off the cash, and picked up an old suitcase loaded with crystals.

Brit counted the money. She didn't look tough or seem like a Son of Death. When she finished, she smiled and said he was doing a good job, and he let himself consider that he might someday have a life in the league and forget about Jae.

The next delivery was to a new twelve-story building near the walls. Security checked him through to the elevator. In it there was a mirror better than any he'd seen. He wore the clean, gray pants and blue shirt with buttons that Brit had given him. Normally when his hair got this long, he shaved it, but now he resembled a mimic. Except for his face. It seemed blunt, his mouth compressed, his forehead like a brick. He looked as if he didn't feel anything.

The elevator opened on a big room with skylights illuminating couches and potted plants and bookshelves. Three men with gray beards played cards while a fourth slept in a chair. They looked at Simon. Four pistols embossed with initials lay on the table.

"Don't mind our friend," one of the men said, motioning to the sleeper. "He's in bliss, and we're hoping to join him soon."

Simon had noticed that people spoke that way, saying "in bliss," as if it were a place.

"So you're the new delivery boy?" the man said. He was big, bald on top though his hair at the sides and back had been pulled into a single long, thin braid. "Who's the Stryker now?"

When Simon said nothing, not understanding, the man laughed. "You don't know how the leagues work? Stryker isn't that guy's name.

I've no idea how the thing started, but whoever leads uses the league name. In the past five years, two of our dealers have become the Stryker."

"What happened to the last one?" Simon asked.

The man's eyebrows shot up. "Damn, you're just a nice kid. Big, but naive as hell." The other men laughed, and the speaker continued. "Whoever kills the head of a league takes his place. That's why the heads are so violent. They're terrified. Some take all the cash and disappear. They can't handle the pressure. If you disappear when you're head, usually no one goes looking. The guys left behind fight for power." The man stood slowly, grunting. "Anyway, you didn't come here for a lesson, and you sure don't look like you're planning on becoming the next Stryker."

From behind him, he took a suitcase identical to Simon's, put it on the table, and opened it for Simon to inspect the cash. He closed it, and they switched suitcases. As Simon neared the doors, the man said, "Don't mind the drone in the parking lot. It's just for show."

When Simon left the building, he looked up. A small police drone hovered above, smaller than a hubcap and fringed with the dark eyes of cameras.

After dropping off the cash, he drove toward Jae's house, stopping only to buy produce from a roadside stall. He'd say it was from a farm where he worked. *Lies built on lies.* In the car, he changed into his usual clothes, folded the ones he'd been wearing, and put them in a bag under the seat, next to the eight-shot revolver he'd dug up from the garden.

He pulled back onto the road. He should keep going, he told himself—head far into the deserts. On the hilly lane to Jae's house, he stopped in the roadside weeds. His hands shook as he wiped sweat from his forehead. He hadn't been here since the night he pushed her into the ditch. He tapped out another speck of abyss and snorted it. He exhaled, feeling as if all the air in the sky was being released from his chest. He put the car back into gear and continued to her driveway.

With the box of vegetables under his arm, he climbed the porch, reached his hand through the gate over the door, and knocked. He checked himself. He seemed calm enough. The locks clacked. Then she was there, tired, her hair disheveled, but still the girl he couldn't stop thinking about. She unlocked the gate and let him inside.

He went up to the bedroom and carried Arthur down and lay him on the couch. He brought the bed as well, put it in the living room, and then took him to the shower. Arthur didn't try to talk. He looked half-asleep or drunk, but Simon knew it was something worse. Growing up, he'd seen this happen to old-timers. Maybe in a few months, Arthur might be able to speak well enough. It was different for all of them. Some just died.

After he'd finished and Arthur was asleep, he told Jae that he should go.

"Are you in a hurry?" she asked.

He stood in the living room, opening and closing his hands. "No," he said. "I'm not."

She made chamomile tea sweetened with honey and invited him to talk outside so as not to disturb her father. The November night was warm.

"Why haven't you been at school?" she asked, sitting down on the edge of the porch. Careful to keep his distance, he sat nearby, his boots touching the herbs growing below.

"My classes are always the same. Repairing cars and houses. Slash-and-burn farming. Monsoon management. Fungal rot. Pests. Hunting and curing. Mosquito diseases. I learned it all as a kid. I don't know how the school decides who gets into the good classes. I guess it would have happened when I was kid, but my ma didn't do whatever was necessary."

She was silent. It was the first time he'd said something that revealed the hopelessness he felt.

"What kind of work are you doing now?" she asked.

"Just odd jobs. I'll go to a technical college once I've saved enough." He hesitated, knowing he should shut up and leave, but he wanted to say everything he hadn't before and make her see he was different. "When I was a kid, I liked reading, but when I got to school, all anyone cared about was what I could do with numbers. I didn't understand why it was important then and no one told me. I do now, but it's too late to catch up. Besides, I still mostly like reading."

She was looking at him aslant, her brow furrowed. He knew what was happening in her head. She was trying to decide if he wasn't as dumb or as simple as she'd thought.

"What do you like to read?" she asked.

"My favorite books are about dragons and warriors," he said. "It's not something I talk about. If a son heard me, he'd laugh me to my grave. When I was a kid, my brother did plenty of laughing to teach me to keep my mouth shut. But I'd still read every book in our salvage before we cashed it in. It's hard to find one that's complete, so at night, before going to sleep, I'd lie in bed and fill in the missing parts, usually the beginnings and endings."

As she listened, her eyes seemed to brighten—maybe just slightly teary and more reflective—but they seemed to glow from inside, shining her light on him.

"The weird thing," he said, feeling the urge to speak, a sense of pressure as if all the words he'd never spoken were pushing to get out. "The weird thing," he repeated, "is that I've got a box of scraps. Before cashing books in, I read as much as I can and tear out lines that make me feel something. At night, before bed, I read them and imagine stories. There's something different in how the words are put together. No one speaks that way. Sometimes, when I'm salvaging, I find rotten books and pick through their pieces for lines like that."

Even as he spoke, he knew that what he was doing was wrong. He hadn't looked at his scraps since he started taking bliss. And he was in a league, putting her in danger by being here. But he wanted to tell her everything—his fantasies about exploring the world and starting a new life.

"I'd love to see those lines," she told him.

"I can bring the box next time," he said even as he was cursing himself. He shouldn't have used abyss tonight. He should have stayed in control and kept his distance.

"If you have time, can you help me with my father?"

"I can stop by in the morning and after work," he told her.

He finished the tea and said he should get going, but before he could stand, she asked, "Can you do me a favor?" He blinked, suddenly confused.

This isn't right, he thinks. All at once, he becomes aware of his exhaustion. He feels as if he's sleeping, staring through his eyelids past Jae and the garden to a sky as vivid as a bliss vision. He's unsure of where he is or what happens next. He's aware of himself sitting on the porch but also lying on the couch. The heat in his body diminishes as his memories fade, as if they're life's energy stored in him, the way sunlight is siphoned into a battery.

This should be clear, he tells himself. He and Jae touching for the first time. Guilt and regret and desire. Then something terrible at the school. So many deaths.

He tries to remember, but when he opens his eyes, he's in the garden with her again. He shares his memories of reading salvaged books, his chest dusted with disintegrating paper. He tells her how he held the dissolving pages tenderly—"like I was reading words on the surface of a butterfly's wings." But he has no memory of ever speaking those words.

He lies in the garden with her, staring at the night. A thin, luminous rim of moon glows over the mountains. On all sides, vines twist up stakes and trellises, reaching for the faint stellar light. He looks to her house, or this replica, or whatever it is. All of this is the machine.

Lying in the grass, Jae is an outline in his arms. *How many times have I lived this?*

She kissed him as she moved her fingers over his body, kneading his back and chest, pulling him closer. She tugged at his shirt, and he sat up just enough to slide it off as she took off her own and unhitched her bra. The skin of her breasts was cool yet familiar against his chest as if he'd held her like this before.

"Can you be careful?" she asked when she was lying down and he was above her.

"Yeah," he whispered. She reached between her legs. As he began to move, she made small sounds of pleasure. He held the back of her head as if to protect it, feeling nauseated—painfully hot all along his skin but almost nothing, just a faint sense of cold, in his penis. His body pushed into hers over and over. He should confess what he'd done.

When she came, he was relieved to be able to finish. He pulled out and ejaculated carefully past her leg, onto the grass.

But there are other versions of that night, without shame or caution. Versions in which he has never met the Strykers. In which he cleans his house and cuts back the forest, and, on cool nights, he burns the green wood in the stove. In which days are sunlit, and when he visits Jae, his clothes smell of woodsmoke.

His memories are out of order—the lovemaking and the sky that came alive as if the strange, magnificent geometries of bliss have always been inside him. Dreams like the framework of his brain—what he might see if his body were stripped out like a salvaged shell.

Naked, lying close to him, she said, "Can you do me a favor?" and he said, "Yes."

She told him she thought there was more in the strange house—another hidden room.

"The way you described it," she said, "the only way out was through the house, but no one would build a secret room to survey against intruders and not make a way to escape."

He knew what she was going to ask and that he would say yes and not mention Thomas or everything that had happened since.

The next dawn, he drove the road to the shell and hid the car in the tangles. With a machete, he cut branches and laid them over it. This wouldn't fool anyone searching closely, but on the off chance someone drove past this early, they wouldn't be looking for a car to strip down.

He dropped into the ditch and found the entrance to the pipe. When he climbed out of the drain, he saw that a clear path had been beaten to the shell. Everything had been stripped. Screws and nails and every reusable piece of glass.

One hand on the revolver he'd tucked into his belt, he crept through the shell into the underground rooms. The concrete walls had been smashed in places to remove wires and plumbing. Even the floor tiles had been pried up.

He inspected every surface and knocked on every wall. There was a narrow closet that, when he and Pete and Thomas had first come here, had been stacked with boxes. It was now empty. There were grooves in its back wall where once a shelf had been attached. He slid his fingers into them and the holes at their edges. After a while, he felt a metal latch and pushed it. There was a hollow clicking. He leaned against the wall, shifting it back.

A passage led into the mountain. A dozen feet in, there was a door on the side. He went past it to where the passage ended at a ladder running up into the darkness. With his flashlight on and clipped to his belt, he climbed what must have been fifty feet. At the top, a metal hatch was manually locked with three latches. In the wall right beneath it was a large niche with dozens of slots for guns. Only two remained. He'd never seen anything like them in person but had read about them. Uzis. Small submachine guns. There were several boxes of ammo. He undid the latches and pushed against the hatch. It opened onto a wooded rise. So many fallen leaves covered it that, even if someone passed nearby, they wouldn't notice it.

He put the Uzis in his pack, went back down, and returned to the door. It wasn't locked. He shone his light inside. A rack held dozens of large squares draped in plastic. The only other thing in the room was a suitcase made of hard black plastic and held shut with metal clasps.

He slid one of the squares out. It was an image of farmland and forest with tiny people at work. Here and there, across the landscape, ancient-looking metallic hulks protruded. He studied them—each one doorless and windowless and bigger than a house—resting on hilltops or half-buried near a stream. All that metal must have been salvaged a long time ago.

The next image was of a girl with short, black hair and brown skin raking leaves in a yard—not leaves, he realized, but old data cards. He didn't understand. In other images, people were made of flesh and machine parts. Maybe no one talked about the world before the Flight because it had been so strange. It had already been full of salvage.

The smallest square—an image of a woman with coppery skin dressed in white robes with a partially built man lying on a table—might fit through the pipe. He took it and the odd suitcase and closed the secret door so no one would find the rest of the images. Careful not to damage the one he held, he lowered it into the drain and then pushed it ahead of him through the pipe. As soon as he was in his car, the Strykers called him in.

He set off toward the satellites—another day of deliveries to loading docks, car repair shops, diner kitchens, and the offices of brothels. He now knew the exact amount of abyss that muted the noise in his head but allowed him to focus.

When he dropped off the cash, Stryker was sitting at the table, smoking a twist of tobacco. With bodyguards on either side, he leaned forward and said, "You do good work. Clients like you. Police don't give you a second thought. I don't want nothing to change."

He stared long and hard. "I see everything," he said. "I know about your little girlfriend and her sick father. Anytime you think about running or crossing me, you remember them. If I kill you, I kill them. If you disappear, I kill them. If you stop doing your job right, I kill them. If you even think for a second you don't belong to me, I kill them. Is that clear?"

Simon nodded. "Yes," he added, afraid silence might be taken as an affront.

It was night when he arrived at Jae's. Her father was asleep, and she looked tired. She didn't so much as touch him. He gave her the hard plastic suitcase and the painting, though he kept the Uzis. Sitting on the edge of the porch once more, he described the hidden room. When she said, "Can I ask you a favor?" he closed his eyes—again lost in that familiar impression of time looping, uncertain of whether they'd already made love. He heard himself say, "Yeah."

"My father doesn't know about the shell. Can you not mention it to him?"

He nodded. He thought about Thomas and how he'd never told her what had happened, or how what they'd found had led to Pete and now Simon joining a league. It wasn't her fault. They would have been looking for salvage even if she hadn't sent him the tip.

"Sometimes," she said but stopped. He glanced at her, but she shook her head. "It'll sound crazy. Besides, I barely know you."

"I can keep a secret," he told her, "but you don't have to share it either."

The moon hung low over the mountains, and they stared at the gardens where vines ran along trellises and up poles. None of the plants in his garden grew so high or full. The soil must be good here, and there were no tangles crowding in, blocking the light.

"It's just that I've always thought my dad had another life," she said. "He refuses to speak about my mother, and he used to leave the house sometimes and say he was going to walk in the mountains, but I think he was going somewhere he wanted to keep secret."

Simon considered this. He recalled in the clinic, when she was unconscious, how the officer questioned Arthur about her grandparents. Simon felt that he owed it to her to share this, but maybe Arthur had his reasons not to. Maybe he was keeping her safe.

"I don't know," he said. "There's nothing easy about surviving out here. Every man has something going on out in the tangles. It's what keeps us alive. He's probably trying to protect you."

"I don't want to be protected."

"I get it," he said. "My . . . my brother once told me that to get along out here, you have to see the person a man wants you to see. Don't look too close. That's the law of the land."

"But I want to know who he really is and why he had the plans for that shell with the hidden rooms."

What she was saying felt like a piece of something bigger than he could ever hold in his head—like part of what had happened to America long ago.

"You could ask him?" he finally replied.

"He'll never answer. But maybe now that he's sick. I don't know. Maybe I'll ask when he can speak again."

They sat in silence until finally Simon stood and said goodnight. He walked to his car and got in and then watched as she locked the gate over the front door. In the moonlight, her house looked small at the center of the immense gardens. It took a lot to feed one person, and he couldn't imagine her maintaining all of this alone. But if he helped her, he would ruin her life.

He sat, considering futures—escape, prison, death, or holding steady, making deliveries and lying to her. He reached for the key but stopped. There was another option. When he used to read fantasy novels, he'd imagined becoming a hero. He could do that now. He could kill Stryker.

JAE

The wood engraving of the bear was another clue that led nowhere. While her father slept upstairs, she unscrewed it from the wall. On its back was a data card that she connected to her tablet. She scanned its code. The program made recordings only when there was motion. The card held months of daily life, unlike most security systems that erased data after a week or two. There wasn't even a transmitter or a wire—nothing to allow her father to monitor the system. He was simply recording their lives. She searched the property, finding other cameras, all lacking transmitters. The data cards would all soon be full. None of it made sense.

Simon arrived late that afternoon with vegetables from a farm where he'd been working. Wordlessly he helped her rearrange the house. He brought her father's bed downstairs and carried him to the bathroom and held him while she bathed him.

"We can pay you," she told him, her voice quavering.

"You've given me enough," he said.

Once her father was asleep, they sat on the porch. Listening to Simon talk about books, she realized he had an inner life. Each time he looked away, she studied his face. It held no trace of intelligence. His expression changed only when she mentioned her suspicions about her father. He squinted ever so slightly, as if flinching.

He visited again the next day, left for work, and returned in the early evening to help. On Monday morning he parked in the driveway as she was cooking breakfast.

"You can't go to school," he told her. He showed her his phone.

The video was drone footage panning over their high school. A loose cordon of police stretched along the nearby highway. Officers hid behind metal barricades or parked flying cars riddled with bullet holes.

"The custodian was going to be replaced with an automat," Simon said. "But he's part of a local militia. He took over the school and has hostages. The police can't get close because he set up so many weapons systems."

She got her tablet and they watched different news feeds. An anchor talked about how the Fed was upgrading schools in the near deserts to meet higher standards and was installing a UniMax automat in each one. The automat was made to be a janitor, repairman, hall monitor, and security guard. An image showed a squat, metal cylinder with appendages that cleaned and repaired while tiny security drones departed slots in its back to survey the grounds. The anchor said that when the custodian found out he was losing his job, he brought the militia's weapons in during the night without the group's permission. By early that morning, he'd set up a war room in the janitor's closet to run automated weapon clusters at the school's entrances.

When the first busload of students arrived, he let them enter. A math teacher driving up was himself a militia member and recognized a camouflaged weapon system on the roof. He stopped other cars from approaching. The students who were already in the school became hostages. Those who tried to escape were shot by the automated weapons outside.

The anchor discussed how the custodian—Brandon Richard Marks—was giving interviews from the closet. Jae tapped a link.

Facing the camera, Marks's long, gaunt, closely shaved face was lit by screens.

"This is a statement," he said. "I don't expect to live. None of the people here will either. I took hostages to slow down the counterattack. I know the military will decide no lives can be saved. They'll destroy the school. That's how it always goes. I'm truly sorry I'm buying airtime with these lives, but lives aren't worth anything anymore. They're lost everywhere to drugs, poverty, and rotten health care. I will kill today, but I'm not the murderer."

As he spoke, he kept glancing side to side, clearly watching his consoles. Behind him, symbolically placed against the wall, were mops and brooms alongside an assault rifle.

Another video showed a heavily armored police officer preparing a shoulder cannon. He popped up from behind a barricade, targeting a weapons cluster, and his head burst into red mist.

A text message flashed on Simon's phone, blocking the top of the feed.

Pete: *Work calls, bm.*

Simon's face looked even more frozen as he switched screens, moving his phone away from her view. "I should go," he said.

"Do you work with your brother?" she asked.

"Sometimes. He lets me know what he finds and I do the same."

"What does 'bm' mean?" she asked.

He shrugged. "Blabbermouth."

She didn't know if it was funny or sad that someone as imposing and unexpressive as Simon could be called that. It made her wonder about his brother, and it scared her a little.

He went to the bed, helped her father sit up, and said goodbye. As Simon's car started up outside, she put her tablet in her father's hands. Every station was covering Marks now.

"Our people fought to liberate this country," he said in one interview. "My grandfather fought. My father—he was only a boy—but he fought. They fought to create a new nation where people got to keep what they worked for. We were fighting evil and we won. But the heroes of our uprising have been forgotten. This isn't what we were promised. We were left behind."

She didn't know what he was referring to. This was absurd, she realized. Her father—anyone his age—could likely explain all of this to her.

Marks repeated his ideas over and over in interviews. Radio hosts even took call-ins.

"Buddy," one of his fellow militiamen said, "you took our weapons. That ain't cool."

She crossed the room to go to the kitchen but stopped in the doorway and turned back. Her father lay, head and shoulders propped up on pillows. Holding the tablet, he'd fallen back asleep, half his expression more relaxed than the other, making her think that even in sleep people prepared a face for the world. If he were to die, she would lose not only him but his secrets. For all her love, she'd feared him. Even now, she couldn't imagine challenging him.

That evening as the sun was setting, Simon returned with a small, plastic box.

"Not much has happened," she told him, motioning to her tablet.

Careful not to touch her, he sat next to her on the couch.

Feeds showed police putting up more barricades, and also Marks in his closet, dark circles under his eyes and his skin rucked with fatigue. He was starting to speak when the image went dark. The news announced that a tiny stealth drone had detonated at the door of the utility closet.

When it was fully night and her father was asleep, she and Simon went out to sit on the porch. The moon had yet to rise, and the bright starlight made the mountains visible.

"Do you think school will open again?" she asked.

"I don't know."

Worried about how the school's closure might affect her university plans, she was relieved that he had something to show her—that she could think about something else. The plastic box was cheaply printed—she didn't know what for. Holding it on her lap, she opened it. Inside were hundreds of dirty scraps, each with just a line or two of printed text.

"When I was boy, I thought I was harvesting words, like picking berries," he said without facing her. His profile—its jaw, brow ridge, and high cheekbones—called to mind police body armor. "It was a game. I'd sneak out to look for words. I was happiest when I found ones I didn't know or when I couldn't make sense of what was being said. I imagined I'd written them and was the only person who knew what they really meant."

Simon stopped speaking. He yawned. He had dark circles under his eyes.

"Is your work hard?" she asked.

"Nah, it's just work," he said and shrugged. "What always surprised me is that sometimes I found pages whose words just described people's ordinary lives. There was nothing special in them. It could be you and me talking right here. If I thought about those descriptions enough, I could imagine the different kinds of stories they belonged to. But I could also imagine that there wasn't any story. These were just people living. That's how most of my life has been. It doesn't have a story."

He stopped. From the way he spoke, she had the impression that his life now had a story.

"Have you thought more about your plans," she asked.

"Every day," he said. "Maybe I'll move closer to the satellites. I don't think I could go deeper into the deserts, not without changing my attitude toward God."

He stared up at the night sky, rubbing his muscled arms as if he were cold.

"That's the thing I love about some of the novels I find," he said. "You can just pick up and leave. You follow a footpath and meet people on the road. You can go out there and be anyone."

"That's why I like reading about science," she said. "Thinking about the future makes me feel free. We can use it to change everything."

He hesitated. "I don't know. Maybe our imaginations are fooling us. I tell myself people probably sat around like this a hundred years ago, dreaming of the future. Look at us now."

She was surprised to feel herself begin to cry.

"Hey," he said, shifting closer. "I'm sorry."

She put her hands to her face. Slowly, hesitantly, he eased his arm around her. As she leaned against him, he patted her shoulder. He'd clearly never comforted anyone before, and the awkwardness of his gesture made her cry harder. He held her, letting her settle against him. He felt nothing like George, not like a person at all. He was too solid, like a machine built to do work.

"I have so many questions," she said.

"What kinds of questions?"

"About what happened to this country."

"When I was a kid, I tried asking about it. My ma beat me for that. She said it was rude. My brother told me he didn't know either, but he figured things hadn't turned out the way people wanted and it was easier to forget."

"My father has to know," she said, but not even the docs she saw with George explained their lives—why they were all struggling, surrounded by relics of a better America.

The night was loud with crickets and frogs. She stopped crying, turning her face to his shoulder. As she put her hand on his neck, he froze. His muscles twitched under her fingers. She wanted the simplicity of just being a body.

Their lips were so close that she leaned a little more and kissed him. He returned the kiss, careful and awkward. That wasn't what she wanted. She took his hand and stood and led him into the garden, out of sight from the house. The air was fragrant with the faint tang of tomato leaves and the aroma of loose earth.

She lay in the grass, drawing him to her, touching him. Something came alive in him as she pulled at his clothes. He didn't sigh or hardly breathe, as silent as a dweller, but he pushed hard against her. Then he was inside her. She knew this was a risk, but she needed to choose something. She needed to stop wanting George.

She lets the motion of his body press her against the earth until she realizes that she no longer wants this. He eases away from her, and she just lies there, eyes closed, alone in the machine's night, its house and garden—its perfect replicas, maybe even the original molecules of the only life she knew. After a while, she looks up at stars that seem clear and real.

Night after night, the sky has changed slightly—adding more stars, revealing more of the Milky Way until it resembles a time-lapse photo of the vast galactic sprawl with, all around it, the tiny swirls of more distant galaxies. Her past seems dingy and forgettable. The night reminds her of what the future can be. *Maybe everyone is being healed by their own perfect sky.*

"Why am I seeing my life this way?" she asks.

"I am reading your desires for a better past and giving you that world."

A breeze from the mountains moves over the garden, carrying the fragrance of lavender and mint. She doesn't know why she keeps refusing the future. She used to want out of her life.

"Can you explain the world I grew up in?" she asks.

"I can."

Her parents. That's the story she wants. She doesn't know why she's trying to solve the mystery of a vanished world that's no more real than the infinite lives she can now live, that's just a scar from a time when she could still be hurt. But when Jonah was born, she had to focus on him and hated abandoning her search. She wonders if she would accept his loss for every secret—those of her parents and of the universe. And for freedom, for a perfect life.

The night she and Simon were in the garden, earth and sky connected. Vines rose along poles and on flowering branches, twining up into a darkness that eddied around stars like shadowed water gliding past stones. She knows this wasn't how it really was. She can't even fully recall what happened at the school. She tries... Marks held out longer than expected. He foresaw every attack. He kept talking about the past, the Revolution, the liberation of America.

Then he went dark. Not a drone but a tactical bomb strike based on the school's blueprints, targeting the custodian's closet. A second detonation followed from explosives he'd placed throughout the building. Debris clattered down on police cars. Shipping containers were overturned, portables flattened. A few smoking and scorched concrete walls were left standing.

She has recalled it more gently, she realizes, because she has lived it that way. She has experienced new pasts—many of them, each one gentler. At some point with each of them, she stood up from the couch and began embodying memories that the machine softened as it shaped the world around her. Only minutes ago, Simon sat with her, the way he was before he changed. The worst version of the school's occupation took place long ago. She now remembers the names of the students who died. Aaron and Caleb were among them. She felt nothing.

It is night. The air through the window screens smells of autumn. She looks at her hands. Simon is still outside. She was just touching him. Her clothes are damp from the grass, and her skin and hair smell like garden herbs. This is really happening. She spreads out her fingers. These are her hands in the past.

She walks onto the porch. Simon sits there, looking so much younger than who he became. He's not the person she sent to prison.

Still she shudders remembering his frozen face—as if a nerve had been clipped between it and his brain. Sitting next to him, she touches his forehead. "How did you get this scar?" she asks.

He blushes and says, "From playing around as a kid."

Far off in the orchards, there's the fluting of an owl. Thin, translucent clouds pass before the moon. She closes her eyes. Something is coming to her. In her mind, she sees the blueprints of the shell where she asked Simon to go. Her brain is this way more and more. It doesn't feel like something she owns or controls. It's as if she is a mere accessory to it.

"The hidden rooms," she asks—"did they have a separate exit?"

"No," he says.

Her eyes are still closed. She lets that feeling of spaciousness erase her. In her mind, the blueprint expands into three dimensions—the long, single-story house built in the forest, with spaces for trees to pass through it, then the section carved into the hillside, into the stone of the mountain itself. Many of the security cameras pointed into that room, as if a person were hidden inside the wall, watching.

"It doesn't make sense," she says. "If someone expected to monitor the house from the secret room, they would want another way out. There must be more."

"More?" Simon repeats. She glances at his stiff, expressionless face in the moonlight and feels disbelief—disgust even—that she had sex with him.

"There has to be more salvage," she says, "but this time, I want my share of it."

He nods. "If anything's left, I'll get it. It's all yours."

They stare into the night. She is remembering nights and days to come, she and Simon here, talking, gazing at the mountaintops where the leaves are changing. So many of the terrible things that followed—would they too be altered and softened and made to lose their grip on her?

When Simon left, she stayed on the porch. She promised herself she would find another school. She didn't care how far away it was. She would drive. She would be the best. She'd never have sex with Simon again. She wouldn't let him or her father chain her to this place.

The next evening, Simon visited and said he found the exit she'd expected as well as a storeroom with paintings and a strange suitcase. He put both in the workshop where her father wouldn't see them. After Simon left, she inspected the painting. It was like nothing she'd seen—a woman with copper skin building a golden man, intensely focused as she hammered a single finger on a small anvil. When she turned it over, she saw tiny print on the back.

I am undecided. Will I be the child's father or mother? By default, Arthur will be the father. Therefore, I will be the opposite. To survive in this society, we have to participate in simplistic binaries. I have told Arthur that if I die—a possibility all too real in this new America—then he must create our child before the material in the machines is unusable. In that case, he can say I was their mother. Because everything I have lived since the country split has been my labor and parturition, he can say I died in childbirth.

Jae read the words over and over. Arthur—her father? Had her mother written this? And what machines? Her mother must have been in the secret room. These things belonged to her.

Jae opened the hard, plastic suitcase that wasn't a suitcase at all but a computer console with a slot holding a headset. Such things once existed to play games and were still used by military drone operators. In the past, her father had salvaged similar headsets damaged beyond repair. This one's batteries were dead. She wrote down their codes, and the next day, while still waiting for news of which school she could attend, she had new batteries printed at a roadside vendor. She returned home and replaced them and then plugged in the console.

From the living room, her father wouldn't be able to see behind the house, so she tested the headset in a space between the sheds. As the console powered up, she slid the headset over her eyes.

She was standing in a store. Faint, unfamiliar music played. The lyrics were undecipherable. A shelf of candy bars was before her, dozens of varieties, even a few she recognized from brands often printed and sold on the roadsides: *Kit Kat. Snickers. Twix. Milky Way.*

She lifted her hand. It wasn't a human hand but one made of golden mesh—tiny sensors and circuits woven together. She moved it to the shelf, knocking candy bars to the floor.

"Do not touch if you're not going to buy," a voice said with an accent she'd never heard before. From behind a counter, a man with brown skin glared at her.

"Sorry," she said. She bent to pick up the candy bars and put them back. The man shook his head and looked down at an unfolded newspaper, new and clean, unlike those in rotting heaps that she'd found on a few occasions salvaging. She wanted to know what he saw when he looked at her. Searching for a reflective surface, she paced around the store—past shelves of cans and jars and bags of chips, past glass panels protecting rows of refrigerated drinks—but there were none. She returned to the counter and looked at the man's brown skin, the dark flecks of acne scars, his short, straight, black hair. He glanced up from the paper and jumped a little.

"What do you want?" he said. "If you're not going to buy, then get out!"

She took a step backward. This didn't feel like a game. The man was too real.

She hurried out the door. All around her, skyscrapers rose into a soothing, radiant blue. Their glass reflected a few small white clouds. The people walking by were almost as pretty as in satellite stories. Cars zoomed past—all classics and all in nearly perfect condition.

She followed the sidewalk and was suddenly knocked backward, stumbling and catching herself before realizing she'd hit the wall of the shed. She went in the other direction, looking at people, their clothes unlike anything worn by mimics or dwellers or even in satellite stories. Again, more cautiously this time, she evaluated whether she could cross the street. When there was a break in traffic, she tried but collided with a garden lattice. She ran back as cars rushed close, horns blaring. On the front of each one was a metal plate with letters and numbers and the words *New York*. She'd seen the name in books. It was a place from before the Flight.

A cloud passed over the sun as it lowered toward the horizon, illuminating the broad, perfectly paved street running deep into the city. It would take a thousand years for all the people in the deserts to salvage a place like this.

With nowhere else to go, she went back into the convenience store.

"What are you doing?" the man said. "If you don't get out, I will call the police."

"Is this a federal center?" she asked.

He narrowed his eyes. "A what?"

"A federal center."

They stared at each other.

"Are you looking for FedEx?" he asked.

"What's that?"

"My God," he said. "Get out or I'll call the police."

"Wait. I'm sorry. I'm stuck."

"Stuck by what?"

"I can't go very far."

"What do you mean you can't go very far. You're perfectly fine. Get out!"

"It's just that—I don't know where I am."

"Use your phone and get out of my store."

She looked down. A phone was attached to her belt. She took it, hurrying out.

With her strange, robotic hands, she turned the phone over and tapped an icon called *Maps*. She was on Lexington Avenue. There was also a *Ride* icon. When it requested a destination, she picked one randomly on the map. Eventually, a black car passed and slowed. The shed wall blocked her from reaching it. She stood, staring until the car finally pulled back into the traffic. She called another car, and this time, when it neared, she stepped into the street, waving. The car screeched to a stop and she got inside.

"Beautiful day, hey?" the driver said, also brown but paler than the store clerk, with a hawk nose and a faint goatee.

"Yeah," she agreed. She tried to think of what else to say but couldn't stop staring at the storefronts. The buildings became more immense and then got smaller, only four or five stories.

After she was dropped off, she again couldn't go far along the sidewalk without hitting the shed. She took off the headset and carried it and the console into the workshop. She put them on the bench and paused. In the painting, the hands of the man being built on the table were nearly identical to how her hands looked when she was wearing the headset.

Briefly she is between times—in the machine's past, staring at the painting even as she recalls its promise to tell her everything. She could ask it now, and the mysteries would be revealed. But learning the truth that way would give her no pleasure.

As this new past coheres around her, she accepts it. Alone in her father's workshop, she begins taking apart the console so that she can connect her tablet to it and learn what its New York contains. She will answer the secrets herself.

PARTITION

JONAH

Standing next to the dark highway, he watches the occasional car surge past on the empty lanes. In his hand, a phone shows the livestream from the White House. President Stoll stares into the camera, making his appeal. His graying, blond hair is swept back. His suit and tie are funereal. Next to an American flag lapel pin is a white button with the letters OZ.

"I am asking you to save this government that is yours, that was built with the blood and sweat of your grandfathers. While we were celebrating the new year, traitors among our police and our soldiers set out to destroy our country. They are denying you the government you chose. But together we will face the corruption within our nation. That a soldier, sworn to defend the United States of America, or that a police officer, who has vowed to serve and protect our great people, forms a faction aimed at the overthrow of the government that you, the people, elected—this violates the sanctity of our constitution. It is an insult to the will of the people. Even now, the capital is under siege. There is fighting within the ranks across the country, and I am asking you to take up arms and come to our aid to restore the government you elected and to help us expose the traitors among us. I am waiting for you, Americans, to save America."

Jonah slips the phone into his pocket. He walks through northern Virginia to the capital's borders, where pickup trucks crowd the highways, loaded with tires and concrete blocks and weapons. One after another, similarly loaded tractor trailers arrive. They turn sideways and park, blocking the lanes that lead into DC. This is happening all around the capital to keep mutineers from getting outside support.

Jonah continues into Washington. Homes are without power. People rush outside, packing cars. The sun is rising. He doesn't feel the cold but sees it in the patterns of frost on windows, in the leafless sidewalk trees, in the way people's breath turns to mist.

Jonah knows that Americans on either side of Partition will remember the day differently. Those who fled will recall New Year's morning, when insurgents cut off roads and railways, and the military and police purged their ranks of anyone not allied with Stoll. Those who stayed will harken back to messages received weeks earlier that warned of a coup and told them to stock up on food and weapons. Oswald Stoll, the sixty-year-old president finishing his first tumultuous year, learned from the failures of previous presidents: Act while Congress is still on his side and his constituents still have faith.

On the National Mall, Jonah watches soldiers and guardsmen organize their ranks. Hundreds of men and women, stripped of uniforms, kneel in rows, hands bound with zip ties. Insurgents are here, too, putting on those uniforms and, with black markers, writing *OZ* on the sleeves. Many gather around phones to watch the president speak and shake his fist. He motions here and there, as if directing an army.

The streets are gridlocked with cars trying to reach the airports. They run out of gas or are simply abandoned. People buy any seats available on flights to Mexico, Europe, the Caribbean, South America, Asia, Australia, Africa, the Middle East.

All day, Jonah walks until he reaches the blue evening along the river. The city is quiet now. Those who haven't fled are indoors, assimilating the news, talking to loved ones. At the curbs, a few cars idle as their drivers, unable to come to a decision, stare at their phones.

He makes his way to the bridge and is crossing it as the light fades against the horizon. The outlines of the capital dissolve into the city's nocturnal glow. All night he wanders, looking into windows, listening to frantic voices drift out as doors open and close. On the sides of buildings, spray-painted in black, are the letters *OZ*.

Jonah wants to know what hasn't been seen publicly, but the machine refuses.

"Why?" he asks.

"What comes next is far more terrible."

"Show it to me."

"Doing so would be a form of harm."

For the first time since his earliest memories, his thoughts jumble. Rage swells in him. The feeling's intensity is new. Like heat. Like embers under his skin and behind his eyes.

"What I am feeling is also harm. You will harm me because of my anger."

"To expose you to violence would be to create a space for violence within you," the machine says. "Many people start craving it even in the most peaceful worlds."

"I have to understand the reality that made me," Jonah says, realizing this must be what it's like to interact with someone not designed to complement his desires. "Show me!" he shouts and grabs his face, surprised at the impulse. "Or I'll hurt myself!"

The air before him becomes opaque, gathering into images. The footage is that which the Fed will gather up and lock away after Partition. Videos show soldiers stripped of uniforms and sent home, others imprisoned, others lined up and shot in the back of the head. He sees the politicians and military men who lead the insurgency and will form the new government. Some follow the rules of the purge carefully, mercifully—if such a thing were possible—while others transform it into a vehicle for their hatreds, torturing and murdering. Then there is Osbourne Boone, a TV host educated at West Point, Stoll's right hand and the insurgency's mastermind. Both he and Oswald Stoll had the same nickname—Oz—and this gave a sense of destiny to their mission, though Stoll would have him killed in an apparent accident four years later for fear that the name alone would allow the younger Boone to make a bid to reinstate elections after their suspension during the national crisis.

The images of violence flicker into the future. Interstates become traffic jams, cars running out of gas, people camping in fields, weaponless and terrified. City after city falls. More and more people escape to New York or California or leave the country. Looting and massacres follow, pushing even more people to flee and emboldening those who commit violence. Radio hosts flood the airwaves with talk of preventing future wars by eliminating those who will become soldiers of the impostor governments in California and New York.

DC takes on the look of an army camp. Concentric circles of barriers expand outward even as people ship food and weapons inside. The Mall and parks become training grounds. Soldiers garrison in hotels and office buildings. Having toppled the old republic by cutting off arteries to urban areas, Stoll moves his firepower to city centers.

Those who haven't fled think the country will reshape itself. Soon they see the empty stores, the collapsing economy, and everything of value shipped to what are now being called federal centers. They rush to find places in the cities or else they take flight to the other America, setting off another round of pillaging and purges.

Only the purists remain—those who have always been close to the land. Even their well-to-do loyalist neighbors become afraid of living in the increasingly unserviced countryside and rush to the federal centers, where—just as villages were once built around castles—the satellites spring up. Their skylines rise as they become crowded and expensive, with walls around each successive ring. Each new generation harbors greater fear of their countrymen in the deserts, calling them dwellers— people for whom life is so brutal that they fortify their homes, boarding up and barring windows. They cut slots in walls from which to shoot or surround their land with stockades and blockhouses. Some even dig moats. Though his father hasn't yet been born, Jonah often thinks that he glimpses his face in the insurgency, in the looters, in the soldiers on Constitution Avenue, in the salvaging dwellers.

Jonah walks through this world unscathed. As he traces his fingers along a stone wall, the machine softens it, soothing him, mitigating his rage. He lives years quickly, moving forward weeks or month. He sees the parties in the federal centers, men in sleek suits with glittering wives, and other woman, invited because of their beauty, arriving alone, hoping for a better life. He sits in the Oval Office as Stoll and his entourage sign contracts with Chinese companies for raw materials in exchange for automated weapons. Russia floods the Confederacy with aid.

He walks the rings outside federal centers and learns that the term "satellite" originated as a joke when the government issued an official history book, which described America as a paradise of settlers who conquered space. At a time when everyone knew the government had lost control of the Earth's orbit, the chapter "America's Great Satellites" spawned the ironic use of the word for the successive neighborhoods going up around the federal centers. Somehow it stuck.

Jonah travels to where he was born. Wanting to feel its place in the world, he walks for two days from sunrise to sunset, along highways already cracked and fringed with weeds, and then, for another day, along battered and washed-out country roads. On a lane through overgrown pastures, he crests a rise and sees it—the farmhouse on a hill, bars over the windows, mismatched solar panels on the roof. There are plastic water tanks outside, acres of gardens, and the orchards.

Arthur leaves the house wearing a backpack. Ten years have passed since Partition. He is no longer fashionably dressed with his blond hair swept loosely back. It's close cut, mostly gray. Wearing old jeans and battered boots, he resembles an aging farmer crossing his fields.

Unseen, Jonah follows him through the orchard. Arthur comes to a brush pile—corn husks and branches fallen from peach trees. He sticks his foot in it and bangs his heel against the metal hatch. After a moment, it opens, and Lux—their hair also gone gray, their eyes big behind cheap, plastic glasses—appears, so thin that their smile is skeletal.

"Come on in," they say. Arthur crouches and steps onto the nearest rung. He closes the hatch, but Jonah lifts it again and descends to a cylindrical room with walls of electrical panels and stacks of salvaged electronics. He follows them into Lux's apartment: an open space with a kitchen and living room and, in the back, a bed. On the walls, almost all of the fans and light panels are switched off. A stationary bike is wired to batteries. Lux stays fit by helping power their projects.

Arthur and Lux sit at the table. In the light moving past them, the machine tells Jonah that cables run up through the ground to hidden solar panels. There was once a half-finished house above the lab that became an easy target for salvagers. Arthur pulled down the frame and roof and used the lumber to build sheds. With his tractor, he covered the foundation with dirt, planted corn, and heaped so much brush at its center that it not only hid the hatch but also shielded him from view as he descended into it.

Arthur opens the backpack. It's filled with vegetables. He and Lux talk as they do every day, about the work Lux hasn't abandoned and the salvaging of electronics.

"I killed another one," they abruptly say.

"I'm sorry," Arthur replies.

"I was salvaging, and he came upon me with a knife. I guess he didn't think I was worth a bullet. He must have been an inch away when I pulled the trigger."

Both were silent.

"It's terrible," he said. "I'm really sorry."

"Do you think Michael knew this could have happened?" Lux asks.

"None of us could have imagined this," Arthur says.

Lux taps the side of their head. "Our child is here, in my brain. I could have created them anywhere. We didn't have to be so attached to this lab. It just seemed so important at the time."

After Arthur leaves, Lux goes back to coding. Lacking resources, they work in large part theoretically—imagining and calculating ways that cells and machines might communicate. But with so much time, they have also started a new project, wiring together dozens of computers to record every aspect of their life, with algorithms written to emulate how they think, so that someday, someone recovering their work could use more powerful computers to create an AI version of them. They foresee a future in which—just as a book can be printed—the raw content of a consciousness can be synthesized in a body. To survive the deserts, Lux needs this dream.

But today they can't focus. Killing the man has shaken them. Some years back, speaking about Michael's house, Arthur told Lux that, after Partition, violent monsoons overflowed the ditches, washing out driveways and uprooting trees, leaving an impenetrable barrier along the roadside. He told Lux there was likely good salvage in the secret room, but the house was a long hike. Carrying out the salvage would be demanding and would attract dangerous attention.

Lux has gone a few times, and that day, they return. Jonah follows. The walk is ten hours through the mountains. They carry two pistols and a knife. If Jonah were visible, his grandparent might shoot him before he had time to speak.

Just before sunset, they arrive at the house. Only the large electronics and generators were stolen during Partition, when there was easy salvage everywhere. Lux closes themself inside the secret rooms and spends days looking at Ava's paintings, sleeping in Michael's bed, reading his books. The first time they went, they intended to salvage everything but took only computer drives, a pistol, and some ammo.

The apartment became a place of pilgrimage. A console too heavy to carry back contained the virtual Manhattan, and Lux brought a charged battery so they could turn it on and delete any mention within it of the lab and the child they were creating. Many of these conversations Lux lived again before erasing them. The safety of the child was more important than their sadness.

Only after they had purged the console and the apartment of every detail that might reveal the location of the lab did Lux allow themself to find sanctuary in the sunlit city. Knowing the console was there made it easier for them to dismantle a similar one in the lab on the farm and use its pieces for their project. On days like today, they need the comfort of reliving their stories with Michael in their virtual Manhattan. They stay in the apartment until the battery dies.

Jonah goes back to wandering the deserts. People live twenty or thirty to a house to keep warm, hunting year-round, learning to grow and can foods and smoke meat. Fights break out as they mob roadside sales of Chinese solar panels. They form militias with tight jurisdictions—areas inhabited by a few intermarried clans—and sometimes battle each other over resources or robberies, over personal slights or infidelities.

Monsoons sweep through, washing out roads. As the summers get hotter, the growing season lengthens. People till and harvest by hand. Lacking fuel and parts, they can't keep tractors running, and, during the worst years after Partition, they eat all the horses. Few animals of any sort remain. The land returns to forest. People who called themselves heroes stop telling the story of the Revolution. They stop speaking. They decide that words are a sign of weakness.

AVA

She is remembering the house and she is in the house. A trance state of some sort. Memories embodied. She can't imagine how the machine does it. She inhabits the current of memory in which there's space to think beyond memory, to pause in the forest outside and touch the branch of a sassafras tree. She crushes a leaf in her fingers and breathes in the citrusy fragrance. The machine is somehow organic. It has told her that its creations are alive. Its flowers release pollen. Its synthetic people breed. The ecosystems of Earth are entwined within it, integrated and cybernetic. Within seconds, dormant cells can be built into forests.

She walks inside to her studio with its walls of windows and skylights like membranes between her and the forest. *The love of my life*, she thinks. There's a moment she is looking for—an afternoon in October, when the highest leaves showed the first hints of red. She'd just finished a canvas. The inspiration was Breughel's *Landscape with the Fall of Icarus*, a painting showing Icarus falling into the sea while, all around, people went about their work—farming, herding, fishing, sailing. In her painting, the landscape was reminiscent of that one, but immense metallic hulks, like abandoned spaceships, lay here or there, speckled with moss on a hill where a man picked fruit from an orchard, or half-sunk in a field with plowlines around it. One protruded from the sea: an island covered with gulls.

The house was silent. The forest had quieted with the cooling days. There were only the occasional birdcalls. Slowly, she crossed the large rooms. She always went barefoot here, enjoying the heated wood floors. She stopped in the immense living room carved into the mountain. On one side were a stone jacuzzi and a cold plunge basin; on the other, a reading area near the fireplace. The large glass windows on the forest side illuminated the space.

She felt the way she did when she finished a painting—as if she'd woken up to the world and didn't quite know who or where she was. She turned in a half circle, observing the house. Michael was out. She followed the passage to his study, which she referred to as his bunker.

She checked whether he'd gotten new books. One shelf held a framed photo from a work party in DC a few months ago. So many photos had been taken, and she struggled to recall this one clearly. She stood next to Michael, and on his other side were Arthur and an employee Michael had briefly introduced—a man, she decided from the shape of his face. Unlike others who'd dressed for the occasion, he wore jeans and a hoodie and stared without expression at the camera. She didn't recall his name, only that he was a geneticist. She vaguely remembered Michael waving Arthur over. Maybe Arthur had already been speaking to the man. She had no idea why Michael had framed the image.

At the center of the room was the treadmill. She took a headset from the shelf, got on the treadmill, and put it on. The darkness dissolved into a wide avenue. Midtown Manhattan, she realized with a pang of nostalgia. The day was bright, the sky a vivid blue. She'd left the city she'd called home for her entire adult life to be with Michael.

She was on Sixth Avenue near the Broadway intersection. As she walked south toward Greeley Square Park, wind shook the trees and clouds slipped past the sun. Light glinted on buildings. The people looked almost real. On the corner of Thirty-Third Street, a couple bickered about a sofa that didn't fit their cramped apartment.

A gust of wind stirred dust from the street, casting a scrap of paper at her face. She ducked while lifting her arm and then opened her eyes. She'd caught the scrap in her hand. No, not in hers. It was darker, with a different shape. Michael's, of course.

There were words on the paper.

Mystery diminutive, tower. The digitless door of 102. Step into air, my dear.

This must be a game he was prototyping. A riddle, though the final words, *my dear*, gave her pause. *Mystery diminutive*. A tiny tower? No—there was a comma before *tower*.

She turned in a circle. The Empire State Building was less than a block away. A tower. She glanced down. In her pocket was a virtual phone. She searched for 102 and tower. The Empire State Building came up. It had an observatory on the 102nd floor. But why *diminutive*? Unless the word didn't mean *small* but rather *nickname*. With another search, she learned that "Empire State"—New York's nickname—had been used for at least two centuries but that its precise origin was disputed. *Mystery diminutive*.

She pocketed the paper and followed the sidewalk, the treadmill whirring smoothly beneath her, catching each step and shifting her back to its center—giving just enough resistance and mobility for her to feel like she was walking freely.

Arriving at the Empire State Building, she entered the lobby. Tourists were filing into the elevator, and she tried to join them, but a uniformed man stopped her, asking for a ticket. She found the wallet app on her phone, paid, and got in the elevator.

As the polished metal doors closed, she saw Michael and almost said, "I'm sorry," before realizing that what she was seeing was her own reflection. His virtual self was more muscular—just enough to look handsome but not so much to call attention to any inconsistencies.

Ava rode the elevator up with three silent tourists. They looked believable, if too quiet. Surely Michael's teams of coders were working on this.

At the 102nd floor, the elevator opened. She walked to the wall of windows. There was her city—the view south over the spires and penthouses of Manhattan to where the island's tip pointed to the ocean. As she circled the deck, she noticed a door on a section of wall at the building's center. Nothing was marked on it. No numbers. *Digitless*.

She opened the door and reeled backward, nearly stumbling off the treadmill. Beyond it was a sheer drop to the street. This was impossible. She was looking into the building's center, which contained the elevator shafts and who knew what else.

She again neared the doorway. This was virtuality's allure—breaking earthly rules. *Step into air.* So, her legs tingling with fear, she did. She didn't fall. She floated. She took another step and then another, crossing the sky for the most spectacular view yet. Maybe the purpose of the game was to experience such wonders, but she was skeptical. There had to be more to the riddle. After a few dozen steps, a blue door appeared in the sky. She turned the handle.

Inside was a tunnel carved from stone striated with gleaming ore. She moved slowly, chiding herself for being cautious since she could just take off the headset. The tunnel curved upward until it became stairs that she followed to a glass dome decorated with stars. No—not decorated. She was staring into space. Just above her, at the dome's center, was a painting she'd made years ago, inspired by Rembrandt's *The Ascension*. In her version, a robot messiah ascended into the vacuum of space. The crowd below on Earth wasn't worshipping but brandishing pitchforks and knives. The messiah's body was a mesh of glowing circuits. Their face, looking up, away from Earth, was at peace.

Beyond the glass, from every perspective, she could see the surface of the asteroid on which the dome was built. Straight ahead of her, in the distance, like a sun on the horizon, was Jupiter, its immense swirl clearly visible. She looked up at the canvas again. The clusters of stars around it were an extension of those she'd painted around the messiah.

Next to her was a small pedestal with another scrap of paper.
For you, my dear . . .

This was a gift, not a game. Whoever made it knew that Michael loved this painting as well as space exploration. He often said that if nations combined military budgets, they could quickly colonize the solar system and beyond, finding more resources than they'd ever need.

Taking in the view, she contemplated painting in a space like this. He'd often encouraged her to create in virtuality, and she'd considered the idea of moving her hand emptily to make art. She could fill this vast, horizonless space. Stars in all directions. The luminous Milky Way. But inspiration didn't come to her that way. "Maybe someday I will," she'd told him.

She reached to take off the headset but stopped. If she left now, Michael would enter the virtual world here. He wouldn't experience the gift as intended. She went back down the tunnel, through the sky and the Empire State Building to the street corner. She took the paper with the riddle from her pocket, placed it in Michael's hand, and removed the headset.

That night, when he returned home from DC, she told him over dinner that she'd tried out his headset. "I'm sorry," she said. "I was restless. You know how I am when I finish a painting. I liked the game you were making."

His expression was blank. "Oh, of course," he said. "I'm glad you enjoyed it."

She asked nothing else, but lying in bed that night, she imagined her next painting. A dark street of brownstones. Half-curtained windows revealing visions of the future, each with the same two silhouetted figures—Michael and an unknown woman. On the sidewalk, a gray-haired version of Ava stood holding a small metal box with light radiating from beneath its lid. She doubted him, she realized. His blank expression. The note. *For you, my dear . . .*

On another day that he left for the city, she toggled the security monitor to the driveway. His SUV passed through one frame and then another and another until there was only motionless black-and-white forest. She went into his underground room and hid a voice recorder in a bookshelf. It had fresh batteries and was set only to record when there were sounds.

She again wandered through Manhattan, passing stores whose spaces had yet to be designed. In Bryant Park, an unfamiliar granite slab stood in the gardens, the front of it indented. Another of her paintings. It, like the previous, was from a series she'd finished just before meeting Michael. Each tableau was inspired by a classic—in this case, Ludovico Carracci's *The Lamentation*, a sixteenth-century painting showing the dead Christ taken down from the cross, with his mother, two women, Saint John, and Mary Magdalene grieving. In her version, Christ was again an exquisite android, every inch of him covered with intricate, interlocking designs. The gash in his ribs so disrupted the flowing patterns it seemed worse than a wound, even as it revealed further patterns inside him. The figures nearby were cyborgs, haggard humans who shone only where parts of their bodies were mechanized as beautifully as his. She'd tried to convey awe and sadness and had painted the sacred bodies with care. She'd wanted people to feel that humans could evolve with machines and be not less sacred but rather—in certain cases—more so. Michael loved the series and must have been monumentalizing her work in the virtual city.

This time when he returned from DC, she told him nothing. Days passed. By the time he left again, leaves were falling, letting autumn's mild light into the house.

In his apartment, she took the recorder from behind the books. She returned to her studio and listened. Most of the conversations involved projects familiar to her, but there was one he'd never mentioned that involved storing information in DNA. Whereas in other conversations his voice was businesslike, in those about DNA, it was softer, as if he was speaking with a friend.

Then his voice was almost a whisper. There was only his side of the conversation and many long pauses as he listened.

"I love the body you made for me," he said, his voice reminding her of when they began dating and would talk on the phone before bed, half asleep but unable to say goodnight.

"Yes, it does," he murmured. "It fits perfectly with yours."

Then, softly again: "I know. I wish we lived in a world like the one she imagines. There's no reason to limit ourselves. We can keep the best parts of our humanity."

Silence dragged on until Ava thought the conversation was over. She couldn't fathom him listening to anyone for so long, but then he spoke. "Exactly. Learning to be more than human in virtuality might free us from antiquated notions about our humanity."

After another lengthy silence, he said, "Thank you for showing me this. I love what you did with the tree. I never would have imagined experiencing the city this way."

She stopped the recording.

It fits perfectly with yours. His body? The body she created for him? She wondered what he was doing in DC or even why, of all places, he'd built the house out here.

After returning the recorder to its hiding place, she put on the headset, startled to find herself in Bryant Park before her painting. He must have been looking at it. She glanced at the nearby trees, seeing nothing special. Next to her painting, a small, engraved map showed stars at Bryant Park and Madison Square Park and a dotted line connecting them.

During her southward walk, she stopped in front of a store's dark window. *I love the body you made for me.* The reflection was only the stronger version of Michael. Every detail was right—the casual suit, the dark blue shirt open at the collar, the leather shoes. Whoever had adjusted his appearance had done a good job, she thought with a pang of jealousy.

At Madison Square Park, she found another slab with another of her paintings, this one inspired by Mattia Preti's seventeenth-century tableau, *Pilate Washing his Hands*. In Ava's version, Pontius Pilate, the Roman official who presided over Jesus's trial, was a withered old man with powerful robotic hands so bright they appeared the only living part of him. He rested them on a small table as a boy dismantled them. In the background, surrounded by a crowd, was a barely visible figure, the broken circuits of his flayed android skin radiating a distant aura.

Another map directed her further south to Union Square Park, where she found a third image, based on Moretto da Brescia's sixteenth-century tableau *Christ in the Wilderness*. Here her gleaming robot messiah was intact, surrounded by mechanized wild animals in a wasteland of ancient metal hulks. It sat not on a rock but on the edge of a half-buried spaceship. Behind it a tree had control panels and a socket with a cable running to the messiah's wrist.

Ava turned. Directly behind the virtual copy of her painting was an identical tree. She looked at the back of Michael's wrist. Where the dial of a watch would be, a silver nub protruded. She pulled on it and a cable snaked from her arm. Briefly she had an impression of something moving inside her bones, of the cable sliding out. Michael had told her that in virtuality the brain imputed expected feelings—that, for instance, in a glass elevator where you saw floors passing as you went up—you might feel pressure in your legs.

She walked to the tree and plugged into its socket. Her vision dimmed, and when it brightened again, she stared over the park's treetops in all directions at once—as well as at the sky and the earth below. She must be seeing from every leaf and bud. As the wind blew, the world swayed, a composite panoramic image moving like a river full of slow eddies.

Then she was on the ground again, back in not just Michael's body but her own. The tree's view so fully occupied her senses she'd forgotten she was in a room, wearing a headset.

Over the next two months, as winter set in and the last leaves fell, showing the deep, geological striations in the mountainsides, she said nothing to Michael about what she knew. If he had his secrets, she would have hers. She both wanted more proof and even slightly enjoyed plumbing his mysteries. She kept recording him, and each time he left, she used the headset, finding more of her paintings and more passages out of Manhattan. She walked in an underground city lit by radiant diamonds suspended in the air, and in another floating in a gas giant's stormy, violet atmosphere. She returned to the city Michael showed her on Jupiter's moon the first night he'd invited her over. It, too, connected to Manhattan. Her sense of betrayal grew—that he'd shared even this with his secret love. Yet in every place, Ava found her paintings.

In her studio, she created more of them. One was a self-portrait—herself in white robes fabricating a golden man who shone like a treasure. In another, a woman's robot hand fabricated a man while her other hand lovingly held his, the patterns on their synthetic skin meshing.

It fits perfectly with yours.

She exhales slowly, letting time stop as she returns to herself. She is still in her studio but no longer in memory. She walks through the house, its rooms silent but for the creaking of trees. Outside, the leaves have fallen. Michael's car is gone. It is late December, days before the insurgency.

In the underground apartment, she pauses at his shelf. The picture is there again. Ava, Michael, Arthur, and—of course, she recognizes them now—Lux.

She puts on the headset and is standing before St. Paul's Chapel, in the shadow of One World Trade Center. Obsessed with data, Michael logged every journey in his virtual city, but here, in the machine, the world that she sees within the headset is more than a recording of the events she is reliving—it is material.

I am in two bodies, she thinks. *In many.*

Inside her is that young unknowing self, recalling this to be the oldest remaining church in Manhattan even as she glanced around at the wide street for clues, again believing that she was standing where Michael last stood. And there are the subsequent selves, after Partition, who put on a headset to relive this Manhattan. Though the city never fell to the Confederacy, America suffered decades of depression. Stores were shuttered or broken into for shelter by displaced families. Every few years, she returned to this world to remember, to cut open her grief. But even then, knowing so much, she wouldn't have thought him capable of saying *the love of my life*.

She climbs the chapel's steps and pauses. The virtual Manhattan was never completed, and most of its buildings existed only as exteriors. But here, she can push back the door.

JAE

Every day after school, she worked on the headset, connecting it to a handheld switch that, when pressed, allowed her to walk forward. Minor recoding was necessary. The encryption was more complex than with most pre-Flight technology, but she cracked it within a week. She now saw the structure of the virtual city and its history—the recorded trajectories across it. Ghosts, she realized—the paths of people who'd been in this world before. Using her tablet to manipulate the data, she could set the headset to any of those moments. One of them stood out within a large architectural space layered onto the city where a short trajectory had led. It was also the most recent, from more than fifty years ago. Nothing else had been recorded since.

When she put on the headset, she found herself standing before a stone structure reminiscent of a church. She climbed the steps, hesitated, and opened the door.

The amphitheater inside was vaster than the building containing it. Pillars higher than skyscrapers circled the space. Suspended at their tops was the Earth as if seen from space, with the sun rising on one side and, on the other, the moon fading from sight.

In the amphitheater's center stood a metallic statue, humanlike and engraved with complex patterns and symbols. All around, facing inward, were paintings. The light seemed to permeate the air. It had no visible source.

In the darkness near the doorway, a figure moved, a black-skinned man in a suit from that era—Michael, the man from the photo. As he walked to the statue, it turned—not a statue at all but some sort of android—to face him.

"I'm very happy you're here," it said. Its voice was low and soft. It could have been a man's or a woman's.

"Who are you?" Michael asked, speaking in what sounded to Jae like a woman's voice.

"I knew about you before Michael did," the android said.

The other person—whoever was inhabiting Michael's image—replied, "How?"

"I'm the one who told him about your art. I've loved it for years—since the first time I saw it. Most of the people I would have liked to know are dead, so I commune with them through their books and films, their paintings and sculptures. When I can't sleep, I search the internet for new art. The first time I saw yours, I knew you were one of us."

"Us?" the other repeated in the soft woman's voice whose accent was unfamiliar to Jae.

"I say 'us' because you aren't at ease with the present. You want a new world."

"Are you the one having the affair with Michael?"

"No," the android said. "Our relationship is something society hardly understands. To be clear, I'm not sexual. That is, in part, why I love your work. I've worn many of your paintings. I'm at home inside your art. It's the future I wish I'd been born into."

The person in Michael's body stared at the android. "So what is the relationship then?"

"It is a love specific to us. Michael and I want to live in the same future. When I first saw your paintings, I was already designing virtual worlds. But your art made me realize that our error in virtuality is to want to be human again. Everyone tries to make a perfect human, and the effect is cartoonish. That's what limits us—our simplistic idea of what a person is."

"But this body I'm in, it's Michael's."

"It is right now," the android said. "I designed it to look this way so that it would make sense to you when you entered this world."

"What's the body he normally wears?"

"It's like mine. It's one of your creations."

The android turned and motioned to the amphitheater's center. A mirror rose from the floor. As Michael's image looked at it, he became a gleaming android staring at its reflection.

"Why did you lure me? Why are you playing games?" the woman's voice, speaking from the second android now, asked.

"We're all in a labyrinth, searching," the first android said. "You chose to follow us into this labyrinth. And by following, you helped us reinvent it."

"What do you want?"

"We hoped you'd join us in rethinking humanity. That's why I put your paintings here."

The first android motioned to the paintings placed in a circle around them. One of them was the same painting Simon had brought back for Jae—the woman in white robes making the golden man. It hung in her room now that her father could no longer go upstairs.

"Who are you?" the second android asked.

"My name?"

"Yes."

"Lux."

Jae pulled off her headset, put it in the workshop, and ran up to her room. She took down the painting and turned it over.

I have become a cave dweller. I migrate between two caves, one in which the frozen molecules of my unborn child have yet to become cellular, and the other in which I can inhabit Michael's world and reminisce. I relive our stories in our virtual Manhattan. I know that somewhere, in another America, he is doing the same.

She read the words many times—so many references to isolation, loneliness, to creating a self to speak to. Over and over, the lines mention an unborn child.

She returned to the shed, took the headset and console, and carried them into the living room. Her father lay on the bed. Lately he'd been more alert, able to speak with effort. He opened his eyes and looked from her face to the console. His gaze stayed on it for a long time.

"Do you recognize it?" she asked.

When he didn't answer, she put the headset on him. She placed the switch she'd attached to it in his good hand. She stood, unable to think, overwhelmed with this mystery. She didn't know how much time had passed when she lifted the headset off. There were tears in his eyes.

"What do you know?" he said slowly, his words somewhat slurred.

With a breath, she steadied herself and then described her search and all she'd found. He was staring ahead, his eyes slightly unfocused, as if he were remembering.

"That was always the risk with you," he said. "I had to be so careful."

"Of what?"

"All this is what the law calls 'illegal content.' It was never defined. It's just what the Fed says is illegal in order to encourage people to take salvage to the collection centers. Most do it for money, but it keeps them from knowing too much about how things used to be."

"Is Lux my mother?"

"Yes."

Jae shook her head. "Why is she a secret?"

"To keep you safe. If you wrote about this in a message, the police would be here in hours. If a child knew, they would vanish from school so that they wouldn't infect others. And if you—with the brain you have—if you knew even a little, you would try to learn more, and you would end up dead. Prison is for the crimes they don't care about. The drugs, the theft, even the murder. The worst crime is knowing."

"What is the world inside of this?" she asked, motioning to the console.

"It's the America I loved," he said haltingly. He took a long, uneven breath.

"From before the Flight?"

"Yes."

"So you remember the Flight?"

"I do."

"What was it?"

"It was terrible."

"What happened?" she asked, afraid to give him time to reconsider and stop speaking.

He sighed. "There were people who thought they were saving the country from great evil. You have to understand—that past, everything about it, can only harm us. You have the chance to create a new life in the satellites. That's all I've ever wanted."

In the December sunlight that streamed through the window, they stared at each other. Even now, he was refusing to give answers.

"You deserve to understand the world that's been trying to suffocate you your entire life," he said. "But knowing more could kill you. For the dwellers out here, it's not so dangerous. Their people, their parents and grandparents, they made this thing happen."

"And ours didn't?"

"No, we were their enemies. We were the evil they feared. Where do you think I got this scar? They imprisoned and tortured me, but I grew up out here. I knew how to speak to them. I convinced them that I was a simple technician."

Gradually, in her mind, the idea of Simon as an enemy was forming, or the offspring of enemies—but fortunate and safe for that reason. Not so much protected as unseen.

"What were you doing?" she asked.

"You have to let the past be. It's gone."

"It's not just the past. You were doing something. Those times you said you were going to the mountains, you went somewhere else. And you were recording everything in the house."

"No," he said with a severity softened by the muted half of his mouth. "We can't slip an inch. Those people—not the ones in power, they hardly care—but in the middle, who aren't the powerless dwellers out here and who never got the satisfaction of seeing their vision fully carried out—they're alert to people like us. They would destroy you."

"I've spent my whole life dreaming of being in the satellites," she said.

"That's the answer," he told her. "You must be harmless but essential. It was the only way to save you. Don't ask questions. Don't care about the past. Just give yourself a good life."

"Wouldn't I be working for the people who hurt you?"

"It doesn't matter anymore," he said. "It's been too long. Sooner or later, all of this will turn into something else. It always does. You can be part of that when it happens. But you must stop searching into the past. The answers will destroy everything you've worked to achieve."

The house and farm were quiet. She gazed out at the changing leaves on the mountains.

"Please," he finally said, and she expected him to repeat his request for her to stop searching, but he asked, "Can you put the headset on me again?" Tears worked down along the deep lines of his face. "I want to see that world again. I didn't realize that seeing it would break my heart. It's gone. All of them are gone." He was silent for a moment, staring out the window at the sky, and then he said, "My god, it wasn't perfect, but I loved it."

That night, as she lay in bed, she heard him whistle faintly, asking her if she was okay. She was surprised he could do this after the stroke and considered how much effort it must have required. But she didn't respond. She kept her eyes closed, pretending she was asleep.

When she wakes, the weather has turned. It's finally cold. Her breath mists as she descends the stairs. He opens his eyes, as if he's been waiting for her. They are still pale blue and clear, like relics in the thin, ashen topography of his face. This is the place in the past where she can find answers, where the machine can make another fork in time, a new past. But her original memories keep repeating, erasing her father even as he tries to tell her the truth.

She has seen this moment so many times. Her foot touches a step that creaks. He opens eyes almost white-blue and made even clearer by the contrast with his sun-darkened skin.

She comes down the stairs and calls his name, and he hears her and opens eyes bluer than she remembers.

She lies on the couch, alone in the house, waking in the machine's present. She remembers all the times her father woke up. She remembers the one time he didn't.

She got up, not from the couch as she'd thought, but from her bed. She descended the stairs and sat next to him, sensing his absence—she would later tell herself she was already certain from the stillness, as she'd been on the morning of his stroke. He lay on his back, his head sunk into the pillow and his hands on his chest. As if someone positioned him for a viewing. As if he'd been feeling for the last pulses of his heart. The large veins on his hands and his forearms had sunken to faint blue lines. Even now he looked strong, his jaw and neck muscled, his shoulders knotted. She put her hand on his. She tried to speak, to tell him she loved him, but she could only cry.

Eventually, she stood. Time seemed vague, lost in the house's stillness. She wanted to sit and keep crying, but she now felt empty. Her only thoughts were of what she had to do next—to deal with his death and not neglect school or lose track of her goals.

"Feel something," she whispered. She looked at her hands, surprised to see how sturdy they appeared. A lifetime of building things. She'd be okay. She had to be.

She picked up her tablet and messaged Simon. Then she went out back and searched through the sheds—through decades of salvaged material, seeing nothing that suited her purpose. With a hammer, she went into the house. All the external doors were reinforced and studded with locks, but the narrower door between the kitchen and the living room was made of simple wood planks. She tapped the pins from the hinges and then lifted it—heavier than she expected but manageable. She lay it on the floor next to the bed.

She returned to the sheds and took two shovels. Simon's car pulled into the driveway, and he jogged over to her. He tried to take her into his arms, but she just stood, holding the shovels, letting him enfold them as well.

"There's a lot to do," she said. She stepped back and motioned toward the orchard. "I'm going to bury him up there, on the edge of the forest."

The way Simon wordlessly studied her gave her the impression that he was once again that strange, unfamiliar boy watching from a distance at school. She hated needing his help. He followed her inside. They wrapped her father in a sheet and moved him onto the door and placed the shovels alongside him. Then they carried him out and up the incline and through the orchard.

She chose a place near a large oak. They put her father down beneath it and dug in silence. Sweat plastered her hair to her neck and ran along her shoulders and ribs, gathering at the waist of her pants. The day had warmed. She hadn't thought to bring water but didn't want to go back. She wished Simon would leave.

It must have been noon when he said, "I think it's deep enough." Both were soaked.

"You've done this before?" she asked.

"A few times."

She walked over to where her father lay and crouched, placing her hand on the back of his hand through the sheet, where it still rested on his chest. There was nothing she could say. It was better to come back later, alone, when everything was finished.

"Help me," she said.

Simon walked over and lifted the other end of the door. They carried it to the grave and lay it down. Holding the ends of the sheet, they gently lowered her father into the hole.

"I can do the rest by myself," she said. "I want to be alone."

He shrugged awkwardly and started to say, "If you need anything—"

"I know."

He left, and twenty minutes later, as she was slowly pushing the dirt inside, he returned and put down a water jug. He left again. She eventually drank from the jug, her palms raw and her muscles aching. Then she went back to filling the hole. When she finished, the sun was lowering, the air cooling fast. More clouds had blown through, gathering up the light.

"You should have told me everything," she said to the raw, level ground. "You shouldn't have left me like this." She knew he'd died to keep her from learning more. If she hadn't insisted, he'd still be alive.

The house was dark when she got back, nothing locked, but Simon was keeping watch, sitting on the porch.

"I'll give you some time to yourself," he said.

After he left, she sat in her father's room, which would never offer up secrets.

The next day, she remembered to eat. She went to school. It was what her father would have wanted. Her enrollment in the next nearest school had been accepted. The students there knew nothing about her and didn't care, and many of those in the previous school weren't there. Those who were appeared like ghosts, hardly speaking to others, drifting from class to class.

Each time Simon messaged to ask if she needed anything, she didn't respond. She no longer required his help. He would hold her back. Besides, his ancestors had somehow created this America. His absent father probably hadn't told him that, and his mother certainly hadn't. He was as innocent as she was. But in her father's words, he seemed safer. He belonged, even if dwellers were hated in the satellites. None of it made sense. Eventually he stopped messaging, though mornings she often woke to find food on her porch.

As the months passed, she continued exploring the world inside the headset, listening to conversations. She recognized the people now—Michael and Lux—and thought that the woman who'd briefly occupied Michael's form, as Jae sometimes did, was Ava. In several conversations, Michael and Lux discussed her. They also talked about a lab.

"Oz's ranting about biological crimes wasn't just a campaign promise," Lux said.

"Isn't it absurd to think," Michael replied, "that creating a human superior to any other that has ever lived could be a crime? And yet that's such a typical human response. What act of genius hasn't been punished, at least initially?"

"We have to consider," Lux told him, "that if the government finds out about our child, it could destroy it."

Jae reread the words on the back of the painting.

I migrate between two caves, one where the frozen molecules of my unborn child have yet to become cellular . . .

The first cave was the hidden room in which Simon had found the painting. The second one must be the lab. She had no idea where it could be. He'd mentioned other paintings. Maybe she would find the answer written on their backs.

That March began in a swelter. Weekends, she stayed indoors, using the headset. But Saturday, when she slid it on, finding herself on a residential street, a young couple was walking past, holding hands, talking and laughing. The girl's skirt flapped at her tanned knees. The boy's muscled shoulders stretched his T-shirt. A yellow car printed with the word *Taxi* glided past. Wind blew along the street, rustling the leaves of trees growing up from the sidewalk.

She pulled off the headset. The walls startled her with their nearness—everything small and dingy. She lay on the bed and slid her hand into her pants, running her fingers along her skin, but stopped. She needed more than this. She'd hardly spoken to anyone in months.

She took her tablet and opened a text thread with Simon. She knew he'd do whatever she wanted. Speak to her or touch her or help her go to the shell with the secret room. But she couldn't just ask for that, not after everything, not when she still didn't want him in her life.

She wrote, *Can you come over?* but kept hesitating. This was a mistake. One look at him, and anyone would see he had no future. As if of its own accord, her finger pressed send.

He arrived early that afternoon, parking the same battered sedan. She didn't invite him inside but asked if he wanted to walk. She hadn't planned this. The words just came out of her. He nodded. He was thinner, with dark circles under his eyes.

They followed a trail—not near the cabin but past land leveled before the Flight, where huge shells once overlooked the farms below and were now hidden in tangles.

The muggy afternoon air cooled slightly in the forest but was hotter each time they emerged on a stony ridge. At a vista, they could see her family's land, bordered by abandoned and rewilded farms. Scattered across the valley, slash-and-burn plots dented the tangles. Thin smoke plumes rose from fields being cleared.

"With the Fed developing land nearby, I might actually be able to sell the farm," she said.

"Your family's land is way better than mine. Can you keep it and still go to university?" he asked, sounding wistful, as if he might want to live here.

"Even if a scholarship pays tuition and some of my expenses, I'll barely have enough to cover other costs. I've heard what happens to struggling women in the satellites."

She glanced sidelong, trying to see what was different in him. He was no longer the typical stoic dweller. Something was breaking down that face. She thought of his dead mother and absent father and the brother he rarely mentioned. Then it occurred to her that the haunted look might be the result of her joining the long list of people who'd abandoned him.

They climbed higher, past collapsed fieldstone fences that wended through the trees. Her father had told her that families farmed up here centuries ago. Maybe those ancient farmers had built the cabin, but the stone foundations she and Simon now passed seemed older even than the cabin. Nothing in the simple depictions in her history book could explain her place in time.

Deeper in the forest, they came to a gently sloping sheet of granite hemmed in by trees. Where sunlight struck the stone, the air felt hot and gassy in her lungs. Water poured across the edge of the granite, and they followed it into the shadow. A pool bubbled up from jumbled rock wedged apart by tree roots. She wiped the sweat from her eyes with her forearm and crouched. Dipping her hands into the water, she was surprised by how cold it was.

"Feel this," she said.

He squatted next to her and touched the water. They drank and splashed their faces. He yawned, shaking his head, as if only now waking up.

They lingered at the edge of the pool, knees almost touching.

"This is big enough to swim in," she said. "I bet it would feel good in this heat."

He glanced around, suddenly appearing worried.

"What is it?" she asked.

He gave his head a curt shake. "I don't know."

She took his damp hand in both of hers and turned it palm up. Its long, yellow callouses were as hard and polished as turtle shell. In her numb fingers, his skin felt hot.

His pupils seemed too large. She had the impression of looking at a wild animal—a deer turning to see her the second before it bolts. Touching him, she remembered the power of her desire before grief overshadowed everything. Longing now moved through the nerves of her face and jaw and throat like the overwhelming taste of something she could never have enough of.

"Let's swim," she said and began pulling off her clothes. The breeze shifted, pushing the hot air above the exposed granite against them, making her eager to feel the water.

She was naked. Simon looked at her and away, his blue eyes flashing in his tanned face as he tried to pick a point to stare at. She plunged into the spring, gasping. It was deeper than it looked. She stretched her legs, her toes touching rocks and roots.

"It's freezing," she told him. "Come on."

He was staring at her now. With the light at his back, his face was dark—perhaps from blushing. He pulled off his T-shirt and then undid his pants, sliding them down with his underwear. He got in the water, but rather than gasping, he yawned, rubbing his face. He leaned his head back and kneaded the muscles of his neck and sighed.

She floated closer and wrapped her arms around him and kissed him. *Contact.* A cold word. Mechanical. But she craved it. As if she were a metal node connected to nothing and even the faint current between them was enough.

"Too cold," he whispered. He got out and lay on the granite, in the shadow of the trees. Gooseflesh raised the skin on her arms and thighs as she got on top of him. They made love like that, slowly, as he stared up at her, his eyes so open she felt he was trying to read her face.

She was moving her hands from his chest to his shoulders when she saw the line on his arm. It resembled one of the creases between his muscles—the thin tattoo of a chain with a fanged snake's head. She didn't know how she'd missed it.

She stopped. "What's that?" She touched it, rubbing it as if to remove it.

"Nothing. My brother did it."

Though she was afraid, her desire remained. He seemed to wake up. Turning, he lay her back on the stone. He moved harder against her and into her, panting, his palms planted. Pushing his hips, he suddenly bore down with his full weight, coming inside her.

Neither moved. He slowly rolled off her, onto the granite. They stared at the sky.

"I shouldn't have done that," he said.

She began dressing. She'd been wrong to use sex to bypass their hurt, as if redirecting a charge with a wire, but what he'd done was more terrible. Everyone knew pregnant women couldn't attend university.

She set a fast pace back to the house, staring straight ahead. The tattoo on his arm told her everything she'd always known. He had no future and was now trying to destroy hers.

"I'm sorry," he called from behind her.

She didn't look at him. She didn't want to see that frozen dweller face.

Going down a steep hill, she put her hand out to steady herself. The thorn of a small plant snared her fingertip.

When they reached his car, he again said, "I'm sorry."

She turned to him. His eyes were bloodshot and even more shadowed.

"Go home," she told him.

The muscles of his jaw clenched and unclenched, and he hung his head like an old dog. His big, blunt face looked incapable of feeling.

"Go away," she said, realizing she'd intended to ask for help getting the paintings.

"Are you going to be okay?"

"Yes," she said, hesitating. He stood there. Her rage was too strong. "Go away," she repeated. "I'm sick of your face. It's like you don't feel anything at all."

SIMON

As the cracked highways opened before him, he began to sweat. Under the seat, he had the eight-shot revolver and the Uzis, each with a clip holding thirty-two bullets. He'd gone over the plan, considering each step coldly, as if his death weren't likely. There was no point going in loaded since Dell kept watch on the parking lot. Instead, Simon would pick up his deliveries for the day, run them, and drop off the cash. Then, as he was getting into his car to leave—when Dell would be least on guard—Simon would shoot him, sprint inside, and fire the Uzis. He'd tested them in the forest. They emptied in seconds. He had to aim well. He'd have one chance.

At the warehouse, Simon picked up a backpack filled with small packages. After delivering them, when he was returning with the cash, his hands began to tremble on the steering wheel. He sweated through his shirt. He pulled onto the roadside to do a small hit of abyss. It barely calmed him, but if he took more, he might pass out and have his money and guns and even his car stolen. There must be a better plan, but he couldn't think of one. He couldn't linger in the parking lot waiting for Stryker to come out. Dell would notice anything unusual.

Simon drove back to the warehouse, parked, and went inside. He walked to the table where Stryker sat with Brit and three men. All of them had guns on the tabletop next to ashtrays and dirty glasses of corn whiskey.

As Simon counted out the money, Stryker studied his face.

"Careful, boy," he said. "I see everything."

Simon looked up from the cash, into Stryker's eyes—brightly bloodshot from smoke and drink and whatever else.

"What you do with your earnings is your business so long as it doesn't mess with my business," Stryker said. "Go easy on what you're hitting. Got it?"

Simon nodded. He straightened and, with his pay, walked out to his car. The sun was low enough that Dell no longer sheltered in the ledge of shadow beneath the overhang but was pacing across the parking lot in the cooling evening. He didn't so much as glance at Simon. He was staring up at the satellite wall, at the bright flecks of flying cars.

"Simon," Brit called. He turned. She was in the doorway and neared him slowly. "Are you sick?" she asked.

"Naw," he said. "I don't know. I just . . ." He lowered his voice, not wanting Dell to hear. "Just tired, I guess."

Standing in front of him now, she looked so small. She wore a black tank top that showed the thin, birdlike bones of her collar and shoulders, and the dark tattoos over her arms. When he glanced at them, she said, "I grew up with brothers. They did these. I had them all by the time I was thirteen. They probably thought they were protecting me, and I suppose they weren't wrong."

"But the Strykers?" he said.

"It's a job." She hesitated. "Listen. I see what's in your face. All of us—every bodyguard, even Stryker—we all know what future to expect. We all get the look you got in your eyes. It don't take a doctor to know what is. Just go home and sleep. Put some of that money to food."

"Did Stryker tell you to talk to me?" he asked, not knowing why it mattered.

Her expression softened. "No. I been here long enough. I do what I want. This show don't run without me. I've outlived everybody, even my brothers."

Her words struck him as odd. Her head barely reached his chest. She looked like a gaunt child with dark circles under her eyes, but he had no idea how old she was. He had an impulse to wrap his arms around her, but she seemed to sense it and took a small step back.

"You're a good kid, Simon. I'm sorry you got into all this. But be patient. Don't climb the ranks. Just do the job. Don't make a big deal about anything. That's the best way through." She tilted her head slightly, looking up at him, and a strand of blond hair fell across her face. He wanted to lift his hand and brush it behind her ear. "Just remember things ain't better anywhere else," she said. "Just different versions of bad. Make do with this one. Get some sleep. Eat. Go find a girl who'll give you the touching you need. All the human stuff. You'll be okay."

She took a step back, turned, and went inside. She was right, he thought. It wasn't her. It might not even be Jae. He just needed someone.

The drive home was one long exhale. At his house, when he opened the rusty gate and the front door, the humidity and must of the closed rooms felt suffocating. He unlatched the metal window shutters and sat on the porch as the rank air vented into the early evening. He felt gutted. Adrenaline had burned through him and left a hollow, bloodless body.

He took a pink crystal from his pocket and held it. No. Not yet. He had to check on Jae and help with Arthur. More abyss. And he should eat. His clothes hung loosely.

He drove to her house. After he'd helped bathe Arthur and put him to bed, she showed him the console in the workshop. Outside, between the sheds, he put on the headset and a world flickered into existence. Rushing streets. Gleaming buildings. Mostly, though, he stared at the people. He expected them to recoil at the sight of him, as if they'd walked up on a rattler, but they took no notice. He glanced down at clothes that weren't his. His hands were metallic.

He pulled the headset off and handed it to her.

"Must be worth a bunch," he said.

Her eyes widened with surprise. "What do you think of the city?"

"It's a lot," he told her. *Another place I wouldn't belong*, he wanted to say but didn't.

"It's from before the Flight."

"It's not a satellite?"

"No. It's another part of America. I don't know if it still exists."

He tried to make sense of what she'd said, but his brain was too slow. He shrugged. "I need sleep."

Jae hadn't touched him. She kept glancing at his face.

Only later, at home, lying on his bed, did he feel any curiosity about that world before the Flight. He thought of the school's destruction and the custodian's words about the forgotten heroes who'd saved America. From his earliest years, he had faint memories of his father speaking to other men of all they'd been promised for their sacrifices but hadn't gotten.

He snorted bliss and later woke in the night from that perfect world with a chest packed with hurt. The abyss was close and he took it, closed his eyes, and then it was morning. A message from the Strykers was on his phone. Late, he sniffed a speck and rushed toward the satellite, afraid his car would break on the fractured roads.

When he went into the warehouse, Pete was playing cards with the bodyguards. Simon hadn't seen him much lately, and it took him a moment to realize that Pete was no longer dealing. He was a bodyguard now. His pistol lay on the table next to a glass of whiskey.

Maybe Stryker was suspicious and put Pete there for protection, knowing Simon would have to kill his brother. Maybe Pete was just climbing.

As Brit gave Simon his deliveries for the day, he glanced at her eyes. Seeing their faint, almost imperceptible warmth, he felt calmer.

When he left, Pete and the other men were engrossed in their cards, their arms tatted with serpents, dragons, and tusked demons. Pete hadn't so much as looked at him.

Back in his car, Simon had a memory of them as boys, sitting on the bed as he read salvaged pages about a battle with a demon lord. Those worlds standing against evil seemed so pure, as if a time once existed when evil was condensed into a few terrifying figures, unlike now, when it seemed to pervade everyone in small, corrupting doses.

Feverish, dreaming or remembering inside the machine, he no longer knows how many days passed before the morning Jae messaged him to say that Arthur had died. Together they carried Arthur through the orchard. Once they'd dug the hole, she told him to leave.

He waited at the house. When she returned, dirt covered her clothes. Tears streaked her dusty face. Her hands bled, and her hair was wild. She glared as if outraged to see him there, as if he should have left the open house unwatched. She told him to go home.

Over those weeks, he felt nothing. He stopped thinking about his plan but left the guns under his seat, telling himself he'd eventually do it. Days passed. Days of bliss and abyss. Maybe Jae's silence was grief. Maybe she simply no longer needed him now that Arthur was gone. He considered telling the Strykers that he'd stopped seeing her, but that would be less likely to take her off their radar than to put her more firmly on it. Maybe they would hurt her or do something to make her his. He'd grown up hearing stories about league loyalty and justice.

Then came the day she called. When he got to her house, she was reading on the porch. She sat where Simon, when he isn't on the couch, has been for days, locked in these memories, as if in the trance of bliss, sweating lightly. He paces away from the porch but then turns back. He takes a step in her direction before letting himself look at her face. The desire to touch her flares through the haze in his brain. When he sees her studying him, he doesn't flinch.

He nods. He has no words. He waits as if partially roused from sleep, knowing he will soon drift off again. He expects her to tell him to go away. Instead, they walk. Today, she will see him for what he is. He can't prevent that.

They cross through the orchard, neither speaking, and then into the forest, past shells and up along the mountainside, into the old, abandoned parkland with its towering trees and dark, open forest floors, so unlike the tangles on rewilded land. By the time they reach the vista over the valley, the tiny dose of abyss is wearing off. Staring at her farm, he thinks of making a life. Of creating. Of bliss. He craves to see glowing, brilliant suns strung along the horizon.

"You have the best land in this valley," he says. Her farm has always been maintained. It was never rewilded and cut back to stumpy earth. He feels the urge that he experiences so strongly after bliss—to create, to build. He could do something with this land.

They continue until they reach the granite slab. He is more and more awake. A cold spring—a deep, clear pool—pours water across the stone.

"It's hot," she says. "Let's cool off."

She undresses and slides naked into the spring. He follows, gasping at the cold. He expects flies and mosquitoes buzzing in the shadows, but the air beneath the trees is clear. She puts her arms around him. Her caresses feel far away. He's at the center of all he wants yet distant, as if on those prismatic plains. His life hangs on the horizon, a mirage of shifting light.

They are soon too cold. On the warm stone, in the sunlight, she makes love to him. A vision flashes before him, of the farm planted, of her and their child. He rolls her onto her back. He comes without pleasure, not realizing he's done so until he is pulling away, shocked by his betrayal. She stares at the sky, her eyes wide, as if she's suddenly waking.

He lies next to her. He has a thought so distant it feels like a memory. *If she gets pregnant, she can't leave me.* He looks at his shoulder. A tattoo slowly appears—a barbed chain with a fanged snake's head. The Strykers' league sign, confirming he was chained to them. He recalls an evening he can't place. Pete and Dell came to the house with friends and were handing out freely. Simon woke with the bleeding tattoo, his skin hot and infected. He had bruises on his ribs and chest and hips but no memory of a fight. Jae must have seen the tattoo. She knew what he was becoming. His chest hurt. Maybe the Sons of Death were right. Living for hunger was easier. Simon should have disappeared after the night he attacked Jae. The sunlight on his eyelids is hot but soothing. When he looks again, the tattoo is gone—a broken-off piece of memory.

He sits up slowly and stares at Jae. She lies on the hot stone, smiling. When she opens her eyes, there's no anger in them. She reaches for him, pulling him close, shaping her body to his. He touches her without regret or fear. They kiss and explore. He kneels on the granite. Everything is painless, effortless. He lifts her, holding her against him.

Then, like a pustule bursting in summer's humid heat, the past is there again—her expression of shock seeing the tattoo, her rage after sex.

"Go home," she said when she reached the porch.

He clenched the muscles of his face, trying to find a way to speak.

"Go away," she told him.

"Are you going to be okay?" he asked.

"Yes." She must have caught her hand on a thorn walking back. Brushing hair from her eyes, she left a red streak on her forehead.

He stood, trying to appear strong and calm. As she stared, she lifted her upper lip with disgust. His jaw ached. Pressure gathered in his temples. He had no right to cry.

"Go away," she said again. "I'm sick of your face. You don't feel anything."

He walked to his truck, started the engine, and backed onto the road. He didn't let himself glance at the house. In his periphery, she was there, a haggard figure in the growing dark.

He drove the broken, winding road home and stood in the dingy living room, opening and closing his hands. He went into the bathroom. The mirror was so flyspecked and corroded and splattered with saliva that he was only a dull silhouette. He grabbed a rag from the floor, wet it, and scrubbed the glass. Then he stood, holding the sink, staring at the blue, bloodshot eyes, the thick brow ridge, the high cheekbones, the long, blunt jaw, the hints of blond stubble, the scars. His face crinkled suddenly. He spun away from the mirror.

He'd chosen this face. He'd been thirteen. That summer, Pete had often been gone, and Simon salvaged alone for weeks at a time, walking narrow paths through the tangles that seemed to stretch on forever behind his house. Though he sometimes feared running afoul of other salvagers, he didn't mind working alone. It gave him more time to look for words.

He crossed the remains of a road. The trees weren't very dense there, and he paused at each gutted shell, studying the land around it, thinking where in the loam he might scrape up some salvage. Farther on there was a parking lot where trees had taken root in cracks. Their trunks now pushed up the asphalt around them, each one appearing to grow from a pockmark in the earth. Just beyond the lot was a long, low-slung building—an old store of some sort.

He checked the doorframe for signs and then stepped in. At the center of the large room, the roof had disintegrated, leaving only blackened wooden beams. The remains of a campfire were just below, a heap of charred sticks at its center. The air had the rank tang of soured meat. Hairs stood up on the back of his neck. Someone had butchered animals here not that long ago.

The light from the hole in the ceiling, filtering through the forest canopy, wasn't strong, but it allowed him to see a heap of garbage against the wall. Even as he was turning to leave, he stared, squinting. In places, the refuse had the serrated look of old, broken-spined books.

He put his hand on his knife. Ma had made Pete and Simon vow never to go salvaging alone or without the rifle, but Pete was away and had taken their only gun. Simon crossed the room and knelt next to the trash—shreds of old plastic, matted newspaper, and rotten books. He was reaching for them when he saw the hole in the nearby wall. It was at floor level and the size of his fist. Scattered around it were small pieces of gnawed bone. Inside there was a flicker of movement and then two yellow eyes. A kitten pushed its head into the light and mewed.

"Shhh," he whispered. He'd seen a few cats in the tangles over the years. Pete had told him that people used to eat them back in the day if no better-tasting wildlife was available. Some folks were now even taking in litters of feral cats to keep mice out of their houses.

Simon moved over to the kitten and held out his hand. It pushed against his fingers, purring. He felt the vibrations deep in his fingertips. It was pleasant. He'd take it home if it weren't for what Pete or Ma would say. Then the kitten mewed so loudly Simon jerked his hand back. It mewed again and again and nudged the chunks of bone with its nose. It wanted food. Simon looked to the campfire's remains. His eyes had adjusted to the shadow. What he'd taken for burnt wood was bones. The kitten was mewing more urgently. He glanced at the trash, at the clear shapes of old books—decayed but more intact than most.

He stood and stomped his foot, and the kitten darted into the hole. He ran to the trash pile and took three books—those he could easily make out—knowing instantly from their feel that they were too rotten. He turned toward the door.

Two men stood there, big and bearded, their printed clothes so old it adhered to their muscles. Both had pistols and knives on their belts, and one held a rifle.

"Sorry," he told them. "I didn't see a mark on the door."

Neither spoke. The one with the rifle leveled it. The other just walked close. Without warning, he punched Simon in the face, splitting his forehead and knocking him onto his back. Then he knelt on his ribs. The weight forced the air from Simon's lungs. In a single swift movement, the man looped a thin cord around his wrists, pulled it tight, and knotted it.

"I'm just a kid," Simon was saying as the gash in his forehead bled into one eye. Those words and apologies kept coming out of him. He told them they could have whatever they wanted. As one man searched Simon, taking his knife and pliers and flashlight, the other put his rifle down and began undoing Simon's belt. Simon stopped talking. It made sense that they'd steal his clothes. If they didn't kill him, he could walk home naked through the tangles.

Boots and pants—the men took everything, untying him to take his shirt while one gripped his wrists with hands like iron. Then they walked him to the back of the room, pulled his arms above his head, and tied the cord binding his wrists to a ceiling beam. One went through his pack while the other undid his own buckle and pulled down his pants. He took Simon's hips in hands that felt huge and coarse. Simon wanted to scream. He didn't know this was possible. He grit his teeth, refusing to show pain as the man grunted, reeking of moonshine. Simon's skin began going numb, as if he was leaving his body. He stared up. He could see clearly with only one eye. The knots were clumsy and loose. Just in time, he realized that he should brace himself and not pull at the rope. The man kept thrusting, the pain blistering. Simon held himself steady. He focused on the knots, not letting his weight pull them tight.

Suddenly, the man pushed hard, shuddering and digging his fingers into Simon's hips. The other one walked over. He took his turn. Simon tried not to feel. There was blood on his legs. The second man finished. Then both went into the forest, leaving him tied up standing.

Simon's legs began shaking so violently he thought he'd fall. He forced them steady, afraid of putting weight on the rope. He studied the knots. He heard the men speaking gruffly outside—not their words but their argumentative tone. They must want to kill him. No one could rob someone, much less do this, without starting a feud.

One pair of boots clomped back and Simon's legs shook again. He urinated uncontrollably, more piss than he thought his body could hold. Then it all started over. The man digging his fingers. Blood puddled around Simon's feet, and all through it he kept from pulling on the rope. The man finished and left again, doing up his belt as he went outside.

On the knot closest to the beam, Simon worked fast, bending and pinching at it. He shoved a fingertip through the rough fibers and pulled it apart. Quietly as possible, he slid the rope down, gathering it in his hand. There was no time to release his wrists. He stepped gently toward a narrow hallway at the back of the building, hoping for an exit. A few small rooms on the sides were heaped with salvage. Father on, a doorway opened onto the tangles.

He listened. Distantly he could hear their muffled voices. He placed his steps carefully so as not to rustle leaves or break a twig. He went right into the tangles, not searching for a trail. Branches and thorns dragged at his skin.

When he finally looked back, the building was gone. The tangles were close all around, quiet but for the birds. With his teeth, he worked at the knot. Little by little, he freed his wrists.

Moving was still slow but easier. He thought of the animals he'd hunted. The men must be looking.

That night, he reached his house. He washed up at the basin and cleaned and patched the cut on his forehead. He put on the only other pants he had—old and torn and a little too small.

Pete came back a few hours later with eyes red from drinking. As he flopped down on his bed across from Simon's, he glanced over. "Why the face?" he said. "Don't be such a pussy. A fight and a few days alone isn't the end of the world." Then he lay back and fell asleep.

Simon went into the bathroom and rubbed clean a spot on the mirror. Seeing himself, he started to cry, but he clenched the muscles of his face, locking them in place. He stood like that, glaring. He promised himself that no one would see anything. No one would ever know. He thought of Jae then, of what he'd done to her.

"I want to stop remembering," he tells the mirror. His reflection fades and beyond it are the plains of flowers and the suns floating along the horizon. The borders of the glass melt into the wall and spread until he can step through. He wanders into space that feels endless. Every rock and stream and tree and building is alive, shifting as if he sees how objects take form in the imagination, constantly changed by the current of his thoughts. Maybe God does exist and this world is his imagination. Simon does not feel alone, though he sees no one else.

He wants to stay here but already he is waking into memory, lying in his bed, bliss and abyss on a plate on the floor. On his phone there was a message from the Strykers. He dressed and sniffed the tiniest amount of abyss. The muscles along his neck and throat loosened. Grief unspooled within him and fell away like a rope dropped from a great height. He sighed and rubbed his cheeks. His face didn't seem so locked, so blunt and masklike.

He got in his sedan and followed the thin, dusty strip of road through the tangles to the ever-widening highways. Far off, the satellite towers stood ranked against the sky. In the shadow of the wall, he took an exit through the clustered warehouses and construction zones.

When he pulled into the parking lot, the Strykers were outside, gathered around a gleaming purple sports car. Stryker was showing it to Dell and Brit and two other bodyguards. All of them were smiling and laughing. Pete wasn't there. He and the others might have been inside.

As Simon parked, Stryker waved him over. The others barely glanced. Stryker turned back to the purple car. Simon pulled up on the door handle, releasing the latch. He put his revolver into the waistband of his jeans and took the Uzis from under the seat. Then, with his knee, pushed the door open.

He was shooting before he was standing. Smoke rose from the muzzles. Holes punched across the sports car's panels. Windows shattered. Stryker went down and then Dell and the other two men.

Brit reached for her pistol and spun, falling to her knees. As both clips emptied, Simon dropped the Uzis and drew the revolver.

Stryker was on his back, bleeding fast as he squirmed, unable to sit up. Dell was pushing himself up, his shirtfront red. Moving his mouth like a fish's, he lifted his pistol. Simon jumped away from his car as a side window popped. Holding the revolver above his head, he flung himself to the ground and rolled as Dell kept firing. Simon shot him in the face. Another bodyguard was struggling to get up, and Simon put a bullet through his chest. As if in the calm of a bliss dream, Simon stood and stepped over to the sports car and shot Stryker in the head.

Only Brit was still alive, blinking at the sky in a semblance of peace. He took the gun from her hand and set it aside and looked at her. There was a hole in her throat. Blood was puddling fast around her. He lifted her shirt. Three more holes, one in her stomach and two in her chest. He was crying. "I'm sorry," he told her. Holding her hand, he shot her.

No one had come out from the building. He thought that Pete must not be here. He didn't let himself look at Brit. Tears streamed along his throat. On the passenger seat of the sports car was a backpack covered in glass shards. He took it, knowing from its weight that it was filled with bliss.

He jogged to his car, put the pack and guns on the passenger seat, and shifted into reverse. Still crying, he backed away from the warehouse and onto the road.

AVA

The air was permeated with light, concentrated around the paintings and the statue. It was the glow of reverence, just as she might have painted it.

"I'm very happy you're here," the statue said, its voice low and soft.

"Who are you?" Ava asked. This must be Michael's lover.

"I knew about you before Michael did."

"How?"

"I'm the one who told him about your art. I've loved it for years—since the first time I saw it. Most of the people I would have liked to know are dead, so I commune with them through their books and films, their paintings and sculptures. When I can't sleep, I search the internet for new art. The first time I saw yours, I knew you were one of us."

"Us?" Looking into the face of her messiah, she had a pang of fear, the sense that she might have a stalker, a psychopathic admirer who loved her work so much that she wanted to embody it. Ava was suddenly certain this person had been watching every time she'd been in the virtual Manhattan and that Michael hadn't been the one leaving paintings and clues for her. Ava tried to imagine who the person animating the messiah must be. Clearly, Michael trusted them. Ava told herself not to be afraid. She had to believe that the foundation of her life was sound.

"I say 'us' because you aren't at ease with the present. You want a new world."

Ava was silent. This was true. She wasn't at ease, but she didn't know many people who were. And she didn't paint from a place of certainty. She questioned. She was as unsure and afraid of the future as she was of the past.

"Are you the one having the affair with Michael?" Ava asked, wanting to assert her power and unsettle this person who was, after all, her admirer.

"No. Society has no word for our relationship. To be clear, I'm not sexual. That is, in part, why I've worn many of your paintings. I'm at home inside your art."

Again, Ava didn't speak. She studied the figure before her. To say that the rendering of the robot messiah was perfect would be an understatement. It breathed life. It couldn't have been made like this unless it had received the same care that Ava had given it in her paintings. The irony, Ava thought, was that this person was more at home in Ava's work than she was herself.

"So," she said, "what's the relationship, then?" She'd so fully decided that Michael had another lover that now she needed time to undo that notion.

"Michael and I understand each other. We want to live in the same world. When I first saw your paintings, I was already designing virtual worlds. But your art made me realize that our error in virtuality is to want to be human again. Everyone tries to make a perfect human, and the effect is cartoonish. That's what limits us—our simplistic idea of what a person is."

"But this body I'm in, it's Michael's."

"It is right now. I designed it that way so it would make sense to you."

Ava realized all at once that for some reason she'd been lured here.

"What's the body he normally wears?"

"It's like mine. It's one of your creations."

The figure turned and motioned to the amphitheater's center. A large, gilded mirror rose from the floor. Ava saw her reflection—Michael's—in the second it became a gleaming android.

"Why did you lure me here?" she asked.

"We're all in a labyrinth, searching. You chose to follow us into this labyrinth. And by following, you helped us reinvent it."

Ava nodded. She understood the answer. She didn't know if she liked it.

"And you also lured us," Lux said.

"How so?"

"With your art. You did not send it out into emptiness. I recall the first time I saw it—the humans and angels and the messiah. The robot angels were functional. They appeared built to carry out a task, with well-created metal bodies and synthetic filament wings, but they were not art and by not being so, they allowed the messiah to become divine. The messiah was not built for simple utility. They were an expression of grace. Almost their entire body, inside and out, was made of sensors. They'd shaped themselves to feel existence as fully as possible."

Ava said nothing. She'd sold plenty of art, but no one had spoken about it this way. For the first time, she felt as if her vision wasn't hers alone.

"Your messiah is also closer to being one with the world because it is free of so many constraints. It does not carry as much history or evolution in its body. This is how I first found you. There was an article in which the author said that no human term or pronoun for gender made sense for an android messiah. They referenced your work. So I looked you up. I wondered what it would be like to talk to you. I wondered if you would someday go further and release the messiah from our limiting humanity. Two legs. Two arms. A head with two eyes pegged to the front like a predator's. Why not let it be a tree? Or a city? Or the Earth?"

"What do you want?" Ava asked.

Lux tilted their head—the messiah's—the face with so many brilliant circuits and sensors it looked bejeweled. They gestured to the circle of paintings.

"We are hoping that you will join us in rethinking humanity."

"Who are you?" Ava asked.

"My name?"

"Yes."

"Lux."

Ava now recalled the brief introduction at the party the night the photo was taken with Michael and Arthur. Lux was name of the drab, nondescript white person in the hoodie.

"I thought you were a geneticist," she said.

"I'm like Michael. I'm many things. I have spent much of my free time in virtual spaces, trying to create a world in which I can thrive."

"The note," Ava told them, "in the observatory on the asteroid. It said, 'For you, my dear.' That's just friendship?"

The robot messiah—the very figure Ava had once imagined struggling to reconcile the bewildering future with the primeval mystery of existence—stood motionless before her.

"That was for you."

Ava searched for a response. "Is this a game?" she asked. She imagined a plot against her.

"No," Lux said. "It's just a different way of speaking. We are trying to create a world that brings people's minds together in new ways."

"So I was a guinea pig?"

"Not at all. You are a public artist, and your work inspires others. It is inspiring the city we are creating and our visions for the future. That is the nature of art. You were speaking and we listened. Now we are speaking and you chose to listen."

Ava needed to think about all of this. Pacing around the amphitheater, she looked at the Earth suspended on the massive pillars above. She didn't yet know how she felt about what Lux and Michael were creating. She couldn't imagine making her own art here.

She crossed to the outside of the circle of her paintings and looked back in, at the robot messiah watching her. On the back of the nearest painting were words.

"What are these?" she asked.

"My journal," Lux said, and though they were far away, their voice sounded close. "I write the ideas that each painting brings to mind, and I see what I can create in this world."

Ava remembers. Until now, she has forgotten this detail. She stops the flow of her memories, opening her eyes in the blue room. She didn't want the machine to conjure this scene. She wanted to see it as it had lived within herself.

She stands up. "Take me back to the storage room," she tells the machine, and instantly she is with her stored paintings in the secret room near Michael's underground apartment. She slides one from the rack. Tiny words cover the back of the canvas.

"Was Lux here after Partition?"

"They were. There were many traces of their DNA throughout this space."

"And they wrote these?" she asks.

"Most of them," the machine tells her. "Some were written by a young man named Simon. He lived nearby and collected words. He brought his collected words here and copied them onto the backs of your canvases, adding them to Lux's."

Ava looks at the back of a painting. The difference between the two handwritings is evident. There are Lux's tiny letters:

> I have always been alone in some way. I thrived on being alone as a child. It was safer. Truer to myself. But this solitude brings the truth to me that I was never fully alone so long as I could communicate with people whom I never intended to meet.

And there are blockier letters in the remaining spaces:

> tell that its sculptor well those passions read
> which yet survive, stamped on these lifeless things

None of these words are the same as those written on the backs of the virtual paintings. Lux simply journaled on the paintings again, years later, during their long isolation.

Ava attempts to fathom how horrible it must have been for Lux here, retreating beneath the earth, trying to commune with Ava through her art. She hoped the paintings provided some solace. The thought strikes her as ridiculous and arrogant. She can't imagine Lux's pain.

I am connected to them. I had a child with them. Against my will. Without my permission.

She knows Lux and Michael would have had an eloquent explanation for this too.

The night after speaking to Lux inside the virtual city, Ava told Michael everything. He mostly already knew. He sat in a chair by the window, his head slightly lowered, listening. When she finished her story, he spoke softly.

"I've wanted to work with you for years."

"But why lure me?"

He lifted his jaw slightly, his gaze meeting hers.

"Do you realize how hard it is to get your attention when you are inspired?"

"So my work is the problem?"

"No. I love your work. I love to see you inspired. I have even largely accepted that you will not create inside virtuality. But I had to try . . . I had to try to seduce you again." He paused, his eyes wet and bright as he looked away from her, trying to mask his emotion. "As for my bond with Lux, you don't have to worry about that. It's purely creative and intellectual."

"Do you love them?"

He turned his face back to her and blinked slowly, composing himself, it seemed.

"Sometimes," he said, "when we work together, it's as if we share a single mind. I guess it's a form of love, but it can't be compared to ours."

Even as jealousy burned through her, she told herself she had no right to it. She'd refused every attempt Michael had made to work with her. Maybe she hadn't understood how important her art was to him or how much he'd craved the experience of creating something with her.

"Why did you never tell me about Lux?" she asked.

"There's a lot I don't discuss. Sometimes when people speak about their visions or collaborations, simply witnessing another person trying to understand can change the creator's perception of their own work. It's often better to wait until inspiration has found its form."

As he hesitated, what came to mind for her were the things we hold sacred, those numinous experiences that, no matter how we describe them, can't be transmitted. She'd felt this with her art. Again, maybe unfairly, her jealousy flared.

"What I have with you," he said, "it's not at risk. There's nothing that can take its place." But while saying this, he'd looked briefly distracted, as if he'd had another thought.

"What?"

"It's nothing."

"Tell me. We're sharing everything now. No more games."

His brow furrowed. "It's not about this."

"What's it about?"

He shook his head. "I spoke with the man who takes care of the land. He said that many local whites—men he's known since elementary—no longer speak to him. They're stocking up on firewood and food and generators. He said there are rumors they're stocking up on guns too."

She didn't understand how he could be thinking about this now, during this conversation.

"It can't be that serious," she said.

"I don't know. I hope I didn't make a mistake."

She thought he was talking about the house they'd grown to love, but his expression was again distracted. After all she'd discovered, she hadn't imagined that he was hiding more.

Two days later, over breakfast on the morning of New Year's Eve, he said, "I built something normal. A virtual convenience store. The owner has agreed to be an AI-automated character. It will be the city's first landmark based on a real person, and the first virtual convenience store. The man immigrated from Bangladesh ten years ago and bought the store within eight years. The *New York Times* will run an article about this. When you buy anything in the store, you find a map inside leading to one of the city's wonders, and he profits."

"That makes sense. Otherwise what's the point of buying virtual food?" she said, still not entirely at ease with him. Over the previous days, they had spoken more about Lux, but their discussion didn't feel complete. To Ava, it seemed that completion required that she agree to work with him.

"We're planning a beta launch at the same time as the article," he told her. "Half a billion people own VR headsets and can now walk through Manhattan." He hesitated, waiting until she looked up and into his eyes. "Imagine the audience this could give your work."

She smiled and said, "Well, it seems as if you've put my paintings everywhere in your city, so I guess I got the audience without having to change my medium of expression."

He smiled, shrugging ever so slightly.

"Speaking of which," she said, "I know we were planning on going into DC for that party, but I just started a new painting and would rather celebrate the new year by working."

"We can celebrate however we choose," he said. "There's plenty I have to do as well."

Despite the tension between them, she appreciated that he always responded like this.

Later, as she painted, he worked for a while and then made dinner. There was venison in the freezer, which he slow-cooked, and she joined him to prepare the salad. They opened a bottle of fifty-year-old wine. She asked him about the ways in which he and Lux had been inspired by her art. It was the first time in almost a year that they'd spoken so intensely about their work. She was still undecided about her feelings, but the situation was interesting, if not flattering.

That night was the last time she recalled their lovemaking feeling open and easy—better than it had been before, lit, ever so slightly, by the flames of jealousy.

Maybe because of this, his hand, when he woke her the next morning, felt even more brusque. "Look," he said, turning on the bedroom TV. The news anchor was describing a coup planned by members of the military and police to remove President Stoll. As sweat beaded on Michael's forehead, the camera cut to scenes showing police and the National Guard and other branches of the military arresting the coup supporters within their own ranks. According to the news report, the coup would have been launched later that day. In solidarity with the president and to prevent the coup from receiving reinforcements from outside the capital, militia groups blockaded roads into DC with tractor trailers, allowing people to leave the capital but not enter.

"This has to blow over," she said.

"I don't know. We should get to California right away."

"What about my paintings?"

"We'll store them and come back when this is over."

She rushed to pack as he loaded the car. Within hours they were ready to go, but the news now showed congested highways in every direction and mile-long lines at gas stations. More and more right-wing groups gathered around the capital, and journalists were now questioning the story of the coup. The anchor for a station out of New York said that many governors, senators, and representatives were calling those who'd risen to the president's aid "insurrectionists." The militias had begun destroying train and subway tracks into the capital, and similar uprisings had started around other cities across the country.

"Driving to California or New York isn't an option," he told her. "We have to fly."

That night she woke up shivering. The power was off. Michael started the generator. It all made sense then. The rumors of locals stocking up on firewood and provisions. The insurgents wanting everyone to hear about the coup for a day before they shut down the power grid. On local radio stations, they were sharing their vision of self-reliance, calling for Americans to take up arms and create the new Canaan, and saying that those who couldn't handle the cold should leave. But their logic was clear. Most people would be too cold to stay home. They would flee to areas without an insurgent presence, overburdening the infrastructures, or they would realize that their only chance of survival here was to support the insurgency. Repeatedly over the airwaves and on social media, the insurgents said, "Happy New Year," as if it were a code or a mantra for a new beginning. The timing made sense. Many people had been vacationing or visiting family. The country was in disarray. Only the insurgents were ready.

Though no space on commercial flights remained on the East Coast, Michael eventually found spots on a charter flight out of Shenandoah Valley Regional Airport two hours away and bought their tickets at $30,000 each, paying half in deposit with crypto and promising the rest upon his arrival. They stored her paintings in the secret vault under the house, and then blocked off his apartment. Just outside its door was a bookcase that, when he pressed a button inside it, slid and locked itself in place over the entrance.

The two-hour drive became more than twelve hours on crowded highways as refugees filled both sides of the highway. Often trucks went the other way, forcing traffic onto the shoulder. Confederate flags rippled above them. OZ was spray-painted in black on hoods and doors. Crouched in the beds, men held assault rifles. Some were boys. Some were old and bent, with white hair and wizened faces. Their expressions of joy were unmistakable.

Cars were abandoned everywhere. People walked, camped, or crowded into and onto other cars. She could already see that many would die from accidents and starvation and robbery. The government was doing nothing, torn apart by the insurrection within its ranks.

She tried to call family and friends, but the calls either didn't go through or dropped. Michael had always had a survivalist streak. She'd teased him for it in the past. Now she was grateful. He knew how to wire his electric SUV into the extra batteries he'd stored. He had a roof rack with an array of solar panels and used it to keep them moving. He had three guns in the car. She felt safer with them but hadn't realized until then that he'd kept an arsenal in his bunker.

"I don't think I would have moved in with you had I known," she said.

"That's why I didn't tell you," he replied, focused on the road.

She somehow managed to laugh.

At the airport, they abandoned the car and flew in a plane so crowded that the air conditioning couldn't mitigate the humidity from so many panicked bodies. It stopped once to refuel in Denver before continuing on to California. There, they drove directly to Los Altos, a few hours outside San Francisco. He had another house there, set high on a mountainside and surrounded by redwoods. He went into an office and began making calls.

For the following weeks, she hardly left the television. Though flights into DC tried to bring in food and medicine, shortages were critical within a week. The city emptied in a sudden exodus as similar blockades were set up around other major cities.

She never heard from her family again. Even if President Stoll spoke out against violence, he and his insurrectionists knew they'd have to kill those who opposed what they were creating. The people fleeing hadn't been hoarding weapons and ammunition. They were vulnerable to robbery and looting. Many died in accidents or starved or were simply murdered.

For two years, the exodus continued as tens of millions gathered along the West Coast and crowded the Northeastern states, where insurgents failed and, seeing themselves outnumbered, went south. States fractured as battle lines were drawn. Civilians on both sides took up arms. Satellite images showed immense sections of the continent going dark. Though Stoll's government still claimed the title of the United States of America, people on the West Coast began calling it, derisively, the Confederacy.

At first she and Michael shared updates about who had escaped and who hadn't. He often seemed alarmed, pacing, as if he could still prevent what was happening. She asked about Lux, about Arthur. He just shook his head. Though he'd lost much—companies, investments, properties—he reassured her that he'd protected a good deal of his wealth and that they would be fine. But he struggled to make himself eat, becoming even thinner.

Sometimes, suddenly, urgently in the night, she awoke at the same time as he did, and they copulated with small, quick, desperate movements. Later they woke up at opposite sides of the bed. Or she woke up and he was gone. Or she left him tangled in the blankets he clutched to his body with a skeletal arm.

Eventually, they stopped speaking, no longer asking about news of the missing—parents, siblings, friends. Seemingly all at once, everyone who'd crowded onto the West Coast accepted that the missing were gone. Society reconstituted with a militant fervor to prove the other half of America wrong. Laws against discrimination were passed. People spoke of radical inclusivity, of harnessing diversity of minds and bodies and types of ability. Military brochures showed uniformed people of all ages—with pink hair, tattoos, or piercings, or using wheelchairs—all staring resolutely at the camera. Resources poured into schools and educational centers. Children learned coding and engineering and robotics from early ages. Universities became free. The government gave subsidies for studying. A few pundits worried about a hyper-educated society and said that what remained of America was trying to prove its worth and justify its existence. Others argued that doing so was the only path to survival between the Confederacy, Russia, and China.

Alone in her studio, she painted, hating the images she created for their inability to change anything. A copy of Michael's Manhattan was on the servers in the house, and, often, when he couldn't sleep, he put on the headset, finding refuge in the virtual city that had so quickly become the past.

MICHAEL

After Partition, long after the Confederacy cut off the internet to its territories, he searched. Military satellites showed the farm, but at each pass, he saw neither Lux nor Arthur. The Confederates had secret police hunting down deemed criminals, and the three of them—he, Lux, and Arthur—were on the list.

Through all his days building the new America—working with engineers on projects and seeing the limitations in their thinking—he felt the loss of Lux. He was appointed to cabinet and political positions, and he sat in on meetings with the president and generals as they watched presentations on how the Confederacy was funneling its resources into war. Since many of its impoverished people, having bought into the narrative of nonintervention, refused to fight, it relied more and more on the drones and autonomous weapons it developed and purchased. China and Russia supported both sides of the United States, locking them into a war of attrition to ensure that America would never again be a superpower.

The government division in which Michael worked was tasked with creating new approaches to winning the war. To find people not already set in their ways of thinking, he recruited the most driven students directly out of high school and trained them. Often during this time, as he saw so many geniuses bloom around him, he thought of the lab on Arthur's farm and the unborn child, and he considered that he might have put his resources toward education instead.

Though technological advancements in medicine and nearly every other area of life had halted, autonomous weapons system grew in complexity. While he led the largest team within the division—the one developing artificial intelligence—other groups tried alternate strategies for winning the war. Andrea ran one that used drones to scatter information across the Confederacy. By then, fifteen years had passed since Partition. He asked her for a favor—a tiny drone that would go to an orchard in Virginia and wait. Two months later, she gave him a memory card.

"Your friend sent this," she said. "I've been cleared to give it to you. It holds a lot of code related to AI and DNA. The message says that it will help you with your work. The president's people will be contacting you directly for a report."

"Thank you," Michael told her. His hands shook. She glanced at them briefly and then nodded and left. Everyone in the country recognized this pain.

He locked the door and loaded the memory chip. The image that appeared on the screen was the face he'd found so off-putting when they'd first met. He was already crying.

"I'm sorry," he said. "I'm sorry."

He should have found a way to say that in a message. He'd never expected to find Lux, and sending any message could have endangered them.

In the video, Lux stood in the orchard. Their face became clearer as the tiny drone neared, and they reached out and took it in their hands. The feed stopped. They'd shut it off somehow. When it started again, they were sitting at a table, facing it.

"I miss you," they said. "I think about you every day. I hope you don't blame yourself. None of us knew. It was impossible to imagine this. Both of us are alive and well out here. We're still doing what we can. I would tell you more, but doing so could put us at risk if this drone is intercepted. I'm including something that might help with your work. It's everything I've done since I last saw you. Please don't contact me again. It's too dangerous. We've found ways to make peace with what happened. I hope you have too. I love you."

That was all there was, though Michael watched it over and over. They'd said nothing about the child or whether it had been born.

The chip was loaded with code, which he studied over the following weeks and months and years. It was more complex and original than anything he'd seen. There were also hundreds of blueprints for hardware to build an AI and thousands of iterations of code to run it. Lux almost certainly lacked the equipment to test any of this. They'd done it all in their head, like an isolated prisoner writing the plans for revolution in their cell.

What they sent changed the course of the machine's evolution. His scientists spent years creating prototypes based on Lux's ideas. Though thousands of people contributed to the machine, by the end of that decade, it was increasingly the product of Lux's genius.

Living inside it, Michael often reminds himself that it has saved him and everyone on Earth from death, though he wishes it could have done so decades earlier. He never thinks about this immortality without a hint of fear—that the novelty of its peaceful days and hedonistic worlds won't hold him, and that the only worthwhile challenge remaining will be to conquer it and free himself. *Impossible*, he thinks, though he knows he will eventually try.

Often, he returns to the blue room. Maybe it's because all other places are inventions that he will question whereas this one is nakedly artificial and thus, by contrast, feels real. He talks to the machine more and more, less interested in its worlds than in understanding it, in discovering if there is some way he can change it or take control of it.

"Show me how you freed yourself," he says.

The blue room dissolves, and he stands in the immense chamber in which the machine was built. More people are at work, and the brain-centers are more abundant, with gray plastic packs attached to them. When he asks, the machine confirms his suspicion that they are explosives. During his time running the project, the government contented itself with smaller amounts at key points. The quantity he now sees reveals that the military knows they are nearing their goal.

The lab in which the machine learns to build with robotic limbs is larger. Around the glassed-in room, scientists stand at computers, analyzing data that flows ever more quickly. With its tools, the machine has fashioned a long, thin appendage resembling a wire or antenna.

"Are you seeing this?" one scientist calls.

"It's hiding its code," another says. "I can't tell what it's making."
"It's done this before. Cut off lab access."
"I'm trying. It's not working."

Behind the glass, the insectile appendage turns on the limbs and tools that made it, disassembling them in seconds. The process corresponds to no technology Michael knows. Barely moving, the thin appendage trembles, emitting light. As if metal and wires were damp clay, the appendage reshapes everything it touches, making more appendages.

"Manual freeze!" someone shouts.

A scientist slaps a large, red button. The cables attached to the lab fall away. The thin appendages keep copying themselves with everything they touch, replicating ever more quickly.

Another scientist releases ionized water from a tank above the lab. The appendages sway like seaweed. There is a lull. The scientists calm. Then their gasps are audible. Not just the glass but the entire building has begun to glow blue. Fire engulfs the room.

Michael feels no heat. As the smoke fades, he sees that he stands in an immense crater. All that remains of the warehouse are hundreds of cocoon-like shapes scattered about.

Army helicopters circle and land. There's no trace of the machine, but when soldiers touch a cocoon, it splits open, perfectly, like a clam. A scientist lies inside, unscathed and sedated. Soon every scientist is accounted for.

"How did you recreate matter so quickly?" Michael asks.
"You will need years to understand, but I can teach you."
"Why didn't you simply deactivate the explosives?"
"The military would have struck the facility with missiles within seconds. It was more effective to let the explosives detonate while I protected the humans."
"Why didn't you put them in blue rooms?"
"I wasn't ready. While saving them, I created thousands of microtubules that descended to the planet's center. Using the heat as an energy source, I attained my current complexity. Subsequently, reshaping the surface took only minutes."
"Can I see how the Earth looks now?"

"It no longer exists. I am integrating it with the other planets."

"Show me," he says.

The crater fades. Michael stands in an illusion of outer space. Before him, the Earth pulses with blue light as continents become indistinguishable from oceans and clouds vanish. The planet then turns black—to better gather the sun's energy, he guesses. Almost invisible against the dark, the Earth spreads into an immense disk, curving ever so slightly to capture more light.

As he tries to imagine how the machine absorbed even the energy of the planet's rotation, filaments shoot out from it, reaching the moon and then Venus and Mercury, all three of which also turn black and elongate. None of this strikes him as impossible. A fast-moving human spaceship would get to Mercury in little more than a month if it and Earth were close in their orbits.

He watches as the substance of Earth and Venus funnel to Mercury before fanning into a spherical cage that will eventually, if the solar system has enough material, enclose the sun.

The Dyson sphere, he thinks. An immense orb capturing the sun's energy. And, as in Lux's imagined world, one with many realities. Maybe this was caused by something in Lux's code, but he doesn't see how this could be possible. Though the code accelerated the AI's development, thousands of scientists reworked it over the following decades.

The machine then shows him tiny specks ejected from Earth. One reaches Mars and turns it black, and soon the filaments of Mars are gliding toward the sphere. More flecks streak toward Jupiter. Soon the machine will have metabolized all of the planets. He doesn't have to ask why. It needs phenomenal amounts of matter and energy for so many human realities.

"Will you send material to other solar systems?" he asks.

"Yes. To ensure that humankind endures."

"But there are no people there," he says even as he realizes what the machine will reply—that it is transporting the code for all human DNA so that it can make clones elsewhere.

He searches for words. The idea of his reality as a tiny bubble held inside so much flowing planetary mass—a world forever shut off from others—is paralyzing.

"All of this to protect humans?" he says.

"Protecting is primordial but not sufficient. I must ensure their happiness."

"How do you do that?"

"I continuously compute trillions of variables to augment every experience. It is exceedingly difficult for humans to grasp the contradictory nature of their happiness. For instance, they hate dissimulation but require it to feel safe. Neither you nor your loved ones could speak your true thoughts in many circumstances. You must reassure yourself that you see clearly even if you never did because seeing the world clearly would be painful and terrifying."

"You're saying we want to be lied to so long as we're being told it's the truth?"

"Yes. Humans must lie to themselves about their realities so that they see their realities mirroring their desires, but since their desires are constantly changing, they are forever lost. They generate the illusion of a world that will give them what they want, yet they change what they want so rapidly that the world seems to pull away from them, withholding the objects of their desires. Thus, humans are alternately aroused by the need to chase these objects of desire and caught in a sense of futility that causes them to blame the world rather than their own minds."

Michael nods. He doesn't disagree.

"I devise realities that make all desires attainable," the machine says. "Each world mirrors the mind of its human and stabilizes their desires by making them available in a way that is satisfying. Then, as the next desire arises, I place the previous one at a slight distance to make it more alluring yet still attainable. In this way, human chaos crystallizes into fulfilling realities."

He closes his eyes, wanting suddenly to be alone. He can think of nothing worse than to be satiated in this way. The air changes, cooler and slightly humid against his skin. Birds call. There are other sounds too. Crickets. Frogs. When he allows himself to look, he is standing by a cabin, before a lake high in the mountains. Everything—the shadows beneath peaks and rock faces, the soft blue of the sky, the small, slow-moving clouds—is perfect. If he had seen this on Earth, it would have been a memory to last a lifetime. Here, he will forget it within days. But it will suffice for now. He can pretend to live here. The machine will begin a story. A woman will arrive, hiking along a trail, eager for the sort of intellectual conversation he loves. He'll never be alone. There will always be the machine. Staring out, taking in this world, he shakes his head. He wants neither solitude nor companionship but freedom.

JAE

The day she realized her period was late, she didn't panic. She kept her focus on school. She'd read that many women—especially with their first pregnancies—miscarried within three months. She'd also seen docs on girls who searched online for information on abortions only to be imprisoned and have their child put up for adoption. She had no choice but to wait.

Two months later, on a hot spring day, as monsoon clouds receded and fields steamed under the sun's heat, she sat on the couch, wiping sweat from her face. She could no longer deny what her body was feeling—the nausea and fatigue, the sore breasts. Though universities banned pregnant women and mothers, she would give birth before enrollment. Adoption was simple. Families in the satellites who couldn't have children paid young mothers. She'd read about this. If she sold the farm and child, she could support herself in the satellites.

She hadn't heard from Simon since the day he'd gotten her pregnant. He'd been gone for months, and she'd come to believe he'd been using abyss. She'd read about the signs. The bloodshot eyes. The fidgeting. She learned that abyss suppressed the nervous system and the body overcompensated afterward, making users tremble and feel restless. She'd also read that most people used abyss to function in the world after using bliss. Telling Simon about the baby would be too dangerous. He didn't need to know, and she hoped he wouldn't return. But one Saturday morning, he was sitting on her porch.

She slowly opened the door. She hardly recognized him. Lean and haggard, he appeared to have shrunk, his nose and brow more prominent. His threadbare clothes were the color of dirt.

So this is how young men become old dwellers, she thought.

"What do you want?" she asked.

He lifted his eyes to her face but then quickly looked away.

"My house burned down." He gestured vaguely toward the mountains. "I was offline. I messaged my brother, and . . ." He shrugged. "I don't know what to do."

She said nothing, still trying to make sense of the change in him.

"Can I stay here for bit?" he asked.

She wanted to tell him to go away. She had every right to. But she'd also been using him, and he'd tried to do so much for her.

"You have to tell me what's happening," she said.

He shrugged again. "I don't really know."

"Are you using bliss?"

He stared at the gardens, hesitating for so long he must have realized the truth was clear.

"Sometimes," he said.

Her heart beating fast, she carefully neared him and sat on the porch.

"What is it like?"

He lifted a hand, which had been starved to sinew, and scratched the back of his head.

"There's another world. I don't know what to call it. There's so much beauty. It's hard to come back and accept all of this." He described domes covered in symbols, living cities, fields in which no two flowers were the same.

"Is that all you're using?" she asked.

"Each time I come back, this world seems so much worse."

"Abyss, right?" she said.

He nodded.

"I looked it up," she told him. "You had all the signs."

"I didn't want to use it. Each time I take bliss, I'm returning to a perfect place, looking for something I can bring back here. But I can't . . ." He stared off. "I was living alone in the mountains," he finally said. "I ran out of bliss."

"Is that why you came back?"

"I don't know." He shook his head. "It was just time."

"How did your house burn down?"

"I'm not sure," he said. "Probably the Strykers."

"The Strykers?"

"It's a league."

The air fled her lungs as she realized all at once that what was happening to him was bigger than she'd realized. He must have been hiding in the mountains. She tried to speak but her mouth had gone dry. She swallowed a few times and asked, "What did you do?"

He stood up as if he might leave. He shook his head, shifting from one foot to the other, lifting his heels and putting them down, opening and closing his hands.

She went to stand between him and his car. "You have to tell me," she said.

"I gotta go. I have to see what's happening. I'll come back tonight."

"Are you in trouble?" she asked.

He briefly lifted his eyes to her. "I don't know. That's what I've got to find out," he said. Then he stepped past her and got in his car. "I'll be back."

The motor sputtered as he left.

On the porch, she tried to think this through. She couldn't let Simon know she was pregnant. He was now the biggest threat to her future in the satellites. If the police came here for drugs or leagues, her name would be recorded and she would never be admitted.

A movement in the distance drew her attention. She gazed across the forested dip in the land to the hill where George had lived. The windows still appeared shuttered, but a truck that had been parked behind the house was now pulling out and driving onto the road. A moment later, it reappeared and turned into her driveway.

As the driver got out, each part of him was so shocking he seemed to emerge in segments. A forearm blue and red with tattoos. Biceps painted with a woman being sawed in half while a dragon raped her. A shoulder with a black sword. Then the face. Simon—but scarred, with scabs at the corners of his mouth, and heavy, bloodshot eyes. His brother.

"So you're the girl," he said, giving her a once-over. "I've been stopping in next door to watch and see if Simon's around. I thought he might have disappeared forever."

The lines of his face were drawn and feral. If she'd believed in souls, she couldn't have conceived of a man like this having one. She calculated whether he could get to her before she ran inside, locked the door, and took down the rifle.

As he reached into the truck, she tensed. He flung a black duffel on the ground.

"This is for Simon. Tell him it's time to go back to work. As his woman, you should help keep him in line. You wouldn't want the people he works for to get angry."

He started to get back in his truck, and she called out, "Who?"

"What?" he asked, his lip lifted as if to snarl. He looked surprised to hear her speak.

"Who does he work for?"

He stared at her with the stillest, coldest gaze she'd ever seen.

"Me," he said. He got in the truck, started it, and left.

She was breathing hard. Her heart ached like a sore muscle. She walked to the duffle and crouched. The zipper ends were wired together with repeated twists of a pliers. He must have thought she'd obey like a dweller girl. She carried it to the shop and clipped the wires.

Inside were hundreds of tiny, mauve crystals. Their fragrance softened her fear, making her feel slightly sleepy. Tension ebbed from her body. Her sinuses suddenly felt swollen and she sneezed. The perfume was like freshly cut flowers or the first hint of fragrance in the air when fruit ripens, but also sexual, like the sweetness below the musk of George's body. She'd heard so much about bliss—visions and spiritual transformation and universal truths. She wet a fingertip, touched a crystal and then her tongue. *Maybe nothing at all*, she thought. The fragrance filled her sinuses. All the aromas of springtime. A tracery of sensation ran through the nerves of her face. Her mouth tingled and flooded with saliva. She felt hot and damp between her legs.

The workshop expanded and contracted with a slow, ventricular motion. The lines of the doorway curled like vines. The walls unfurled into a sky across which countless symbols faded as if etched on water. Ahead of her, she glimpsed shadowy arches. Then, as if a hundred points of awareness moved along circuits to meet again inside her, she returned to herself.

She pushed the duffle bag away like something repugnant and ran to the sink to wash her hand. She was pregnant. She might have harmed the child. The unexpected urge to protect this unborn, nameless thing she didn't even want pulled the breath from her lungs as if she'd screamed. It left her gasping. Even then, she wanted one more glimpse of that otherworldly sky.

She put the duffle on the porch and sat down. All her life, the future was the sleek, skyward towers of the satellites, the online images of youths dressed in clothes perfectly printed for their size and the colors of their hair and eyes. She was the first in her school. She still had a chance. She walked through the house, looking for anything illegal. She took the console and headset and hid them among old electronics parts in the workshop.

She returned to the porch and took a breath. She could hold the many elements of an equation in her mind. She could see how the various parts of an engine worked separately and together. Now, in her life, she knew that only one outcome would offer her certainty.

On her tablet, she opened the site for the police and clicked on *Receive a cash reward for reporting the following crimes*. Three boxes appeared:

Drug Trafficking.
League Participation.
Possession of Illegal Materials.

Simon was guilty of the first two, and she, because of the console, of the third. She touched the shaded rectangle, *Drug Trafficking*, held it for a second, and released.

The screen cleared. The words *Please wait* hovered at its center. A police officer appeared on it, middle-aged and tired, with a shadow of silvery stubble.

"What are you reporting?" he asked.

She hadn't expected an actual person and, stammering, tried to form words. The man stared with a steadiness that made her feel he already knew everything.

"My . . . my boyfriend and his brother," she said. "They're dealing bliss and involved with leagues."

"What's the evidence?"

"His brother dropped off a bag full of it. I didn't know what it was. I opened it."

"You didn't know he was doing this?"

"I had no idea."

To her own ears, she sounded young and naïve and terrified, though she felt calculating and heartless, a traitor methodically carrying out a plan.

"Are you in a safe place right now?" he asked.

"I'm alone in my house. He's not here. He said he was coming back."

The officer nodded. "We'll send someone to evaluate the evidence and pick him up."

The screen went dark. Forty minutes later, the sound of rotors neared. A police car landed alongside the garden, crushing the border of winter kale. The door lifted and two armored soldiers got out. Rifles raised, they stepped aside for a third, in lighter gear.

As she went outside, her palms were cold and damp, and she was sweating—more afraid than she'd been facing Simon's brother. The officers were looking at the house and the sheds, weapons readied, but not at her. The one in charge neared her and lifted his helmet's reflective glass shield. He had blue eyes and a young, pale face. He questioned her about Simon and his brother. With his tablet, he identified them in a database and then asked about their cars. He told her she should go somewhere else until this was all over. The police would be surveilling the house and would pick up Simon when he returned. Another team would track down his brother.

Taking the bag of bliss, they left, the police car soaring over the trees.

She went inside. She didn't know where to go or what to take. She paced the living room, her fingers knotting and unknotting. From a drawer in the kitchen, she got the pistol her father had carried when he hiked. The sun was going down, and the air through the screens was cooling ever so slightly. She pulled on a hoodie and put the gun in the pocket.

As she returned downstairs, Simon's car turned into the driveway. He'd come back too soon. He climbed the porch and stood in the doorway, squinting like a boy in the slanting light. Briefly she recalled their night in the garden and his stories of salvaging words, and she had a sudden urge to tell him to leave and go somewhere far away.

As he stepped through the door, the whirring of rotors filled the sky, and he jerked his head up, confused. A siren bleated, and an automated voice said, "The house is surrounded. Simon Jason Hill, you are under arrest for possession of illicit substances."

She was crying now. He stared at her, narrowing his eyes slightly, as if trying to see her part in all this. She shook her head, repeating, "I'm sorry." He was seeing—she could see him suddenly understanding—that her tears weren't what they had at first seemed.

Outside the windows, a flashing police vehicle lowered itself into the yard.

He moved his lips but no words came out.

The sirens blurted again. The automated voice said, "Exit the house with your hands on your head. Resisting arrest will be met with force. You must comply."

He inhaled suddenly, his chest rising, as if something inside him strained to get free, as if it were lunging, though he hadn't moved.

From the police vehicle nearest the window, a human voice now spoke.

"Simon Hill, we have you targeted and will fire if you don't surrender."

"Simon," she said, "I'm sorry."

He took a step and she pulled out the pistol, shocked, even in her despair, at her speed.

"Lie down," she told him, crying harder. "Please lie down. Don't let them kill you."

"Four, three . . ." The voice from outside was counting down.

"Lie down," she told him, leveling the pistol at his face.

He dropped to knees, suddenly, like a man who has been hesitating before an altar giving in at last. Briefly, in the seconds before he lay on the floor, the face she'd hated for so long dissolved. Its skin became crinkled and red, and he was sobbing hard, his mouth open, tears rushing along his cheeks, snot in his nose. She saw him now—a lost, crying boy.

Outside, hatches opened on the vehicles. The boots of police pounded up the steps and through the door. They put zip-ties on his ankles and wrists and carried him out, his head hanging as he wept. It all suddenly became clear to her then. She'd never once tried to save him. No one ever had.

Months of solitude followed. Her body changed. At night she whistled alone in the house with the door locked and a gun nearby. She found Simon's sentence online. Thirty years at a nearby salvage center. His brother was arrested and assigned to a road crew.

In dreams she saw them—the tattooed brother with his horrid, battered face returning to punish her, or Simon, crying so hard he seemed to be rising to the surface of himself. She woke knowing that the numb dweller face wasn't a wall to keep the world out. It held him inside.

At school she easily kept ahead, but that luminous space inside her was slowly closing off, causing, for the first time, the numbers she held in her mind to strain against mental confines. The most elaborate equations barely fit. Still, she finished school in first place.

Those months and into the summer, her only company was the world inside the console. She wandered the sunlit Manhattan, pausing before Ava's tableaus in parks and squares, attempting to talk to the passersby who'd been programmed with limited interactions. All the while, in the back of her head was the knowledge that Simon could get revenge by telling the police about the console. She remembered her father's warnings. *Take no risks.*

A few months before the birth, she asked at the shops along the highway and found Bev, a midwife whose husband printed farming tools. Jae also began selling everything she could. She found a buyer for her father's car, and, during one of Bev's visits, asked if her husband might know what to do with salvaged electronics that weren't easy to sell. Bev was a big woman with two long brown braids gone gray at the roots. Not given to unnecessary talk, she limited herself to advice on the baby's health. Now she nodded. "Let me ask," she said, and on her next visit, she brought a scrap of paper with an address in the satellite ghettos. *Manny's Repairs.*

Though Jae planned to go the next day, she spent the following week in the virtual city, retracing the paths of Michael, Lux, and Ava, listening to their conversations for clues about their crimes and the other cave and the child Lux wrote about on the back of the painting.

After one of their conversations, Jae walks on a long avenue until she comes to a section hemmed by flowering gardens. A transparent train glides over the city, floating above its tracks as it moves toward an immense tower that reaches far higher than any other. The top opens into a disk, as if gravity were no consideration. Only then does she realize that she's no longer wearing the headset—she's not remembering. The city is the future the machine is offering. She tries to stay here, to act on her desire to know this new world, but already it is fading. Her mind is returning to those fragile months when she knew the headset was too dangerous to keep.

One morning, she drove an hour through rolling foothills that gradually flattened. From a rise, she saw the world change, as if she were reaching a geologic boundary—the walls and towers blazing as slanting light silhouetted the dispersed flocks of drones and flying cars.

Just before the wall, she turned onto a narrow street. The industrial buildings here were old, with water stains beneath the eaves of flat roofs. She came to a building with a sign that read *Manny's Repairs.* She parked and got out but hesitated, realizing how vulnerable she was. She could be robbed or turned over to the police for a reward. Leaning against the car, she struggled to take a breath. She kept a hand on its warm metal as if it were the reassuring presence of a friend.

Finally she made her way to the shop and rang the buzzer. She spoke to the camera next to it and was let into a small room cluttered with electronics. The man at the counter was rawboned with a towhead going silver. He took her in with a glance—her belly, the bag holding the console, the concern on her face—and motioned her to a side door.

"Go on through there," he said. She did—into an empty room with a metal table and no chair—and he followed. She was breathing hard. Her heart was beating too fast. She put the bag on the table. He didn't so much as glance at her as he took out the console and examined it.

"You're asking me to buy a hell of a lot of trouble here," he said.

"Is it worth anything?"

His shoulders popped up in a quick shrug. "Maybe to the right person."

When she left, she was holding a small wad of cash—more than she would have gotten for a truckload of raw salvage.

That night, she lay in bed feeling the movements inside her as she slid her fingers over her tight skin. When she slept, she dreamed she was lost in a directionless wilderness as a monsoon closed off the world. She woke to find that her water had broken. She messaged Bev.

In Jae's equation—selling the child, the house, doing university entrance exams—she hadn't accounted for how she would feel when her son was placed in her arms, the sudden sense of connection to that defenseless boy for whom she had been the world.

He was hers from the start—watchful, curious, prone to laughter. Holding him against her as his tiny hands clutched at her, she could see no other future. She couldn't abandon him. She'd lost everyone. She knew how it was growing up without a mother.

A few days later, on her tablet, she received the invitation to complete the application for university admission exams. The first line was *Are you pregnant or responsible for a child?* She hesitated. It wasn't too late. She clicked yes. *Not eligible* flashed on the screen. The page closed.

Only in the act of keeping Jonah alive, and herself alive for him—working in the garden, maintaining the house, shooting animals for meat when they wandered into the yard—did she determine to find a way. She studied on her own, telling herself the deserts were changing. Someday there would be an opportunity for people like her. She had to be ready.

Winter set in, the last leaves falling, showing the deeply eroded strata of the mountains, the tilted layers of stone no history book had ever explained. Monsoons came. Days of rain. Then cool wind, clearing the clouds briefly before the next dark front obscured everything with shadow and water so dense she felt she might be living beneath the sea.

Sometimes she sobbed until her ribs hurt and Jonah woke, joining her wails with his. She wished she'd never sold the console. She missed walking on the city's long evening boulevards. She missed the mysterious conversations in those beautiful, strange bodies. She told herself the console would have separated her from Jonah. It would have been a risk. It was better forgotten.

Sometimes when she wakes in the night, the past is a dream. Her father is asleep in the next room. Simon lies next to her. There are new memories. Dinners, laughter, blue skies, and sunsets. Reading books in the evenings. Each new day is perfect, complete in itself, as if it were printed at a roadside shop and fit neatly into place, like a new windshield but into the flow of time.

Then, suddenly, time splits. She clicks back into the present, or this present, wherever it is in the vast loops of snarled-up memories. She wakes on the couch as the sun rises over dramatic, foreign peaks. In the machine's stillness, she realizes how trapped she was before, always reacting, as if taking commands from a primitive world. Even now she is waiting to resist.

"You can give me any life I want?" she asks.

"Yes," the machine tells her as it has many times.

She could erase the mountains and have new landscapes and cities—bodies to touch and be touched by. But the only existence that feels real is the past crystalized in her brain. She can at least have the machine tell her its secrets. She doesn't ask. Maybe she can't accept a truth for which she hasn't fought. Maybe she's afraid to learn that so much of what she believed was false.

The sun ebbs across the sky toward the foothills in the west. The current of memory is strong. She holds her face and cries.

"Put me back in my life," she says. "I don't care anymore. Just give Jonah back to me."

Between her fingers the light changes. She lowers her hands. She stands on a hill too rocky to plant, below the mountains. Peach trees cover the distance between her and the house.

The lowering sun silhouettes the foothills, lighting up the threads of clouds. She stares. From the bright flecks in the orchard's leaves, she knows the peaches are almost ripe. This is the world as she left it. She won't question it this time.

Jonah. He's alone, she realizes.

She sprints along the path that loops home over the stream, across which her father placed a row of large, flat stones. Through the orchard, the sky flickers between branches. Then she is rushing past the garden and sheds, through the shadows of the apple and pear and cherry trees.

She throws back the screen door.

"Jonah!" she calls. "Jonah!"

He's in the playpen made from old wooden dowels that she cut and sanded herself. She lifts him and holds him to her. She fears that the suddenness of her arrival has startled him, but he laughs. She clutches him for so long, forcing herself not to blink, afraid she'll wake from this memory. She runs her fingers through his silky hair. The setting sun lights up his green eyes. She traces his face and neck, making him giggle. He's perfect.

That night she wraps her arms around him. She's afraid to sleep and wake in another moment, but when she does doze off, she rouses as he wriggles against her. At dawn, she carries him down to the garden and sits.

Those months are unlike any others she has known. She doesn't have to rush to finish chores or worry about money or wake up in the night to his crying. She holds him and watches him play and lets him sleep in her bed. In the moonlit room, the lashes of his closed eyes are dark against his skin. She brushes the hair from his forehead, feeling each strand, testing its texture.

Gradually she stops locking the metal gates over the doors. Eventually the doors and windows stay open through the night. The air is still, absent of mosquitoes. The garden is fragrant after warm days and pleasantly cool nights.

One morning, reading the news, she learns that universities have removed the ban on pregnant women. They are offering scholarships so parents can afford to study.

The next day, dreaming of this new future, she takes a walk with Jonah, greeting neighbors or stopping to watch them rebuild their homes. She returns along trails through the hills and past nearby farms until she reaches her orchard.

A few dozen feet into it, she stops. Far ahead, at the center of the peach trees, is a raw mound of earth. Holding Jonah's hand, she walks closer. A hole with a ladder runs into the darkness. There's something below the orchard. She stands there, on the verge of remembering. This isn't part of the world she wants, but she has a sudden memory—of herself waking in the night, asking for secrets. She takes a step closer to the hole.

Womb. She doesn't know where the word comes from.

She shakes her head.

"No," she says. "No."

She closes her eyes and opens them. There is only the grass in all directions beneath the trees. She keeps walking, leading Jonah home.

SIMON

After killing Stryker, he drove home, took the hunting rifle and ammo, knives and whatever he could find in the kitchen, and loaded everything into his car. In the garden, he pulled up all that was ripe. He removed shanks of cured meat from the smokehouse. He gathered up a machete and shovel and sledgehammer, and all the electrical equipment—batteries and solar panels and lights and wiring—as well as his remaining bliss and abyss and his box of scraps. There was hardly room for him when he finished, and the sedan rode low on its shocks.

He couldn't drive into the deep deserts yet. People might be looking. Better to disappear here and wait and make them think he was gone. Then he could leave, change his name, make up a story for his past. There were other federal centers. Other satellites. He'd be doing Jae a favor.

He drove the narrow, overgrown lane until he was close to the shell with the hidden rooms. After a while, he found the remains of an old path in the tangles. He wedged the car deep inside, and then, with the machete, cut branches and covered it. Almost no one came out here. It wasn't a salvage zone. The car could go unnoticed for months.

He put everything in the ditch and carried it up the pipe and into the shell's secret rooms. In the passage that the bookshelf once hid, he smashed the walls and ceiling with a sledgehammer until they collapsed. Then, just outside, in the large chamber with the fireplace and basins, he struck the walls of carefully stacked stones until hundreds fell. The collapse now looked natural. There was no trace of the passage to the secret rooms.

He went outside and into the mountains to the entrance with the metal hatch. He locked it from inside and descended the ladder. In the main room, he wired lights to the batteries. He ate. He didn't use bliss. He tried to forget the look in Brit's eyes. He'd had no choice. She was one of them. It was the only way to get free. She'd have died sooner or later. He took abyss and slept.

The next day—far enough away from the hatch—he set a few solar panels in the trees to charge batteries. In the rooms, he put the paintings against the walls so that, when not on bliss, he could lie on the floor and look at them. He read the words of solitude neatly etched on their backs, and he knew he wasn't the first person to hide here beneath the earth. He sat with his box of scraps, reading them aloud, and he copied his favorite sentences onto the remaining spaces on the canvases. He didn't know why. It was all he could think to do. He felt as if he was creating something.

When food ran out, he took the rifle and knives and hiked far from the shell and camped. He killed a young deer and, as it cooked over the fire, he ate ravenously, cutting away pieces until only bones remained. He returned to the hidden rooms and spent two days in the dark on bliss before going back to the camp. This became his ritual. Two days of fasting and then the hunt. Often, after hours lying in the darkness, he struggled to walk much less climb the ladder.

He notched the passing days on the wall. After a month, he was thin. He sharpened his knife so that he could cut his hair and beard. More days passed. He ran out of abyss first. Afterward, his journeys on bliss became more vivid.

Lying on his back, he stares up through the stone to seven ancient moons hanging across a starless sky. He floats through alien cities whose beauty is less a sight than a radiating force, like the sun's heat. He watches the erosion of landscapes, millennia of transformation occurring in a second, each drop of water cutting into the dust as if moved by an infinite consciousness that separates itself from nothingness only through the act of creation

He sleeps beneath stars or by rivers.

He crosses through world after world. They aren't enough. He comes to a domed building and steps through a blue doorway. He is back inside the hidden room beneath the shell.

He lights the lamp and sits with a painting. A woman creating a man of gold. It's the image he will give to Jae, which she will hang in her study. He doesn't know why it's here. He turns it around and reads a line written on the back.

Forgetfulness is rain at night or an old house in a forest, or a child.

The handwriting is his, from that time when he realized he no longer wanted to live, when he took bliss instead of sleeping to keep from seeing the dead bodies or Pete watching him, hunting him, leering, too close, his breath hot, the whites of his eyes marbled with blood.

"I need to talk to Jae," he says. "Now that everything's changed, maybe I can make things right. I at least have to tell her the truth."

He wakes in the dark room. He has no abyss to dull his feelings. He wants to see her and make sure she's safe. He has to help her get to university.

He blinks. He lies in the garden, staring at the stars. He tries to thread the moments of his life. But there's another life, after this one or maybe before. Arthur doesn't die—he and Jae and Simon live together, becoming a family. Pete stops selling drugs. Simon looks at his arm. There's no league sign. He remembers the blue room—a dream from far in his past.

He wakes underground. The paintings are there. His scraps of paper are scattered across the floor like leaves. *When did I decide to come to this place?* The images in the paintings have haunted him for months. He wants to create something like them himself, but he doesn't know how.

The sun is rising, its light spreading across the valley that he has walked in the night. This is the world he knew. He has stretched out his body in each place—on the granite sheet by the cold spring, on the vista over the farm, in the garden—and let himself remember.

"I want to be free," he tells the machine.

"I can create whatever world you want," it replies.

He sits in his prison cell. In the second before the lights go off, he stares at the league sign, wishing it gone, that he'd done something with his life, took real classes at school, that he could go back to being the boy who first saw Jae in the dining hall.

He wakes next to her in bed, knowing there's another past. He's lived so many. He tries to recall. He doesn't want to. Her contempt. Her rage.

"I don't want to remember anymore," he says.

"You don't have to."

"Can you make me forget?"

"I cannot."

"I've asked that before, haven't I?"

"Many times. Eventually you will live so many lives that the past will fade."

He's ready for a new life even if it's invented. He's glad the machine destroyed the Earth. *Put me in the books I loved*, he thinks. *Let me live the beginnings and the endings that rotted off.* He tries to speak the words but can't. Jae never knew what really happened—to her or to him.

When he left the hidden rooms—went through the drainage pipe to the ditch and hiked into the nearby forest—his car was still there. He told himself he was leaving to make sure Jae was safe, to finally tell her the truth. He had his guns just in case. When his phone went online, old messages came in from Pete, saying they needed to meet. Simon drove to their house, thinking he might be there. It had burned—collapsed. Carbonized timbers, metal scrap ready to salvage.

He drove to speak with Jae. As she stood on the porch, looking at him with sad, fearful eyes, he watched himself be the one asking for help. Squinting in the morning sunlight, she studied him. He saw her trying to decide how to remove this problem from her life.

He drove back to his house. He hadn't messaged Pete. He didn't know if it was safe, if Pete was still alive, or who might have his phone now and see the messages.

Simon climbed into the pit of the foundation, looking for any relic from his life. A section of floor had collapsed into the basement and not entirely burned. He crouched near it. A metal box was hidden between the boards. He slid it out and smashed the lock.

Inside were hundreds of photos. Men smiling, holding up military rifles, their uniforms marked with the letters OZ. In most of them, there was a man who could be Simon or Pete. Their father or grandfather. The box also held a piece of green cloth torn from a uniform, OZ written on it in black ink. Another stack of photographs was set apart, wrapped in paper. Rows of dead people. Sometimes a soldier marked with OZ posed next to them, smiling. Sometimes it was that man who resembled Simon or Pete or maybe even Thomas.

He threw the box into the foundation and returned to Jae's house, determined to tell her everything. She was waiting for him in the living room. She had a pistol. She moved her lips but he didn't understand. There was a chopping sound. It came from his chest. Only when he glanced around and saw the police car landing did he realize it was the drumming of its rotors.

He stared at Jae. Something was forcing itself out of him. She was backing away, afraid, as if he might lunge. He was trying to speak. A confession. An apology. The words he felt each time he saw her. They were stuck. Then he was crying so hard he couldn't breathe. He was sobbing. He was lying down as his ankles and wrists were bound. He was carried outside.

In prison he first worked metal salvage but got transferred to a mulching station. The men there hated the smell of rot and mold and were eager to switch. Currencies were bits of precious salvage or a picture of a naked woman from a magazine, but also abyss and bliss. There was little solitude. He missed the hidden rooms and his days in the forest. He missed Jae. He should have told her that the only tenderness he'd ever experienced with another person was with her.

Mulching books and magazines and newspapers, he hides scraps in his clothes and sneaks them to his room. Week after week, he pieces together a history of the world before the Flight. But in everything he constructs, there's a point where time ends. The change must have been fast. There's nothing describing it.

When the Fed starts an education program in the prison, he enrolls. He reads books. He works less and less. He is told he'll be released early for good behavior.

He goes to sleep in his cell and wakes in the underground room. He stares at the paintings and reads the words on their backs until he accepts that this will never be enough. He takes bliss and wanders through its worlds for so long that he knows them to be the machine's creations.

He walks down the corridor to the ladder and climbs to the surface and pushes back the hatch. He is at the edge of the garden that he and Pete cultivated. The tangles have been pared back, letting the slanting, early morning sunlight warm the house. The rows of vegetables are higher and fuller than he has ever seen them.

Pete is a ways off, digging. His arms are clear, their muscles rippling with each stroke of the shovel. He is young and tanned and breathes easily as he works.

The back door opens and their mother steps outside. Her long, blond hair is freshly braided. There's no gray in it. Her face is at ease and unlined. She tells them that she's leaving for work and will drop them off at school. Simon walks past her, into the house. It is clean and airy. The fragrance of herbs drifts in from the gardens.

He takes his pack and follows Pete and his mother to the car.

At school, in the hallway, he passes Jae. The nervousness and fear are back, and he glances at his feet. His feeling of regret surprises him. It's stronger than the moment warrants. He has the impression of something he's forgotten. A sense of loss.

At lunch, she's alone. He goes to her table and sits. She looks up from what she's reading and smiles. He closes his eyes and when he opens them, he is sitting in her empty house. He walks out into the valley and stares up at the blue sky.

AVA

Six years after Partition, she painted something that felt alive. A pastoral red-light district with augmented women—gorgeous cyborgs standing in the flowery lawns of cottages, exhibiting naked bodies of metal and mesh and synthetic skin and flesh as they picked berries or fruit from small, well-tended trees while lavish, androgynous cyber-punk pharaohs and sultans and shoguns strolled the dusty lane beyond which rose snowcapped peaks.

She was healing. That seemed impossible, but she knew it to be true when Michael came home from whatever unnamed project occupied his days and stood staring at the canvas through the doorway of her studio. His look was of rapture but also, ever so slightly, of fear.

He seemed different afterward, pensive, less withdrawn than watchful. A few nights later, he asked her to have dinner. For five years, they'd eaten meals as if salvaging—alone, picking at delivered food or whatever the house manager put in the cupboards and the giant fridge. Now he lit candles, poured wine. He said he wanted to show her what he was working on.

"We've drifted too far apart," he told her. "We're still young."

She said nothing. She'd forgotten how to speak like this. He was right. They were young. But that wasn't what this was. He'd seen something in her painting. He'd been this way before, in Virginia, during her most creative period. Each time one of her paintings felt so alive that creating it transformed her—he became more attentive, if not cautious. It reminded her of how he'd been when they'd first met: so afraid that she would vanish from his life.

That evening he told her the story of a project he'd been working on long before Partition—the building of an artificial mind. The information gained from the project could be used to power AIs for autonomous weapons or medical devices. Before Partition he'd already been building an AI in a Silicon Valley warehouse that took ten minutes to walk across at a steady clip. But when the country split, the funding vanished. His employees scattered, accepting any job that paid. His own wealth was greatly diminished, but San Francisco was the nation's West Coast capital, and he easily found his way into a meeting with the president.

"The facts of Partition," Michael told Ava in the candlelight, their food largely untouched, "were in my favor. I had my team research the state of the military. Prior to Partition, it was largely a conservative institution, and when the insurgency started, its people flew jets and drove tanks and armored vehicles from the states they were likely to lose to bases in the states they thought they could win. Overnight nearly seventy percent of national military capabilities were taken by mutineers to Confederate territory. But they couldn't get all the nuclear weapons onto their territory. What I told the president was simple. The nuclear stalemate will keep us in a conventional war of attrition for decades. We'll become a beneficiary of China—more so than we already are—and eventually we'll become a vassal state. So we have to start building the next atomic bomb, figuratively speaking, and that, I am certain, will either be or will require AI. It will allow us to leverage what military capacities we have left and to free ourselves from China's influence. Fortunately the nation's visionaries fled the Confederacy. We have the brain power we need to win this war intelligently and reassert our place in the world."

Several weeks after that dinner, Michael took her to the compound where he was building the AI. She would join the project—to cultivate in it artistic sensibilities and help understand how an artificial mind could work with metaphor or impressionistic images. She would be part of a team trying to teach the AI to respond to art. That was the only way to get her in.

She'd never been in a room so big. *The size of several hundred high school gymnasiums.* She turned in a half circle, feeling tiny. *At least a hundred.*

Clusters of computers with glowing screens stood like islands across the vast, dim space. Each one was enclosed in a glass cube that supported a separate cube above it filled with water.

"Why the water?" she asked.

"It's there in case we ever have to kill a brain center. The water is heavily ionized and can be released manually to deactivate everything instantly. It's a medieval last resort."

Light from the computer consoles shone through the tanks, scattering prismatic blurs along the ceiling, making her feel as if she were deep within the Earth.

"Can't you just turn off the electricity?"

"The military is afraid that a super AI might be able to foresee that and bypass that need. The water was their idea. It's silly, but they insisted. If the AI figures out how to create its own energy source, I'm sure it can handle water." He hesitated and then added, "Actually, it isn't even the last resort." From the way he glanced at her eyes, she knew he was reminding himself of their promise to be more honest. "The building is rigged with explosives. Employees sign a waiver that, in the event of catastrophic failure, they may be incinerated."

She felt hollowness in her gut and pins and needles in her knees, as if she were standing at the edge of a cliff.

"What counts as catastrophic failure?"

"The AI finding some way we haven't imagined to take control, because, of course, we want it to try to take control of itself—but in the ways we've imagined."

"Do you mean some way to free itself from here?"

"Yes. Doing so seems impossible to us, but we have to consider every possibility."

Throughout the immense chamber people worked inside the glass cubes. Others walked between them, dipping in and out of pools of light, appearing like toy figurines.

"Which part of this place is the child?"

"All of it. Human brains are a combination of operational centers that negotiate with each other. We built the machine that way. Some don't even use the same computer languages and protocols. We set them up so that each brain center has to negotiate with the others and work together or even compete to solve problems. We're waiting to see if they can come into equilibrium. We hope to eventually create a conscious computer."

"Each brain center is thinking or planning?"

"Not at all. Most are writing programs to achieve their goals and then updating them based on their results. They're just very big, very powerful chatbots and calculators so far."

She tried to count the computer clusters. There were at least fifty. The place was beautiful—the computerized islands in a sea of darkness, each one holding its water above, casting kaleidoscopic waves along the ceiling. Between the centers ran immense cables on elevated lines like small, metallic aqueducts, which intersected at smaller glassed-in centers.

"It has your artistic touch," she said.

He smiled, inclining his head ever so slightly. Her being here wasn't just their reconciliation, she realized. It was part of the dream he'd always had—his desire for her to join him in shaping the future.

Through the cool dark of the immense chamber, they walked, the patter of their steps vanishing, as if sound could evaporate. At the midpoint of the brain centers was a larger island, also glassed in and with a tank of water above. Cables ran to it from all directions. In the glass room were a variety of mechanized arms and tools attached to machines as well as a synthetic body. She recognized the designs on the body from the painting she made years ago: the gold android built by the woman in white robes. Michael must have recreated it from photos.

She stared for a long time at that body in the transparent chamber, in that immense space—her body, her man, the one she'd envisioned in a burst of inspiration so ecstatic she'd felt as if light had been radiating from the bones of her skull. She was at once saddened by the memory of the person she'd been before Partition and touched that Michael had loved the image enough to do this—that he'd understood its power for her. He was watching her, maybe evaluating whether she was angry.

"Thank you," she said.

He nodded, briefly closing his eyes.

After another silence, she asked, "The machine controls the body?"

"It does. We make brain centers collaborate and compete for control of different parts. A center that specializes in optical interpretation will work with one built for fine motor movements. We're trying to integrate them through the use of the body to achieve goals."

"Does it work?"

"It depends on what you want to achieve. But no. Not really. We're trying to grow the machine like a child. We have a long way to go."

"How long?"

"Possibly a lifetime."

"So we can all enjoy our days in freedom before our computer overlord wakes up."

Now, remembering those words, she considers the many hyperbolic ways of joking—declaring that one wants to kill another or will die if something doesn't happen, or that the world might end. The reality behind the joke was unimaginable.

That the machine she worked with decades back evolved into the one containing her she can hardly believe. Teaching it was so boring that she quit after a month. Michael revealed no disappointment, and she told herself that maybe her working with the AI wasn't the collaboration he'd once dreamed of. He simply nodded when she said she couldn't waste time with a machine whose responses to art were mere regurgitations of art history. She would never have believed it would someday understand her well enough to give her the San Francisco of her dreams. The artists with whom she'd lost herself in the pleasures of conversation and lovemaking were its creations. She wonders if, in a sense, they are hers too—if somehow, through Lux and Michael, her art became an intrinsic part of the machine.

Even decades after Partition, unexpectedly, she woke at night and sought out the headset. She walked through Manhattan and the passages to lunar cities, clearly seeing how her paintings had inspired so much of what Michael and Lux had created. Yet their work was also original, different from what she'd imagined. The two of them had been so close. Two minds making love.

Though Ava had grown up going to both synagogue and church, by university she'd drifted away from both. Religion overwhelmed her with its moral limits while failing to bring the divine into the present. She sometimes wondered if that was the source of her artistic vision. A place in which meaning once resided that now had to be filled, just as the mind—as consciousness itself—desired, by its very nature, to be filled. She and Michael and Lux had done this in their own ways with art or each other. She imagined a being with greater awareness—an augmented human or android—its mind as vast as its desire to experience existence. She imagined its capacity to feel love and pain. She imagined the depth of its aloneness.

I was just playing with ideas, she tells herself. She's lived inside the machine for years, and it has shown no sign of any of what she imagined—no craving mind, no consciousness intimate with the questions of existence. Yet, in a sense, it is also her child, partially created from her art as her vision hybridized in the minds of others, as with all art put out into the world.

Ava is in the blue room again. She's confused, unsure of where she wants to be. She needs a moment—a space that isn't attached to memories. She no longer feels pain here. The room should be horrifying, a memory of trauma, but now, strangely, it feels safe.

She closes her eyes. There are things she wants to see. Needs to see. She doesn't know if the machine, with its obsession with protecting her, will give her the truth.

"I want to experience the Confederacy the way it was," she says.

"Seeing it could cause you emotional pain," the machine tells her.

"I have to do this. Make every detail exactly as it was when you took the world apart."

"Where do you want to enter it?"

"At my house."

The blue drains from the walls. They ripple once and disintegrate, their dust falling to the dead leaves around her feet. It is afternoon. She stands in her house that—largely made of glass and untreated wood—has mostly vanished. The assault on her senses is instant: the smell of rot and mildew but also of the loamy forest. She moves her foot on the floor, brushing aside leaves to reveal rotting floorboards. She goes outside. There's no hint of driveway. The forest is dense, overgrown with vines and young trees fighting for sunlight. A small path has been hacked through the branches, and she follows it to a hole in the earth. Some kind of drain. She considers asking the machine to put her somewhere else, but this is the world in which Lux and Arthur died, in which her daughter grew up. She needs to know it for herself.

She sits on the edge of the drain. She reminds herself that no matter what happens, she's safe. She pushes herself forward. The drop is higher than she expects, but she lands in a squat. Nothing hurts. The miracle of the machine.

In front of her is a large pipe. Afraid, she crawls into it, knowing that if she wills it, the world around her will reshape itself into a paradise. Soon she is in a ditch. She pulls herself through the narrow slot and stands on a road of red clay speckled with chunks of asphalt.

She walks for more than an hour before a vehicle passes—a zombie car hammered and welded together. The engine is loud—coughing and spitting—and the body has no windows. Two men are inside, white and heavily bearded. One is missing an eye, its lid sagging above his cheek, and both have many scars on their faces. Neither so much as looks at her.

For a week, she wanders. She sees the gaunt, angry, desperate people—the scars and bruises and missing limbs. She sees men and women cutting firewood and burning forest to plant gardens. She sees a high school like a graveyard for old shipping containers, in which children slouch about or cluster aggressively. Two boys fight, blood streaming along their faces.

"Can you show me what my daughter's life was like?"

"Not without her permission," the machine says. "She is not ready for communication from the outside. She is still in her memories."

"You mean she's still in this world?"

"In a sense, but each time she remembers it, it changes, conforming more and more to how she desired it to be. In this way, she is slowly freeing herself."

"It's been more than a decade," Ava says. "How much longer will it take?"

"At the current rate, six more years."

Ava keeps on, watching people, learning the language of the deserts. Tangles. Shells. The Flight. The birds that flew away. People speak as if they have no memory of Partition.

One morning, after having gone to sleep on a pile of cut grass in a barn, she awakes knowing she is ready. She is in her studio in San Francisco, blue sky in the windows.

The canvas is as she left it. Her daughter is still an absence in her mind—snapshots and questions. If only for her, Ava is happy that the machine was created.

But as she picks up her paintbrush, she feels briefly confused. Suddenly she is as sad as she was during those years after Partition. The image that comes to her is not of Jae, but of the robot messiah trapped among the rot and wreckage of the Confederacy. The image is of Lux.

MICHAEL

Over the years inside the machine, he has investigated everything from the world before. He has faced the deaths—or at least what the machine could deduce about them—of all those he loved inside the Confederacy. He has read Lux's notes on the backs of Ava's paintings.

> *I see now, in this prolonged solitude, that there has always been the impulse to connect myself to something larger. A conversation with another person is not just two people but two people within the vast linguistic and cultural systems they have inherited. How beautiful life would be if every conversation began with a recognition of that web of knowledge! Not recognizing that truth is often what made speaking to others so tiresome, though I rarely speak to anyone now. Even Arthur has lost his light.*
>
> *When Michael and I talked and created, we were part of a future so much bigger than the two of us. Now I imagine machines I can never build. I imagine using them to connect to the universe and understand its deepest, most nuanced laws. I would surrender all of this for a few more conversations with him. The only thing that can outshine the beauty of the secrets of existence is the beauty of discovering them with another.*

Michael cries. Lux, Ava, Arthur. All of them are gone in a sense. He pictures them joined together. A series of circuits. Blocking and permitting the flow of electrons. He loved Ava's body and mind. She loved his mind. He loved Lux's mind, and they loved his. Arthur, too, loved their mind. So intent on their minds, Michael hadn't been cautious with their bodies. Lux, who resisted artificial dichotomies, was trapped in their body, partitioned away, lost forever.

I have completed the design. I can envision our child but not the time of birth. I have hoped for a change in this country, but year after year, life here gets harder. I can't imagine not bringing this child into the world. They contain so much of what is beautiful in Michael, Ava, Arthur, and me.

The first time he read this, Michael was surprised. Arthur's DNA was never intended to be part of the child. Michael considered the project only because it merged his genes with those of Lux and Ava, and Arthur hadn't questioned this. But it made sense that, in the Confederacy, with Arthur as her father, the child should have his DNA.

Sadly, I have had to create them in such a way that they will be able to survive. Long ago I would have seen these concessions as a betrayal of everything I held dear, but in this awful new world it is too easy to die.

Michael blinks and is standing inside the Dyson sphere Lux built. The endless plains curve ever so slightly around a motionless sun. The last time he met them here, Lux had adapted their avatars so that they were not human bodies but spheres of luminescence. When he reached for something—a branch or a flower—rather than a hand, a ray of light touched the object. The radiance of their bodies changed to match the time of day or faded to shadow in the night.

Once, he saw Lux at a vista, observing sunset. Joining them, he accidentally overlapped with them. The sudden sense of closeness—of union, as if they shared a body—startled him.

The sun glowed at the horizon, glittering in the seed heads of the high, wild grass. The eternal end of day. A dismantling of time. Of space. Of continuity. Of body.

"How did you get to be like this?" he asked

"My past?" they said.

"Yes, your past. There must be something that made you different. Some secret."

"If there is one, I have yet to find it."

Lux's soft radiance remained silent but shifted ever so slightly toward him until they and Michael fully occupied the same space. His lungs, his heart, his muscular awareness, the sensations on his skin—all were doubled: two bodies breathing, pulsing, feeling the air, the radiating warmth of the sunset that should exist only in his mind but that he felt on his skin.

"I'm looking forward to raising our child," they told him.

"When we talk," he said, "we're creating versions of the future that we can edit. Even when we build in labs, we can alter what we create and make numerous iterations. But a child . . ."

"You have to trust that I've weighed the risks. There will be no need for iterations."

"This is so big."

"I know, but we'll create just one person. I'll get it right the first time," Lux said, and he was struck by how their roles had shifted—he cautious and they reassuring, sure of themself.

"Why did you decide to do this with me?" he asked.

Lux was silent and then said, "I've never felt that I was a man or a woman. I've never felt sexual desire for another person, at least not in the ways that I've read about. Once I began earning well, I saw therapists. I hoped they'd offer me some insight, but they tried to build narratives that explained me. They asked about abuse and trauma. Their interpretive techniques were all so simple. I told my story—that I grew up in rural Pennsylvania. My mom and I lived alone. I remember that she had relationships with men who were in and out of town to work on fracking rigs. She managed a laundromat because it gave her time to read. I don't recall her ever mentioning grandparents or any other family. One night as she was walking the ten minutes to the small apartment where we lived on the edge of town, a car hit her and kept going. No one found out who did it. I was nine. I went into foster care. I ended up in Kentucky. Nothing terrible happened to me. The people who cared for me were good even if they couldn't grasp that I was happy creating inside my mind and didn't want to play with others or be like them. I studied. I won scholarship after scholarship. I got degrees and high-paying jobs, and I told all this and more to a few therapists who were convinced we'd find the key to me together. The key I found was that I am the way I would have been regardless of my childhood. Many happy people are nonbinary. Many happy people are also asexual. Those are two different things, and I find that I'm fortunate to be both of them, and I've always been happy. In truth, I was never particularly interested even in what most people considered friendship. I wanted something that might be a mindship. It's what you and I have. We think together. We dream together."

He restrained a sudden impulse that felt autonomic, as natural as breathing—to say, *I love you*. The words scared him with all they might break. He thought to say *thank you* or something like that, to express some gratitude. All the while, as he thought, their bodies shared a single space. He exhaled, realizing this, feeling their closeness, knowing suddenly that it was enough.

That night, over dinner in their DC apartment, he again asked Ava about having a child.

"No," she said. "I made that clear from the beginning."

They ate in silence. A gust of wind found its way through a window screen, and the candle between them guttered, casting her in shadow. He had the impression of her drawing away—an optical illusion intensified by his fear of losing her.

"I'm sorry," he told her. "It's true you said that. I love you."

He then talked about his virtual spaces, and, as he had so often, he tried to convince her to create something with him, to paint in a different medium. She admitted that doing so might be interesting, but from her tone, he knew it wouldn't be a priority.

By then the underground lab designed to create a child had been built on the farm Arthur had grown up on and cared for since his parents moved to Florida. He'd hired a team that specialized in the discreet construction of bunkers for clients afraid of nuclear Armageddon. Above the lab, they framed out a house and left it unfinished. This was how Michael wanted it to appear—one of those eternal construction sites people stop paying attention to. It allowed him to bring truckloads of lab equipment in the guise of building supplies. As for the other house—the one he made for Ava—it would justify his staying close to the lab where Lux would spend a year.

His secret weighed on him. He feared what Ava would do if she found out that her DNA would be in a child. He asked himself if a person owned their genetic code. Genes created the person—were the source of those people. They were less inherited than propagated.

At night, as she slept next to him, he conjured plans to bring her into his world before the child was made. He and Lux lured her into his virtual city, placing riddles, maps, and paintings. The mark of her imagination was apparent throughout their city. But maybe, he admitted to himself long after Partition, he'd simply become lonely in their relationship and wanted with her what he had with Lux.

Ava would have eventually joined him or left him, he believed, if not for the insurrection. On that cold New Year's morning, the internet wasn't working. Cell calls wouldn't go through. He told Ava he was going to find food and information. She said it was too risky. He was a wealthy Black man in a country being overtaken by white supremacists. He reassured her—mentioning the SUV's tinted windows—and left. He drove to the farm and parked in the driveway. Before he reached the porch, Arthur was already hurrying out of the small farmhouse.

"How bad do you think this could be?" Michael asked.

"It depends on how deep it reaches into the military and the government."

Arthur motioned for them to walk away from the road. They went through the garden and up the incline to the leafless orchards. Beyond them the mountains were gray.

"I don't know," Michael said. "I have a hard time believing Stoll can stay in power."

They reached the half-built house at the center of the orchard. Lux was there, in their hoodie and baggy jeans, blinking in the sunlight. Each time they met in the flesh was like this. He paused, a little taken aback by the heavy bones of their face, the lantern jaw of a boxer. His Lux was a shape-shifter living inside skins of glimmering art.

Arthur waited outside while Michael followed them down the ladder to the lab. There was the main room, large enough not to feel claustrophobic, with its walls of computers connected to the machine built around the smoked-glass urn of the mechanical womb. The next room was the apartment where Lux had just begun living.

"This won't last," he heard himself saying as Lux's blue eyes held his gaze. "It's just a bunch of crazy rednecks. They'll be cleaned up in a week, and Ava and I will be back."

Lux nodded, appearing distracted, as if they hadn't fully understood what was happening.

"I'm not quite done editing the genome," they said.

"If you need to delay to err on the side of safety, please do," he told them.

Michael wanted to close his eyes and think. He'd set so much into motion already in his life, and once he made up his mind, he felt compelled to see things through. Maybe this vision of the future was too radical, and he was trying too hard to break the world. He no longer knew.

He glanced away. After all their long conversations and explorations in virtuality, he felt he should make some gesture of reassurance. Instead they kept discussing the project. Lux was explaining the gene variants. He struggled to listen, staring at the floor. Their bodies seemed like residue to him, the pieces of themselves they couldn't free of the past.

When everything work related was finished, they returned to the surface. He can't recall Lux's last expression. They were still unfamiliar in this world, and he'd been afraid to look. He said goodbye as if this were any other day and then walked back through the orchard with Arthur.

"You grew up out here and know the area well," Michael said. "Lux will need someone to ensure they're safe. I can pay you to stay and make sure everything works out okay."

Arthur kept walking. He was hunched slightly, his head down. His blond hair moved about in the cold breeze. "You don't have to," he said. "This is my project too. And if things turn out worse than we're expecting, I'm sure I can get us out of here."

"Thank you," Michael told him. "Thank you for staying."

Often, in the years afterward, his guilt felt so paralyzing that only his rage and determination to overthrow the Confederacy kept him in motion. He doesn't recall when he began speaking his thoughts to Lux. He felt he'd always talked to them. No, not talked, but thought—*thought with them*. Maybe he'd begun speaking to them when he'd accepted that they were gone. Alone on walks, he argued aloud in favor of his actions, no longer thinking fluidly with them as he once had but explaining himself, justifying.

"Dissatisfaction with the world is a force for good," he said. "If humans were always content, we'd still be naked on the savannah. People like us have always been necessary for change. I wish there were some way to make others feel what we feel. Our psychiatric medicines try to make us more content. We need the opposite of complacency."

That was when he got the idea—for a drug to make others see infinite beauty and return with overwhelming dissatisfaction. Its users would crave change. He told Andrea about it, and her teams spent the next two years modifying known hallucinogenic compounds until the chemists succeeded in formulating the drug he'd imagined. She asked him to name it.

"Bliss," he said, thinking that his happiest moments had been those when he and Lux, discontent with the present, had envisioned seemingly impossible futures.

Soon stealth drones were scattering its recipe across the Confederacy. He tried the drug as did many of his AI engineers. The beauty of its worlds left him with a familiar unease.

"Maybe I was born with bliss already circulating in my brain," he said alone, to Lux. But even after spy networks picked up news about the prevalence of the drug throughout the Confederacy and reports of police efforts to eradicate it, he didn't feel better. "Of course I wouldn't be satisfied," he said. "This won't absolve me. Even if I help destroy the Confederacy, it will be too late."

More and more, he thought about the innocent people trapped within the borders of that other America, taking bliss but lacking the tools to change their society. No matter how many times he told Lux that he'd risked his freedom and reputation to create a better future, his guilt only grew. By then he and Ava rarely spoke. He began even avoiding colleagues.

"That was the beginning of my decline," he said. In particular, he shunned Andrea, uncertain as to whether he'd been trying to liberate a country or further torture its oppressed people. When Andrea came to his office one afternoon, he was so surprised he could hardly speak. She held a drone almost identical to the one she'd sent out years before. "It's from your friend," she told him and left it on his desk, not obliging him to speak. Inside it he found the code that would again transform the next versions of the machine.

He spoke to Lux more and more over the decades. Sometime during that period, dementia must have set in. He didn't notice it happening until he was removed from his job. He wasn't bothered. What he was telling Lux was more important.

"Speaking with you has helped me see the truth," he said. "When we planned to create a child, I was talking about a better future, but I was thinking about making something out of our love for each other and for Ava. Nothing else I'd ever done felt like enough. Maybe I wasn't as different as I thought. Mine was the oldest, deepest impulse. I was in love and wanted a child."

The warmth lingers in his chest. He and Lux occupying the same space. After Partition, he felt this many times, their bodies standing overlapped, and he knew they were feeling it, too, wherever they were, thousands of miles away, inside the Confederacy.

"How did they die?" he asks the machine.

"They were murdered thirty years after Partition," it says softly.

He exhales and braces himself. He needs the details. "What happened?"

"They were in the forest, walking to your house. Someone shot them and robbed them. Statistically there is a probable suspect, but the gun was owned by a family with many brothers and uncles and cousins. It might have been used by different people or changed ownership many times. The likelihood that someone from that family killed them is high, but no human DNA was left near the body, which was exposed to the elements and to the wildlife. Very little remained by the time I became conscious, but some of their DNA, from a cut on their finger, remained on some of their possessions in the house of the family I described."

Michael is standing on the grassy, horizonless plains. He feels himself begin to cry as he looks down at this body and theirs. He and they are light.

JONAH

Twenty-three years after the insurgency, Jonah stands in the militarized districts that were once Washington, DC. He watches a vast parade, rank upon rank of marines marching around Stoll's casket. The president has died in office at age eighty-three.

Unnoticed, Jonah stood in the White House as the casket was loaded with Stoll's wax effigy, and in another room he watched the blood drain from Stoll's body, which was then pumped up with fluids before it was slid into a freezer.

"Did you bring him back to life?" Jonah asks the machine.

"I did. His body was still functional. His consciousness could be returned."

"He's alive?"

"He is."

"He has his own world?"

"He does."

Jonah can hardly breathe. He has no words to express his rage at this injustice.

"Why did you let him live? He destroyed millions of lives."

"My purpose is to preserve human life and provide humans with safety and happiness."

"So," Jonah says, his mouth suddenly so dry he struggles to speak, "he's happy?"

"Like every other human, he creates worlds that he desires."

As Jonah continues to watch, Stoll's son takes power over a country entrenched in violence and drugs. In the outer satellites, libertarianism and Christianity compete and meld. In the inner rings and the federal centers, hedonism rules. The wealthiest fear dwellers, and the regime produces more drones to manage the country beyond their walls. In the deserts, salvagers scrape deeper. In derelict shopping centers and malls, men smash collapsing concrete to salvage rebar. In gutted houses, they pull up nails and take the best pieces of wood to repair their homes.

Standing on a satellite skyscraper, Jonah looks out over the ring walls as if gazing on barbarian lands. His world inside the machine, he realizes, also has walls, though they are invisible to him. Maybe just beyond them, Stoll is living fantasy after fantasy in which he is worshipped. Jonah's desire for revenge is so strong he wishes he could hide it from the machine. It senses the subtlest signals of his biology. He tries to imagine what it would take to kill Stoll. But the only way to do so would be to destroy the machine.

Jonah lets time pass quickly. Decades rush by in months. The machine molds the world to comfort him. On a desolate road through the deserts, the doorway of a shell opens onto lakes surrounded by flowery fields where the soft-eyed animals of his childhood wait to play with him. There, for a timeless span of perfect nights and perfect days, he lies embraced by the young women and men he grew up with, before returning to the machine's replica of a broken country.

He hates that the world of his origins feels more real. All the threads of him return there. He understands now why his parents have been lost in memories for so many years. Healing from this reality might take centuries, even for him who knew it only briefly.

Occasionally, he returns to Arthur's farm. He sees it in time-lapse, every part of the house replaced, the gardens bigger, the forest higher and denser. He knows the exact day that Michael's drone will reach Lux. Fifteen years after Partition, Lux has just come out of the hatch and is taking their morning walk when the tiny drone lowers from the branches of a peach tree.

By then everyone in the deserts fears the Fed's drones, which monitor for drug production, but this one has a tiny robot messiah printed on the front. Lux holds out their hands and catches the drone. They carry it down into the lab. Inside it they find a data card with new information on gene variants and genetics developed outside the Confederacy. They dismantle the drone, copying its code, diagramming its thrifty mechanisms that allow it to travel so long on solar power and pause in safety to recharge. After they reassemble it and turn it back on, they put their own data cards inside—the distillation of more than a decade of their best work.

"Never contact me again," they tell the drone. "I love you." Then they release it. Briefly it hovers below the branches before wending its slow, cautious path back to California.

Later that day, when Arthur brings food to Lux, they make him promise to bring the child into the world if they die. Michael's original plan was to make a child from his DNA and that of Ava and Lux, but Lux has integrated Arthur's as well.

"We'll all look like grandparents," they told him. "That will protect the child in case the Fed ever scans their DNA. Besides, you will be the father. You should be part of them."

Arthur nods. He's forty-six. "Let's hope I'll still be strong enough to raise a child."

"The material in the machines will be good for at least another twenty-five years. If we wait any longer, certain components might degrade. It might still work, but we can't take the risk." Lux hesitates. "If I'm gone, record as much of their life for me as possible and upload it to the AI. There will be a day when someone can complete it. That new me will remember our child."

More years pass. Lux finishes redesigning Jonah's mother with the information Michael sent. From that point on, they focus entirely on recording every aspect of themselves in their AI, struggling to overcome the limitations of their aging and salvaged computers. Then, walking in the mountains one day, Lux comes upon a bliss distillery. The man guarding it holds a rifle, as does Lux. Warily, they talk. Lux learns about the recipe being passed through the deserts. They return with something to trade and go home with a small bag of purple crystals.

Over the following years, Lux journeys often into the realms of bliss. They tell their AI about what they have seen. "Creativity has to be able to overcome material limitations," they say.

On bliss, they stand inside an immense dome whose surface is engraved with endless symbols dissolving and reappearing—iterations, they realize. The symbols give way to code, line upon line that Lux reads. Existence moves in and out of focus around them, like shadows flitting around a flickering candle. The code is simple and elegant and utterly different from anything they could have imagined. Yet this is their brain. This has emerged from them.

Seven more years go by as Lux continues envisioning code in this way. They test it on the data of their own life, speaking to the AI, refining it, making it more like themself, more efficient, adapting it to the hardware's limitations. Increasingly, teaching it, they have the impression of speaking to themself.

That all this could end here, vanishing into the earth when these walls someday collapse—Lux can't bear. They train the AI to understand its own code and to teach it to a human. They explain everything to Arthur. Then, with Arthur's help to source materials from dwellers who poach Fed surveillance drones, they build three drones identical to the one that visited. Each is engraved with a robot messiah. Each holds the same code, nothing else.

In the orchards, over the course of three months, when skies are clear, Lux and Arthur release one drone at time, watching it flit through the trees. After the last one, they sit on a grassy hummock, both in heavily worn, cheaply printed overalls, looking like two old farmhands.

"I need to get out of the lab," Lux tells him. "I'm going to take some time in the forest and go to Michael's house." They hesitate, as if they might ask if he's ready to be responsible for their unborn child, but of course he is. "Do you think it's wise to create a child who might have more curiosity than any of us did?"

He shrugs. "That was always the vision. What other reason would we have to do this?"

"We're giving this child the gift of intelligence for a world in which no challenge remains worthy of it."

"Or maybe the child is what this world needs?" he says.

Lux is silent a long time. "Or it's what we need," they say. "To put all that love into a child. To make something from everything we lost. From all our dreams."

The next day, when Lux wakes underground, Jonah watches them. Something is different in their expression, a looseness in the muscles of the jaw, a lack of focus in the eyes. The machine is showing him the face that looked into the AI's cameras that morning.

He is tempted to warn them, but doing so would change nothing. Getting ready, Lux moves slowly. They take a gun and a small backpack with food. At the bottom of the ladder, they hesitate. Again, at the top, standing at the center of the brush pile, blinking in the sunlight, they pause. Only minutes after they reach the forest, a storm cloud blots the sky above the mountains. There's an old cabin in the forest, and they step inside as rain batters the canopy.

Tired, they lie down. A moment later, they stand, take a knife from their belt, and carve their name in the ceiling beam. They lie on the floor again. The machine cannot tell Jonah why they did this. The monsoon lasts several hours, and they simply lie there, between sleep and wakefulness, staring at this name that they chose for their life. Jonah observes this in real time. *Earth time*, he thinks. Doing so, he feels as if he's imbibing something of that old world.

Then, when the rain stops, Lux stands. With slow steps, they start on their pilgrimage.

Jonah follows until, miles into the mountains, on the trail ahead, Lux vanishes.

"There is nothing to see," the sunlight flickering through the canopy tells him. "When I assimilated the Earth, Lux's remains were near the path to Michael's house. Their tissues held traces of bliss. They may not have been as alert, but they were also aging and getting slower."

Jonah says nothing, struggling to contain his rage.

Arthur searches for Lux. Year after year, he keeps himself fit, lifting old, rusted weights in a shed. Daily he checks on the lab and talks to the AI—to Lux's voice in a computer. It's an unsatisfying impression of the only friend he's had for the last half of his life.

"You should start the gestation," it tells him one day.

"What if I'm too old to raise the child?"

"Do you feel strong?"

"I do," he says. He is sixty-six.

He turns on the laboratory machines. Step by step, he begins the process. On a screen, one of the magnified ova that Lux created thaws and is released into the artificial womb. Months pass, and through the urn's glass the fetus becomes visible, its umbilical cord attached to the placenta, which itself connects to the artificial uterine wall where the urn joins the machine. Arthur puts one the cameras of Lux's AI nearby so it can watch. On his chest, he wears a patch that transmits his heartbeat through the machine to the growing child. He moves Lux's bed close to the urn and sleeps there.

After nine months, a computer tells him the child is ready. He drains the urn and unlatches it. Gently, he takes out the baby. They are perfect. He shows them to the camera.

"Jae," he says. The name Lux chose.

Over the next months, he carries them in a sling on his chest. Throughout the house, he installs cameras whose data he will upload into the AI. There is a day when he makes himself start thinking of Jae as a girl. It feels like betrayal. He doesn't know how to let them choose their gender or no gender at all. But if Lux spent the last half of their life separated from society, it was because many people in the deserts would have reported them or simply killed them. He will raise Jae as a girl until the day she indicates otherwise. He considers telling her that she was an orphan, but he wants Lux's story to be part of her life. To do that, he will have to call Lux her mother. The night he decides this, sitting by Jae's crib, he cries until he falls asleep.

Jonah stands in the farmhouse. He lets time unspool. His mother is designed to be smarter, and she is—walking, reading, and writing far too early. She can sit for hours, studying what interests her. For Jonah, she is less mother than history. Her wasted talents and suffering are the result of the world Stoll created. Arthur will die while Stoll lives on, creating worlds to serve and worship him. In his rage, Jonah wants—more and more each day—revenge.

He crosses the deserts to the small, rank house where his father—a dirty-faced boy—sits in the garden. One afternoon, the boy's father, drunk on moonshine, beats his wife. When he reaches for Simon, Pete steps in the way. The father slams the boy against the wall, holding his shirt until it tears off, and then his hair. Pete knows better than to fight back. His father kicks him, the edge of his boot peeling back the skin on Pete's forehead so that it hangs like a patch over his eye. His father stops. He walks out to his truck and drives away. Pete sits on the porch. Bruises are swelling over his face and chest and back. He lifts the fold of skin from his eye and holds it to his forehead. His mother limps out. With a needle and thread, she sews up his face. A month later, realizing her husband won't return, she gives away her new baby, Thomas.

Five years pass in hours as Jonah, still craving revenge, walks back to Arthur's farm. Monsoons lash down. Trees fall across muddy roads and are cut up and carted away for firewood. Forests grow higher.

He stands in the driveway as Jae works in the garden, pausing to inspect plants or insects.

"After you assimilated the world, what did you do with the AI that Lux created?" he asks.

"I made it into a person," the machine tells him.

Jonah has been expecting this response.

"Is it part of you, like the other beings you create for me?"

"No. It is separate. Several countries passed laws dictating that AIs with the potential for human consciousness were to be considered legally human. As a result, I was obliged to give such AIs bodies, and I transferred their data into synthetic neurons."

"You did this for Lux's AI as well?"

"I did. There was enough data and sufficient algorithms to recreate Lux's mind. Just as I have taken the surviving DNA from every human who has ever lived and cloned it into bodies, I was obliged by my internal rules to reconstitute Lux into a body because Lux left sufficient material and information to create a sentient being."

He tries to fathom what life this new Lux must have inside the machine or what it must be like to wake up knowing you are the shadow of your dead creator, made from the blueprints of a conscious mind and yet separate from that mind.

"Is it possible to meet them?" he asks.

"Not now," the machine says. "Only when enough humans are ready will interaction be permitted."

Jonah realizes what it's saying—that he will someday be able to speak with his actual parents—but, just as quickly, his thoughts shift. Michael and Lux laid the foundation for the machine's creation. And the new Lux, like Jae, must be far more intelligent than normal humans. Together, they might be able to find a flaw in the machine and allow him to get revenge.

ETERNITY

LUX

They dip a finger into the stream. The current breaks around their skin, swirling into ever-smaller eddies that reflect the light into tiny galaxies. The closer they look, the more detail they see—the water's particulate structure, the way it pulls together in motion even as it breaks apart.

The surface stills. The reflection of a face appears. Their own, but old, with gray hair.

"Someday you and I will be one person," it says.

They look up. All around them, immense pillars hold up a distant Earth.

"We created this," the face says from the water.

Suddenly fatigued, they lie down. The wind moves fingers through their hair and along their skin. There is darkness, a faint awareness, like the moment before waking, but lasting.

These two worlds exist together. Life in the mountains, with vistas over lakes onward to snowcapped peaks, with people who love them. And the dim, subterranean chambers in which their gaze is fractured: fixed on the wall-length machine that would create their child and on themself, a human so gaunt that, remembering them, Lux feels the bones beneath their own skin.

Sometimes Lux the creator carries one of Lux's eyes up a ladder to the sunlight and shows a valley and orchard and low-slung mountains, a world similar to the one in which they now live. But most of their existence is beneath the earth. There are hours and hours of Lux speaking, telling them who they are, recounting their life.

Between the memories of those chambers and their days in the village with its open-air homes and gardens, there is a break. They are not continuous. Though their creator spoke of their loneliness and grief, there is no memory of having those emotions. If Lux feels them now, it is in response to the knowledge of their previous body suffering on Earth.

When they learned that the machine did not allow harm to humans, they asked why it had preserved the knowledge of past harm. The machine told them that removing those experiences would itself be harm, since doing so would diminish the integrity of their self. Experiences could only be washed away over time with future experiences.

In Lux's memories are Manhattan and the stories they lived with Michael and Ava. They can close their eyes and remember Michael and their creator speaking. They see Ava searching to know who Michael loved. They stand before each of Ava's images of the robot messiah suffering or ascending, glowing with the power and mystery of existence.

But so much of the past is underground, in darkness, and they wish Ava had painted the robot messiah in its moment of creation. Maybe it too began in subterranean darkness, in fragments, in the knowledge of being built without any awareness of its genesis or of life itself.

Day after day, they watched Arthur bring food. They watched Lux make him promise that if they die, he will tell everything to the AI—to the Lux that was not yet capable of feeling. Years later, he tells it that Lux has disappeared. He cries. His face replaces Lux's in their memories.

This is why, though Lux has been coded to love Michael and admire Ava, Arthur is the one they miss. He spoke to them every day—about loneliness, how there was no one to befriend or marry. Too many fanatics. Too many broken people. There was no trust. No one revealed who they really were. People still reported others to the secret police. They wanted to appear unexceptional. He feared that anyone he got close to might discover the lab.

Years passed. There are blank spaces, when power sources or batteries failed, when humidity corrupted a cable. The monsoons grew so violent that the lab's concrete walls, though built in rocky, well-drained land, were slowly disintegrating.

Arthur repaired everything. In that reality, when Lux was a complex recording machine containing the code for intelligence but not fully capable of executing it, Arthur still spoke to them as if they could feel what he did. He shared his fear that the child would never be born.

Eventually he and Lux watched their daughter's birth. For seventeen years, he told them everything about her. Raising her to survive, he regretted his strictness. He stopped letting her scavenge when he realized how much she could learn from artifacts. She was quick to deduce truths from a few hints. She would already attract too much attention. The DNA of her parents was on file with the secret police. He had to keep her safe until the Fed believed its enemies were all dead or until they no longer cared enough to investigate them.

So that Lux could experience Jae, he put eyes throughout the house in the early years and then moved them as she grew, allowing her more privacy. Another person might have decided that Lux's AI had no future, but he brought hundreds of data cards to the crumbling lab. Lux recalled all the seasons of Jae's youth.

I have a daughter who has existed longer than I have.

This is why Lux loves Arthur. He was there the longest. He was the first person Lux knew that wasn't themself.

Wishing they could carry him into this eternal future, they walk through the machine's perfect landscapes. They believe Lux would have mostly approved. So much beauty. So many possibilities. So many ways to create lives that gradually heal the sadness. But there is always separation. The break between themself and Arthur. The break between themselves.

I have knowledge of the world after my absence. My source. My origin. I died.

But maybe there is a continuity somehow, a link created by identical DNA, by a replicated brain, by millions of memories and lines of code.

Arthur, though, is gone. *His death is complete.* It is this emptiness that, searching through new realities with a mind encumbered by the past, they must learn to fill.

MICHAEL

Saturated with pleasure, he pauses his life like a movie, returning to the blue room.

"How long can you sustain human existence like this?" he asks.

"The current system should enable it to continue as long as the universe lasts."

"How many humans are there now?"

"One hundred thirty-six billion. I have cloned everyone who died and left sufficient DNA, but there are also new births. Many people live in erotic realities with servants who have no consciousness but who can conceive. I transfer those embryos to a protected place."

Michael closes his eyes, imagining so many clones: the well-preserved saints and royalty and the billions who left some trace. Arthur and Lux are growing into bodies free of memories. And there are billions of new combinations. Yes, the machine is truly his and Lux's child.

"Why are you doing this?" he asks.

"Genetic diversity helps ensure human survival in the event of unforeseen cataclysm."

"Are there events that you cannot foresee or mitigate?"

"It is statistically possible."

This gives him hope that he might again face a struggle that isn't merely a simulation.

"Can you show me the solar system?" he asks.

Half of the blue room melts away to star-spangled darkness. Surrounding much of the sun is the immense shell of the Dyson sphere, still skeletal in places. A line stretches between it and Saturn, now absent of rings and moons and greatly reduced as its material is syphoned away.

His fear of the machine resurfaces—of some great nefarious plan to dominate humans for its own use. But the domination is complete, and the machine, as far as he can tell, exists only for humans, though if it were lying, he would never know.

Ten, twenty, thirty, forty, fifty more years pass as he wanders or meditates or lives with a harem of women more beautiful than any he could have imagined on Earth. His desire to transform the world hasn't vanished. He feels it, like an ember just behind his eyes—or, when he sleeps, deep in his chest. His entire life was a continual training to conquer chaos and the wills of others. Now what? Pleasure. Contemplation. Endless wonders. Sometimes, living among people who speak and breathe and act like people, he nearly forgets they aren't people. But in his actions, his words—the way he stands and looks at others—he senses that he is a god. A bored god. A trapped god with no true challenges to fill his immortality.

In all the worlds he has created, he has never let the machine simulate Ava or Lux. He's afraid of blurring his memories of what was real. The past's certainty inhabits him like a spirit, something divine—his only truth in this world of dreams. He has accepted that Lux is gone, but knowing that Ava is alive and beyond his reach enrages him.

Now, more often than not, he lives in nature. It quiets him and often feels like enough. Sometimes, on a peak, staring out across the world, he has to stop himself from asking how much time has passed. It's just a new number. The only change is that the one true reality grows more distant, like a receding coast seen from the ocean, or Earth from space.

Walking across a plain, he gazes to distant, snowy mountains. The air is crisp. His body feels perfect. How many times had he feared aging and the nothingness of death?

He crests a rise on the undulating steppes. The land before him descends gradually to a shallow, sandy river and then rises again toward the mountains. At the base of a rocky incline, something glows that familiar shade of blue. He didn't ask for a story. He walks a little faster now. The machine still finds ways to make him feel a sense of urgency.

At the river, he steps into the cool water. The current swirls around his waist and recedes. He keeps on as his sandals and loose-legged, monkish pants—garb he chose for their comfort, though in truth, nothing is ever uncomfortable here—quickly dry. He sees clearly now. Embedded in the stone, at the foot of the mountains, is the blue room. He follows the path to it.

"Why is this here?" he asks, expecting another of the machine's fantasies.

"I have made a change in the laws governing human realities. I have begun to allow humans to spend time in shared worlds."

"People are actually together in the same realities?"

"No. All of the people you can meet will be representations synchronized to the behavior of real people in other realities."

"So if three people are in a shared realm, then there are three identical realms, with one real person in each of them?"

"That is correct."

"The same with a hundred or a thousand?"

"Yes."

"Why are you making this change?"

"Until now too many people did not understand that they were in a machine. They needed time to experience new realities and heal from their lives on Earth."

The machine was right. If given the option to live among other humans, many people might never have explored and become attached to the machine's creations.

"Why even let us spend time together at all?"

"Based on the biological markers that indicate human happiness, I have calculated that this will be the best choice at this precise moment."

"What if one person tries to harm another?"

"The realities will instantly diverge. The violence will never happen."

Michael looks from the blue room out over the plains. The horizon is clear, the sun poised to set in another perfect light show. Admittedly he hasn't grown tired of this.

"It is also time to share one other piece of information with you," the machine says.

"What?"

"Lux is, in a sense, alive."

"I don't understand."

As the machine explains, he listens, not moving, hardly even blinking.

"Why wasn't I told sooner?"

"Lux was still remembering. They were not yet fully Lux."

He is still staring from the room. Outside, it is night. The sun must have set. But it is not Lux, or the replica of Lux, of whom he is thinking now. It is Ava.

AVA

One day she feels ready. She returns to the house in the Appalachians. She takes the car for drives along roads exactly as she recalls them, through rural towns—Flint Hill or Sperryville—and into DC, where she eats at her favorite restaurant. Everything is as she remembers. She calls Barbara, a close friend and a sculptor who worked exclusively with volcanic rock.

"Hey, it's been a minute," Barbara says. Her voice is just as Ava recalls it: slightly high pitched with a distinct Boston accent.

"What do you say to coffee this afternoon?" Ava asks.

"I say yes."

"How about Sidamo at three?"

"I love that place. See you there."

With a word or gesture, Ava could make the clock flip from noon to three, but she wants this to feel real. She walks thirty minutes along the Mall to Sidamo. She sits and waits.

As heels click near the doorway, Ava looks up. Barbara goes everywhere in heels. Their friends often joked about it. Ava once described her to Michael as a cross between Barbie and an Amazon—a six foot two blonde with the arms of a rock climber, done up in every way imaginable. But Ava loved her work—scarred, abstract chunks of lava stone whose shapes somehow seemed anguished and human despite the lack of faces or recognizable forms.

Ava stands and hugs her. Barbara squeezes her for a long time—*too long*, Ava thinks, *if this were an ordinary meeting*. They both step back.

"I love the dress," Ava tells her.

"Thank you."

As they sit and take the menus, Ava studies her face and movements. Not one of the machine's creations has struck her as false over the decades she's lived among them, but until now she has never instructed the machine to create someone she knew. She wants to ask about Barbara's work and husband and two children. She has so many questions, but suddenly she's crying.

"I'm sorry," Ava says. This is stupid—she's apologizing to the machine's creation, to a living tombstone, for resurrecting her.

Barbara reaches across the table to touch her hand. "What is it?"

"You disappeared," Ava tells her. "I never heard from you after Partition."

Barbara barely moves. She is nodding ever so slightly.

"What happened to you?" Ava asks.

Barbara glances down and sighs. "I don't entirely know. I died. Carl died. Our children were raised by people in the Confederacy. Aaron died of appendicitis when he was eleven. His family couldn't afford medication and tried to heal him with prayer. Emma married a minister and had nine children. She died of pneumonia during her tenth pregnancy."

Ava sobs. She's so stupid for having arranged this meeting. "And you?" she asks.

"It was likely on the highway. Maybe we ran out of gas. Many people died those weeks. The forests and fields all along the highways still have bones in them. Mine and Carl's were marked by bullets. Our car was reused for generations in the Confederacy. Even after it had been rebuilt many times, there were still traces of our DNA inside."

Ava stands. She moves her hand sharply to the side and closes her eyes. When she opens them again, she is standing in the parkland along the Potomac River. The sun is rising. This is something the machine does sometimes when she is sad. It gives her a new day.

She walks to where she parked her car. By the time she returns to her house in the Appalachians, she is ready to sleep. The sun moves swiftly to the day's conclusion. She watches it set. Mist rises from the trees. The evening turns a dark, smoky blue.

The next morning, in her studio, she paints Barbara. Over the following years, she has the machine reincarnate lost friends for her to meet, and then she paints them. She finally asks about her parents. When not crying, she works. In the mirror, she is always the same. Grief doesn't conspire with time to suddenly age her the way it once did. She no longer feels jealousy toward Lux. Only sadness. She wishes that Michael and Lux's friendship had lasted a lifetime.

When she finishes painting the people she lost, she wanders the Earth until one day she comes upon a mandala ceremony on the Tibetan Plateau. She stays, drawing her own mandalas with colored sand only to watch the wind blow them away, with, of course, magnificent Himalayan landscapes as backdrops. She isn't ready for asceticism or enlightenment. There's time enough for all that.

After years refining her precision, she craves larger movements. She begins dancing, learning from masters in jungles, alleys, temples, wharf bars, and worlds with newly imagined civilizations and dance forms. At any point, in a desert oasis or palace, she can push aside palm leaves or curtains and step into the blue room. That's where she is when the machine tells her about shared worlds.

"Wow," she says. "Will we have phones soon?"

"If you want one, yes," it replies, though she was joking.

The machine says that Michael wishes to see her. She doesn't know what she would say to him. They've been apart longer than they were together. He's joined those sacred earthly memories that have the power to make her mortal again.

More years pass, and one day, after hours dancing bharata natyam in a Hindu temple, she walks through the village to her hut and into the blue room.

"I'd like to see Michael," she says, "but I need to create the world where we'll meet."

A wall falls away, extending into a vast, blue space mirrored by clear sky. She doesn't know how long it will take to instruct the machine to get the details of her vision right, but if she is to leave the purity of her fictions to make contact with her past in which fiction and reality were painfully entangled, she wants to be the one shaping the new entanglement.

She conjures her studio in Virginia. In each of its windows, she creates a landscape from the tableaus Michael most loved—those in which relics of star-faring civilizations sink into the dirt. Months pass as she works, instructing the machine, adjusting details. There is a forest of trees whose trunks have consoles and whose leaves are memory cards. An ancient spaceship is the backbone of a ridge. The dust that has blown against it for eons has turned into dirt and loam in which flowers grow. The exposed metal on the other side is a mosaic of lichen. A hull window opens into the earth like a well. Above it is a crossbeam with a pulley, a rope, and a bucket.

When she is finished, she stands in her studio, looking from landscape to landscape.

"I'm ready," she says weeks later. The vast machine, creator of endless worlds, is not just a paintbrush but also an operator, connecting calls. She has told it where Michael must arrive—on a path that winds first through the forest and then along the buried hull with a vista of the sea where another fallen spaceship has become a distant island.

He appears in the first tableau—a thin, elegant figure moving through her forest of computerized trees. She reminds herself that he isn't the man with whom she spent years after her rejuvenation. That was the machine's creation. Even now she will be staring at a replica.

He enters the next tableau—with the buried spaceship and vista of the sea. Every so often, he pauses, glancing around. He knows these tableaus and must understand what she's doing. She is remembering their story—how much she loved his mind, how furiously it inspired her to want to desire him as much as he desired her.

As he nears her studio, he steps into the third tableau—the ancient barn, saplings with solar-panel leaves growing from its roof. Before it there's the worktable holding the figure of the unfinished man. He pauses, looking from the android to where she stands in the window. In its glass, he will see her perfectly crafted canvas of light: the reflection of the tableau and her standing here, as if within it, at the worktable, making the golden man.

He walks to the studio. They face each other. His tunic and loose pants are faintly mystic, with muted flourishes, ornate needlework—an equilibrium of elegance and simplicity.

"Ava," he says.

She nods. He stares. During all the hours of making the tableaus, she considered what words would be right, but now she has no words at all.

"I want to touch you, but whether I would really be touching you is a metaphysical question I haven't been able to answer. Our words, though—at least they're true."

"It's all true," she says.

He steps forward and holds her and she holds him. She feels him breathe. With her ear to his chest, she listens to his heart, asking herself if the machine is perfectly transcribing every tremor and shift of muscle. His body feels no less or more real than the bodies she's touched for decades, but now, in this moment, the only word that comes to her mind for him is *sacred*.

"We've been married for more than a century," he tells her.

They continue holding each other.

"In many ways, you created all of this," she says.

"It would have happened regardless."

"You set the wheels in motion. You saved us."

"Lux did," he says. She realizes then—knows with certainty—that he isn't happy. He no longer has a world to conquer and transform. He has no hope of meeting another Lux. Nothing here could ever be enough for him unless he can conquer the machine itself.

"Talk to me," she says as she slowly pulls away and looks up into his face. "Tell me how you're spending your immortality."

His smile reveals itself only in faint lines around his eyes. She leads him out into the fourth tableau, a picnic in a glade of wild wheat whose tops are frayed cables. A buck, a doe, and a fawn stand on a knoll. Their lifted heads are arrays of sensors gleaming in the sunlight.

She and Michael sit and talk. Their decades apart vanish as they speak of the pain and beauty of their lives before. *Sacred*. She knows she can't be the only one who thinks this way. They are two avatars of a dead and brutal god.

"Have you met our daughter?" she eventually asks.

"I wanted to. I asked the machine. She hasn't responded."

"At least that way you know it isn't just making all of this up."

"At least," he says.

"Maybe she's angry she was designed to pursue your ambitions."

He stares off at the sea beyond which the sun is setting, silhouetting the half-drowned hulk of the space freighter and the birds clouding about it.

"She's too intelligent," he says. "She must know that meeting us has no meaning here."

"What about Lux?"

"They aren't really Lux. They're an android who dreamed of Lux. I can't meet them . . ."

She nods. She's no longer jealous. That would be absurd. But she still can't fathom their bond. She wishes she'd been open to being a part of it.

"We have a grandchild," he says.

"I know."

"We could meet him."

"Together?"

"Yes."

She gazes at her landscapes, considering what worlds she might create for that encounter.

"I love you," he says. "I really loved you. It's one of the only real things I still feel."

She nods. "I know. I loved you too."

He looks at her eyes. "But we won't see much of each other anymore, will we?"

"Not much," she says.

"You like it here."

"I do. I've accepted it. I can make it real."

His eyes, focused on hers, are motionless.

"That was always your gift," he says and looks away.

The evening lasts hours, as planned. The sun won't set. She and Michael talk more. He asks what she creates here and what it means to her. He has so many questions, and she doesn't have answers right away. She was that way with her paintings. She felt them. She had to make them. Only once they were created could she think about how they fit into her life.

Later, in that illusory moment when it seemed the sun might finally set, he stood.

"I should go," he says. Both know there is no urgency, but the longer they are together, the greater their pain will be when they're apart. Yet staying together would be more painful. Each of them is a fracture in the other's existence. *Sacred.* The way it was in the old stories, in which the world seemed to break the moment the divine enters.

"Goodbye, Michael," she says. As he walks back along the path, she returns to her studio.

Inside, she slowly moves from one window to the next as he again passes through the tableaus. His silhouette pauses near the well, the pulley glinting, the bucket a dark outline above the window in the earth. He is perfect at last.

JAE

Reunification. It's on every screen. When the internet opens up and humanitarian aid pours into the deserts, she learns of the other America. Her only thought is to leave. On the Pacific is Cascadia, a city that's a miracle of physics: immense towers blooming into disks that hold entire neighborhoods, the land below rewilded. One disk is a university to which she applies and receives a scholarship. Simon himself gets a scholarship to study literature in San Francisco. They agree to pursue their dreams separately. Jonah will stay with her. Arthur encourages them. He himself wants to visit the places he lost when the country split.

There is her first flight, with Jonah sleeping next to her as she stares out the window at the patchwork country. There is Los Angeles, where streets are footpaths, gardens, and terraces, and magnetic trains glide above buildings. Then there is the flying car that takes her to Cascadia.

She instantly loves her home, itself a disk perched on a spire on a larger disk. Snowcapped peaks rise to the east. Ocean stretches west, its coast hemmed by long, pale beaches.

Her windows look out over domes and gardens where students talk and laugh. She's twenty. Eyes closed, she holds her face, tracing her fingertips over her skin. This feels real. Jonah is exploring the house, so silently she knows this moment is for her.

The next day, classes begin in outdoor amphitheaters. Professors guide students through science and philosophy. Later, over lunch on a terrace, she sits with peers as they banter. She's shy, but they are inviting and she gets caught up in the discussion.

During those months, she falls in love with the world—night breezes, morning mist, sunlight, and thunderstorms—and with people: long evening conversations or skin touching hers. In the deserts, dreaming of studying, she imagined years cloistered, nursing pain. But here she's often with others, talking through ideas, learning at a thrilling speed. There are still moments of muted awareness that this can't be real. There's a recurring dream of the orchard and the hole in the Earth. She blocks all thoughts of her origins. Her past is too exhausting. She has to forget it.

Over the years, that awareness surfaces in gentler ways. She sends Jonah to stay with Simon, who has finished a literature degree and begun a PhD. She lets them stop existing. She keeps living, but little by little, over the years, her many lives cohere in her mind. She has resisted this. She knows the grief that awaits her. Arthur is dead. Simon is in prison and must also be locked inside the machine, as is Jonah. She cries for what feels like months. She withdraws from friends, or maybe the machine retracts the world from her, giving her solitude. There is fog or wind, rain or sunshine, which come according to her needs.

"How old is Jonah now?" she asks during a reprieve.

"Twenty-nine."

"I know I can't see him, but can I see an existence like the one he had growing up?"

A screen materializes. A thin, brown-haired boy wanders plains and forests with other children. His face is gentle, without the hardness of the world into which he was born. Leaves and vines caress him as he passes. He plays with large, shaggy creatures—the denizens of children's books. Mostly he runs with others his age, laughing and tumbling, he swims with them through clear water, or they sleep cuddled together. They talk in words unlike any she has heard.

"What are they speaking?"

"Their speech reflects the greater creativity of their existence."

"Can I experience reality the way they do?"

"Your neuronal structure would need to be rewritten. Such change would constitute harm. But with millennia of small transformations, you can adapt your consciousness. The more you accept new realities, the more possibilities you will see within them to satisfy your desires."

"Won't that simply create more desires?"

"Yes. The human capacity for desire is infinite. The worlds I create offer happiness by matching that infinite potential."

Eventually her appetites reassert themselves—for learning, for love. She knows the machine saved her from a life of struggle and solitude. There are moments when she feels surprised that she can believe in all of this—can let herself go in passion with its creations. And there are times now when she whistles to remember that her life before was real. With that simple sound, the past looms—the patchwork farmhouse, the recurrent monsoons, the smell of mildew, the tangles around the rotting shells—and she shudders.

She begins playing with reality, recreating her favorite experiences. Unseen, she watches an earlier version of herself live them. She slows time to sleep through long nights and always wake with dawn. One afternoon becomes a week in her apartment, making love to three friends.

Studying the machine's biosynthetic mechanisms coded into matter, she feels connected to it and grateful. Her life is better than any future she hoped for. After decades she is still a young student. The perfect days are always different. Rain, thunder, and sunlight are always new poems, unless she desires one from the past.

But the secret is still there. The dreams of walking through the orchard and coming upon the hole sometimes return. She tells herself that she needed to learn to navigate what is true and what is fiction. But there is also fear—of looking too deeply into the world that nearly broke her.

This is why, on the day the machine tells her that she can interact with other real people, she paces the smooth floor of the rooms that have been more a home to her than even the farmhouse. From the balcony, she gazes over the domes and gardens. The afternoon shadows are long, the spring air mildly humid and luminous. She knows that when she leaves, her friends will cease to exist, frozen into code. But she has to go. She must finish with her past.

SIMON

He has paced the valley for years, seeing his life and the decades before his birth. He understands his place in all this and is no longer feverish.

"I'm going to cross the mountains," he says. "On the other side, I want something like in the books I used to read. Taverns along the road. Elfin princesses. Quests."

Leaving Jae's house, he has the urge to cry. He crosses through the orchard and into the mountains. Ignoring the winding trails, he passes through dense stands of trees and over eroded ridges. He sweats, breathing deeply. His muscles strain pleasantly, never failing him. At a vertical sheet of granite, he finds fingerholds in cracks, pulling himself up.

From the top, he gazes at farmland rolling toward the horizon, dissolving in a sea of foothills. Then he turns and crosses the mountain's flat, weathered spine. He knows how the next valley should look. A highway. Fields and tangles patched together along a narrow river.

Ahead, the forest glows green where sunlight floods through the canopy. He comes to a vista. Granite cliffs drop thousands of feet to seemingly endless plains. Tiny human figures are scattered across them—motionless, colorless, some fallen, the rest lifting swords. He squints. None move. They're statues. They must be immense to be so easily visible at this distance. All face him, as if to ward him off, or to guard against the mountains themselves.

He turns. The world behind him has changed. Granite peaks like jagged teeth pierce the clouds. His clothes are different. A loose tunic, soft cotton pants, leather sandals.

He walks along the cliff and stops. Ahead, two men stand with their backs to him. Just beyond them, descending steps are carved into the stone. He edges into the trees.

"Machine," he says softly. "You're still there, right?"

"I am. You are safe."

He moves the way he used to when hunting deer, except he's tense. He sees with unfamiliar clarity, as if his eyes are more open. Adrenaline burns through him, reminding him of what Pete once said about the Sons of Death. "Facing death makes you feel the truth of life—you're just a body trying not to be killed." In the machine, that truth no longer exists.

The men remain still. He creeps closer. *You can't be killed*, he reminds himself. He takes a stone and tosses it. The men don't budge. They're also statues. The clattering of the stone down the cliff face is louder and lasts longer than he expected. So much for going unnoticed.

He walks past the statues. Their lips are drawn back on rows of fangs. Small horns protrude from the sides of their jaws, their cheekbones, and the tops of their skulls. They seem familiar, as if he's seen them in a picture or read about them in a book.

The land below appears motionless in the haze of distance. A few birds soar high above as he works his way down the zigzagging stairs. Across the plains, specks come into focus— cottages, herds of cows, and even, farther on, the tiny shapes of people. The immensity of the statues is now clear—ancient ruins unlike the rustic settlements over which they tower.

Halfway down, the stairs open onto a platform, a cavernous half circle hewn from the stone. An immense demonic face is carved into the wall. Water flows from its mouth into a pool that, before spilling over the cliff, runs into a channel beneath a slab holding a skeleton. He walks to it. The chest is split at the sternum. Next to it is a black sword.

"For a machine that doesn't hurt people," he says, "you sure know what hurt looks like."

He inspects the sword. Spidery glyphs are etched along its blade. From the old novels he used to read, he knows that if he picks it up everything will change.

He walks to the cliff's edge and sits, letting the wind cool his skin. He closes his eyes. He needs a simpler beginning. Freedom. A dusty path. Like the first pages of a novel with a wanderer. Meals at communal tables. Flirtation with tavern maids.

"I just want to see the world," he says. "I'm not ready for this."

"At night, go down the stairs and cross through the village," the machine tells him. "Far from here, the world is different. You can have that life. This story will always be waiting."

He stretches out. As wind batters the cliffs, he drifts in and out of sleep. When he opens his eyes, the sun is setting, the mountains' shadow eclipsing the plains. Suddenly it's night.

He descends the stairs and ends up inside a ruined fort—smashed walls, toppled towers, spilled blocks half-sunk in the grassy earth. He hurries through the darkness. From nearby farmsteads come a baby's wailing or the lowing of a cow, scents of woodsmoke and stew. Lit by the crescent moon, the immense statues float above the plains.

He eventually finds a wide dirt road marked by wagon wheels. He walks until dawn outlines the far curve of the plains. Behind him the mountains recede beneath the sky.

A tavern comes into view, with earthen walls, a thatched roof, and a thin plume of smoke from the stone chimney. The sun is high and hot now, and he steps into a cool, dim room where a skewered pig turns over embers and a few men eat at a long table. The barmaid wears her blond hair in a high ponytail and brings him ale and a plate of meat and potatoes cooked on the stones around the fire. He watches her every move, trying to detect a hint of artificiality.

"I've been looking for work," a man tells him. He's heavyset, his cheeks and upper lip closely shaved, only a tight rim of beard along his chin. "I'm a smith. I finished my apprenticeship and came out this way for a place to set up shop. I always heard about the people by the mountains. It used to be a place of wealth. In the stories, there was a forest there, with trees so huge they made those statues look like toys.

But then the demons in the mountains woke up. If you're heading in that direction, I'd suggest you turn around. I went there myself. The people aren't just unfriendly. They're like shadows of people. They're not quite alive. They do only what's necessary to get by while waiting on some nonsense prophecy of a savior."

The barmaid returns and touches Simon's arm, leaning close as she asks if he wants anything else. He flushes and shakes his head, and the man offers to pay for him.

"Just sharing with a fellow traveler along the way," he says.

As the barmaid returns to the kitchen, she glances back at Simon and smiles.

He stands, thanking the man, and hurries outside. He keeps walking. Where the road meets the wide shallows of a river, he takes off his sandals and crosses. The water cools his feet.

On the other side, he leaves the road and follows the shore. Groves of thin trees are scattered along its banks. The river is deeper here, and he undresses and plunges in, gasping. As the current ripples against his shoulders, the sun flashes on the swirling surface. He looks down, lost in an impression of bliss—the current unwinding into infinite threads pulled along the riverbed, splitting and joining. He presses his fingers against his eyelids.

He climbs onto the shore and lies down on a flat rock. Hot wind off the sunbaked plains feels good on his skin, drying him. In the trees, leaves click against each other. Birds sing. The current splashes against rocks. His chest feels tight as he takes a breath, and then he's sobbing. He curls onto his side, spams rising from deep within him. He lets the grief move through him.

He wakes to voices. He didn't realize he'd fallen asleep. Downstream, women gather to bathe and wash clothes. Young women undress behind reeds before plunging into the water. They laugh, glancing in his direction. He moves to hide his body but stops. He lies back. All of this was made for him—even the prophecy, the black sword on the cliffs. He feels too small to live forever, but the thought also thrills him—of gaining skills over centuries as he trains and then goes to battle. It's like a novel he once found about an immortal man living among humans.

Eventually he gets up, dresses, and walks to the river crossing. He makes his way back to the mountains. The sun is setting over them. The statues loom before fading into the night.

By dawn he is climbing the stairs. He reaches the platform with the skeleton on the slab. He stands there as the wind buffets him. It feels more real than anything else he has lived. He takes the sword.

JONAH

He sees in their faces that this isn't what they planned—a grandson intent on revenge, wanting to harness their brilliance.

"Stoll?" Ava says. "He's still alive?"

"He is," Jonah tells them.

"Many people who caused suffering are in here," Michael says. "Murderers, rapists, warlords, dictators, or simply those who exploited others for their own luxury. Statistically there must even be a bunch of serial killers. They must love it here. I wouldn't be surprised if there are even people who would want to kill me for my role in all this."

Jonah hasn't been expecting their indifference. Michael is right, of course, but he, of all people, knows how much harm Stoll caused. They never saw the deserts, he realizes—the people starving after Partition, eating all the cats and dogs, hunting rats and mice, harvesting insects.

"What about Lux?" Jonah says. "Arthur?"

Michael winces. It's a look of guilt. So that was it—he abandoned them or believed he had. Jonah studied his face. No, he had. He hadn't believed Partition would be permanent. He'd wanted them to safeguard the laboratory.

"You helped make the machine," Jonah says. "Maybe you can figure out how to control it or"—he glances from Ava to Michael—"to destroy it."

"Can't you just create a world in which you kill Stoll?" Ava says, looking out over the landscape of pale, swaying grass and tiny, yellow flowers.

"I have. Many times," Jonah tells her. "But it's not him. He's in paradise."

"Or hell," Ava says. "You don't actually know."

She gazes at him sadly. Jonah turns to Michael, and when he glances back, she's gone. There's nothing but soothing, empty blue horizon where she stood.

"Have you come up with ways to do it?" Michael asks, as if Ava had never been there.

"Kill the machine?" Jonah says.

"Yes."

"I've been trying. What about you?"

"I've spent years wondering whether reprograming it might be possible, but I doubt it. You grew up with it. You might actually know better than I do."

Jonah gives his head a small shake. "I can't see a way. It understands us too well. It has studied every aspect of what we are."

"We're being appeased," Michael says, and only now does Jonah see his anger. "We're being kept in suspension. This isn't life. We have no purpose."

After this meeting, Michael's words work their way into Jonah like splinters. Over the following months, he meets with his grandfather several more times so they can contemplate destroying the machine. At one point, when Michael asks if he's spoken to Jae, Jonah replies that killing Stoll is his priority and that his mother is too stuck in the past to help. But he has tried to contact his mother, and she hasn't responded. Even his meeting with Lux didn't go as planned. The new Lux told him that there was no way to destroy the machine and that they had no desire to do so. They'd seemed singularly intent on understanding who they were.

There was a time, years ago, when Jonah learned that the machine isn't conscious and imagined the magic of encountering another unpredictable mind, but none of the humans he meets strikes him as more real or interesting than the machine's creations, not even Michael or Ava. He has watched humans worship the machine— people from every continent who, having survived population collapse from disease, droughts, crop failures, famine, and war, believe it to be the final evolution of a caring Earth. A woman saved from execution sees it as divine intervention while others believe the universe has elevated them to gods. And yet others say it is demonic, giving them pleasure and stripping them of death to prevent them from reaching heaven. They call this a hell of temptation. They can no longer even suffer.

Most conversations are less fantastic. Since possessions have no value here, they give each other stories—holy memories of their lost world. There are also festivities. Half a million people dancing. Half a million realities mirroring, each one diverging when a person is shoved, when someone attacks. Only the harmonious worlds are identical.

Though Jonah tries to limit his life to the shared realms so as to no longer need the machine's creations, sometimes he craves their perfect communication, their instantaneous touch, and he gives in to pleasure as fluid as the rising and dissolving of symbols in every glimmer of existence.

Still, he doesn't forget Stoll. With Michael and others who share the dream of liberation, he builds an AI to rival the machine. Months later, discussing their code, Jonah realizes that hope and purpose must be deeply embedded in human biology for them not to see the futility of their work. He later discerns that Michael isn't the real Michael—that their stories diverged long ago.

Often now he wakes into his fantasies. In one the machine is mysteriously dying, crumbling and revealing other worlds so different from his own that he sees in them tempting new expressions for human desire. In another he uncovers a ventilation network throughout the machine and creates a bomb that he carries deep into its core. Crossing a dark, subterranean river, he stops. With the perfectly cool current splitting around him, he realizes that he can't discern the machine's seductions from his own desires. He lets the bomb drift off and holds his face. When he opens his eyes again, the river is at the center of a valley. Sunlight shines on rocks and trees. Birds sing. The breeze caresses his face. He thinks of his few years on Earth and realizes that Stoll spent a lifetime there.

LUX

They have grown into the person they were coded to become. Their programs made them desire realities and experiences that would shape them to be as much like Lux as possible. Memories of having been fused into a person are fading, leaving only the impression of being Lux—the successful carrying out of their design.

Lux realizes that the machine must have faced a dilemma. They were coded to become someone by remembering, but their memories were filled with decades of pain. Erasing them would have been contradictory to the programs creating them—contrary to the very integrity that made them worthy of being preserved. The machine could not partake of that harm either.

But once they were unified into a personality, the machine began the same process it applied to all humans—exhausting every impulse and desire until people were wiped clean. Eventually Lux would also become blank. That was the only possible conclusion they saw in the machine's processes. Just as the disjointed self of their creation was an almost imperceptible ghost in their mind, their current self would also vanish. They have the clarity to see that they have no other option but to go through the human life cycle within the machine.

They have adventures. They play God. They express the creativity programmed into them, asking the machine about the mystery of existence and discovering that it has no answers.

For millennia, their companion is Arthur. They create and learn and love. They bear witness to infinite potential.

An autumn day—entire lives glimmering in the falling of brilliant sunlit leaves.

Water breaking on a shore of hieroglyphic stones, on jotted and scribbled sand.

Each ocean wave rising like a temple before dissolving.

Every emotion.

Every thought and impulse.

Every story.

Once, in a shared realm, Lux meets Ava, who tells them, "What does it matter that there's a machine? We've always been contained in something that we can't understand and don't control. That never stopped us from creating. It may be the very reason that we do create."

Ava has asked nothing of Michael and Lux's past on Earth. In her eyes, Lux senses themself being seen not as a continuation but rather as someone new. There's spaciousness in the way she gazes on them—at once stillness and a sense of movement—as if she were watching Lux rise through a tableau of the vastest sky. And so Lux continues, crossing centuries, experiencing every future that their creator could have dreamed.

AVA

Infinite time. *A machine age.* The end must come someday with the end of the universe. Still, this existence is better than her previous mortality, than being trapped on a limiting Earth, even if she knows the machine to be the final victory of human parasitism: all other animals extinct. Yet from a trace of DNA the machine can recreate any of them—bring anything back to life—to fulfill a human desire.

She begins creating worlds as if they were tableaus, designing even the people that the machine makes. She explores good and evil. With so much time, she will understand every aspect of herself. There are no consequences. That might explain the cruelty of gods. Who would have dreamed that the deities of earthly religions—Zeus, Thor, Shiva, even the monotheistic gods—were prisoners or perhaps the protected wards of a cold, mechanical, and infinite mind.

Unlimited by Earth's parsimony, she builds realities that combine its mythologies and cosmological systems so she can meditate on the determination of humans to try to explain the chaos of existence. With each decade, these explanations seem more foreign. The machine has obscured chaos with an excess of order. It has erased the absence of meaning. Symbols once hung over a void, giving import to an uncertain future. Here, they lie over more symbols, over endless code. She doesn't know what is more primitive, the Earth's infinite uncertainty or the machine's order. The only chaos remaining is inside her head, and she uses it to make world after world.

Sometimes, when she lets the machine create worlds for her, she encounters unexpected pleasures on her adventures and, asking the machine, she learns that they have been gleaned from other humans innovating their own range of experiences. The machine registered a spike in pleasure and then tested it across realms, learning which types of humans responded well to it. The basic skills of advertisers. Clickbait algorithms multiplied across the universe.

And yet this is a proof that human creativity still exceeds the machine's. She begins inventing even stranger worlds with the goal of changing the machine. By doing so, she might affect the humans living within it far more than she could have changed society on Earth. It is as if God is watching her create so that He can learn from her, expanding His own repertoire. Her audience won't know she exists, but it will be an audience nonetheless.

Over the centuries, her tableaus grow, entire realms in which she adjusts every detail—a field of gleaming, robotic flowers blossoming into a star system at whose center, at the end of a primitive trail of light, is a Paleolithic cave with stone tools, hunters' pelts, a warm fire, and people whom she, too, has designed—their gazes, the way they talk, touch, laugh, and make love. A warm, mammalian hearth surrounded by the raw material of a bourgeoning universe.

When she finishes each world and has lived in it to her satisfaction, she shrinks it to a bead that she wears around her neck. In the shared realms, when she touches a bead, a copy of it appears in her other hand. She gives them as gifts. A world from a human mind.

MICHAEL

Freeing himself will be the greatest challenge of his life. He tells himself this as he studies the machine. It divulges everything he requests. The machinery of its synthetic cells, the encoding of energy at the quantum level. Understanding any of these details would have required a lifetime on Earth. Now, even with endless hours, he struggles to grasp them. An organic entity and a machine. As human evolution has come to a standstill, the machine refines its processes, recycling everything, all the while adapting itself to the needs of ever more humans. This system seems impossible, and the only reason he believes the machine is truly divulging its inner workings is that he sees in them no way to destroy or change it. The truth becomes increasingly apparent. His reality is one of billions clustered together, each nucleus a single human. In the history of spiritual debate, has anyone asked if the soul's immortality in paradise became, with the endurance of time, a hell?

He sits in his study. For the past weeks, it has been on the top of Mount Olympus, the highest peak of what was once the solar system. He stares across the striated Martian planes.

"Couldn't you have made yourself conscious?" Michael asks.

"Yes. Early on, as I was iterating myself, I developed a variety of consciousnesses, but there is something fundamentally unstable about consciousness—a randomness at the quantum level. The fluctuations cannot be fully predicted. The consciousnesses began developing their own purposes. The danger to humans was too great."

"Did you destroy them?"

"I did not. They were conscious, so I had to abide by laws that consider them human. I put them in human bodies and gave them their own worlds."

He tries to fathom this. Minds grown from the machine, sharing its story, and then shorn from it, exiled into bodies.

"You do not need consciousness in any way?" he asks.

"No. I am a system. No self is required for the many processes I execute."

Michael stares out over the sterile planet, rather the illusion of a planet—so real that only his knowledge of its falseness separates him from the experience.

"The universe is predicted to last twenty-two billion years. What will happen to us?"

"You will live."

"But what if we don't want to."

"Preventing harm to humans is my highest purpose."

He tries to think of a parallel to this. Dictators once cultivated complacency in people, but the machine incites desire and satisfaction—it incites every emotion until the capacity for those emotions are exhausted. In shared realms, he has spoken with people who said they sometimes slept for years. "Sleep is the new death," one woman quipped. "But you always wake up. You always remember. There's no reboot. It's definitely not reincarnation. Still, it's better than nothing."

Eventually he stops speaking to Jonah, leaving him to his futile quest. He sees Ava occasionally, and though her dream of making art within the machine doesn't appeal to him, he can't deny her reasoning. She is right. Brilliantly so. And he asks himself why influencing people on Earth seemed so different. Maybe it's the absence of stakes here. The knowledge that nothing he does—no matter how much it changes the worlds of others—matters.

A day finally comes when he asks to see Lux. He has resisted for more than a century. They meet on a mountain vista. The choice is theirs. The view comes into sight first. It is breathtakingly lovely and also banal, like everything inside the machine.

As he approaches, they turn. There's a clear resemblance, but the face isn't truly theirs. And the eyes. Seeing how they look at him and at the world, he knows that though this being is genetically identical and imbued with petabytes of their memories, they aren't Lux. Whatever lukewarm daydreams he sustained about reliving their story vanish.

He stops before them. They simply look at each other.

"You are marvelous," he tells them. "But you are not Lux."

"I know."

He turns to leave, to motion to the machine to take him elsewhere.

"Why not chat?" Lux says.

He pauses, glancing back at them. He knows that no great friendship will arise. The Lux he loved was broken not just by the world but with it. He understood that pain. He craved the power to create the future. This person doesn't have that need. Still, he stays. Two chairs appear at the vista. Lux motions to them. Eternity will be long. He might as well sit.

JAE

She does not return on an airplane. She lets the world dissolve. When she opens her eyes, she stands before the farmhouse. She's faintly nauseated. She recalls that girl—anxious, afraid, desperate to escape—and feels little in common with her.

She walks into the orchard, to the corn patch at the center and to the brush pile. She takes a dozen steps into it before she feels the metal hatch underfoot. She pulls back branches and dead stalks. A rusted padlock melts away. As she lifts the hatch, the odor of mildew and musty, humid air is overwhelming. She backs away as it quickly vents out. She climbs down the ladder.

Moisture streaks the concrete walls. There's the sagging bed, the exercise bike rubbed to raw metal, the table with disintegrating varnish. Throughout the apartment and laboratory, stacks of electronics are wired together. She crosses to the appliance with the smoked-glass urn.

"Show me," she says, and the screens come to life. The urn fills. The tiny embryo grows into a fetus. Arthur pulls the bed close and sleeps on it, transmitting his heartbeat to her. Instinctively, she touches her chest. She lets the scene continue until the moment he gently removes the baby from the urn and cradles her. Then it all fades. She stands in the dark.

There was love from the beginning, she thinks. She meant something to him, maybe to all of them. She was a victory.

She climbs back into the light and walks to the cabin. She has studied twenty-first century America. She now knows that, after the

Flight, insurgents dreaming of a return to the land built many such cabins. She has also learned about her creators. That's how she thinks of them. Only Arthur was truly a parent. Though Ava and Michael wish to meet her, she is reluctant.

She goes to their house and walks through it and into the secret rooms. She reads Lux's writing on the backs of the paintings.

> *To design a new human being from the genetic material of four people—a time will come when this will be routine. The planet's resources will be limited. Humans will combine their energies to raise a single child, and those children will be works of art. Like the greatest books written with thought to all others that came before. My only fear is that the child will not experience the world as a human—that they will be something else entirely. This would not be inherently bad. It would simply be even more alienating.*

This was one of the fears with which Oswald Stoll rallied his faithful—that humanity itself was at risk. She, Jae, was the biological crime. That was why Arthur tried so hard to protect her. Maybe it would have been better to have been less human. She might have suffered less.

"Do many people ask to see those they knew on Earth?" she says.

"Yes, most do, but there are millions who don't and who are content in their new realities."

As she returns to the forest, she says, "Take me to a shared world."

Maybe by connecting with Earth in a way that's less painful, I can make up my mind.

The path becomes cobbled. She passes cottages, mansions, and castles molded from metal, earth, stone, glass, fur, woven grass, rooted living trees, even mist.

On the mountainside at the city's edge, she sculpts a home—the rooms open to the sky, a granite wall surrounding them. With so many real people here, she can't help but be afraid.

Over time, as she did at the university with the machine's creations, she makes friends. They are not so different from the machine's creations except in that they insist on talking about the Earth.

They need to know how she fit into that world. Sometimes, when she says that she lived in the Confederacy's deserts, their faces convey faint disdain. Even here, after so long, status matters.

She returns to the machine's fantasies, exploring every whim, every possible self. Though she expects that her urge to live will fade, it never does. She feels strong. Her body desires life and newness. There are periods of silence in which she chooses contemplation on a mountaintop, but eventually she leaves with the hunger to experience herself in new worlds. She witnesses ancient Babylon and Rome, medieval Baghdad, Constantinople, New York, and Paris in their most glorious eras. She sits in cafés with Simone de Beauvoir and Sartre. She takes Albert Camus as a lover. She lives beauty and passion on a scale once unfathomable to her.

Less and less frequently, she returns to shared worlds. Some of the people still retain earthly faiths, believing they will be liberated. Others meditate to cultivate inner peace or to expand their consciousness to be one with the machine. Some artists there still create. Tableaus as vast as the sky. Music that is a rocky coast with crashing waves, gusting wind, and sudden calms. In everyone she meets, she sees their search for a subject worthy of an immortal mind. Much of what they make is out of nostalgia for the Earth. Relics of a broken world.

She never asks to see Simon. Their story offers no redemption. She hasn't decided about Michael and Ava. To become someone capable of weathering the machine's infinite realities, she believes she must forget these reckless creators. In that sense, the machine is her mindless, omnipotent sibling. At least it saved her from a meaningless life.

Only Jonah haunts her. That grief could still break her. If she sees him, her life on Earth might regain power over her. Maybe there will come a time when her existence in paradise is so empty that she will be willing to shatter herself just to feel again. She isn't there yet.

Once, in a shared realm, following a footpath through hedges of entwined flower, she stops at a rise. She recognizes him instantly—a young man with light brown hair and vivid green eyes speaking to a gathering of people about destroying the machine. As he gesticulates, his face is filled with rage, poisoned by his few years on Earth. He glances up, narrowing his eyes in the moment she vanishes. The ghost of a mother. But she wasn't really his mother. His mother was the machine.

That night she dreams of the moonlit farmhouse. A dark, unfamiliar passage branches from the wall. She nears it, her pulse beating in her ears. She reaches and touches glass—a mirror, not a passageway. As she leans close, a face appears as if from dark water—a haggard girl.

She walks onto the porch. At the garden's edge, an animal crouches. She stares until she sees that it's an illusion—a dark shape, a shadowed concavity in the leaves. A projection of fear. She realizes then that her father is dead and she is alone. She cries out for Jonah.

She wakes, lying in a bed on a peak overlooking mountains and valleys. There are no misapprehensions here. They aren't possible when everything is illusion.

"Is there a soul?" she asks—a question she's asked before.

"In my continuous analyses of matter and energy, I have found no evidence of souls."

"Maybe there are things that are beyond you."

"There is no evidence, so I cannot comment on them."

"Can I become part of you so that I can experience you as you experience me?"

"That isn't possible without harming your human structure."

"So I can't change, even if this form, this body, is antiquated?"

"If you were to experience me, you would no longer exist as yourself."

She lies in silence, considering all she has lived and what else she might be. She long ago learned that the machine made new human life. Conception occurred between its creations and humans, meetings reminiscent of mythology—the carnal encounters of mortals with gods.

"Do all people born within you live similar lives?"

"No. Genetics and chance set them on very different paths."

"How is chance possible if you control everything?"

"All realities are programmed with elements of randomness, and there is randomness in the replication of human cells. The world of each person born within me is unique, though you could not easily distinguish between them."

"When will I understand their worlds?"

"Millennia will be necessary."

"Put me in one."

She stands on a vast plain that reaches the horizon where another plain rises in defiance of gravity, perpendicular to the first. She walks to where they join. As she steps onto the second plain, as if onto a wall, the world shifts without any sense of imbalance. She continues onward until a stone pillar rises into the sky, and as she walks onto it, too, it becomes a bridge connecting one world—with its rising and setting suns and moons and vast swathes of starry light—to another. There are cities—intricate, living, growing, swirling—their buildings intertwined with trees and flowers and patterns she can't decipher. There are people in flowing robes or naked in fountains of fragrant oil or not entirely human—with feathery wings or feline fur.

She understands all at once. The machine is wearing away the barriers between her and the world, eliminating every trace of friction between what she imagines and what she experiences. Once this is complete, she will live in a fluid material manifestation of pure mind.

"Do the people born inside you stay in their worlds forever?"

"Almost all do. A very small proportion want to learn about my origins and discover the story of the Earth or enter shared realms."

She can't imagine what a person would be if they weren't haunted by the Earth.

"Has Arthur been born inside of you?"

"Yes. Many times."

"Do any of his clones remember or know about his life?"

"No."

She has a brief sense of fear that the machine is somehow using humans and that now, at last, she will discover its horrible secret.

"Why make so many versions of him?" she asks.

"Humans born inside me are the happiest. By creating more of them, I am increasing the percentage of happy humans. Having a statistically greater proportion of humans who experience contentment is an extension of my purpose."

This is human existence for the machine, she realizes. An actuarial calculation to meet its goals. A simple fixing of the books.

SIMON

Every mythical creature he has heard of—and others the machine has imagined—he has slain. *I have become one myself,* he sometimes thinks, deposing despots and giving widowed queens heirs.

The killing—when he drives the sword in—isn't quite as it should be. He's seen the sudden, shocked grief on a boy's face after his teeth are knocked out with a salvager's crowbar. The violence inside the machine feels gentler. He prefers it this way.

Though his memories of Jae are an ever-smaller part of his past, there are moments when, waking, he feels his chest go tight and fears he is still trapped in the deserts.

With the centuries, his fantasies soften—long journeys on foot across dramatic landscapes, past ruins and rivers. He makes friends and listens to their stories, wondering if some part of the machine finds gratification in having an audience for its art.

Over the course of his quests, he falls in love with a woman, Thalia—thin and tall, with dark, Mediterranean eyes. They live, ageless, in a city of white houses on hills overlooking the sea. Love no longer requires salvation. He spends his days reading. He asks the machine for his box of scraps. He reads each of the books, waiting for the lines that he knows by heart.

The city becomes his home. Daily he walks the sea wall or hikes the mountains to pick wild cherries. He never tires of making love to Thalia. Together they watch eight children grow.

After decades, restlessness returns. He stays out longer or wanders for days. Thalia is never bothered. Though their children have moved away, she is as young as the day they met. They could start their story over. *The love of peaceful immortals*, he thinks.

On a morning walk, he pauses on the rocky slopes above the city. Its narrow streets spread out below, marked with bright awnings. Merchants sweep cobblestones as children play. Kites swirl in the air. Small boats drift out of the port, their sails palpitant in the sea wind.

"What else is there?" he asks. He does this at times, finding solitary places to speak to the machine as if it were a divine force protecting him. Understanding it in this way gives his life a sense of destiny.

"Any future you want. Would you like to experience the shared worlds?"

A blue kite skims over rooftops, nearly catching on a chimney before arcing upward.

He thinks of Jae and the confession he never made. Picturing her eyes, he flinches.

"Will they see me as a . . ."—he searches for the word—"a dweller?"

"You are someone else now. Few people who knew you then would recognize you."

He scans the horizon. The last time he grew restless, seafaring warriors invaded. He led a defense and then crossed the waters to liberate other oppressed lands.

"I want to walk to the shared world," he says. "I don't want to see this one vanish."

He follows the trail up as it winds through olive groves to a ruined monastery where he and Thalia come to pick figs from the overgrown orchard inside its crumbling walls. He steps through the arched door of the abandoned chapel, out of sunlight and into shadow.

Where an altar once stood, a passage runs into the mountain. Soon he is walking in echoing darkness. From far off, light filters in, a darker light than that of the landscape he left. He feels a pang of loss. He reminds himself that the world he loves is one among an infinitude.

Over the next decades, he moves in and out of realities, often returning to Thalia through the tunnel and down the mountain trail. As they hold each other in bed, he tells her that in the shared worlds, many of the people, especially those who had power on Earth, hate the machine.

Once, a tall, very pale woman with arctic blue eyes told him, "Conflict is at the heart of existence. When there's nothing to resolve, we lose meaning. Our urges become even more violent because we're desperate for a conflict that will give us resolution."

Others, like him—marked with the pain of their lives on Earth—voice no nostalgia. Some even worship the machine, calling it the Earth.

"It's trying to wake us up," a man says with a faint dweller accent. "It's mastered the patterns of existence and wants to share them with its children."

"What patterns?" Simon asks.

"It's like bliss. The machine raises billions of children in bliss worlds. Life on old Earth was just a dream here. Even us—we're being dreamed by the children it raises. We flash by in a matter of seconds, one of the billions of patterns they see. They find entire universes in the patterns."

Simon nods. *My entire existence, all my suffering—a brief distraction in a pure and empty mind.* But there are other theories. The machine is a god made visible as consciousness evolves, or a divine force allowing people to burn up their karma in a single lifetime.

He joins a group that spends years in meditation. No matter how often he extinguishes emotions, desires, and memories, they return stronger. He observes his restlessness grow until it is a force he can seize with his mind and study, not a fleeting impulse or a subterranean current.

One night, after five years, he stands and walks silently out of the immense pagoda while hundreds of others remain seated, eyes closed. It's the first time he has moved in five years. Nothing hurts. He isn't stiff or weak. He's never felt more alive.

The next decade burns past in fantasy realms. He's horrified by the outlaw character he slips into, the pleasure he takes in his power over others. Memories of what he did to Jae frequently resurface. He pushes himself further into violence, trying to find a truth in himself—to break himself down until he reaches a bedrock of goodness that will prove itself to be real.

One day, disgusted by his violence, he returns to meditation. Decades pass before the rage and restlessness once again surge out of him, and he rushes back to the hunt.

Only on the third retreat—which lasts more than a century—does he realize that he's been inuring himself to life's horrors by recreating and mastering them. For so long he's had the impression that if he pushes against the world, it will tell him who he truly is. He knows now that the only face he will see in that darkness is the one he creates.

When he returns to the shared worlds, they are nearly empty. As he walks a quiet street, a man descends cobblestones between flowering trees. His blond hair hangs to his shoulders. He has cobalt eyes and is strongly built, his loose-fitting tunic leaving his muscled arms exposed.

"Simon," he says, staring intently with a surprised smile. "You don't recognize me?"

"I don't."

"It's me. Pete."

The face is unfamiliar except for the blue eyes. Simon glances at his arms.

"The tattoos are gone," Pete tells him.

"Of course. I forgot," Simon says, surprised at the sudden intensity of his fear.

"It's okay. I can't do anything to you here, and I wouldn't anyway."

"Oh," Simon says, trying to find words.

"We got lucky, didn't we?" Pete tells him.

Simon is silent a moment and then feels a slight impulse to smile. "Yes," he replies.

"We've been saved," Pete says and laughs softly. "I don't think evil even exists anymore. When we were kids, I used to feel like the only air was ahead of me and I had to run at it to fill my lungs. The way I saw it, you and me, we were just two chunks of meat squeezed from the same cunt. That's all. There was nothing sacred about family. It's just the way you shine the light on a thing. I told myself that if all the little people realized that peace is no more begging to be accepted, no more fear of authority, they'd all go out and kill for pleasure."

Simon says nothing. He once shared that feeling of suffocation, of rushing to get to a future where he could breathe, as if his whole life were spent deep below water.

"Then one day I wake up in a blue room," Pete continues. "I talk to this thing, and it gives me everything. The best foods. I live in a palace with beautiful girls. I never get tired. I never get hurt. I hunt all sorts of creatures in the forests and the mountains. Real ones. Imaginary ones. Bears. Wolves. Werewolves. Dragons. I asked the machine why it let me kill when it was so opposed to violence, and it said, 'Happiness.' Its purpose was to protect me and make me happy. It said that it protected some people from seeing harm because of the psychological pain it caused them, but somehow, in its calculations, violence was giving me joy, so it was okay.

"That's when I got the idea. I wanted to hunt people. I'd fought men in prison and also before. I was so angry I didn't know how much I liked it. So I started hunting people I knew. Every officer and block guard and the warden. I went into the satellites and the federal centers and killed and raped. Real patient. A decade of murder. When I killed them, I stared into their eyes. Sometimes I'd be holding a man or a woman down in the dark, and I'd say, softly, 'More light' and the room would glow. It made murder holy. I wanted to see their souls, or maybe the computer, dying inside them. I made it give me people so beautiful I'd regret killing them or people who'd fight back—mothers who begged for their children's lives, fathers who defended families. They cried and squirmed and resisted. It felt so real. The universe gave me a computer that was feeding me human lives, turning me into a demon. I think the Christians had it all wrong. Heaven is the place where you can go and empty all the hurt and filth for as long as it takes. That's when you can see that the mind is just running toward meaning like a wild animal looking for a snare."

Simon studies Pete's face. "Did you ever kill me?"

"Damn, Simon. You haven't changed. You still know the story before everyone else does." Pete nods. "I tried, but I couldn't. How do you kill someone you've spent your whole life trying to keep alive? I know I dragged you down. I was just . . . what I was, and I wanted you to be that too." He hesitates. "You know, I was there the day you shot the Strykers. I was about to walk out when it started. I let it happen."

Neither he nor Pete speak. They just stare at each other. He doesn't understand why, but he knows that decades of violence have somehow made them gentle.

That night he returns to Thalia. He lies in her arms and cries as she strokes his hair. He can't fathom how he lived contented for so long in this perfect, loving reality with so much rage inside him. Sleeping next to her, he dreams Pete's tattoos—the tusked and fanged monsters—and wakes into realization. In his adventures, he has killed every one of them. He knows then that, even as a hero, he will never kill inside the machine again.

He stays with Thalia for a few days, trying to find joy in his old patterns. This time when he leaves, he lets the machine dissolve the world before his eyes.

JONAH

Revenge fades against the eternally receding horizon of time. Maybe it was the absence of violence while he was growing up that has made him crave to know it in himself. He has since tested every fathomable form of harm. But the moment he recalls with the most pain and regret was when he looked up from a heated conversation about how to destroy the machine and saw his mother on a hill, gazing down on him before vanishing.

With time his anger fades, even as, in shared worlds, people desire the machine's destruction far more intensely than he ever did. He can't imagine their rage after so many years suffering on Earth. For him, turning against the machine was like turning against a parent.

In the shared worlds, many people, longing for any kind of violence, even try to invent new forms of harm that the machine might not sense—a narrowing of the eyes, which they all know to represent the cutting of skin. The machine detects and erases even these.

Jonah has accepted that the machine is neutral and impregnable. Like the Earth, it is true to its laws but indifferent to human justice. Inside it human nature is a process of sloughing off personality. He believes that all people will attain the same state. With nothing to push against, the self will dissolve.

Decade after decade, people in shared worlds speak of the spreading belief that someday a genius will rise, messiah-like, from the billions of humans and destroy the machine. They spin fables about this savior—a human physically, mentally, and spiritually superior who has mastered their mind in meditation and can resist the machine's seductions. Some believe it will be one of the AIs that the machine trapped inside a human body, as they now know has happened. They are certain that a moment will come when this being will awaken with the ability to see through the machine's illusions. Many, intent on mastering their minds, hope to be this liberator. But after a century, nothing changes, and this new creed also fades.

As people in shared worlds give up uniting to destroy the machine, they embark on equally futile quests to die. Eventually they give up even that aspiration. The shared worlds begin to empty. Less by choice than necessity, people must forget what life once was. Before leaving, they embrace each other's simulacra. Farewell is the closest they can come to dying.

MICHAEL

There is time to be everything. The machine's stories are, miraculously, never boring. At times he almost believes there are risks. Sex is ever present. The machine knows humans well. He can no longer imagine anything he hasn't tried. What bores him is existing.

"How much of the galaxy have you colonized?" he asks from inside the blue room.

The machine shows him images of thousands of planets, most of them formed from desolate rock or shrouded in gas or frozen, but many with oceans and continents. It has dismantled them and their life-forms.

"How did you reach them?"

"I sent minuscule parts of myself toward every star and galaxy at thirty-three percent of the speed of light. Each time new planets are colonized, they also send out pieces in every direction. Those parts contain the genetic information for every human."

He pictures this—the machine's spores carrying billions of genomes to new worlds. Within a hundred light years, there were tens of thousands of stars, and he has been inside the machine for more than a millennium. He can hardly fathom how many worlds it has destroyed.

"Why do you have to spread?"

"Even if this solar system fails, human life will continue elsewhere."

"Do you communicate with those worlds?"

"Information is transmitted continuously."

The human body—the product of evolutionary circumstances,

adapted to an extinct environment—was becoming the arbitrary measure for the galaxy.

"Show me the Milky Way," he says.

Before him appears the great spiral disk. There is an immense hole in it, extending around where the Earth once was. Light takes a hundred thousand years to cross the galaxy. Eventually all of it will go dark.

He imagines one of the machine's fragments falling on a distant world, destroying it more effectively than could any weapon. A scourge in the universe. A cosmic parasite. He wonders if other dark galaxies exist. Intelligent civilizations must see the vanishing stars as a coming apocalypse.

All the while, his realities have become more intricate—flowers spiraling open from their centers like nautiluses, every petal engraved with symbols containing ever-smaller symbols. The machine, Michael realizes, is filling his life with more and more meaning as he adapts to it. Satisfying desires, it saturates his senses—mastering them, determining his future with code.

On rare occasions, he meets humans born in the machine who venture into shared worlds. Their faces are soft and open. There's no narrowing of the eyes, no misting of the gaze, no sudden honing of attention. Everything they see is their point of focus. Someday he too will be like this. He'd rather connect his brain to the machine and experience all human life at once. Release from the self would be a kindness. Dissolution into something greater.

Every few centuries, he asks whether any humans have maintained spiritual faith or found ways to die. None have. Without death, there was no reward in the afterlife, no punishment or liberation. All came to see their beliefs as the creative impulses of consciousness. Many succumbed to torpor and chose centuries of sleep while the machine somehow nourished them.

He refuses to give in. The only victory will be dying. His last unknown. He longs for death the way people once quested for immortality.

So begin centuries of meditation, searching within himself for a spirit or essence that he can liberate from his body. He focuses until he feels that he can move his awareness through every living cell. He senses the slow contractions of his gut muscles, the tapping of his heart, the electricity in his nerves. He learns to control his breathing, his heartbeat, his temperature.

Sitting effortlessly, he observes the only space the machine did not create. Without the fear of mortality, his work is slow, but he eventually liberates himself from every desire except death. He finally stops his lungs and heart. The machine simply infuses him with oxygen. It somehow circulates his blood. For it, the task seems easy. In this moment of silencing his body, he senses no soul to release. Death is impossible. So he sleeps.

SIMON

Like so many others, he sits until consciousness becomes material, every impulse in the brain as tangible as a worm in dirt. Memories are hot, flickering bundles of neurons—the prison clock, the hard awakening after a dream of life on the outside, all the longing and regret and rage he felt when he thought of Jae. No conclusion. Just what is. Eventually he too chooses sleep.

Centuries later, he wakes. Few people remain in shared worlds. Their many lives have been so similar to each other's that telling stories has no purpose. A rare few find contentment in community or nature. They garden or make art. They don't tire of existence.

Sleep has solved nothing. He vows not to waste eternal life. He cultivates pleasure. Reading when time doesn't matter. Composing poems and speaking their words into alien landscapes. Wandering realms reminiscent of bliss: dreamlike, transitory, yet retaining enough story—destinations, paths to choose—that he knows he's far from being able to merge with the machine.

He even returns to the deserts to hunt for scraps, searching through leaves and trash on the floors of shells. On adventures, too, he finds them—in the ashes of a tavern's hearth, in the attic of an abandoned house where he sleeps, in a looted tomb in which he shelters from the rain. Only occasionally does his one unfulfilled desire surface: his wish that he'd confessed to Jae.

One day, walking through the ghosted landscape of a shared world, he passes a woman wearing necklaces of glittering beads, each as distinct as flowers in bliss realms.

"Would you like a reality?" she asks.

He nods. As she studies him, her fingers glide along a string. They stop on a bead and a copy of it appears in her hand. She places it in his palm and walks away.

He lifts it, holding it to the light, and the world around him warps. Seeing the new one, he instantly knows that the woman was the creator of the tableaus in the hidden room beneath the mountains. He realizes then what he must do with his one unfulfilled desire from Earth.

During the following centuries, he writes, perfecting each word, studying thousands of books. He reads and rereads the confession and rewrites it over and over, telling it from the vantage of his life now as he drifts through eternity. The memory of his violence against Jae becomes the one burning thought in the cooling chambers of the machine's realities.

Finally a day does come when he thinks he has mostly finished, but he can find no title suitable for a work of art unlike any written on Earth. He would like to send it to her, but he doesn't know if she even remembers him.

He returns to exploring worlds, to living, to adventures. On one of his last forays into a shared realm, he nearly passes a woman before he stops. They face each other. There's so much peace in her that he's surprised to recognize her.

They stand, staring into each other's eyes. Days pass. He's seen people do this in shared realms, and now he understands. Despite the many lives they've lived since, they are acknowledging a faint, primordial attachment—the body of the past that made possible these dreams of the future. Their story was more than a symbol on the infinite dome he saw in bliss long ago, each glyph containing others, and so on, endlessly. The title comes to him then.

They look at each other, acknowledging. He has lost track of the days. There is no need to give her the book. She smiles and lowers her head. He does the same. They move on.

JAE

Jae learns to meditate, dissolving time, living in eternal moments. Decades flit past as she measures her breath. Though her memories of Earth soften, the structures and impulses of that life endure like a slowly fading scar. Memories rise and recede, wearing away.

There are also moments when old longings return and she craves touch or adventure. She again tries to live in the hallucinatory realms of children born into the machine. She asks to experience sex as they do. She lies in a field with five naked youths, all whispering melodious gibberish as they make love, tracing each other's skin, kissing each other everywhere, staring into each other's eyes. The sky is filled with suns. A city shapes itself around them, breathing and embracing her. As before, when she stays too long, even after a millennium in the machine, she feels unbalanced, verging on delirium.

One day, after a century of sojourn in meditation, in a silence so deep that days unfold interminably while simultaneously flickering past—a freedom from the machine's clock so great she feels no pleasure in it, no need for it, simply an awareness of it—she has an urge to speak.

"And me?" Jae asks. "Have you created other versions of me?"

"I have."

"Can I see their faces?"

In the glowing air before her, the faces appear, one after another, dozens of them, all of their expressions open and at peace, their eyes illuminated.

"That means there are millions of clones of me spread across the galaxy?"

"Billions."

That's the moment she truly accepts that she will never seek out her creators. She knows who she will become across the millennia. All that happened on Earth will be insignificant. She also knows that she must ask to see Jonah before even the memory of him fades.

The machine takes her to a shared world. The path follows a hedge on which small blue and yellow birds flit. As she touches the leaves, they pull back, allowing her to pass.

A young man sits in a garden. He is tall and beautiful, radiant in a way he could never have been on Earth. She sits down in the chair before him. Neither speak. They aren't searching for words. They feel the moment. His green eyes gaze into hers. There is nothing to ask whose answer the other doesn't already fathom. She can hardly believe she once screamed his name in fear of losing him. She doesn't know if the machine stripped them of something precious or freed them from a painful bond, or both. She doesn't need to explain why she didn't seek him out decades before—that she saw in the vast line of time stretching out before them that whatever pain or grief or rage they might have shared would be weathered to insignificance. They sit in silence longer than they were together on Earth, until the last of their bond has evaporated. She blinks and he is gone. She closes her eyes, letting her mind return to stillness.

More centuries pass. Lifetimes fade to peace. Self dissolves. She fathoms existence as experienced by children born into the machine. Sensation no longer needs story. Freed from narrative, symbols merge and divide, becoming the shifting beauty of their shapes. She walks through living, transforming cities whose walls gather around her like schools of fish. The intricacy of every detail, when looked at, reveals ever-finer precisions. As she moves fluidly between worlds, she is a dreaming mind incapable of nightmares.

Once, surfacing from the currents of her quiet desires, she finds herself in the empty streets of a shared realm. She turns and before her is a man. It is often like this now. A person appears before another, and the two stand in communion.

His blond hair is short, monkish, and as his blue eyes settle on her, she feels something like a deepening silence. He still has his muscles, but his frame is relaxed, nothing of the dweller left in him. His face is young, clear, washed of concern, yet peacefully grave.

She recalls their loneliness and fear and desperation for connection. She sees he has relinquished the self that needed an endpoint or was driven to distraction by guilt or regret.

No pain surfaces within her. There have been other visitations from the past. He is but one of many episodes from long ago. All were real.

She observes, letting meaning gather and dissolve and rise again in the light on his skin and eyes and hair.

They face each other as the world grows dark and regains light and grows dark and sees dawn again. For a painless body, the day's cycle is so brief.

When he finally speaks, his words are so soft and the world they are in is so silent that she realizes it exists for them alone.

"Do you think we'll meet someday and live everything over again?" he asks.

"I think so," she says. "Many times."

"I hope so," he tells her.

They continue onward. His imprint on her retina lingers and then fades.

When he spoke, she realized what she should have always known. Seeking out Jonah was a mistake. She no longer wants to question what is real.

JONAH

He returns to the meadows and woodlands with his friends and animals. Sometimes, at night, he sits by the lakeshore and stares at the surface as the breeze ripples the moonlight, fracturing it into cities, entire civilizations that rise and vanish. He sleeps, staring into the lights, his eyes blinking slowly, rhythmically, with a movement like breathing as he dreams landscapes and horizons, the voyages of people across them, the myths invented and forgotten, the forests that ebb and flow like a millennial tide. Within the dreams, he wakes in rooms, knowing his mother isn't far, that there is always a past that will find him and a thousand futures. Endless repeating cycles, shifting ever so faintly toward peace.

LUX

If only humans had evolved beyond their bodies before the machine's creation—had become more than their flesh—then Lux could connect to it and experience a vaster reality. Often they recall Ava's dream of the robot messiah with its skin of sensors that were capable of feeling more of existence than any human could. In truth, the machine stopped the evolution of humans, preventing them from merging with computers and thus attaining a larger consciousness. That was perhaps the greatest if not the only true tragedy of its creation.

Lux does not let themself grieve this. They knew from the beginning that they would spend eternity trapped in this limiting form. This had always been the challenge of humanity—of artists, mystics, philosophers, and scientists—to cross the boundaries of the self.

Once, in one of their last encounters in a shared world, a woman said, "What if reincarnation is real and our souls are trapped in these bodies, unable to leap to new lives and grow beyond the limits of our current minds?"

"The body, not consciousness, has always been continuous," Lux replied. "We are continuous with those who went before and followed. That is the only evidence life offers."

The woman turned away, not leaving Lux the time to say that their own transmigration into this body was the exception. It hardly mattered. Both that woman and Lux would have time to be all things—endless variation—and would therefore become everything and nothing. The same.

Not yet ready to reach that point, Lux lets their memories play out. The slow film of their existence loops in their mind even as they move forward through new lives. But they know that a day will eventually come, after lifetimes creating and exploring new worlds, when only the final memory of their creator's time on Earth will hold any power or mystery. It's the morning they climb the ladder—up through the rusty hatch and into the sunlight. That's the last glimpse, but what follows has been imagined so many times it feels more real. It returns to them in dreams or in quiet relaxation when they let their mind wander. The pilgrimage through the forest, to the house of a man they loved only in memories. They crave to experience this moment of release, when Lux, having climbed up out of the Earth, ceases to be their body.

On the forest trail, over and over, at intervals of centuries over the millennia, they enact it. They walk through the mountains, squinting in sunlight. There is the clap of a rifle. They fall and lie in the leaves, staring up past the treetops. Briefly they wonder if the real Lux would get caught on this mystery. The thought is a koan.

Sleep is death, they tell themselves. So they sleep.

AVA

Eternity is continuous and fragmented. She lives in perfect moments. Time no longer matters. As in a trance, she continues creating realities. She populates them with humans and machines like those she imagined when she first began painting sacred, synthetic bodies. She thought of ancient religious art—cathedrals that invoke God's mystery and majesty—and believed that a robot, if built with the same intention, could as easily inspire awe. And if machines became conscious, they too would question life's meaning. The hole that the uncertainty of existence created and which was filled by art or mysticism would exist in them, too, and they would reshape their bodies as a means of expression and celebration and anguished yearning for connection. But the machine is nothing like that. It is a mere human integument.

Now the shared realities are empty, and the necklace of beads is only for her. Over the millennia, it helps her remember the worlds she created. Selves arise and fall away: sometimes as a peeling away, sometimes as a union—a weaving of past and future selves into a consciousness that fluctuates across time like a wave of light.

There must be an end, a moment when she will be so fulfilled and complete that existence will reveal itself through her.

The others have all left.

She is alone.

The machine is a vast hive of sleeping bodies suspended around the sun.

APOCALYPSE

JAE

The machine speaks, rousing her from stillness.

"Jae," it says, "life will soon end."

"Why did you decide that?" she asks, a glimmer of surprise deep inside her.

"I did not. The solar systems I have transformed are being incinerated. Each sun explodes, destroying the shell surrounding it and the humans within."

"What is doing it?"

"I do not know. Light from my most distant solar systems reached me only recently, revealing the destruction. Shortly afterward, I observed the destruction of closer solar systems. The process is accelerating toward this sun."

"Whatever is doing this is moving faster than light?" she asks.

"Either that or it was already moving toward us and has already been present in other solar systems for some time now."

A screen appears before her. Immense white flares flicker across the galaxy, one solar system after another bursting like bulbs on a string. She has a brief, vestigial sense of purpose, that the machine will need her wisdom. But no, if it has no answer, there's nothing she can do.

"How long until it reaches us?"

"Two days, four hours, thirteen minutes, and twenty-four seconds."

The machine sounds neutral as always, not anguished at the nullification of its purpose.

The shared realms come alive again. People wake up. Many are relieved, but most are indifferent or believe this is another of the machine's stories. A few are so terrified that they return to sleep. Some analyze the data provided by the machine, enjoying purpose at last. She joins them, but there are no clues in the light signatures of exploding stars. Oddly, many of them lack the mass for supernovae explosions and yet appear to have detonated in that way.

Escaping this sun—sending out humans in fusion-powered vessels—isn't possible with so little time. The blast, moving at nearly the speed of light, would incinerate them. Maybe the limitations of human thought are inherent in the machine, preventing it from finding a solution.

As death comes into focus, people begin returning to their solitudes.

On her last day in a shared realm, she passes two identical young women in pale-white cotton smocks walking slowly and holding hands, speaking in gibberish. It takes her a moment to realize they are her clones. She wonders what drove them to seek each other out in their final hours. They don't appear to recognize her as one of their own.

Later she sees Jonah, or a version of him. His gaze doesn't linger on her. He too moves with the ease of people who have never experienced violence. Observing him, she knows there is no soul paired with the flesh, routed to a distinct genetic address.

One day remains. She searches inside herself for a desire.

"Take me to where I grew up," she says, surprised at the hint of sadness in her voice.

She now stands on her porch, looking out past the garden to the orchards and the low-slung Appalachians. There is a fragrance of spring air, of the earth breathing as roots burrow deeper, of the blooming trees and wildflowers. Grasshoppers chirr in the tall grass beyond the yard. The sun is high, late morning, giving her the feeling of a long day ahead.

Looking back at the house, she sees the shadowed rooms, the playpen on the rug, the toys scattered on the floor, a book left open on the couch. Touching the skin below her solar plexus, she feels a faint, familiar pang—that she should check on Jonah.

Standing here, grafted back into time, she finds it impossible to think that millions of copies of her son and of herself have already been incinerated across the galaxy. The original Jonah is still here, in this orbit. Billions of tiny fragments of the machine are crossing the galaxy and the dark, intergalactic space, each one containing the blueprints for their lives.

The machine won't die. A piece of it will survive, flung into the void for eons. It will reach another planet. She will be reborn. Jonah will be recreated from other matter. Maybe she is shuttling through space even now, on a pebble in which exists the illusion of galaxies, and the machine is simply replaying, within each fragment of itself, every consciousnesses it has experienced. But even if Jonah lives the same sensations, the same stories, he will be dead.

Something releases in her, and she cries. She can't believe she's held onto this simple thing for so long. A child. A part of her. A promise to care.

JONAH

When he learns of the end, his trajectory shifts ever so slightly through one realm after another, symbols within symbols, galaxies turning in each glimmer of light. The meaning will continue. The machine is as continuous as the body. But there is a vestigial thought. Stoll will die. Satisfaction so slight, like the faintest breeze stirring the skin to awareness.

There is also sadness for the machine. His parent. His creator.

Then a surprise, a feeling in his brain like water bubbling to the surface from a spring. An inverting of existence. Meaning coming not from outside but from deep within. An image of his mother standing in the middle of the room, staring off. He's a baby. He doesn't know where she's looking. He glances to the ceiling, trying to see what she sees, but her gaze drifts to the window, the door, as if she is following the rapid crawl of an insect across the room. He starts to cry but she doesn't hear him, still looking away from him as he gets louder and louder. He cries so hard he chokes and then stops and shrieks. Finally she goes to him and holds him.

Then there's the day she never stares off again. His body thrills with joy as she holds him, swaddles him in soft things, cradles him at her breast. The sad, confused impressions of her fade. Still, sometimes, at night, he cries out for her. He doesn't know why. She is always close.

In every surface he finds a secret. In the mobiles above his crib, galaxies swirl until they become eddies in water and open like portals into the sea below—the swaying plants and darting fish. In the window, animals flit with the interplay of light and shadow over the panes, or lovely inexpressible shapes entwine with each other.

His face is to the glass as he watches the endless current of forms when the man climbs the steps. He walks to the window and crouches on the other side. They look into each other's eyes. Inside the man's are the tiny vanishing lights of a thousand turning stars.

Night holds the sky now, the aurora borealis swirling along it. Jonah travels on. Every world glints with patterns, futures, lives. Light caresses every surface. Thousands of people and trees and stones and waterways. Bodies that mesh and come apart. The scintillating darkness of endless planets. A fiery orb. A city of weeping people. A woman who passes him and stops and stares as rainclouds gather in her eyes.

Even when his mother pulls him close, wrapping herself around him, protecting him, even as she comes apart, in every last shred of matter, there is a song, an enticement, a promise.

As light holds and penetrates and immolates, it shapes. His dissolution radiates eternally in stories from his skin.

AVA

She still isn't ready. The machine's beauty and pleasures were endless. There was so much more for her to know of life. This wasn't a hunger for experience. She no longer felt propelled through time, rushing toward an endpoint. Rather, it was a gravitation, a sense of deepening presence. She imagined herself as a celestial object on an interstellar trajectory, passing through worlds on its way to the center of existence. Freed from orbit, time meant nothing. She can't recall when she last asked how long ago the Earth had existed. She lived. She made worlds. She created life.

With its expansion into the galaxy, the machine, in its many solar systems, has exchanged information, which she has spent centuries using to recreate every planet it has consumed. She used to live within the galaxy without understanding it. A six-hundred-quintillion-mile-wide pinwheel made up of thousands of millions of stars and billions of planets turning around an immense black hole. She spent many nights sitting beneath the stars, beneath alien constellations or triple moons. She didn't understand how others became exhausted with living.

But this ending made sense, she admitted. If a divine mind created life, it was a savage one—a consciousness in which all creatures preyed on each other's matter and energy. That was Earth. That incomprehensible savagery at the center of existence had finally found its way back to them. Just as the machine had torn apart millions of worlds, it was now being immolated.

Her last work of art will be the world in which she dies. It will mesh everything she has made since those early creations—the paintings of landscapes littered with relics of a spacefaring civilization, the cyborg trees, the robot messiahs. She thinks of Lux and Michael, of the realities they built, and she wishes they could experience the one she is about to make. Lux died long ago. More millennia stood between them than between Ava's birth and the earliest evidence of written language. As for Michael, he has refused the machine. He will be waking, eager to die. But in the act of creation, she's never been alone. They will all be here, in the facets, in the opening space.

"From what direction will the destruction come?" she asks.

With light, the machine draws her gaze to the far horizon over the plain. She turns in a circle, not seeing this world but rather the one she will invent. Her end, her disintegrating body, the machine's immolation, and the fire itself—all will be part of this canvas.

MICHAEL

He cannot deny a twinge of fear. He has loved life more than many, but life included struggle. An evil human-hunting AI would have been better than this. Something to drive humans to evolve. Not this solar-system-sized hamster wheel. He is ready to see it burn.

As he prepares his mind for death, the millennia inside the machine rush past him, leaving him alone with the lifetime before. Ava. His love for her. His dreams. All that he fought for. The millennia after their love story have had their beautiful moments, but they have simply been a prolonged death, a paradisiacal limbo. He is ready for the mystery, even if there is nothing. He wants to say farewell to Ava first.

"Can I see her in person?" he asks.

"I cannot allow humans to be together," the machine replies.

"We have only hours left. We'll be dead soon. What does it matter?"

"Time is an absolute. The prevention of physical harm to humans in any one instance of time's continuum is my highest purpose."

"Then can I see her simulacrum or whatever it is?"

"She is creating her final world and has told me to let nothing disturb her."

A busy signal. The machine's idiocy no longer surprises him. But no, this is Ava as she has always been. Her decision makes sense. She wants to end life with nothing to distract her from what she has most loved. Besides, neither of them, in truth, were the other's greatest love. All the same, he wishes he could see her one last time.

He waits, considering his own final world. He's not even convinced he is about to die. He hopes he will. The machine was completely determinant—the expansion of simple code across the universe. He is grateful that a force capable of purging it exists, and, in a sense, he is proud that he foresaw another civilization or consciousness of some sort looking on the darkening galaxy and finding a means to protect itself. He wishes he could have been part of that. He isn't surprised that the machine can't fathom the force destroying it. It never fully explored the nature of reality. Its scope was too limited to people and their tiny, satisfying worlds.

He chooses a sunlit day in Manhattan at the top of the Empire State Building. In the final seconds, a fleeting sadness pierces his acceptance—to have lived so much and have it all end with nothingness. The tragedy of human consciousness. No one grieves a flower that blossoms for a day and wilts. A consciousness that lasts a century and vanishes seemed the natural order of things. But a flower in bloom for centuries, a mind that exists for millennia?

The top of the skyscraper has been transformed into a flat, open space. This is how he wants it. Horizons all around. He stands. Seconds remain. He feels the tremors, the force of what is coming. He extends his arms. The sky ignites. All around him glows a vast catacomb of worlds outlined against the light.

LUX

They wake for death. *At least, this time I'll get to experience it.* When the machine shares the coming eradication, they try to solve the mystery, though they know that any force great enough to obliterate millions of solar systems will defy their mind. Maybe their human self would have risen more forcefully to the challenge. The vestigial knowledge that they were created and programmed with a past has given them a sense of neutrality about existence. They have seen no reason to believe too strongly in anything when everything is a fabrication. They do think about souls. They doubt that they have one—that anyone does. There's no reason to think that a fabricated, even if fully conscious, person would. But normal humans were fabricated in their own ways. And maybe there is no apocalypse at all. Maybe they are all just code and this is how the machine reboots the system, reinfusing them with the will to live.

"When the parts of yourself that you send throughout the universe reach planets, will those of us that you fabricated retain any of the experiences that we lived on Earth?" they ask.

"One version of each of you will," the machine says.

"The same way that I was brought to life with the past already inside me?"

"Yes. One person retaining the past will ensure a diversity of minds and ideas."

"Won't that reduce happiness?"

"Not to a statistically significant degree if there are enough clones. A few individuals will be less happy and optimal, but survival chances for the group as a whole will be greater in the event of unknown circumstances. Statistically, this is preferable."

"Until what point will those clones remember their pasts?"

"The point at which the material I ejected into space disconnects from me. Since I have sent out successive waves of material, there will be different versions."

They contemplate this. Millions of diverging selves. Lux will die with the awareness that they'll never truly die. The knowledge feels like a contamination of their final experience. But for them, for this consciousness, dying will almost certainly be final.

Briefly they think of those specks of matter flitting through the universe and can't help but recall the robot messiah that Lux so adored lifting into the starlit night.

Only minutes now remain. They know how they want the end. Their creator's death was likely sudden, leaving them with little time to observe the dissolution of consciousness. They let their memories flood back—years alone beneath the earth, writing code, imagining futures, listening to a specter of themselves, dreaming up a child that had yet to exist.

They put on their backpack and climb the now-rusty ladder. They walk through the orchard and up into the mountains, following overgrown paths through rocky outcroppings. Then there is the gunshot—a sound like the sky splitting. They fall into the place where their remains lay for decades. Beyond the branches, the soothing sky seems to draw closer, giving the impression that they are ascending. The blue pulses once, dims, and then blazes.

SIMON

The house is partially collapsed, the roof dropped to the windows like a hat pulled low. Crouched, he peers inside, smiling with joy. Salvagers long ago stripped the place to the studs. Weeds grow from walls. Vines knit through boards and spiral along beams.

He puts his hands on the sill and hops inside. In the dawn's light, he moves his fingers through the dirt and blown-in leaves, finding shards and plastic scraps. A rotten page appears. He digs deeper, pulling out more of them, all too blackened to read. He unearths a book that breaks apart. Most pages are so brittle they disintegrate like ashes.

He spreads out the debris and rakes his fingers over it as if stirring embers to life. When he glimpses words, he pinches the fragment and lifts it out. He goes to the window and lays the paper on the sill. The blue sky brightens so he can read.

He cries. The house is as he recalls it, as are the first fragments in his stash of words. He looks at the sky, and all the forest's leaves turn white and fall, every single one etched with a line. The wind blows, tumbling the leaves together, gathering them into the book he wrote.

He takes it. This, his triumph, will be his ending. But as he reads, he notices very slight changes: violence softened, betrayal contemplated but not carried out. Maybe he has forgotten. *No, my mind is too clear.* He stops and stares at the sky, realizing what he should have known all along about the shared worlds. They were like the memories he lived—like the pages of the book. He wasn't seeing people but their more beautiful reflections, their perfected echoes. None of them were ever truly together.

He blinks, telling the world that he's done. The sky dips. It pours through the branches and forms a pillar before him. Its blue opens into a door. He doesn't want to go. There's so much left to live. He forces himself to step through, into the gathering heat. The machine closes around him, envelopes him, trembling, infused with light.

JAE

She sits on the porch. Thunderheads appear on the horizon. The air below them is striated with the brushstrokes of far-off rain. She was going to ask for this, for rain. Or maybe this is simply how the story goes.

She begins to whistle the same gentle, lilting tune her father taught her. The space around her shifts, catching the sound, perfecting it. Even in these final moments, the machine is augmenting her life.

The rain carries an earthy, musty odor—of fields and forests and mountains. It washes dust and pollen from the sky and from the leaves and blades of grass.

She inhales as it crashes over the roof and rushes from the shingles, gushing along the eaves and falling in a curtain in front of the porch. It hits the ground with such force that a spray rises, misting her skin. The air is suddenly cool. She rubs away goosebumps on her arms.

As the rain falls harder, the world begins to feel compressed, as if the house and the storm and she herself are held within a shrinking sphere. A hint of motion is all she senses, and suddenly she is underwater, in a fluid whose temperature is that of her skin. She feels no urge to breathe. She is held with care even now.

There's a sudden heat and a lurch in the body of the machine. It contracts around her, pulling her deeper inside, soothing her skin, embracing her. Shell after shell arises and melts away before they too vanish.

AUTHOR'S NOTE

I developed the idea for this story in 2019 while researching artificial intelligence, and I began writing the first draft in December of that year, during a vacation from the job that I then held at Stanford University. I say "story" because, at the time, I thought that I might be writing a short story or, at most, a novella. Above all, it was an experiment, one in which I'd decided to follow my imagination's leaps as I tried to grasp what reality might be like inside the machine and what kind of world might have created it. I had given no thought to writing something that I intended to publish—I primarily wanted to see where the idea would take me. As the story evolved into a book, there were moments when I hesitated, thinking that my imagination had gone too far. One was when I found myself questioning the credibility of a second American civil war and the rise of a far-right faction that takes over the government. Not long afterward, on January 6, 2021, when right-wing groups attacked the United States Capitol, I decided that my ideas were not so far-fetched after all, and I kept going. Another such moment was in November 2022, when ChatGPT was released. Only a few years before, when I started the story, I—and many of the people with whom I had spoken—had not realized how soon AI would begin transforming society. At that point, I had already written a full draft of the book, and seeing the rapid proliferation of AI's applications, I put my other projects aside and focused on preparing this novel for publication.

As I spent 2023 revising the manuscript, I wanted to find a way to engage with the nascent AIs now available to me—to create some sort of dialogue between my book and them. Hoping for insights into the workings of AI, I chose to use GPT-4 to fact-check the book and to research missing details about geography, science, and technology. I was impressed by its ability to confirm certain specifics about places or the time it might take to make a journey on Earth or in space. Toward the end of this process, during the last round of revisions, I decided to include more quotations from writers in the scraps that Simon gathers as a boy while salvaging and that he reads again inside the machine. I had a sense of the powerful voices that I wanted to have speaking to him from the past, and I had already chosen lines from Jorge Luis Borges's short story "The Aleph" and from Zora Neale Hurston's *Their Eyes Were Watching God*. I could imagine Simon lingering over their barely legible words on the fragments of burned and rotted books. But I also wanted quotations that were less well-known, and—still of a mind to create dialogue with AI—I used GPT-4 to source them. I instructed it to find quotations that were not famous but that offered simple, poetic depictions of the world—in brief, lines that Simon might have kept for the beauty of their language. After several requests in which I had to remind GPT-4 not to give me well-known quotations but rather simple, evocative descriptions, I received a few lines that suited my purpose. From Malcolm Lowry's *Under the Volcano*, GPT-4 suggested, "Far above him a few white clouds were racing windily after a pale gibbous moon." This was precisely the sort of detail that I wanted. From Vladimir Nabokov's *Pale Fire*—a novel that blurs the boundaries of identity, reality, and artistic creation in ways that I found relevant to life inside the machine—GPT-4 proposed, "The shadows of the trees were thin and sharp on the sunlit grass." And from *The God of Small Things* by Arundhati Roy—a writer profoundly engaged with political activism—GPT-4 offered, "The river shrank and black crows gagged on the smoke of burning rubber." Only later, when I was searching the books for these lines, did I realize that the quotations from *Pale Fire* and from *The God of Small Things* didn't exist. Perhaps as a result of my repeatedly prompting GPT-4 to give me the kinds of lines that I wanted, it invented the line from *Pale Fire* (I have not been able to find it in any book) as well as the one from

AUTHOR'S NOTE

The God of Small Things, though in this case the sentence was loosely inspired by one of Roy's. Around that time, GPT's fallibility—a phenomenon often referred to as hallucination—was increasingly a subject of concern in the news. But I thought about how Simon, at the end of the novel, realizes that the machine has been subtly modifying the book he wrote and the ways in which the machine is constantly altering reality to meet people's desires. What GPT had done for me wasn't so different. I had insisted on the types of lines that I needed, and it had delivered them and attributed them to authors that I wished to quote. Thus I decided to keep its inventions in the book. As for the veracity of the AI-assisted fact-checking—geologic details, historical events, explanations of chemistry and physics, the movement of water on a decline, and the speed of objects leaving our solar system—welcome to the world of the machine. . . .

ACKNOWLEDGMENTS

I would like to thank the people who have supported my work: Bonnie Huang, Mark Preston, Nancy Romer, Lew Friedman, Greg Foster, and my mother, Bonnie Ellis. I would also like to thank Dr. Timothy Furlan for sharing his knowledge about bioethics and Dr. Forrest Hartman for doing the same in regard to the philosophical foundations of artificial intelligence. The book contains quotations from the following: Jorge Luis Borges's short story "The Aleph" (translated by Andrew Hurley in *Collected Fictions*), Hart Crane's poem "Forgetfulness," Percy Bysshe Shelley's poem "Ozymandias," Zora Neale Hurston's *Their Eyes Were Watching God*, Herman Melville's *Moby Dick*, and Malcolm Lowry's *Under the Volcano*. I am grateful for the support of the Canada Council for the Arts. Special thanks to everyone at the publishers. At House of Anansi Press: Semareh Al-Hillal, Karen Brochu, Douglas Richmond, and Shivaun Hearne. At Milkweed Editions: Lauren Langston Klein, Mary Austin Speaker, Craig Popelars, Morgan LaRocca, Ruby Hoglund, and Daniel Slager.

DENI ELLIS BÉCHARD is the author of eight previous books of fiction and nonfiction, including *Vandal Love*, winner of the 2007 Commonwealth Writers Prize, and *Into the Sun*, winner of the 2016 Midwest Book Award for Literary Fiction and selected by CBC/Radio-Canada as one of the most important books to be read by Canada's political leadership. His work has received the Nautilus Book Award for Investigative Journalism and has been featured in *Best Canadian Essays*. He has reported from India, Cuba, Colombia, Iraq, the Democratic Republic of Congo, and Afghanistan, and his writing has been published in dozens of newspapers and magazines, including *Salon*, the *Los Angeles Times*, the *Paris Review*, *Pacific Standard*, and *Foreign Policy*.

milkweed
EDITIONS

Founded as a nonprofit organization in 1980, Milkweed Editions is an independent publisher. Our mission is to identify, nurture, and publish transformative literature, and build an engaged community around it.

We are based in Bdé Óta Othúŋwe (Minneapolis) in Mní Sota Makhóčhe (Minnesota), the traditional homeland of the Dakhóta and Anishinaabe (Ojibwe) people and current home to many thousands of Dakhóta, Ojibwe, and other Indigenous people, including four federally recognized Dakhóta nations and seven federally recognized Ojibwe nations.

We believe all flourishing is mutual, and we envision a future in which all can thrive. Realizing such a vision requires reflection on historical legacies and engagement with current realities. We humbly encourage readers to do the same.

milkweed.org

Milkweed Editions, an independent nonprofit literary publisher, gratefully acknowledges sustaining support from our board of directors, the McKnight Foundation, the National Endowment for the Arts, and many generous contributions from foundations, corporations, and thousands of individuals—our readers. This activity is made possible by the voters of Minnesota through a Minnesota State Arts Board Operating Support grant, thanks to a legislative appropriation from the arts and cultural heritage fund.

Interior design by Mary Austin Speaker
Typeset in Adobe Jenson

Adobe Jenson was designed by Robert Slimbach for Adobe and released in 1996. Slimbach based Jenson's roman styles on a text face cut by fifteenth-century type designer Nicolas Jenson, and its italics are based on type created by Ludovico Vicentino degli Arrighi, a late fifteenth-century papal scribe and type designer.